A LOG IN THE SPUTTERED AND FELL...

The glass fire doors were trimmed with brass, in which was reflected a man and a woman.

She was in some kind of white sweater with a lacy open weave. Her head was tilted, her hair fell away from her shoulder. Her earring was a pearl, and at her throat her pulse throbbed. She was trembling.

How easy it would be to tighten his hand over hers and pull her to him.

Joe broke free and stood up. "I'd better be going."

Tory looked up at him. Her eyes were green, brighter green than he had known eyes could be. He had thought that before.

"I'd better be going." He had already said that.

"You aren't going to make a pass at me?"

"No."

"And if I should make one at you?"

"I guess I'd want to make very sure that I wasn't dreaming."

"Oh, you aren't dreaming." She held out her hand. He took it, pulling her up...

KATHLEEN GILLES SEIDEL

DON'T FORGET TO SMILE

W♦RLDWIDE

TORONTO · NEW YORK · LONDON · PARIS
AMSTERDAM · STOCKHOLM · HAMBURG
ATHENS · MILAN · TOKYO · SYDNEY

First published September 1986

ISBN 0-373-97025-0

Printed in Canada

For
Anne Stuart
Beverly Sommers
Deirdre Mardon
Donna Ball

One

A LOT OF DIVORCED WOMEN these days are doing things that their mothers never planned for them, but even so you'd be excused for being surprised that Tory Duncan was running a bar in Oregon.

Not that there was a thing wrong with Tory's bar. It was almost entirely respectable, and since the original owners had intended the place to be a health food restaurant, the outside was rather pretty with a stone foundation and timber siding.

But this was not the part of Oregon where you would expect to find a person like Tory Duncan. She wouldn't have been such a surprise in Portland, which has its share of designer sportswear, young lawyers, and BMW dealers. And she would have fit in on the coast too. Interesting people move to the coast, coming up from San Francisco to build interesting houses, strange shapes that jut out into the ocean. In fact, Tory had spent a year on the coast, the first year after her divorce, not doing much, mostly admiring the scenery and letting her standards drop.

Then she left the coast and moved inland. Her bar was in Sullivan City, a pine sawmill town on the eastern slopes of the Cascades. When people think of the Cascades, they think of the western slopes with the magnificent Douglas firs and the dense undergrowth, a tangle of ferns sometimes higher than a man's head. You can't see the sky in the western forest, and the air is thick and soft. But on the other side of the mountains, the eastern side, there's not so much rain; the forest is pine, sunny and parklike—much more ordinary than what they've got in the west.

Sullivan City is a pretty ordinary place as well, one more working-class town, big enough to have a high school, a Pizza Hut, stoplights and a fairly good fabric store, but not at all the sort of place where anyone would ever want to own a stone-and-timber health food restaurant. Tory bought her building before construction was finished, and she opened it as a bar for loggers. The men who worked in the woods came here; the guys from the sawmill and the planing mill went to Robertson's. At Robertson's, the bartender was exactly what you would expect a bartender to be.

Tory was not. She was from South Carolina, a graduate of the University of South Carolina, a Kappa Delta, and before she had gotten divorced, she had been living almost like a Tri-Delt—the Tri-Delts were the debutantes, the only thing above the K.D.'s. And she was beautiful. Her face had clear, delicate lines and high cheekbones that caught the light; her eyes were a vivid green, and her hair blond, a swirl of honey and wheat that fell to her shoulders and curled under at the ends. She had the clean, open sort of all-American beauty that did as well with the four shades of eyeshadow, silk shirtwaist, and linen blazer she had once worn as it did with the neat jeans and light flick of mascara she wore now.

In college, Tory had been the perfect Southern coed. Her mother had taught her to be ever the good listener, to be endlessly cheerful, interested, sympathetic, always willing to adapt her mood, interests, values, and beliefs to whatever company she was in. A perfect Southern coed—and now one hell of a fine bartender.

Other people might think that that was coming down in the world, but Tory didn't. Not even close.

It was the last Sunday before the start of hunting season, and through the first half of the NFL game, things were pretty quiet in Tory's bar. Tory suspected that her Sunday regulars were home, working their way through lists of chores their wives had made up, hoping to buy themselves some free time next weekend. It was just as well that things were slow because Tory's second bartender, Pete Miller—known around the bar as "Rich's father"—had asked for the afternoon off. Tory and her waitress, Nancy Smith, were handling what business there was alone.

Which wasn't difficult because Nancy was a good waitress. She always arrived early; she never forgot who ordered what, and when she had time she was nearly as good a listener as Tory. She didn't greet the customers by name as Tory did or comment on their problems, because when Nancy had taken this job she made it clear she didn't plan on talking. Ever.

Nancy stuttered. It was a godawful stutter, a real jackhammer of a thing, and she had dropped out of high school as soon as the law had let her. She got her G.E.D. and lived at home, doing correspondence courses. At twenty-two, she was on her way to being one of the better educated people in town when Tory, who had frequently seen her at the post office, had offered her a job.

Nancy smiled at customers instead of asking them what they wanted. She wrote down the orders and passed them to Tory. This system worked nicely when Rich's father was on duty. Just as Nancy didn't talk very well, Rich's father didn't hear very well.

During halftime on this Sunday afternoon, people finally started drifting in, grumbling about the gutters they had cleaned, the screens they had put up, the cars they had washed. Tory and Nancy took their orders and listened to their complaints. Tory drew beer, poured chasers, mixed Seven-and-Sevens and bourbon-and-gingers, and changed the channel when the NFL game was over. It was just a usual Sunday afternoon at Tory's, a decent working man's bar.

This was when the gunmen came in.

Of course, no one knew they were gunmen. There were two of them, just kids really, looking like anyone else—faded jeans, straw-colored hair, wispy beards, a type that was a dime a dozen both on this side of the mountains and over on the coast. But they were young and seemed nervous.

Tory thought nothing of that. Looking like she did, she made a lot of men nervous.

"Can I see some I.D.'s?" she asked. The drinking age in Oregon was twenty-one, and Tory carded people.

One of the kids pulled down the zipper of his grey sweatshirt and reached inside. Tory expected a driver's license. She got a gun. A big black metal gun. She stepped back, lifting her hands in the air.

She heard a shriek. It was Nancy. The other kid had stuck a smaller gun, a Saturday night special, in the girl's ribs and was prodding her toward the wall.

The men in the bar were on their feet. One started forward; another thrust his arm out, stopping him. Tory's regulars all hunted; they knew guns. And when someone was pointing a gun at you, you did what he told you to.

Which was just fine with Tory. She had spent years doing exactly as she was told; she was hardly going to quibble now. She looked at the gun; the barrel was a black circle pointing at her. Why was this happening? Just when she had finally gotten things going well, so well that neither her mother nor her ex-husband had anything to feel smug about . . . at least not until now. This could turn into an "I told you so" of major proportions.

Tory kept looking at the gun; it was quivering. The kid's hand was shaking; he was nervous.

Oh, great. Just her luck, to be held up by a bunch of amateurs.

Listen, we're all a bunch of amateurs too. My waitress stutters, my bartender can't hear, my janitor is an ex-junkie out on parole, and I used to twirl a baton for three hours a day. Give us a break.

Then Tory realized that the gunmen hadn't said anything. Weren't they supposed to tell her what to do? "Your money or your life" or something like that. Didn't they watch TV? Isn't that what TV taught— how to hold up banks? Not that this was a bank, but surely a little elementary reasoning suggested that the principle was the same.

But Tory was fast suspecting that elementary reasoning powers were not something with which her two gentlemen callers were particularly well endowed.

She glanced over at Nancy. The girl was trembling, almost crying, her eyes dark splotches in her pale face. Tory smiled at her, trying to reassure her. Nancy wasn't exactly the world's most adventurous person.

Tory was starting to feel a little foolish standing here with her hands in the air. It was like the whole bar had assembled to watch her nails dry.

Why didn't someone say something?

At last she noticed some movement over by the dart board. A man had stepped forward. He had his hands in the air. He was new, not a regular. He had come in with—who? With Davy Nelson. The two of them had been putting up mirror tiles or something like that. He was one of the Brighams. Tory tried to remember. Joe—that's what Davy had said—Joe Brigham.

Why didn't someone say something?

At last Joe Brigham did. "Now if everyone keeps calm," he said, "no one is going to get hurt."

Tory wondered how he knew that.

He came forward, speaking to Sweatshirt. "Would you like her to open the cash register?"

"We don't want to hurt anyone," Sweatshirt said. It was the first time either one of the bandits had spoken.

"I know that." Joe Brigham's voice was calm, comforting. This was how a daddy talked. *I know there's a monster in your closet, but you can still go to bed* . . . "Would you like the money?"

Sweatshirt nodded.

Slowly, Tory turned. Now was the time to sound the silent alarm button that would alert the local SWAT team . . . except Tory did not have a silent alarm button and she couldn't imagine that Sullivan City had a

SWAT team. Instead she depressed a button on the cash register and started gathering up the bills.

"I'm sorry there's not more," she apologized. *I sound like I'm handing out trick-or-treat candy.* "But I just opened up a couple of hours ago."

"What about the safe?" Sweatshirt asked. "Where's the safe?"

"Upstairs," she answered. "In my apartment." Now why did she say that? Why didn't she just say that she didn't have one? Oh, well, it was too late now. What a mess this was. Robbers too stupid to ask for money, and a victim too stupid to pretend that she didn't have any.

Tory looked at Sweatshirt to see what he wanted her to do. He seemed to be waving the gun as if to direct her somewhere. Although she wondered if perhaps his hand was just shaking, she went down to the end of the bar, lifted the hatch, and came around the front, ready to be herded upstairs at gunpoint.

Sweatshirt was looking around for the stairs. "Oh, we have to go outside," Tory explained. "The stairs are outside."

"Wait a minute," bleated Saturday Night from the other side of the room. "You promised we'd stay together. You *promised*."

"But we both can't go," Sweatshirt reasoned. "If we do, these other people will leave and get the cops."

The bar was four miles outside of town, set back from the highway in a little stand of pines. It wasn't like they could step outside and wave to Patrolman Pete.

But this did not occur to Saturday Night; he was starting to sound a little desperate. "Could we send her up alone?"

Sweatshirt shook his head. "I don't think that will work."

"What are you going to do then?" Saturday Night looked like he wished he had stayed home.

Once again Joe Brigham spoke. "May I make a suggestion? Why don't we all go? Then we can stay together, and you can be sure we won't do anything you don't want us to."

The two gunmen looked at each other, but before they had a chance to say anything, Joe started directing traffic. He nodded at Davy, who crossed the room, propped open the vestibule door with a chair, and held the outer door open himself.

"You go first," Joe told Tory. "Wait in the parking lot for the rest of us."

Tory and Sweatshirt set off, threading their way around the tables and the silent customers. Davy grinned at her when she got to the door. She went out into the parking lot, and as the other customers filed out—there were perhaps thirty of them—they formed an orderly double line in front of her. She felt a little like the last baritone in a church choir.

It was cold outside, and Tory was getting tired of holding her arms in the air. She lowered them, tucking her hands up against her sides, hoping that Sweatshirt wouldn't think she was reaching for a shoulder holster.

He was looking at her. "You're very pretty," he said timidly. "You look like someone on TV."

"Why, thank you," Tory replied. "It's ever so sweet of you to say that." *But I've promised this dance to someone else, and, oh my, I do declare, why, my whole dance card is full, for the entire evening. Truly it is . . .*

Nancy and Saturday Night came out, followed by Davy and Joe. Davy went up to the front of the line with Nancy, and Joe came back to join Tory. "Is everything all right?" he asked.

Tory wasn't sure if he was speaking to her or to Sweatshirt, but she didn't suppose there was much chance Sweatshirt would answer so she did. "We're having just a lovely time."

He ran his hand over his mouth—Tory wondered if he was hiding a smile—and then he stepped out of line and called up to Davy, "We're all set back here."

"Wagons, ho," Davy shouted and they started to move.

A path ran around the building to a set of redwood stairs that led up to a dormer jutting out from the sloping roof. Keith, Tory's janitor, had mulched the path the day before, and the men's boots crunched against the pine chips. Keith wasn't here; Tory had made a deal with his parole board—he could only work for her if he wasn't around when the bar was open.

Joe Brigham was walking alongside Tory, almost, but not quite, between her and the gun. He must have noticed her shivering because he started to unsnap the down vest he was wearing but she shook her head, stopping him. She would be a whole lot colder if a sudden movement made Sweatshirt nervous.

The line was long enough that they were still on the path when Davy, Nancy, and Saturday Night had reached the little porch at the top of the stairs.

Davy reached out to open the door. "It's locked," he called down.

Tory cursed herself. What an idiot she was. "The keys are back in the bar."

She had visions of them all turning around, trooping back inside the bar while she got the keys, turning in formation, and marching out again. But Joe Brigham had what he probably thought was a better idea. "Break the glass," he called up to Davy. Then he turned back to Tory. "That's okay, isn't it?"

"Why, certainly."

Davy pulled off his wool shirt, covered his hand, and broke a pane on the door with such efficiency that Tory wondered how he had misspent his youth. He reached inside, unlocked the door, and held it open as everyone filed in.

The regulars looked around, interested. None of them had ever seen Tory's home before.

"I'm sorry it's so cold," she apologized. "If I'd known you all were coming, I would have turned up the heat."

Her safe was in the spare bedroom. She went in and knelt down in front of it. Sweatshirt and Joe followed. She noticed that Joe turned away as she started to spin the dial. Sweatshirt, however, kept staring. Oh, well, it wasn't likely that he would be able to remember the combination.

She handed him two small canvas bags and then closed the safe. "That's it."

They went back into the big room and everyone looked at each other for a minute or two.

"Now what?" Saturday Night asked.

"We leave," Sweatshirt answered.

"But won't they call the cops?"

"We could cut the phone line."

While Tory was impressed that one of them had shown a little mental initiative, she couldn't say that she approved of their plan. Ever since the phone company had broken up, you couldn't count on Ma Bell to rush out in two hours and fix everything for free. She spoke politely. "I'd really rather that you didn't do that."

Saturday Night looked stricken.

Encouraged, she went on. "Why don't we think of something else?"

Sweatshirt and Saturday Night instantly turned to Joe, waiting to hear what the "something else" was.

He thought. "Why don't you unclip the phones and take them?"

Tory thought that was an excellent idea. She owned her phones, and they were probably insured under her homeowner's policy. She told Davy where her phones were, and, in a minute, he collected the three of them.

But Saturday Night still looked unhappy. "Won't they follow us?" he asked Sweatshirt. "Our car don't run too good."

Sweatshirt thought. "We could slash their tires."

There was an immediate stir among the hostages. While they were willing to wait silently while Tory was robbed of her phones and a Saturday evening's receipts, they weren't going to stand around while someone slashed their tires.

Joe spoke quickly. "Why don't you have us take out our distributor caps? By the time we get them back in, you'll be long gone."

That idea was greeted with great enthusiasm. So the hostages, the gunmen, and Tory's three phones got back in line—they were getting good at it—and headed down the stairs.

But the line halted before they were in the parking lot. Joe, Sweatshirt, and Tory went up to see what the problem was. Saturday Night had stopped in front of a green MGB that was pulled into a little drive off the main lot. It was Tory's car.

"You're welcome to it," she said. "But it 'don't run too good' either. It doesn't start in the rain."

"It doesn't start in the rain?" Joe turned in surprise. "What kind of car doesn't start in the rain?"

"A British one," she answered. "That's why I had to move here from the coast. Too much rain there for my car."

He shook his head and then looked up at the sky, squinting a little at the sun. "It could cloud up any minute now," he said to Sweatshirt. "So you probably don't want this car. Let's go ahead with the distributor business."

Bill Gottfreed and Tommy Halsey began taking out distributor caps. Tory could see that it was going to take a long time. She leaned against the hood of a pick-up. Sweatshirt stepped forward to follow her, and the receiver dropped off the phone he was carrying. It swung around his ankles, and he couldn't replace it without letting go of the gun. Tory bent over and did it for him. He thanked her.

"Are you all from around here?" she asked.

"From Tramlet, ma'am."

"How nice." Tramlet was another sawmill town about twenty miles north of Sullivan City. The two towns were virtually identical, at least as far as Tory had been able to tell.

Sweatshirt was staring down at the ground, running the edge of one shoe back and forth across the asphalt. "I'm sorry about your money, ma'am," he mumbled.

What do you say to that? "It's okay."

"You know how it is... I mean, we couldn't find work or nothing..."

"Weren't there any openings at the mill?" The economy of the Northwest was not in great shape, but it was better than it had been a couple of years ago.

"They'll only hire you if you're in the union," Saturday Night answered, "and me, I ain't joining no union."

"Why not?"

"Just don't like it, that's all... But we got plans, we're going south. We hear there's lots of jobs down there."

Tory gathered that she was financing this venture. "Where are you going to go?"

"Don't know.... Just south."

Clearly they had never found out if there were actually jobs in the South, if the jobs required skills, or if they were steady work. The two kids were just going to show up and trust their luck. Tory had a feeling that their migration was going to be a waste of her money.

Bill and Tom finally finished with the cars. "That took us a long time," Bill told Sweatshirt. "You'll have a good head start."

Saturday Night looked happy.

"So why don't the two of you run along?" Joe suggested.

Sweatshirt touched Tory with his gun and she stepped away from the pickup. He wanted to use her as a shield until he got to his car, a beat-up Tempest. Since the two robbers were carrying guns in one hand and phones in the other, Tory and Nancy had to open the car doors for them. Saturday Night took the wheel, and Sweatshirt astonished them all by having the sense to roll down his window and point his gun in everyone's direction. Saturday Night put the car in reverse and backed it out of its spot.

"If I ever rob a bar," Joe remarked, "I'd back my car in. It would make the getaway easier."

"What do you mean if you ever rob a bar?" Tory waved goodbye to Sweatshirt and Saturday Night. *Y'all come back now, ya hear?* "It sure seems to me you were the brains behind this stick-up."

Joe shrugged.

The Tempest turned out of the parking lot, and as soon as it disappeared into the trees Tommy and Bill broke for the cars and Davy dashed for the bar.

Sweatshirt and Saturday Night neglected to consider two things. First, while it did take a good bit of time to strip the distributor caps off a parking lot full of cars, it hardly took long at all for two men to put a distributor cap back into one car—and one car was all that was needed. Second, while Tory no longer had phones in her apartment, there was a pay phone in the vestibule of the bar. Tory had little doubt that these two rather pathetic villains would soon discover that they had the right to remain silent.

She was suddenly weary, wanting only to sink down onto her parking lot and sit quietly for a while. But her parking lot was covered with oil stains, and her customers were all heading back into the bar. She had to get back to work.

First she went after Joe Brigham, who was headed for one of the cars. She hoped he wasn't leaving; she wanted to thank him. No one was hurt, and she was sure that that was due to him.

But before Tory could speak, Joe did. "Do you have a phone in the bar?"

She nodded. "A pay one out front, and one behind the bar."

"I assumed you did." Joe bent over and pulled something out from under the car. It was her kitchen phone. "But I thought we ought to hang on to this just in case."

Tory now remembered that each gunman had left with one phone. She had had three. She shook her head. "What if they had been able to count to three?"

"I was willing to take my chances."

Tory laughed and, as they walked back toward the bar, looked at Joe Brigham with more interest than she'd had when Davy had introduced him an hour ago.

It was clear that he was a Brigham. The Brighams were probably the town's largest family. They weren't "important" like the McKechnees who owned the mills. They were simply numerous, something that was particularly noticeable because most of the men looked quite a bit alike with thick, straight hair, somewhere between blond and brown. Their eyes were light blue, and their faces were slightly round with a pleasant, boyish air that lasted well into middle age.

They weren't a family who went into bars much; this was Tory's closest look at one of them.

And while this Brigham might look like half the town, he certainly seemed different from anyone Tory had met here.

"Who are you?" she asked suddenly.

"Joe Brigham."

"That doesn't tell me a lot."

"You're right," he agreed. "There are three of us."

She didn't understand; was he schizophrenic? "Three whats?"

"Three Joe Brighams. I've got a first cousin and a second cousin with the same name."

"That's handy. Which one are you?"

"Bob's second boy."

Bob's second boy? Tory let him open the door of the bar for her. Bob's second *boy*. What kind of grown-up called himself that?

One from a big family, she guessed.

Tory only occasionally admitted it to herself, but she was fascinated by large families. When she was growing up, there had been only her mother and herself. Her mother had been young, trapped in a routine job; Tory had been the most interesting thing in her life. Tory now wondered what it would be like to grow up in a noisy house with a dad and dogs, with brothers and sisters who might provide some shade from the overpowering glare of a mother's attention.

TWO POLICEMEN ARRIVED SOON, and obediently and succinctly, Tory answered their questions.

"Why didn't they have everyone empty their pockets?" one of them asked.

"Because," she answered honestly, "Joe Brigham didn't suggest it to them."

Then Tory stood near Nancy as the girl nodded her head through her questioning. The police knew Nancy and her stammer; they settled for a yes or a no. A reporter from the local paper showed up; he too seemed to know a thing or two about the abilities of the folks in town for he immediately zeroed in on Joe Brigham.

Tory hitched herself up on the bar, swung her legs over it, and dropped down to her usual place. She started filling pitchers and shoving them across the bar. She rarely gave away free drinks, but she was pleased to have survived the last hour with all of her own blood. That was worth a keg or so of beer.

People kept telling her that they were sorry about the money. "It's okay. I've got insurance," she kept saying. "No one was hurt, that's all that counts."

In a couple of minutes, she went over to the end of the bar where Davy Nelson was sitting. She liked all her regulars, but she found talking to Davy more interesting than most. He was brighter, funnier. She doubted that his life was anything great, but he never complained.

"You seem all right," he said.

"I'm fine." Once she'd started working, the weariness had passed. "It could have been a whole lot worse."

"Joe sure came through, didn't he?"

"Yes . . . Who is he? Is he on one of the crews?"

Davy shook his head. "Joe doesn't work for the company anymore."

"He doesn't?" Then Tory remembered. "Oh, that's right, one of the Brighams is in business for himself, isn't he? Fences and siding? Is that Joe?" It would make sense; he might well be the one man in here with the nerve to start his own business.

"No, that's his cousin, Dennis Colt."

"Then what's Joe doing?"

"He was elected fin-sec—financial secretary—of our local so he's the business agent."

Tory wasn't sure she understood. "So he's on the union payroll?"

Davy nodded. "Just started a month or so ago. He's doing a great job of it too."

And then Joe Brigham appeared, taking the stool next to Davy. Tory drew a beer for him.

"So what did you find out?" Davy asked.

"The cops said our boys were from Tramlet," Joe answered. "I don't know how they knew that, though."

"Oh," Tory said, "one of them told me. I asked him and he told me."

Davy grinned. "As long as you were at it, why didn't you get fingerprints and mug shots?"

"I will next time," she promised.

"Were they out of work?" Joe asked. "I thought there was some hiring going on in Tramlet a couple months back."

"They didn't want to join the union."

Tory assumed that this would provoke Joe Brigham into a pro-union stump speech, but he only grimaced and said, "You do hear some complaints about that local, but I don't know much about it."

THE HOLD-UP was terrific for business. Half an hour after quitting time on Monday, Tory's parking lot was as crowded as it was on a Saturday night. Tory normally took Mondays off, but when she saw cars pulling up on the grass to park, she thought she'd better go downstairs and help out Pete and Nancy.

Everyone had heard that the two desperadoes had been caught, but Tory was able to add, as she filled pitchers, that though they had wanted to confess, their court-appointed attorney wouldn't let them.

"I suppose they'll plea bargain," someone groaned. While Tory's regulars were generally solid law-and-order types, she herself was perfectly content for the two unfortunate creatures to be sentenced on a few hand-gun violations rather than on armed robbery. She just wanted her phones back.

Yet she listened to the complaints about the nation's criminal justice system, automatically glancing up every time the door opened. She hadn't been behind the bar too long when Joe Brigham walked in. He came over and sat next to Davy.

"Welcome back," Tory said, meaning it. She was grateful to him. Yesterday seemed funny; it might not have.

"You do run an exciting place here," he remarked.

"We try our best. Now what can I get you?"

He ordered a beer and they chatted about the robbery. Tory soon realized that she was disappointed. Yesterday he had impressed her, intrigued her. He had been the one who had stepped forward, who had managed to keep the phone line from being cut, the tires from being slashed. She had felt a certain intimacy with him as they had maneuvered their way through the hold-up, but now that was gone. He was quietly responding to her, not exactly seeming shy, but certainly not volunteering much that was interesting.

Well, what did she expect? Why should he be any different from anyone else in here? Her regulars were all union men, married with kids. They hunted and fished, talked about chain saws, carburetors, and four-wheel drives. There was no reason to think that those topics weren't what Joe Brigham was interested in too. And that was fine; Tory hadn't opened this bar expecting to find friends.

"So, Joe, do you have kids?" It was a question she might have asked anyone.

"A little boy," he answered. "He's about to turn six."

Once again he spoke quietly, but this time his expression changed. He must be one of those men who were crazy about their kids. "Is he in school?" she asked.

"Kindergarten."

Tory wasn't surprised that a child nearly six would only be in kindergarten. In Sullivan City people didn't push their children. The fall birthdays waited the extra year before starting school.

"Does he like it?" she asked.

"He seems to."

Before Tory could say anything more, Junior Rogers, frequently one of the first of the evening crowd, came up to the bar. As Tory was getting him a beer, he spoke to Joe. "I didn't know you came here."

"This is my second time."

"Well, do you have a minute? Something happened today that I think you ought to know about."

Joe excused himself, and the two of them went over to a table to talk.

THE SAME THING HAPPENED AGAIN on Wednesday. Joe came in with Davy Nelson, but before Tory could deliver their beers, Carey Bonner came over and spoke to Joe, and they took a table together. When Carey was finished, Marge Busch and John Steckler sat down. It was almost businesslike, Joe listening while the others spoke, their faces serious, intent.

No, Tory realized, it wasn't *almost* businesslike. That's what it was.

Tory knew that across the country, union membership was dropping. Younger workers—Tory's regulars—weren't as confident about unions as their fathers and grandfathers had been. They didn't take their complaints to their shop stewards, they didn't go to the monthly meetings. But talking to someone in a bar would be a lot easier than going down to the union hall. A person wouldn't even have to admit to himself that that's why he had come. *Let's try someplace different,* he might say and twenty minutes later he would find himself telling Joe about how the company had violated one of the work rules. If Joe had as much sense as he had displayed last Sunday, Tory thought, he would pick a bar and start going there regularly.

Around nine, Joe came up to the register to pay his check. For all the time he had been there, he had had only two beers. "Sorry about that," he apologized.

"I don't mind," Tory answered. "Just so long as you don't forget your waitress."

That was Tory's rule. Lots of times guys hit a rocky patch and had to cut back on their drinking money for a while. If someone came in and spent the evening with only one beer, it was okay with Tory. She figured they would come back when they were flush again. But she did let the guys know that if they used a table all evening, they had to tip Nancy like they had been drinking all evening.

"But what about you?" she went on. "Weren't you supposed to be home for supper?"

Oh, my wife's taken the kids to her mother's for the evening—that was what Tory expected to hear, but what she got was an expressionless Joe Brigham.

"No," he said.

JOE BRIGHAM HAD A GREAT DEAL of sense indeed. He came to the bar quite often over the next few weeks, varying his times so that he would see as many different people as possible. But he didn't come in on Friday or Saturday nights, which made sense—he went to the bar to work.

Although Joe was very reserved, Tory soon found that she liked him as much as any of her customers. She generally had to be careful about the way she talked around the regulars. During her marriage, she had picked up a rather ironic air, but irony was something that the people around Sullivan City were not very comfortable with—they said what they meant. With Davy, Bill Gottfreed, and one or two others, she could relax a little, and with Joe, she quickly discovered, she could say whatever she pleased. Irony never confused him.

Other than that, she didn't know him very well. He never talked about himself, but then he didn't talk much at all. He listened. And his stillness was more than verbal. Although he was clearly fit—as well he should be, he had been behind a desk for only a month or so—he wasn't one for a lot of unnecessary movements. He didn't gesture much; he never fidgeted or squirmed. When he did move, he didn't throw his whole body into it. When he reached for a mug, only his arm moved; he didn't hunch forward with his neck and shoulders like other men did.

Maybe he was still trying to learn this new job of his; it was like he was always waiting, observing, gathering data, thinking. Tory did not think he was a weak or an indecisive man. He was steady, patient, slow to worry or anger. He took his time.

FINALLY TORY GOT TIRED of waiting for Joe to explain why he didn't have to be home for supper, and she asked Davy about it.

"Oh, didn't you know?" he answered. "Joe's divorced."

"Divorced?" Tory was surprised. "A Brigham?" She had thought that the Brighams were all very straight-arrow, traditional types.

"It did knock the family all out," Davy acknowledged. "Not that they didn't side with Marianne though."

"Good heavens, what did he do to her?"

"It was the union business—how involved he was getting. It took all his time. He was on every committee there was, and then they started sending him to Portland for these deals—leadership training seminars, they called them. He would be gone a couple of days, and Marianne really didn't think that was right. I couldn't figure it myself. She never said a word about hunting trips and still doesn't if Dennis goes on them now. I can't say that I see the difference between going hunting and going to Portland, especially when someone else is paying for Portland."

Tory smiled as if she agreed, but she didn't. She could see the difference. This was a blue collar town. Most people still thought of life as a struggle; work and family life took enough out of a man, why take on more? Lots of women around here didn't think people ought to stick their necks out; it was asking for trouble. Joe's wife probably worried that his union work would somehow all end terribly, with him out of work, them poor, and their baby going to sleep hungry.

Such attitudes kept the town the way it was—pleasant, safe, and, to a half-outsider like Tory, unspeakably bland. No one sunk, no one soared.

But she didn't say that to Davy. "Who's this Dennis you mentioned? Has Marianne remarried?"

Davy nodded. "About a year and a half ago, as soon as the divorce was final. She married Joe's cousin, Dennis Colt, and of course, his little boy lives with them."

Tory whistled. "That must be interesting."

"Joe hates it—not that he ever says a thing about it. The Brighams all stick together, and Dennis is a Brigham even though his name is Colt."

This Tory could not understand. But she wasn't exactly the world's expert on family unity. She hadn't seen her own mother in two years.

ONE MORNING in early December as she was opening up, the bar's phone rang. To Tory's surprise, it was Joe Brigham.

"I'm sorry to bother you," he said. "Do you mind if I meet with some people at your place this afternoon?"

Of course she didn't. "Do you need me to do anything special?"

"Why, no." Joe sounded surprised at the offer.

But Tory's response had been automatic; arranging "something special" had once been her profession.

Tory had done what she considered to be an extraordinary number of odd things, but what had to be at least the second oddest was that during the last few years of her marriage she had been a party consultant. She had worked out of an exclusive stationery shop with lists of caterers, waiters and musicians. She helped people choose their menus and their flower arrangements. She told them when they had bought the wrong size of candle. She was so good at it, so quick and decisive, that her clients assumed she had been a debutante.

Which she hadn't been, not at all, but she had enough sense to have read the etiquette books, she had a good eye for color and proportion, and above all, Tory was good at making people think she was something she wasn't.

From the beginning, Tory had thought that being a party consultant was silly. Who cared how tall the candles were? If they started out too tall, they would burn down to the right height soon enough. And why on earth would anyone want to have a party with a theme? Or decorate around the colors in a dress? Most of the parties Tory worked on she wouldn't have gone to if she had been paid to... and some of the clients tried to do just that.

After a year or so of party planning, Tory stopped thinking that her job was silly. It was worse than silly—it was wrong. People said that they used a party consultant because they were busy, but Tory knew that it wasn't true. People used a party consultant because they were intimidated. They were new money trying to pretend to be old money, and the shop had made them think that they weren't capable of putting on a party by themselves. Tory got very tired of seeing people wig out over having a few friends in for dinner. Being a bartender was a lot more pleasant.

Joe arrived a little after lunch hour. "I appreciate this," he said. "This meeting is pretty unofficial, and it seemed like a good idea to get together somewhere neutral."

"Is something important happening?" Like every other business owner in town, Tory did not want to see a strike.

Joe was shaking his head. "A couple of people are going to mind, but if it gets handled right, that will be all."

And, Tory thought, with Joe Brigham around, there was a pretty fair chance that it would be handled right. "Will you be wanting a pitcher?" she asked him.

"Coffee for me. In fact..."

He stopped, but she understood. He didn't want anyone to drink. Some of these people would have to go back to work this afternoon, and the mill was a lot safer place when everyone was paying attention. "Do you want me to simply put coffee cups on the table and leave it at that?"

He looked up, surprised, pleased. "What a good idea."

Tory moved off to get the cups and the cream. Even a logger bar could sometimes profit from the services of Atlanta's best party consultant.

She didn't know the names of any of the people who came in although it was easy enough to pick out the company man. She tried to ignore their conversation, but when she went to refill the coffee cups, it was easy enough to tell what they were talking about. The company was considering hiring someone from the outside for a supervisory position. In the past, they would have taken someone off the line.

"I don't know," one man was saying, "why you think some college boy will know more about this than someone who's worked on the green chain for years and years."

His voice was resentful, and Tory was not surprised. Many of her customers were easily threatened. On some matters their self-confidence was sure. Logging was one of the nation's hardest jobs and perhaps the most dangerous, and they knew it. Fit and agile, with extraordinary physical courage, they were proud of themselves, believing they were good at the things a man ought to be good at.

But they also sensed, with varying degrees of consciousness, that most of the country, the people in the cities and suburbs, held to different standards, standards that judged success by education and income, by strange sets of letters—L.L.D., D.D.S., M.B.A.—by incentive compensation plans, stock options, and windowed offices. These Oregon loggers didn't agree with those standards, but they knew that when judged by them, they did not fare well, and they didn't like it.

After they left, Joe came up to the register to pay for the coffee. "Do you have an expense account?" Tory asked.

He blinked. "Not for this sort of thing."

"Then forget it, it's on the house. But tell me, how did your meeting go?"

"Okay."

Tory wouldn't have been surprised if he had said nothing more, but he stayed at the bar, running his hand along the edge. Then he spoke again. "Actually, it was great. They may not go through with it. At the end, Ross said he was glad we talked this week instead of next. I can't quite believe it. In fact—"

He stopped, seeming a little embarrassed, probably feeling as if he had been bragging. But why shouldn't he brag? Davy had said that he had only taken this job early in the fall. "That's really terrific," she congratulated him warmly. "Can you tell me about it?"

"I suppose it's really nothing dramatic." Then he confirmed her impression that it had been about hiring an outsider. "I can't imagine why they thought they needed a college graduate for the job." Suddenly he looked up at her. "Did you go to college?"

Had she gone to college? Tory paused. No one in the bar asked her personal questions. She wasn't sure why. She didn't know whether it was because they didn't feel entitled to or because they weren't interested. She hoped it was the latter. She would like it if her regulars thought of her as they would a TV game show host—pleasant, personable, and incredibly uninteresting. She liked being incredibly uninteresting. She didn't exactly want to tell the world that she had been a party consultant. But she guessed she could manage this one question.

"As a matter of fact, I did," she answered, trying to make college sound as if it were an odd accident in her life as opposed to the inevitable, necessary step that she and her mother had both considered it to be.

"Did you like it? Was it worth all that money?"

"I liked it well enough." Whether or not it had been worth the money was a different question. Tory's education had been financed by an array of scholarships, the source of which she was not about to discuss.

"What did you study?"

"I majored in psych. Psychology, I mean. That's the study of—"

But Joe was nodding; he knew what the word meant. "That must have been interesting."

"It was." And although she was growing uncomfortable with this conversation, she mentioned some of the courses she had taken. Apparently one of the union training seminars Joe had been to in Portland had covered some psychological material.

"It sounds like you learned a lot more practical things than I ever did," she had to say.

He dismissed the idea. "That can't be true."

Well, it was. Tory hadn't learned much in college. That wasn't why she had gone.

"Did you live in—what do they call them for girls? A sorority?"

A sorority? Miss Victoria Caroline Davidson? Not be in a sorority? How unthinkable! "I was a Kappa Delta."

That couldn't mean a thing to him.

"Were the other girls like you?"

Like her? How could she answer that? And what business was it of his? "Yes—" she heard her voice; it was tart, brittle, a voice she hadn't heard from herself in a long time "—in that we were all there just to get husbands."

Under the counter, the small refrigerator switched on, the motor chugging to bring down the temperature. Nancy had just come on duty, and she was working across the room, putting clean ashtrays out, the glass of each making a sharp little click as it touched the table. Tory didn't say anything. Joe didn't either, and, in a moment, he glanced at his watch and said he had to go.

TORY FELT BADLY. She should not have spoken to a customer that way. It was the first time she had done anything like it. She had been firm at times; it wasn't easy to refuse to serve someone or ask his friends to take his car keys away, but she had always been able to do it with a smile. She had never been snippy to one of her customers before, not ever.

Was it that Joe had been prying? No. His were reasonable questions from someone who was only beginning to deal with college graduates. And anyway, hadn't she gone behind his back to find out from his friend that he was divorced? She knew all about him; why shouldn't he know about her?

But Tory wasn't ready for that. Staying behind the bar was safe. For most of her life, people had expected her to be perfect. Although she had known—although she had been achingly aware—that she was not perfect, she had tried hard to make it seem as if she were. That was over now. She didn't want to be thought of as perfect anymore, yet she wasn't quite ready to be thought of as flawed.

And here was Joe Brigham, the one man in her bar not willing to take things for granted; he had wanted to know more about her, and for a moment, that felt dangerous. So Tory had lashed out at him.

She wondered if he would ever come back.

BUT JOE HAD NO CHOICE. People came to Tory's expecting to find him; he had to be there. The very next day someone whom Tory didn't know came in during lunch hour with some papers for him.

"Is it all right?" the man asked. "I meant to run them into town, but we've got a fully loaded semi out there and she's acting like she doesn't know her front from her back."

Tory had trouble picturing that. She took the manila envelope. "Does Joe know that this is here?"

"Yeah, he does. He said to tell you he'd be in later on to pick it up."

"It will be here."

For the next few hours, the bar was almost empty. Tory supposed that a fully loaded semi who didn't know her front from her back was providing the afternoon's entertainment for everyone not at work. When Joe came in, she had the local newspaper spread out across the bar and, having already examined the list of hospital admissions and discharges, was to her complete self-disgust reading the names of the entrants in the Miss Sullivan City Pageant.

She spoke to Joe quickly, almost wishing she could apologize. "Did you know there is a fully loaded semi out in the woods who doesn't know her front from her back?"

He laughed. "That's an interesting way to describe the problem. But your information is dated; she's now half-loaded."

"Is that good or bad?"

"Bad. The timber is all over the road, and nothing can get around."

"Was anyone hurt?"

Suddenly he smiled, a small, dry smile that Tory hadn't seen before. "With our union's standards of safety?"

"I do apologize," she drawled in reply. She turned and picked up his envelope. "If there are illegal drugs in this, I want a cut."

"What if there are a lot of boring forms to be filled out, do you want a cut of them too?"

"'Cut' is exactly what I would do with them."

Joe laughed and turned to leave. But just as he was pulling open the door, Nancy touched his arm, which was a little surprising since Nancy rarely initiated anything. Tory watched them. Joe was listening patiently, having picked up one of the bar's unspoken rules, that no one finished Nancy's sentences for her.

He nodded, and Nancy looked relieved. She moved off to finish setting up the tables, and Joe started to leave again. Tory whistled, calling him back over to the bar.

She spoke softly. "What did Nancy ask you to do?"

"Just make a call for her. She's afraid that she might have to testify if those two go to trial," he said, referring to Sweatshirt and Saturday Night. "She asked me to ask them—whoever 'them' might be—not to call her."

Tory had already guessed that Nancy was worried about this. "Don't do it."

"I beg your pardon?"

"Don't talk to anyone for her." Tory was unusually serious. "Listen, all her life everyone has always protected Nancy because she stutters. Her parents— everyone—let her get away with not talking so she doesn't, and she has simply no confidence in herself."

Tory was hoping that eventually Nancy would agree to see the speech therapist down in Klamath Falls. Tory hadn't mentioned it yet, knowing that, at this point, Nancy would refuse to go. She would think it useless; she couldn't imagine getting better.

Joe considered what Tory said. "But the case will probably never come to a trial—they'll plea bargain. And anyway, no one who's spoken to her for three seconds would ever put her on the stand. They don't need a call from me to figure that out. All I'd do is get a confirmation on it, just to save her the worry."

"She could ask them herself."

"That's true."

"You know I'm right."

He didn't answer for a moment. "I don't like seeing women unhappy."

Well, you couldn't quarrel with that, Tory thought. "If you find out who 'they' are and what times they're in, I'll take her down there and she can ask them in person."

"Sounds fair."

Tory guessed that he would look into it that afternoon. "If you're so hell-bent on making women happy, I know what else you can do."

"What?"

"Are you related to one Lisa Brigham?" That was a dumb question; of course he was related to her, the only question was how closely.

"She's my baby sister."

"No, she's not." Tory tapped the newspaper that was still spread out on the bar. "Not if she's entered in this pageant, she's not. This is a Miss America-affiliated contest. She can't be your baby sister anymore."

Joe paused, apparently doing some mental arithmetic. "Good God, Lisa's eighteen. How did that happen?"

"The Lord works in mysterious ways," Tory told him. "Tell me about her. Is she pretty?"

"Is who pretty?" Ed Bauer, always the first of the after-work crowd, asked as he sat down.

"My little sister," Joe explained.

"Doesn't she work in the diner?" Ed asked, and when Joe nodded, went on. "She's real pretty. She certainly has the looks in that family."

And that, Tory reflected glancing at the girl's brother, must be a lot of looks. "Is she blond like you?" she asked Joe.

"No, she's got Mother's hair. She and Cheryl— that's my other sister—always thought it was pretty unfair that all the boys in the family were blond and that the girls were dark.''

Little did Miss Lisa know—and Tory hoped that she would never learn—that there was one time when it did a girl no good to be a blond. ''What's her talent?''

''Talent? Lisa doesn't have any talent. None of us do.''

''In a Miss America-affiliate, you've got to have a talent, it's two-thirds of it—until the Atlantic City semis, that is, then it's only a third.''

Joe clearly did not follow a word of what Tory had said. ''If Lisa has a talent, no one told me about it ... Is she the woman that I am supposed to make happy?''

Tory nodded. ''Do you have any interest in being the world's most wonderful brother?''

''I probably wouldn't mind.''

''Then send your sister flowers tomorrow night.''

''Flowers? Like a corsage?''

''No, an arrangement for her dressing table. Half the girls will get them; half won't. And don't take them yourself; pay the extra for delivery. The girls notice things like that.''

''How do I find out where to send them?''

''The florist will know...and be sure and insist that her arrangement is different from what the other girls are getting.''

Joe pulled out a pen and jotted down some notes on a napkin. ''Have them delivered...have them strange...'' He glanced up. ''And, I suppose, have them expensive?''

He was a quick learner. ''You got it,'' Tory said.

"Anything else?"

"No, strange and expensive should cover it."

He tucked the napkin in his pocket and got up. "Why do you know so much about this?"

"Oh, no reason." She turned and started to wipe off the counter behind the bar—not that it needed it. "I guess I was sort of interested in beauty pageants once. Aren't all girls?"

"Are they? I didn't know that. But if you're interested, why don't you come tomorrow? I imagine the JayCees are concerned about the turn-out."

"Me? Go to a beauty contest? Not on your life."

In the bar mirror, she saw that he was looking at her above the reflection of the bottles, but when he spoke, his voice was as mild as always. "Well, I can understand that, I certainly wouldn't be going if my sister weren't in it."

Joe left, and Tory took Ed Bauer's order. She asked him how things were. They weren't great, he answered. His daughter wanted braces, and the union dental plan didn't cover braces. The girl's teeth really weren't that bad, no more crooked than her mother's, but . . .

What possessed you? What's it to you whether or not this Lisa Brigham got flowers?

. . . Ed had some money, the wife worked, after all. He'd been saving for a new fishing boat.

That's why I'm not going. Because I don't care, I'm not interested. Beauty pageants are boring.

. . . but Susie and the girls didn't care about a fishing boat. Maybe it would be different if he had a boy.

You put your past behind you. And this past was definitely something worthy of being put behind, stomped on, incinerated, even disinfected.

. . . oh, well, a man had to sacrifice for his children. That's what it was all about, wasn't it?

Ed stood up and thanked Tory.

"Bye now," she said . . . and thought that a person who had really put her past behind her probably wasn't afraid to turn and look it in the face.

Two

WITH TWENTY MINUTES TO KILL before he had to leave for Lisa's pageant, Joe thought he would drop by Tory's and give her the phone numbers of the various attorneys who could assure Nancy that she would not have to testify.

"Will you look at that?" Hank Newman called out as soon as Joe stepped into the bar.

"Joey, baby!" This was from Bill Gottfreed. "A coat and tie. Who's the lucky lady?"

Joe didn't like this. You did one thing the least bit different, and everyone noticed. "My kid sister," he answered, looking around for Tory. "She's in this beauty pageant."

"*You* should be in the beauty pageant. That's some suitcoat."

Actually, it was a blazer. One thing that Joe had heard over and over at the training sessions in Portland was that a union leader was every bit as good as the management on the other side of the table. So Joe had looked at the way the guys on the other side of the table dressed and now he was slowly starting to dress that way too. At first, he hadn't been comfortable in a coat and tie since Brighams wore them only to church, but they were beginning to feel pretty routine.

Rich's father was behind the bar and he, too, wanted to know why Joe was so dressed up. Patiently Joe shouted an explanation he could hear. "Well, you wish her luck for us," Rich's father answered. "Nobody from the union has ever won that."

"Then I don't imagine Lisa will," Joe called back, "but I'll tell her you're thinking about her."

Rich's father used to run the planing machine at the mill. It was encased in soundproofed housing now, but it hadn't been when Mr. Miller ran it. Joe asked him about Rich's wife and kids. Rich Miller had been a couple of years older than Joe, but he had been killed in Vietnam. That's why his father was working for Tory, even though his disability pay was pretty good; he gave money to Rich's widow.

"Where's Tory?" Joe asked.

"She took the night off."

That was a surprise. It was a Thursday, and Joe had never known Tory to deviate from her Mondays-off routine. He wondered what she was doing. He had never heard about her going around with anyone in town, having dinner with someone, going to a movie.

Joe found it amazing that they all knew so little about her. No one even seemed curious, except him. Here she was, the most beautiful woman any of them had ever seen—what on earth was she doing in Sullivan City?

Joe's only guess was that she was divorced, and somehow that had led her from whatever she had been doing—which could not have been tending bar—to this. But that didn't seem right. Even though she had told him that story about having gone to college to get a husband, he couldn't believe it, it didn't sound like her. And it was hard to imagine her married, grocery shopping, cleaning house, ironing shirts, doing all the things that the wives did around here. She seemed so above that somehow.

As Joe was crossing the parking lot, pulling his keys from his pocket, he heard a grinding sound. Someone was having trouble getting his car started. He looked around. It was Tory's little M.G.

He leaned down, rapped on the window. She unrolled it. "Do you need a jump?" he asked.

"No, I need a new car."

"Oh, that's right. Your car doesn't start in the rain." It had rained that morning.

"I thought it would have had time to dry out, but I guess not."

"My grandmother has arthritis. She doesn't work so well in the rain either."

"I'm thinking of getting a Japanese one next time."

"A Japanese grandmother?"

Tory laughed. "You're quick, you know that?"

He shrugged. "I'm no different than anyone else . . . but can I give you a lift? I'm off to this pageant thing of my sister's. It's at the high school so I can drop you anywhere."

"Believe it or not, that's where I'm going too," she said. "You don't mind the drive back?"

Joe was surprised. He had thought she had been set on not going. "I don't mind a bit."

He opened the M.G. door for her, and she got out. Instead of a coat, she was wearing some sort of white wrap with one end tossed over her shoulder. Her hair was caught back with a pair of silver combs. She looked spectacular . . . but then she always did.

"What do you drive?" she asked.

Joe pointed out his Cherokee Jeep.

"It does look a little more useful than my car," she remarked.

Joe shrugged. "I hardly know. I haven't had a chance to find out. I inherited it from my older brother not too long ago." Frank still borrowed it for hunting and fishing trips; Joe never seemed to have time for those anymore.

Turning out of the parking lot, Joe headed toward town. The highway was two lanes; his headlights picked up the center yellow line in the dark. The forest along this stretch had been clear cut years ago, and the lumber company had replanted so the pines were all the same height and the same distance from one another. It didn't look like a real forest, but when the time came, the trees would be easy to log.

Soon the highway became Fifteenth Street, the town's strip, running at a right angle to Main Street. It wasn't anything much, just a Pizza Hut, a McDonald's, a couple of auto body shops and a discount grocery store, but it was where the kids cruised on Saturday night. Joe himself had done just that in the old green Bonneville that he had shared first with Frank and then with his younger brother, Jim.

"Is anyone else from your family going to be there tonight?" Tory asked.

Joe glanced at her. What was she thinking? That Brighams were in beauty pageants so often that no one could be bothered? "My immediate family will be there."

"Who does that include?" she asked.

There were five of them. Frank was the oldest, married to Karen. Cheryl was next; she was married to Don. Joe was right in the middle. After him was Jim, whose wife's name was Debbie. Jim was the only one who didn't work for the company; he was a mechanic down at Roe's Garage. And Lisa was the baby.

"And your son? Will he be there?"

"Who, Max?" Again Joe was startled. Tory sure didn't know much about kids. "It's too late for a school night, and six-year-olds aren't great at sitting still for three hours."

"Oh." She sounded as if she knew she should have known that. "You said his name was Max?"

Joe nodded.

"That's an unusual name. I thought a lot of you guys name your boys after yourselves."

"I figured Sullivan City could get along without another Joe Brigham."

When Max started kindergarten, Marianne had tried to register him as "Max Colt," instead of "Max Brigham." Fortunately Joe had heard about it.

"It will make everything so much simpler," Marianne had said.

"Forget it," Joe had said.

They were at the high school now, and as they walked across the parking lot, Joe looked at the cars. There were more foreign automobiles than ever would have been parked outside Tory's: more Datsuns, more Toyotas, even the town's only BMW. This wasn't a union crowd. Joe recognized his family's cars: Dad's Buick—what a great car it had been all these years—Frank's green Maverick, Don and Cheryl's new Citation, Jim's beloved '57 Chevy... and a blue Capri.

Oh. Joe hadn't expected the Capri.

Tory must have noticed his slight hesitation. "You know that car?"

"I paid for it." Marianne had had a car of her own. His sister Cheryl didn't have her own car, nor did Karen, Frank's wife, or Davy's wife, Polly. Times hadn't been good enough recently for families to have two cars. If a woman needed the car, she had to drive her husband to work. But when Marianne had been married to him, she'd had this Capri. Of course, it had been used, but they had bought it from the original owner, and Jim had been the only mechanic to work on it. When Jim had heard it was up for sale, he'd told the rest of the family, saying it was one of the best buys he'd seen. It had been a good car. Joe hoped that Dennis was taking good care of it.

"So your ex-wife's here?" Tory asked.

Joe glanced at her. She must know all about Marianne and Dennis. He wondered who had told her. Probably everyone. "It's no surprise," he lied. "They are family."

Which was part of what made it all so tough. It was okay when Joe's mother would have him over for Sunday night supper; Joe would pick up Max, and the two of them would go over to Mom and Dad's together. But most family gatherings were at Grandma's, and she was Dennis's grandmother too. He had as much right to be there as Joe did. So on Memorial Day and the Fourth, Thanksgiving, Christmas, and Easter, Joe got to see his son arrive and leave with another man.

"Get your coat, Max, it's time to go." "Do you have all your presents?" "Give me your hand; there's ice on that step." Now it was Dennis who said these things.

Really, he shouldn't complain. After all, Dennis was doing fine by Max, no question about that. And Joe did admire anyone with the guts to start his own business, but still . . . maybe if it were someone other than Cousin Dennis it wouldn't be so bad.

Dennis had always been in and out of Joe's family's house because he was Brother Frank's best friend. Frank and Dennis, Dennis and Frank.

Joe, two years younger, had admired them, envied them, resented them. He had wanted to be like Frank and Dennis. Life would be perfect if he could just be like Frank and Dennis. And all that had happened since—Dennis marrying his wife and becoming stepfather to his son—had not particularly improved Joe's feelings toward him.

At least Max wouldn't be at the pageant tonight. That would make it a little easier. It would just be Dennis and Marianne, arriving in the car that Joe had bought for her, going back to the house where he had lived with her.

There had to be better ways to spend an evening.

Just inside the door, two girls were sitting behind a metal-rimmed table, selling tickets. Joe didn't recognize them, but he didn't suppose their dads belonged to the union.

He noticed Tory start to take her purse from under her arm. He wasn't sure what to do. This wasn't a date, but still . . . "I'll get it," he said quickly.

"Thank you."

He was grateful that she didn't make a big deal out of it.

The pageant was in the school cafeteria, a room with several uses. At one end were the steam tables; at the other a stage so that when folding chairs were set up in rows facing it, the room was called an auditorium or sometimes even a theater. On senior prom night, the chairs lined the walls and it was a ballroom.

Tonight the chairs had been turned to face the center of the room, and someone had pushed together the lunch tables so they formed a runway jutting out from the stage. The sides of the tables were draped with crepe paper, but you could still tell that they were lunch tables. Joe wondered if it were safe.

He saw his family. They were all sitting together and there was one empty chair next to Cheryl. She probably had her purse on it, saving it for him. But there was only one place, and he could hardly abandon Tory, could he? So he found seats on the other side of the runway.

Tory untangled herself from her white wrap and let it drift over the back of her folding chair. The rest of her outfit was also white. Her skirt was very straight and shorter than Joe had seen recently (which was entirely fine with him). Her top was cashmere or something, shot with fine silver threads, all loose and full, the sleeves and the bodice part flowing into one another. Joe felt like he was staring at her. It was hard to believe that one woman could always look so consistently terrific.

He decided he had better look around the room. His mother caught sight of him and started to wave, but then she saw Tory. Her mouth dropped open and she nudged Cheryl, who looked and then nudged Don, who looked and nudged Karen, who looked and nudged Marianne...

Joe turned away.

"Do you feel like you just walked into church with the town whore?" Tory asked pleasantly.

Joe shook his head. "They're just surprised to see me walking in with Miss America herself."

Tory tucked the end of her wrap into the chair so that it would not touch the floor. "Second runner-up," she said.

"I beg your pardon?"

"Second runner-up," she repeated. "I wasn't Miss America; I was just second runner-up."

He looked at her, confused, waiting for her to explain the joke.

And then realized that she wasn't joking. "Are you serious? You were in the Miss America Pageant?"

She nodded.

"The Miss America Pageant?"

"In a former life, yes."

"*The* Miss America Pageant?"

"Will you stop looking at me like I crawled out from under a rock?"

"In Atlantic City?"

"Joe!"

He blinked and tried to speak normally. "I'm just surprised, that's all. How come you never said so?"

"It never came up. And you never asked."

"That's true," he admitted. He didn't exactly make a habit of going up to people and asking them how they placed in the Miss America Pageant.

She opened the program and started paging through it, looking at which businesses had taken ads. "They didn't call me; I guess it's because I run a bar. That's why towns with any sense have these things in December, you know, so people will buy Christmas ads.''

"The Miss America Pageant?''

She looked at him with a sidelong glance. "It was almost worth letting that out just to see you finally react to something.''

Joe found it amazing to sit through the pageant with Tory. She knew so much, and apparently there was a great deal to know. He had thought he had a pretty good notion of what to look for when a girl in a swimsuit walked by, but it turned out he was miserably ignorant.

"Breasts don't matter too much,'' Tory whispered, "so long as you don't look deformed. It's legs, bottom, and back.''

A couple of the girls Tory instantly dismissed as BFCB—Built For Child Birth. Some of the thinner girls had chicken wings for shoulder blades; she wrote them off too.

"Do you know why they have the swimsuit competition?''

"Yes,'' he answered bluntly.

She laughed. "You're wrong. It's to demonstrate the contemporary woman's interest in physical fitness.''

"Is that so? Then I was wrong.''

Lisa had, Tory told him, a terrific back, the best back there, but she lost a few points on her rear end. "It's not bad, but she's a bit of a Miss Fanny Overhang.''

Joe considered that portion of his sister. He thought it was pretty cute or at least, he amended prudishly, that's what he would think if it weren't his sister's. "Why is she wearing such an ugly suit?" he asked Tory. It was a one piece, sort of frumpy number.

"They're all wearing ugly suits. That's part of the ordeal. You have to walk down a runway in front of all your friends and family, wearing a pair of three-inch heels and a swimsuit you wouldn't otherwise be caught dead in. Then if you win your state, you get to do it in Atlantic City on prime-time television. If you can do that, you can do anything."

"Like get held up at gun point?"

"That was nothing compared to my state pageant interview."

Legs were important. Tory told him how thighs, knees, and calves should lightly touch with a little gap between knee and calf and then between calf and ankle.

The girls posed and then filed off to change.

"Your sister won the swimsuit."

"She did? How do you know?"

"I just do. She's got a nice body, and she seemed to feel good, and she was able to project it. That's what really counts. You need to feel fabulous, sparkling and glowing, completely confident."

Which was exactly how Tory always seemed when she was behind the bar; it was what made Tory's such a good place. "Well, Lisa did seem happy...but Rich's father says that nobody from a union family has ever won."

"That's no surprise."

"Why not? Are the judges prejudiced?"

Tory shook her head. "No, they usually want the best girl, but to be the best . . . I mean, how important is this contest to your mother?"

"To Mom? Not at all. But what does she have to do with it?"

"Everything. A girl can't do this on her own."

In the talent competition, Lisa sang, and she sounded good enough to Joe, although he would have been the first to admit that he knew nothing about it. He got a little bored during the other selections and found himself looking around the room.

Particularly across the runway to where his family was sitting...to a head of honey-brown hair and a pair of soft, dark eyes, eyes that caught his and then nervously looked away.

Next to Tory, Marianne's looks were nothing; of course, next to Tory, everyone's looks were nothing. But Marianne had an air about her, a soft and gentle prettiness, a touching vulnerability, that . . .

It had been two years since she'd asked him to leave. Two years already, and every time he looked at her, he wondered if he still loved her.

He had been so surprised when she'd told him that she wanted a divorce, that she wanted to marry Dennis. The family said it was entirely his fault; if he hadn't been so absorbed in the union, he would have noticed how unhappy his wife was.

Like most of their friends, Joe and Marianne had married right out of high school, a week before Davy had married Polly. Joe and Davy had gone to work for the company. They wanted to be out in the woods, where the work was less repetitive and more of a challenge. But there weren't any openings for loggers, so

Davy started as a pond monkey, herding logs from the pond into the mill, and Joe drove a lumber hauler in the yard. At least they were outside. The mill was full of clattering machinery, dinging bells and grinding gears, logs scraping and slamming into each other. The noise was so loud that the men on the line could only signal to each other; they couldn't hear.

As a driver, Joe moved around and could speak to more people during the day than someone with an inside job. So he started doing some chores for the union—finding out what the men thought about things, doing some informal canvassing.

He had enjoyed it, and each year he had become more involved in union activities, serving as shop steward, volunteering to be on committees—the safety committee, then the negotiating committee. First he was just a member, then he was chairman. Yes, he was young, but the field rep from the International staff kept encouraging the local to give the younger men and women more responsibilities.

Spots opened up on the logging crews and Joe took one. He liked being in the woods, but he missed the union activity. Marianne knew why he transferred back to the mill, but she didn't say a word.

Now Joe guessed that the family had been right, that he should have realized how unhappy he'd made Marianne, but still he had to wonder if she weren't to blame too. At the end, she'd said that she'd hated his union work from the very beginning. But in the early days, every time he would get back from a meeting, she would be waiting, smiling, ready to fix him something to eat. He had had no idea that she didn't approve.

Maybe if she had said then, "Joe, I hate this; it scares me," he could have quit. But for years she had said nothing, waiting until he got on the negotiating committee, waiting until this work had come to matter to him. And then she was so mild about it that he really didn't take her seriously. . . until it was too late.

Of course he had been blind and selfish, everyone told him that, and he probably agreed with them, but still he wished that Marianne had started complaining just a little earlier and a whole lot louder.

Joe felt Tory stir in the chair beside him. He glanced at her and, a little embarrassed by his thoughts, spoke quickly. "When you were in the Miss America Pageant, what was your talent?"

"Baton twirling."

"Baton twirling? You're joking."

"Being a baton twirler is not the sort of thing one would make up about oneself."

Joe admitted that he had never had the least impulse to tell someone he was a baton twirler.

"It's not a good talent," she said. "The judges don't really like it; it has a bit of a low-rent feel to it. Only the accordion players have it worse."

"You seem to have done all right with it."

"Not well enough."

The girls were now filing by in their evening gowns.

Tory didn't pay much attention to the evening gown competition. "You're picking up your points from your interview here."

The interviews between judges and contestants were really the heart of the competition, Tory explained, although officially they were not judged. The scores on evening gown competition always reflected how a girl did in the interview. That was why swimsuit and talent winners were announced, but the evening gown winner was not. "Except Utah—they're so prim they don't announce the swimsuit winner either."

Joe was baffled. "That's funny about the interview being so important. I talked to Cheryl—she's my older sister—this morning. Lisa said she did great in her interview because she knew it didn't count so she was relaxed. She couldn't figure out why everyone else was nervous."

"Then Lisa's ignorance will get her into the finals."

And indeed it did. The five finalists were the daughters of a cost supervisor, the shoe store owner, a contractor, a company v.p., and Lisa, the only union girl. Each was brought on stage alone and asked why she wanted to be Miss Sullivan City.

It was the most standard beauty pageant question, Tory whispered. "And the answer is because you 'want to help other people.'" Suddenly she started mimicking herself. "Why did I like baton twirling? 'Because through my baton twirling, I can help other people.'"

"How does baton twirling help other people?"

"Don't ask me; I haven't a clue. Unless it is that baton twirlers wear very short skirts."

"I can see that," Joe agreed. But before he could say more, Lisa came on stage.

"Why do you want to be Miss So-and-so?" might have been a standard beauty pageant question, but it seemed to surprise Lisa. "I don't know..." she said slowly.

Joe felt Tory wince.

"I guess it's coming from a big family, I want to do something that no one else has done—"

Tory was shaking her head.

"...and, I guess, that coming from a big family, I'm used to having people look at me as the representative for a whole lot of others, and I try hard to live up to that...and, well, I think I would be as proud to represent all of Sullivan City as I am to represent my family."

Joe couldn't help looking over at his family. They were all clapping madly, except his mother who looked liked she was about to cry. He wished he were with them.

Tory leaned over and spoke in his ear. "That was a terrific answer."

The five finalists filed out on stage, and one by one names were called, until only Lisa and the contractor's girl were left. They gripped each other's hands, and the next name called was Alison Hicks.

Poor Alison got shunted off to the side while the M.C. and last year's Miss Sullivan City draped a sash around Lisa and balanced a rhinestone crown on her head. A spotlight shone on her as she walked up the runway and then back down to a throne, which was a folding chair emerging from wings made of chicken wire and Kleenex roses.

"South Carolina takes its beauty pageants more seriously than Oregon does," Tory commented.

The M.C. made a little speech, and people started to leave. The other finalists had to gather around Lisa while pictures were taken. Joe imagined that they all felt pretty bad, but he was pleased that it was Lisa who would be sitting in the center of the photographs.

"Do you mind if we wait?" he asked Tory.

"Goodness, no."

They went over to where the rest of the family was milling around. Joe approached Dennis and Marianne first. He always did. And he tried to seem pleasant and relaxed when he talked to them. It looked better that way. It wasn't easy, but it looked better.

He introduced Tory to them although they knew who she was.

"I sure do hear nice things about your little boy," Tory said to Marianne.

"He's at my mother's tonight," Marianne answered.

She sounded defensive. That was crazy, Joe thought. Tory wasn't criticizing her for going out at night. Did Tory spook Marianne a little? Was Marianne uncomfortable because Tory looked so great?

What could he say? *Yes, she's beautiful...but you're you.*

It was the truth, but he couldn't say it. So he spoke to Dennis. "How's business?"

"Well enough."

Just then the new Miss Sullivan City pushed between Dennis and Marianne and flung herself on Joe. "Oh, Joe, they were from you, weren't they? It said 'All of us' on the card, but it was your handwriting, I could tell!"

"What are you talking about?" Cheryl asked.

"Flowers, Joe sent me flowers."

"Why, Joe—" His mother patted him on the arm. "What a nice thing to do."

Joe hated to take credit for the idea, but he didn't want to insult Lisa by saying he had been acting on orders. He flicked a grateful glance at Tory, and her green eyes danced. She understood.

"I'm glad you liked them," he said.

"Liked them? I *loved* them!" Lisa gushed. "They had set up all these long tables in the girls' gym for us to dress at, and Kim and Alison and Cassie—that whole crowd—they all had flowers, and none of us did, except Annie whose mom had brought by some carnations in a mayonnaise jar. And about half an hour before it was time to start, the delivery boy came with two arrangements. One was for Alison—it was her second one—this was from her grandparents, and the rest of us just felt awful, like it was really stupid of us to even bother to come because one of them was going to win for sure. Then Miss Edwards pointed to me, and the boy brought the flowers over to me... I couldn't believe it! I felt so wonderful! During rehearsal everybody was always telling us to remember to smile, and I always forgot, but I guess I must have smiled—I mean, I wouldn't have won if I hadn't smiled, would I? But if I did, it was because I just kept thinking about how lucky I was to get flowers, and how they were just as pretty as anyone else's—even prettier, they came in this sweet little basket, and everyone else had these same green vases, and—"

As Lisa described her flowers, Joe glanced over at Tory.

She had known. She had known exactly what would be happening back in the girls' gym, and she had made sure that Lisa would have flowers. She had made sure that Lisa wouldn't have to remind herself to smile.

Joe felt a touch on his arm. It was Marianne.

Marianne.

Neither of them said anything for a moment. Joe always hated that, when they couldn't think of what to say to each other. "This sure is a surprise," he said at last. "Lisa winning, I mean."

Marianne nodded. "But she's always been very pretty... That's a new sport coat, isn't it? It looks nice."

"Thank you. This new job, you know. I have to dress up more."

Joe could tell that she wanted to know what it cost, but she was embarrassed to ask. Which was fine, because he would have been embarrassed to tell her. She was so frugal about everything; she would have been shocked.

"Is it still okay if I pick Max up after school tomorrow?" he asked, just for something to say. Of course it was okay.

She nodded, not seeming to hear. Then she spoke so quietly he had to bend his head to hear her. "Tory Duncan is very pretty."

Joe looked over at Tory. She was talking to the pageant M.C. "Very pretty" didn't quite cover it. He thought about how her eyes had danced a few minutes ago. He had never seen eyes as bright as hers. They were such a pure, vivid green; he supposed they could be called emerald.

He turned back to Marianne. "Did you know that she was second runner-up in the Miss America Pageant?"

"What? The Miss America Pageant... the real one?"

Joe nodded. "The one in Atlantic City. Isn't that incredible? I can't figure out what she's doing here."

Marianne looked a little sick. She didn't say anything for a while, and then, "Do you see her a lot?"

"I go to her bar a lot. It's a good way to talk to some of the members."

"That's not what I—"

But then Frank and Cheryl's husband Don interrupted, drawing Joe aside. Since he had signed the card "From all of us," they wanted to pay him for a share of the flowers, but he wouldn't take any money from them. He didn't want to say it—hell, he didn't even like *thinking* it—but he had more money than they did. The union paid well, and except for a couple more payments on the Cherokee, Max's child support, and his rather minimal rent, he didn't have the sort of obligations everyone else did. In fact, that's how he'd gotten the Cherokee. He hadn't "inherited" it, as he'd told Tory. Frank had gotten in over his head last year and had trouble with the payments so Joe had bought it off him.

In the car on the way out of town, Joe thought of hundreds of questions he wanted to ask Tory, but when they were stopped at the Pizza Hut light, he settled for something simple. "Were you one of the ones who got flowers or one of the ones who didn't?"

"Who, me? I got enough flowers to swamp a mid-sized aircraft carrier. My dressing area always looked like I just died."

There was so much he didn't know about her. "I take it that you had a mother who cared about this sort of thing."

"Cared? My God, it was what she *lived* for."

Joe didn't know what to say. He wasn't sure he understood. Neither of them said anything until they were beyond McDonald's, and then she spoke. "I really don't think the whole world needs to know about this Miss America thing."

"Why not? It's not something to be ashamed of."

"No, of course not. It's just that people sometimes act a bit strange when they hear about it."

Well, yes, he had acted a bit strange. "Are you sorry you told me?"

"I can't imagine what came over me."

"I did tell my wife," he admitted.

"Your wife?" Tory's voice was dry. "I didn't know you were married."

"You know what I mean."

Joe glanced at his watch as he turned into the parking lot; he had time for a beer. He parked, held the door of the bar open, and followed Tory in. He watched her as she crossed the room. Miss America? It was still hard to believe.

Joe sat down next to Davy, who didn't usually come in in the evenings. "What are you doing here?"

"What am I doing here?" Davy demanded. "What about yourself? Look at you. Are we starting to dress up around here, or what?"

"I went to a beauty pageant; my younger sister was in it."

"A beauty pageant? How was it?"

"Very strange, but Lisa won."

"Well, good for her. Three cheers for the home team." Davy waved his mug in salute and then set it down. "Tory went with you?"

Joe knew she wouldn't want people knowing why she had gone. "She's got a business," he improvised.

"And since she couldn't take out an ad in the program, she went instead."

"With you?"

Joe looked at him... and realized what Davy was asking. "Oh, come on. Me and her? Are you kidding?" Of course, his family had been a little surprised at first tonight, but Davy ought to know better. "I just gave her a ride, that's all. We were in the parking lot at the same time, and there was something wrong with her car."

Davy did not look convinced.

"You need to have your head examined," Joe told him.

"That's right," Davy agreed. "Every so often I get these dizzy spells and start thinking that you aren't a married man, but, then again, we all know you are."

"Oh, for Christ's sake..."

BUT DAVY WAS PROBABLY half right, Joe reflected as he drove home later. He wasn't married, but he still felt married, and he certainly wished he still were.

He simply could not imagine a life without Marianne. He had been so busy with work the last two years that he hadn't thought much about the future, but when he tried to imagine some other woman, he couldn't.

God knows Marianne had her faults. She was too cautious, she was a bit of a martyr, she worried about what other people thought. She was just one more American housewife and mother, and he had loved her since she was fifteen.

Tory Duncan was beautiful, poised, a Miss America candidate, as nearly perfect in looks, manner, and bearing as anyone Joe had ever met. And Joe had to admit that he'd caught himself having some thoughts about her he wouldn't care to have anyone know about.

But such thoughts, such fantasies—and he supposed everyone in the bar had them about her—had nothing to do with real life. Miss America? Prime-time television? What did that have to do with the day-in, day-out routine of Sullivan City?

Real life was explaining to a guy you'd grown up with that the union wasn't going to appeal his grievance for him; real life was driving a car your brother still considered his; real life was trying to figure out what's the point of being a father when your son has a perfectly good stepfather.

Three

THE NEXT AFTERNOON, Joe drove to the block where he used to live. It was a working-class neighborhood with one-story houses and waist-high chain link fences. The houses were small, they didn't have foyers, garages, or dining rooms. The front doors opened right into the living rooms; people parked on the street and ate in the kitchen.

But none of the homes needed painting. There weren't any battered cars rusting at the curb; nobody left old refrigerators out on the back porch. In the summer the grass would be mowed every week; in the winter the sidewalks would be shoveled. The people who lived here knew how lucky they were to have their own houses.

It was still early, just about three-thirty, so there weren't too many cars on the block. Joe guessed that Tammy Jennings must have driven Steve to work; their Pontiac was in front of their house. And two doors down was Marianne's car, of course . . . and Dennis's truck.

Joe was puzzled. Why was Dennis home? Did the siding business have such good hours?

But before he could think much about it, the front door opened, and a towheaded, blue-parkaed, miniature kamikaze pilot bombed down the front walk.

Joe reached across the car to open the door, and Max launched a flying vault. For a moment, it looked like the gymnastic feat might end with a triple back somersault, but Joe caught a parka sleeve, keeping his son from tumbling back on the curb.

And people said that logging was dangerous.

"Hi, Dad."

"Hi, Max." Joe rumpled the boy's hair and leaned across him to wave at Marianne who had stepped out on the concrete slab that served as a front porch.

Max Brigham was commonly described as a pistol, a handful, a real firecracker, and those weren't descriptions that his father could quarrel with. Max was energetic, imaginative, and aggressive, tough, talkative and feisty. He was capable of being a good little boy when he had to be, but the effort wore him out. He behaved himself in kindergarten all morning and then came home and fell apart. In fact, when Joe heard that the International staff liked him because of the way he kept people calm, he figured that if he could, the reason was that he'd had six years of practice on Max.

"Are we going to work on the bird house?" Max asked.

"If you want."

For his sixth birthday last week, Joe had given Max some wood and a few light tools of his own so that the two of them could build a bird house together. Marianne had doubted that Max would have the patience for it, but he was doing surprisingly well.

"Then what are we waiting for?" Max wanted to know.

"For you to put your seat belt on."

"Oh, do I *have* to?"

"Yes."

Max groaned and let Joe help him with the seat belt. He then slumped down as low as this instrument of torture would permit, a picture of revolution in defeat.

Joe pulled away from the curb, trying not to smile. "What did you do in school today?"

"Nothing."

Joe doubted that; Max would have ended up dismantling the school building if he had had to sit still doing nothing for three hours. "You didn't draw any pictures or hear any stories?"

"We heard a story."

"Do you want to tell me about it?"

"It was about this bear who ate a rowboat. It was pretty neat, Dad. He swallowed it whole, just like *that*, and there it was inside him like this—" Max stuck out his stomach, demonstrating the effects of swallowing a rowboat "—he was huge and he didn't feel so good and then the people whose rowboat it was..."

The story lasted until they reached Joe's house. Joe lived in a four-room rental near one of the elementary schools. It was just a little box, a real nothing of a place, and Joe was the first to admit he had not done a thing with it. It was very sparsely furnished, having curtains only because his older sister, Cheryl, who was a little on the bossy side, had been so outraged at the way he was living that she had sent Lisa over with a few pairs.

But Joe didn't mind—he didn't care where he lived—and Max adored it. He could shout and run in these almost empty rooms. There was nothing to break, nothing to get in his way. And when he slept over, he got to use a cot and a sleeping bag, an arrangement he described with such enthusiasm to his cousins that they all envied him for being so very blessed as to be the victim of a broken home.

Joe and Max worked on the bird house for twelve, maybe thirteen minutes and then went out in the tiny yard and pummeled each other for another hour or so. It was an entirely satisfactory afternoon.

After times like this, Joe wanted to keep Max for supper, but Marianne thought that she, Max, and Dennis should eat "as a family"—a phrase that Joe wasn't exactly crazy about. Reluctantly, he tucked Max's shirt in and forced him into the bathroom to wash the topsoil off his hands and face.

Joe leaned against the doorjamb, watching while Max earnestly turned the bar of soap around in his hands. He didn't have to use a stool to reach the sink anymore.

"You've got new shoes on," Joe noticed. It had been dry all day, and Max was wearing sneakers, new navy blue ones, instead of his boots.

Max made a face. "Yeah."

"What about your running shoes? I thought you wanted running shoes this year."

All last summer Max had wanted Real Running Shoes, not Cruddy Old Sneakers. He had tried hard to make life intolerable for the adults around him, but the best he had been able to manage was the pledge that when he outgrew his sneakers, he could have running shoes with ridged soles and contrasting leather trim. But he was wearing another pair of thin-soled sneakers.

Joe was surprised. Marianne didn't make promises lightly; as aggravating as Max was capable of being, she never made promises just to buy herself some peace. If she said she'd do something, she did it.

Max stared down at his feet in disgust. "Mom says that running shoes are too expensive. She says I don't really need them."

Well, that was true. Max didn't need running shoes; he was hardly training for a marathon, although sometimes it seemed like he was. And running shoes did cost more than sneakers, almost twice as much.

But there was no reason not to let him have them. Max was not an indulged child, and there was money enough. When Joe started making more, he had increased his child support proportionally, even though there was nothing in the divorce decree making him do it. He wanted his son to be able to have things like running shoes once in a while.

Marianne was funny about money. She was unbelievably frugal. They used to fight about it when they were married. Like with babysitters—if her mother or Joe's mother or Lisa couldn't babysit, then Marianne would rather stay home than pay someone. It wasn't that she didn't trust the sitter, but she could always think of so many other ways to spend the money. She would buy a nice cut of meat, and just when Joe was complimenting her on the meal, asking for seconds, she would point out they wouldn't be eating it if she had used a sitter last week.

Marianne had meant well, but remarks like that had sometimes made Joe want to strangle her. He certainly hoped she wasn't doing something like that with Max's shoes.

As Joe drove Max home, he decided he would ask her about it. He always went up to the door with Max anyway, and Dennis always asked him in. Of course, Joe never went in unless he had something to talk to them about.

Max turned the knob and pushed the front door open. Dennis was standing up, waiting for them.

"It's good to see you, Joe," he said. "Won't you stay and eat with us?"

Joe glanced over at the chair that he had once considered his own. A magazine had been dropped in the seat; a can of beer sat on the little table nearby.

"Not this time," he answered. Since Dennis and Marianne had gotten married, Joe hadn't even had a cup of coffee in this house. "I just have a couple of questions to ask Marianne if she's got a minute."

She came out of the kitchen, drying her hands on her apron. "Of course," she answered, then turned to Max. "Go wash up for supper."

Max began to protest that he had spent hours and hours with a bar of soap, but Marianne would have none of it. A person washed his hands right before supper. As soon as the boy was out of the room, Joe spoke. "Why didn't Max get running shoes this year?"

"Max doesn't need to have everything he thinks he wants." She turned and went into the kitchen as if that was all there was to say.

Joe followed her. "No, he doesn't. But we promised him he could have those shoes, and I don't see any reason why he can't."

"They're expensive. He doesn't need expensive things."

"But we told him he could have them, and that was even before I started working for the union. There's more money now."

Dennis had also come into the kitchen. "That's right, I'd forgotten. We did tell him he could have running shoes, Marianne. Joe's right. He should have them."

Marianne made a funny, sick noise and turned away. Joe was surprised; she seemed tense and white. Nervously, she started putting supper on the table. He watched, confused, wondering why she was suddenly upset. She took a Jell-O salad out of the refrigerator and then a bowl of canned peaches. She opened the oven, started to slide a casserole out, and then suddenly shoved it back in like she didn't want Joe to see it.

But he had. It was a macaroni casserole.

Jell-O and macaroni. She was serving Max Jell-O and macaroni for supper.

Joe reached for Max's glass, picked it up, and sniffed at the milk. It was dried skim.

This didn't make sense. Food was important to Marianne. She had always been proud that she could serve interesting, nutritious meals without spending a lot of money. The only thing that could be said about this meal was that she hadn't spent a lot of money.

"What's going on here, Marianne?"

"Max likes macaroni." She knew exactly what he was talking about.

"And he's just crazy about dried skim milk." Joe didn't want to get angry with her, but this dinner looked like they had all been on strike for three months. "Why aren't you serving meat?" She had al-

ways served meat before. She had never believed the
people who said you didn't have to have meat every
day.

"Meat's expensive."

Meat was expensive...shoes were expensive...
"Sure it is, but we all have work, don't we?"

"Now, Joe," Dennis said, "if you have any complaints about the way Marianne's using your check,
you know she'll sit down and explain how—"

"Dennis!"

Joe stared at her. She had never sounded like that
before—so quick, so defensive. It was almost as if she
was attacking Dennis for having spoken, as if he had
betrayed her, as if he had—

And then it all made sense—complete, perfect,
sickening sense. No, they didn't all have work. He did,
but Dennis didn't. That's why the truck had been
home at three. Dennis's business was going nowhere.
How could it? It was December. Who put up siding in
December? Or ever? Not around here. Joe had seen
the new fences that went up last summer. Sure, people had ordered their stuff from Dennis, but they'd
done the work themselves. Nobody in this town was
going to pay someone else to dig a few post holes for
them, and Dennis had been a fool to think they would.

So there wasn't much money coming in...except
that nice, fat, regular monthly check from Joe. Marianne was running the whole house on Max's child
support check. Some weeks that was probably all the
money she had. Joe was supporting all three of them.

Terrific.

Joe turned on Dennis. "It sounds like it's you who
owes me an explanation."

"What are you talking—"

"My hands are clean, Mommy." Max came in, his arms outstretched, showing his hands to Marianne. She dropped down to her knees in front of him.

"Come on, Max," Joe said abruptly. "Get your coat. You don't have to eat in this house."

Max shrieked and raced for his coat.

Marianne was still kneeling on the floor. She looked up, her hand to her throat. "Don't take him to your mother's. Please, don't take him to your mother's."

"I'll take him wherever I goddam please."

He'd never spoken like that to her before. But he'd never been this angry at her before. Using his money on Dennis. Spending the money for Max's food, Max's clothes, on the three of them. Did she really think he wouldn't mind?

Max rushed back into the kitchen, struggling with his parka. "Are we ready? Can we go now?"

Joe put his hand on his son's shoulder. Marianne didn't say anything. She started to take Max's place off the table. Joe watched her as she scooped up the silverware, the plate. She carried them to the sink. He knew her; she would wash them even though they hadn't been used.

"Come on, Max, let's go," he said.

Outside, he asked Max if he wanted to go to Grandma's or to see Aunt Lisa at the diner. Max chose the diner; Joe had known that he would.

Aunt Lisa, a.k.a. Miss Sullivan City, recommended the blue plate special, which was pot roast, and in a fit of nutritional self-righteousness, Joe ordered her to leave the mashed potatoes off Max's plate and give him extra green beans. While Max ate and chattered away to Lisa, Joe glowered silently, feeling sorry for himself because his poor son was being starved to death by his witch of a mother.

He was still angry when he dropped Max off. He went up to the door with the boy but left without speaking a word, even though Dennis tried to talk to him.

Joe went home and paced around his four little rooms, unable to decide if he was angrier with Marianne or with Dennis. It had been really stupid of Dennis to start a fencing and siding business in a town like this. People always did all their own work. Joe had wondered about it at the time, but Dennis had seemed so sure. And Marianne too. She had seemed happy and proud that her husband was starting his own business. Her second husband, that is. She hadn't wanted her first one to do a little union work; she thought it was too risky.

But look at how things had turned out.

What was Joe supposed to do? That's what made him so mad, there wasn't a thing he could do. He couldn't stop paying child support. That would hurt Max more than anyone. But why should he support Dennis and Marianne too? Didn't he have any rights here? A way of insisting that the money be spent on Max and only Max?

Joe didn't know the law, but the law didn't matter. He couldn't take Dennis to court. The man was family. You don't sue family. Joe was powerless, absolutely powerless.

He turned on the TV, watched five seconds of a jeans commercial and turned it back off. What in the name of God was he supposed to do?

Answer the door, he guessed. Someone was knocking.

He flipped on the porch light and looked out through the little window in the door. It was Marianne.

She almost never went out alone at night; she didn't like to. She must be coming to apologize. Her head was bent, she was looking down so she wouldn't have to meet his eyes through the window. Joe opened the door.

"I'm sorry for dropping in like this..." She sounded nervous. "But I ... Joe—"

"Come on in."

She did and for a moment said nothing, glancing around at the cheap sofa, the wood grain Formica coffee table, the pole lamp. Joe knew that she didn't like the way he lived.

At least he paid his own way. That was more than could be said for some people.

Without speaking, Joe took her coat from her and hung it up in the little closet that jutted out from one of the corners of the living room.

She was still looking around the room. "How can you stand to live like this?" She said this every time she came in.

"I don't mind." That's what he always said too.

"But it makes you look like you're poor."

She hadn't said that before. She was nervous, distracted; she probably didn't even know what she had said.

Makes you look like you are poor.

Was that what had bothered her about his home? Not that it seemed temporary or uncomfortable, but because it made him look poor?

Of course, now that he thought about it...of course, that was what she didn't like about this place.

Nothing frightened Marianne as much as poverty. It was not simply a matter of money, but of character. In her mind, poor people beat their children and shouted at the supper table. Poor people didn't keep their houses clean or tell Christmas stories about the Baby Jesus. Poor people had to lie because they couldn't pay their bills.

And for these last few months, Marianne must have felt poor.

Joe put his arm around her. Her words came out in a rush. "Oh, Joe, you have every right to be mad at me." She was crying. "I knew it was wrong, I knew it wasn't fair, but I didn't know what else to do. I said I'd go back to work, you know I would have been happy to get a job, but Dennis kept saying he'd give up the business if it came to that, but now you're angry with me and he's angry with me—"

"Dennis? Why is he angry with you?"

"For using your money for all of us. He didn't know. He didn't have any idea until today."

"How could he not know?"

"All he thinks about is the business. He doesn't pay any attention to the house money. He asked once and I said I'd been saving and not to worry—"

Joe could understand. He had always turned his pay check over to Marianne every Friday; that's the way things worked around here. The wives handled the day-to-day managing of the money.

Marianne had had a system worked out with all these little envelopes, and she had done a good job. Joe had never had to pay much attention. Once or twice she'd told him she had some money left over; she wouldn't need his whole paycheck that week, and he should use some of it on himself. He hadn't questioned her, and the times when she'd asked him to pick up some extra overtime, he'd never challenged her on that either. He had trusted her, he had respected her ability to manage their family budget.

Dennis must be sick about his business. He wouldn't want to worry about domestic finances, and Marianne would make that easy. What she must have been going through.

"It's been bad, hasn't it, babe?"

She leaned against him. "Oh, Joe, it's been awful. You can't know how awful it's been. I've felt so alone. Dennis can't stand to talk about it, and I feel so ashamed that we don't have any money. I think I would die if anyone knew. I feel like I have to smile all the time so no one will suspect, but I just don't know what we're going to do about Christmas. I lie awake at night thinking about Christmas, about how everyone will find out then."

"It's nothing to be ashamed of. Businesses fail, Marianne. It happens."

"And the other night, when we saw you at the pageant, you had on that new jacket and you looked so nice and so rich, and you were with Tory Duncan... She was wearing such beautiful clothes and all evening I had been so worried that my mother would notice that Max needs new pajamas and that everyone would think I was such a bad mother because—"

Joe couldn't stand it, her being so miserable. He put his other arm around her, pulling her to him. "Oh, babe, you don't have to cry. No one would ever think you're a bad mother."

She shook her head, her hair brushing against his chest. "Your mother would have...if you'd taken him there tonight...if you'd said that I wasn't feeding him right."

"I wouldn't have done that. I'd never do anything like that to you." He was holding her; she felt familiar, precious.

"Dennis said you might be able to take us to court."

"I'd never do that either. Never. You know that." His voice was low, soothing. He could feel her against him. "It's going to work out. You don't have to worry. I'll always take care of you and Max, you know that."

She tilted her head back. "But that's not right." her eyes were dark, soft with tears.

Joe didn't care what was right. He only knew that he could not stand to see her unhappy again. He was brushing her hair off her face, kissing her forehead, trying to comfort her, to let her know that he cared, that he wouldn't let anything happen, that he would help her through Christmas.

"Oh, Joe...I've just been so miserable; all I think about is money. I feel like I can't remember what it was like to be happy...or if I ever was happy."

No, she was wrong: they had been happy, the two of them. There had been happy times. Joe could remember: when they had gotten married, when the bank had told them they could have the loan for the house, when Max had been born...those had been happy times, she shouldn't forget about them.

This was why being poor scared her. Being poor made her forget about everything except money. Poverty numbed the soul until a person could care about nothing but the body's survival. Memories, dreams, hopes shriveled and froze.

So Joe sat down with her and helped her remember all the warm, wonderful memories of when they had been a family, of when they had loved one another. He told her how he remembered when Max was a baby, how peaceful, how precious, the two of them looked, how he could never believe that they were his, how he wondered what he had done to deserve them.

And long before that, she had made him feel like a man. He had only been eighteen, but she wanted to be his wife, to live with him, to rely on him, to entrust her well-being to his care. He had loved her for it, and now he told her about it.

"Do you remember the night we first made love?" he asked softly.

Of course she remembered.

"You didn't like it much, did you?" he whispered.

"I liked it that you did."

He certainly had liked it.

"I'd never seen a man before," she said shakily. "I couldn't believe that you were actually going to—"

"And I couldn't believe that you were going to let me."

They'd been so young that night in the back seat of the old Bonneville—young, afraid, and so much in love. She was the only woman he had ever loved; she was the only woman he had ever made love to. And she was here again, in his arms. It didn't matter why she was here; all that mattered was that she was.

Joe tightened his arms around her and bent his head down to touch hers. Her kiss was soft, familiar. He wanted her. He loved her. She was trembling, responsive, willing.

And married to his cousin Dennis.

He sat up. It was a moment before he could speak. "I'd feel guilty," he said slowly, "but you'd want to kill yourself."

"Oh, Joe..."

There was nothing to feel guilty about. They had just kissed, that's all. They hadn't made love, they hadn't come close. There was nothing to feel guilty about. But Joe felt terrible...and he knew Marianne felt even worse.

There wasn't anything to say.

"I guess I'd better go," she said at last.

He walked her out to her car, opened the door for her, and then spoke. He knew he shouldn't say it—it was really wrong to—but he was going to anyway. "I've missed you, babe."

She stared down at the door handle. "And I've missed you."

"I don't think we're talking about the same thing," he said quietly. After all, she was married; he wasn't.

She didn't answer, and then he realized he was wrong. They were talking about the same thing.

"Aren't—" he stopped. He didn't know how to put it.

She shook her head.

Joe did not know what to say. "He's busy. The business... He must be worried all the time." This was crazy—here he was trying to apologize for Dennis.

She shook her head again. "No, it's not that we don't...it's just that when we do, it's never... I mean, even before the business, it was never the same as with you."

"Marianne..."

When they had first been married, they had lived with her parents and that had been hard—the walls were thin. But then they had moved into the house, and they had their own home, their own bed. Marianne was always there, always willing. He couldn't imagine that anything could be any better.

But Marianne read paperback romances, and one day, when he was home sick, he was bored and restless and picked up one of her books just because he couldn't find anything else.

It had made him very uncomfortable. What happened between the man and the woman when they were in bed together did not have much to do with what happened between Marianne and him. What happened in the book was a whole lot better.

He felt like they were constantly surrounded by visions of things that they could not have. Every commercial on TV showed people moving about in a world of spacious kitchens and new cars. Even in the detergent ads, each woman had her own bright laundry room. TV housewives never went to the laundromat as Marianne did.

Joe had hoped that someday Marianne would have her own washer and maybe even a dryer, but she'd never have a separate laundry room with a rocking chair and a window seat and blue gingham cushions. That was crazy.

They'd never have a wide-screen TV, a side-by-side refrigerator-freezer with an automatic ice-maker, a Cadillac with cruise control. But surely this was one part of the package that they could have. Surely sexual pleasures were not restricted to the rich.

And so, to Marianne's absolute horror, he drove to another town where no one knew them and bought a few straightforward marriage manuals. It was the first time Joe had ever decided to change something about himself. It was the first time he had decided to start being good at something.

Marianne was embarrassed; she called the books pornography and refused to look at them. Joe said nothing more to her. But he did a great deal, and she responded in ways she never had before, bringing them a rapture they had not dreamed possible.

He missed it. And apparently she did too. He wished he didn't know that. He really wished he didn't. She still felt too much like his wife.

He watched the red taillights of her car turn after the stop sign. He checked in his pocket for his keys and started for his own car.

It was for moments like these that God made bars and bartenders.

"I DON'T THINK I've seen you in here on a Friday night before," Tory said as she sat a beer down in front of him.

Was it Friday? "No, maybe not."

Tory Duncan wore running shoes. Whenever she wore jeans, she wore running shoes. With corduroy slacks she wore loafers or leather moccasins; with jeans, she wore running shoes. She had who knows how many pairs, and some detail on the shoes always matched something else she was wearing. If she had on a green sweater, the shoes would have a strip of exactly the same green.

Joe thought his son was the most imaginative person he had met, but it had never occurred to Max to want two pairs of running shoes.

"You've been married, haven't you?" he asked abruptly.

"Yes."

"You're divorced?"

She was looking at him. He didn't understand her expression; it was almost as if she didn't have one. "Yes," she said.

"You didn't have kids?"

"No."

"Do you see your husband much?"

She shook her head. "Never. We lived in Atlanta; he's still there."

How odd—to have been married to someone and now never see him. Would that be better...or worse? Joe didn't say anything.

In the mirror behind the bar there was a double row of bottles on a shelf, one row real, one row reflected. It was hard to tell which was which. Above the bottles was the smooth swirl of Tory's hair, gleaming in the dim light.

"What's up, Joe?" he heard her ask, her voice unusually low.

She knew that something was wrong. "I about did the stupidest thing a man can do."

"What's that?"

"Going to bed with my ex-wife."

And right away he wished he hadn't said it. It sounded so...so...

But Tory didn't even seem surprised. "I imagine that sort of thing happens all the time."

"It didn't actually happen."

"No, but I don't suppose that makes you feel much better."

He picked up an ashtray, set it back down. "That's for sure."

"How did it happen?"

"Well, Marianne came over to apologize, and..." Joe found himself telling Tory all about the money, about how Marianne was using his check for all three of them.

Tory leaned back, her arms folded, listening. She shook her head as he finished. "The poor kid."

"Oh, Max is okay," Joe assured her. "He wasn't—"

"No, not him. Your ex-wife. What a miserable situation. What's she supposed to do? Buy steak for Max and serve her husband meatloaf stretched out with bread crumbs?"

"I don't know what any of us are supposed to do."

"Well, if I know you, you told everyone to stay calm and take it one step at a time."

Joe shook his head. "No, I got very angry with her."

"You did?" Tory looked surprised. "I didn't know that you got angry."

"Everybody does sometimes. I'm no different."

"You aren't angry now."

"It didn't last. Not when I realized how miserable she's been." He stared glumly at his beer, thinking about Marianne. "I had no idea."

"She's probably been hiding it from you."

"She's been hiding it from everyone. She didn't want anyone to know that they didn't have enough money."

"I suppose she feels like she's on display, that she can't make any mistakes because everyone is always watching her."

Joe thought about what Marianne had said about trying to smile all the time, about how worried she had been about his mother finding out. Yes, that's how she'd felt . . . on display. Lisa had to walk down that lunch-table runway for only one evening, but Marianne felt those same curious eyes every time she left her house.

"How did you know?" he asked Tory.

"My divorce was no fun," she answered, "but I can't imagine being the first Mrs. Brigham in Sullivan City to get one."

"Oh." Was that it? Had Marianne felt that she had to be a better mother, that she had to serve better meals, have a cleaner house, because she had been divorced? Did she feel like everyone was watching her, waiting for her to make another mistake?

Tory went on. "I think you need some time after a divorce to sort yourself out, to overreact, to do something the exact opposite of what you did in the marriage. I don't see that your ex-wife ever had that time."

Joe thought about what Tory was saying. "No, I guess not. One day she was married to me, then she was married to Dennis, living in the same house—"

sleeping in the same bed "—doing all the same things."

But Joe had had two years of doing something different, of living in a nearly unfurnished house, not having to be home for supper at exactly five-thirty every single night, being able to work as late as he wanted, to start as early as he wanted. He'd thought that the way he was living was somehow defective; his family certainly believed that it was, but Tory . . . she was telling him that it was necessary, even good.

She understood. She understood how hard it had been, how lonely. She understood because she had been there herself. And suddenly it didn't matter that she was beautiful, that she had been to college, that she had been in the Miss America Pageant. For a moment, none of those differences mattered. She was just another person.

"What about you?" he asked. "Did you overreact after your divorce?"

"Did I ever."

"Were you in Atlanta?"

"For a few months, and then I came out to the coast and fell apart. I gained weight, which I had never done before. I stopped wearing makeup; I must have looked like hell. I lived in a real junky place and slept with some people I hardly knew. It wasn't until I got the money from our house and bought the bar that I started to get myself back together."

Slept with some people she hardly knew? Did women admit things like that? "I imagine your standards of looking like hell are quite a bit different than the rest of ours," he said instead.

She shrugged. "Perhaps. But I certainly looked like hell for someone who used to wear cream blusher, powdered blusher, two types of eyeliner, and four shades of eyeshadow just to go to work."

"Four colors of eyeshadow? You're joking!"

"I wish I were, but listen, Joe, I know you feel sorry for your ex-wife—I do too—but maybe you ought to—" She broke off. "No, forget it."

"Go on," he said.

She shook her head. "No, I was way out of line. It's none of my business."

"I don't mind."

She sighed. "Oh, all right. It just seems to me that maybe you ought to think about what she wants from you. This almost letting you go to bed with her. Was it purely nostalgia or was there some motive behind it? Was it the money? Did she want you to keep quiet about it? Does she want more?"

"Oh, no, not at all," Joe spoke quickly, not wanting Tory to think that Marianne could be that manipulative. "It's that she and Den—"

He stopped, flushing, horrified at what he'd been about to say.

Tory was studying him, a teasing question in her green eyes. Uncomfortable, he looked away. She was wearing a crewneck sweater the color of Max's plum crayon. The collar and cuffs of her shirt were white with pinstripes of plum and grey. "So," he heard her say, "you're good in bed."

"Tory!"

"Well, are you? Is that what it was all about? That you are better than the guy she's married to now?"

Joe could not believe this. With the occasional—and very occasional, at that—exception of Marianne, he had never spoken to a woman about sex. And to have Tory Duncan, who was suddenly no longer just another person, standing there, speculating that he was good in bed, it was, well . . .

"I wouldn't have thought it," she continued matter-of-factly, "that any of you guys were. You all seem to be such prudes about sex. Everybody talks about how the NFL cheerleaders are built, but is mighty quiet about everything else."

Joe did not know what to say.

"But I guess," she went on, "if anyone were going to be half-way decent, it would be you."

"Me? I'm no diff—"

She waved her hand, interrupting him. "I don't want to hear it, Joe. Of course, you're different than everyone else."

What had gotten into her? Why was she talking like this?

She went right on. "Why do you find the notion that you're exceptional so threatening?"

"I don't," he protested.

But he knew that he was lying. He didn't want to be different. He never had. He had wanted to be like Dennis and Frank.

Four

TORY WANTED to shoot herself.

She had embarrassed one of her customers; she had mocked him, taunted him.

She never talked about sex in the bar, never, not even in an abstract way. It would have made her customers uncomfortable. They told her many of their problems, but never this one. Occasionally, they would hint at how worried they were about their teenage daughters, but they never spoke about their wives.

Joe was the first who had done so...and Tory had humiliated him, a customer. How could she have done it?

Because every so often Joe Brigham stopped feeling like a customer.

Tory was astonished at what she had told him in the last two days—about being in the pageant, about all the mistakes she had made on the coast. These were things she thought she would never tell anyone, but now she had told him.

When he'd come in this evening, she'd known immediately that something was wrong. She didn't know how she knew, but she did. And being so concerned about him, she did not evade his questions about her marriage and divorce as she would have if anyone else had asked them.

She was fond of Joe, she cared about him . . . not exactly as a friend, but more as . . . well, a patroness, an aunt, a coach. But when he began talking about sex, she found herself thinking about him, how he sat so still, and how when he did move, everything was slow, controlled. It made her wonder if he was always that slow, always that controlled.

And she had punished him for it, speaking of his private life as if it were something vaguely amusing. What had he ever done to deserve that? It was hardly his fault that she liked the way he looked.

Such were Tory's thoughts during the grey hours before dawn. Not since she had decided to buy the building and open a bar had she lain awake, criticizing herself, castigating herself. It reminded her of the time in her life when every night had been like this.

JOE BRIGHAM might have been impressed by a second runner-up, but Tory wasn't. She was supposed to win; that's what her mother expected. To be second runner-up was to lose, to fail.

After Atlantic City, she was still Miss South Carolina, and her mother was determined that if she couldn't be Miss America, her reign as Miss South Carolina would be the best ever, and to this day, no state queen has equalled Tory's schedule of appearances.

So she saw very little of Ned Duncan, the boy she was dating that year, but when she did, he seemed sunny and natural, loose, relaxed, always the life of the party, the one with a good story, the one who remembered all the jokes. Tory, troubled with self-doubt for the first time in her life, sometimes thought that Ned should have been Miss South Carolina, not her. So seven days after she crowned the new Miss South Carolina, she married him...without knowing anything about him except his lively, charming manner.

But Ned's history was important, she now realized. When Ned was small—and called "Eddie"—his father bought half of a swampy island a few hundred yards off the South Carolina coast. It was a miserable spot, but Mr. Duncan had heard that a developer was going to build a bridge and drain the land. Such a developer never materialized, and Mr. Duncan held on to the property, paying the minimal tax, because he was too stubborn to admit he might have made a mistake.

Nearly fifteen years later, the developer did appear with plans for a golf and tennis resort. Mr. Duncan, feeling cheated of a decade and a half of affluence, added punitive damages to his asking price...and got them.

The Duncans moved from one side of town to another, and their only son changed high schools, now attending the one with cleaner halls, a bigger parking lot and better band uniforms. Ordinary, faceless Eddie became Ned, the one with the newest car, the most drinking money.

It was a transition he never felt secure about. Ned had to be the life of the party because he didn't believe he deserved the invitation. He laughed at himself because he worried about someone else doing it first. He married Miss South Carolina because he wasn't sure that he could.

As a wedding present, his parents made the down-payment on a big, new house with a split foyer, a sitting area in the master bedroom, a dressing room off the master bath, an eat-in kitchen with ceramic tile and a trash compactor, a home with every amenity except solid construction.

Tory and her ever-present mother spent the first year or so of her marriage decorating the house. Just as they had once shopped all day for pageant clothes, now they looked at wallpaper books and upholstery swatches. When they finished decorating, they thought the house perfect. The drapery fabric was repeated in the throw pillows, the ashtrays matched the wastebaskets.

During that time, Ned was working in a large, competitive advertising agency, and Tory was not paying enough attention to realize it was the worst possible place for him. No one adored him, no one reassured him. The agency expected him to do more than just be fun.

When the house was finished, Tory started working, and her success as a party consultant seemed unfair to Ned. She was being mentioned in society columns just when he had to watch people being promoted around him. He comforted himself by criticizing her.

He fussed about their grocery bills, saying she spent too much, and then ten minutes later, he would sit at the table and demand to know why she had bought sirloin steak instead of filets or Delmonicos. He would jerk open her closet door, complaining because she had so many clothes, and at a party at his boss's house, he would get impatient because she wasn't wearing a new dress when everybody else's wife was. In their private moments, he grew glib, ironic, and Tory didn't stop him because, by then, she felt like she deserved it.

Finally she left him, although it was really not so much him she left as herself. She didn't hate Ned; she hated herself, she couldn't stand the person she had become. She lived in a cheap furnished apartment for a few months, then moved to San Francisco and finally drifted up to the Oregon Coast for her year of compulsive self-destruction.

Two months after she'd moved to Sullivan City, Ned shipped her all her clothes. She had no idea if he was sending them vengefully or if he honestly thought she would want them.

He'd called on her birthday last spring. He had a new job, with a small public relations firm, and he liked it a lot. He was back to being a big fish in a little pond, back to somewhere where his money and friendly charm were enough. In a small, safe job, he could be nice again, and Tory hadn't minded speaking to him on the phone. She certainly didn't want to be married to him anymore; she wasn't even sure she wanted to have lunch with him, but phone calls she could handle.

Which was a great deal more than could be said about her relations with her mother.

IT ARRIVED IN THE MAIL exactly a week later, an application from Dennis R. Colt, 347 Oak Street, Sullivan City, Oregon, for reinstatement in the union. Joe was in his office at the union hall. He smoothed the creases in Dennis's application, read through it, processed it, and felt terrible.

So Dennis was solving all their problems. He was getting his old job back at the mill. The money for Max would be spent on Max. Joe didn't have to worry anymore. He knew he should be glad that everything had been taken care of, but part of him resented it—the way Dennis had stepped in to make everything right.

Once, when they were kids, Joe and Davy couldn't get a kite out of a tree—they couldn't reach the lowest branch. Dennis and Frank, with two years' more growth, had come along and had easily swung themselves up to retrieve it. Joe would have almost rather not have his kite back than have Dennis and Frank get it for him.

But we aren't boys; these aren't kites. Dennis had owned a business. He was the first Brigham to have his own business. And now he didn't have it anymore. . . because Joe had complained.

JOE WENT TO THE BAR that night.

"This makes two Fridays in a row," Tory remarked as soon as he sat down.

He didn't answer. Why was she making such a big deal out of his coming in on Friday?

"The usual?" she asked in a minute.

"Not just yet. Maybe later."

He swiveled a quarter turn away from the bar, staring across the room. He ran a hand down his leg.

"What's wrong, Joe?"

He looked over his shoulder at her.

How had she known that anything was wrong? "Dennis filed an application to be reinstated in the union this morning."

"And you feel like you've forced him out of business."

"That's right."

"But, Joe, what did you do? Did you stop Max's check? Did you threaten to take them to court? Did you make any demands on them whatsoever?"

"No, of course not."

"Put yourself in his shoes. Would you want him to support you?"

He didn't have to answer that. "But it's different. He's always wanted his own business; I don't mind working for a wage."

"You don't?"

He glanced up at her, surprised. "No, of course I don't. I'm not doing it right now, but I will again someday."

"You'd go back to the mill?"

"Well, maybe not that," he admitted. "But I'd go on a logging crew in a minute. It's not like I quit working in the mill because I hated it or anything. I'm only doing this because the executive board asked me to. They said there wasn't anyone else."

Tory started to say something, then stopped. "Oh, well, have it your way."

The bar suddenly grew quieter for a moment; that always happened when the door opened, people stopped talking for a moment to see who had come in. Joe didn't bother to look, but Tory did. She went over to the tap, drew a beer, and put it down in front of him.

He hadn't ordered it. "What's this for?"

"Sustenance. You're going to need it. Half your family just walked in."

He turned to look. Standing just inside the door, nodding to the people they knew, were his brothers, Frank and Jim... and his cousin Dennis.

Joe certainly hoped they weren't going to make a habit of this.

He went over to them. Frank and Dennis were the last people he wanted to see, but they were Brighams, and Brighams stick together.

"How's the Cherokee?" Frank said right away. "Did you check the anti-freeze, put on the snow tires?"

It was December. Of course he had checked the anti-freeze. Of course he had put on the snow tires. Every sixteen-year-old in town had enough sense to do that. Why didn't Frank mind his own business?

"Sure," Joe said anyway. Then, as they sat down at a table, he started talking to Jim. He liked Jim, especially now that he had forgiven his younger brother for being good at something.

Was it different for you, being the Brigham who was great with cars? Did it keep you from envying the two of them the way I did?

But Joe didn't ask. People didn't ask each other questions like that, at least not around here they didn't.

"How is the Cherokee?" Jim asked softly.

"Good enough. I wish the steering were a little tighter though."

"Yeah, he should have bought a Blazer." Jim was partial to Chevys. "But you know Frank, you can't tell him a thing."

Yes, Joe knew Frank.

When Nancy came over, Joe ordered a pitcher straight off so that she wouldn't have to say anything. Tory didn't want people doing that, but right now Joe didn't care.

"I didn't know she worked here," Frank said as soon as Nancy left.

"She's a good waitress," Joe said.

"I'm surprised her folks let her work in a bar," Jim said. "I thought old man Smith was pretty strait-laced."

"She's over twenty-one," Joe answered. "She doesn't need their permission."

Dennis didn't say anything.

Nancy brought the pitcher and mugs. Jim asked her how her grandmother was. "B-b-b-better" was all she said, but she looked at Jim when she spoke, not ducking her head and staring at the floor like she used to.

Dennis still hadn't spoken.

Frank poured the beer and handed the mugs around. Joe took one and asked Jim, "How are Debbie and the kids?"

"Fine, but one of those dogs is in heat. It's driving us all crazy. That's why I let Frank and Dennis talk me into cutting out tonight. There're already enough males hanging around that house."

"Have her spayed," Joe suggested.

"Are you kidding? And lose the money Debbie makes on those pups? I'd have to get a second job."

Jim's wife loved dogs. Even when she was a little girl, Joe remembered how she would always have a dog or two with her. Now she bred her two Brittany Spaniels every year. It was a lot of work, but it paid for all their kids' clothes and toys—which made her the family's only successful entrepreneur.

At last Dennis spoke. "You want to play some darts, Joe?"

That was easy: No. No, he didn't want to play darts with Dennis. First of all, Dennis would beat him, and second, Dennis would feel like he had to say something, apologize for something. Dennis might have mailed his union application instead of bringing it in in person, but he was no coward. He had the guts to say something to Joe's face.

Joe wasn't entirely sure he had the guts to hear it.

Oh, well, they might as well get it over with. Joe picked up his beer and threaded his way through the tables to the dart board.

They played a round almost without talking. Dennis clobbered him.

As Dennis was pulling the darts out of the cork board, he spoke. "Nobody in the family knows about the child support, not even Frank."

"They won't find out about it from me."

"Marianne appreciates that . . . so do I."

And then it came, Dennis's awkward, uncomfortable apology. He offered to pay Joe back. It would take a while, but he could do it, he wanted to do it.

"It's okay," Joe kept saying. "It's over, let's forget it."

"No, no . . . and I don't want you blaming Marianne either. It was my fault. I knew that everything couldn't be all right, but I wanted to believe it so I let her pretend that it was."

Joe really wished that he were somewhere else. "I can understand how that would happen. But I'm sure sorry about your business," he added awkwardly.

"I don't know..." Dennis spoke without looking at him. "I guess Marianne was right. It's a mistake to stick your neck out. You're just asking for it."

"Marianne? But I thought—"

"That she wanted us to have a business?" Dennis shook his head. "No, she hated the thought of it; she never wanted me to do it. She was just pretending for the sake of the family. I suppose she felt like since she had tried to stop you from doing something, she didn't dare do it twice."

Joe didn't know what to say. He had resented how pleased Marianne had seemed when Dennis left the mill. "I didn't realize that."

"No, you wouldn't. She's good at pretending."

Joe started to nod, then stopped. Dennis's voice was very flat. What had he been thinking about?

Marianne would never say it, she would never say "Sex was better with Joe than it is with you." She would try to hide it, she would try her best, but it wasn't just money she had to pretend about.

Joe felt embarrassed. Knowing about other people's sex lives was not all it was cracked up to be. He gestured at the darts Dennis was still holding. "Do you want to play another round?"

Dennis shook his head. "I'd just beat you."

"You've been beating me at games my whole life. I can take it."

TORY WATCHED as Joe took the darts from Dennis and began to play again. What a strange family they were.

She could barely make it through a phone conversation with her mother. They had nothing in common anymore. Now that Tory was no longer wearing four shades of eyeshadow, they hardly spoke at all. Tory preferred that to the polite inanities her mother was so good at.

But here were these two men, with every possible reason to avoid one another, here they were, playing darts. They had to hate it, both of them. Why did they bother?

Tory leaned against the back bar and listened to the familiar sounds: the scrape of chairs against the floor, the clink of mugs and pitchers, the sharp slam and jingle as someone hit the side of the cigarette machine—the only way to get it to work—and above it all, the steady roar of men's voices, of men's laughter in the dark, smoky light.

She remembered the picture of the four Brighams in the doorway tonight. Frank, Dennis and Jim had been standing at the door, dressed in jeans and wool pea jackets. Their collars were turned up, and beads of water glistened on their shoulders. Joe had gone over to join them. The light from the entranceway shone on their oat-colored hair, on the rounded planes of their faces. They were so clearly kin, so clearly of the same blood, a force united against outsiders.

Frank's hair was the darkest, Dennis's the lightest; Frank was the tallest, Jim the shortest. Joe was in the middle in every way—height, age, coloring—every way except ability.

Tory looked across the room to where Jim and Frank still sat. A few of the other guys were now lounging around the table; Frank was talking to them. Jim, the youngest brother, caught Tory's glance and, picking up his empty mug, came over to the bar. She drew him a refill and set it down in front of him. They exchanged a few pleasantries. He complimented her on the bar; she asked about Miss Sullivan City.

Tory's impression of Jim was the same as it had been when she'd met him briefly at the beauty pageant. She liked him, although he wasn't anything like Joe except in looks. He talked more than Joe, he didn't have Joe's reserve or Joe's presence. Jim was straightforward, untroubled, uncomplicated.

"Joe says you drive an MGB," Jim said. "How does it run?"

"Awful," she answered pleasantly. "I've been through three alternators."

"It's the electric system? Those foreign cars..." He shook his head. "You just don't know what kind of trouble you're going to have. Even the Japanese ones, your parts are going to run you high. But it sounds like what you need to do is put in a whole new electrical system, an American one, from the ignition switch on up."

"You don't understand. I like having a car that doesn't work in the rain. Then I don't have to go out in bad weather."

"I'm serious," he protested. "Have Joe bring it in sometime, and he and I can work on it after hours; we'd just charge you for parts."

Tory smiled and shook her head. Surely Joe Brigham had more important things to be doing with his evenings than being a volunteer grease monkey. His family might not know it, but she did.

To Tory's surprise, Dennis Colt came into the bar after work a few days later. He was by himself, and for nearly the first time, Tory hoped that a new customer would not like the place. If he started coming, Tory knew that sooner or later Joe would stop.

She drew a draft for him. "I was sorry to hear about your business." Its failure was common knowledge now.

"Thanks," he said, "but I don't mind. There are a lot of headaches involved in having your own business."

"Isn't that the truth?" Tory had a business; she knew. "Owning a bar was nothing like I expected it to be."

"But you seem to be doing okay."

"Sheer luck."

Dennis curled his hands around his mug. "I thought working hard was going to be enough."

What an American attitude. "Unfortunately, it's not. A lot of other things need to fall into place too."

But, Tory thought, those things falling into place weren't entirely luck. Yes, she had bought this building on impulse—the Atlanta house had sold well and she needed to do something with her share of the money—and, yes, she had decided to turn it into a bar on impulse, but after a while, all the old habits took over, and she started planning, preparing.

While she was still on the coast, waiting for the paperwork to be completed, she paid two bar owners to walk her through every stage of their business. She read every book ever written about owning a bar. She went to bartenders' school. She spent hours with an accountant who did cost projections and worked out a business strategy. She learned all about Sullivan City, finding out that the loggers—the guys who worked out in the forests—were starting to feel like the mill workers were getting a better break than they were. Some friction was developing between the two groups, and Tory decided that the loggers would be glad to have a bar of their own. During her opening week, she made sure that her free-drink cards made their way to the logging crews.

Her accountant told her she could survive eighteen months without making a profit. She started turning one in six. Sure, luck had been a part of it, and God only knew how hard she had worked . . . but she had also planned, practiced, prepared.

"What made you decide to go with fencing and siding?" she asked Dennis now.

He curled his hands around his mug. "I've always liked working outside."

And he was probably good at it; Brigham modesty would keep him from saying that. But liking something and being good at it weren't enough to start a business. That was like robbing a bar and deciding to go south. You had to do market research. Did Sullivan City need another fencing and siding installer?

Tory listened to the guys in the bar talk; they liked working on their houses. They hung their own paneling, they replaced their own furnaces, did their own wiring, poured their own concrete. This was a blue collar town; the service economy was weak. People didn't like to spend money on services, on cleaning ladies, gardeners, housepainters, carpenters. They did the work themselves.

Dennis hadn't had any more of a chance than Sweatshirt and Saturday Night had.

The afterwork crowd was starting to show up, singly, in pairs. There were men—and one or two women—in green twill work pants, with layers of shirts, wool over flannel. The white ribbing of their long underwear showed at their cuffs, under their open collars. They wore stocking caps which they pulled off when they came into the bar, stuffing them into their back pockets.

Tory was busy filling pitchers, chatting, taking orders. She kept her eye on the door; she liked to know who was in her place. Soon, a stranger came in, wearing a green parka and a black stocking cap pulled low over his eyes. He looked around the bar and then down at something in his hand. Tory tried to send a glance of helpful query across the room.

But it was Dennis he was interested in. He came over to the bar, cleared his throat, and when Dennis looked up, asked "Is your name Brigham?"

"No," Dennis answered, "but my mother's was. My name is Colt, Dennis Colt."

"Oh," the stranger said and looked back down at the little bit of paper in his hand. It was a picture torn out of a newspaper.

Tory could guess whose it was. "If you're looking for Joe Brigham," she said, "he's not here yet, but I imagine he'll be in soon."

"Will you point him out if he does?"

"Sure."

Once the man went off to a table, Dennis spoke, "Does that happen often, people coming in here looking for Joe?"

"Fairly often."

Nancy needed two pitchers. Tory filled them and slid them across the bar.

"On union business?" Dennis asked.

It took Tory a second to realize that Dennis was still talking about Joe. "Usually."

"Everyone says he's doing a great job."

"That doesn't surprise me."

Dennis paused. "No, no, of course not. Except..."

"Except what?"

"I don't know...it's just hard to think of him that way. For so long he was just a nuisance of a little kid. At least Jimmy left Frank and me alone—he was always off tinkering with cars. But Joe—we were constantly trying to think of ways to get rid of him. And now..."

Yes, and now. Joe was hardly the little brother anymore. Tory knew about the Cherokee, how it would have been repossessed if Joe hadn't bought it from Frank. And in Dennis's case, not only had Joe been his meal ticket, but if what she guessed from Joe's half-finished remark were true, Dennis was finding that as a husband, Joe was a tough act to follow.

"You spent a lot of time with Frank and Joe when you were all kids?" she asked.

Dennis nodded. "My father wasn't crazy about it, but I did."

"Why did he mind? I thought Brighams all stuck together."

"My dad's not a Brigham."

Oh. How interesting. *My mother was a Brigham, but my name is Colt.* Had Dennis's father resented his wife's family? "Did your dad want you to start a business?" Tory asked suddenly.

Dennis was surprised. "How did you know that?"

She shrugged. "Is it true?"

"Well, yes. And I think he's unhappier about losing it than I am. He keeps telling me how disappointed he is. He always said, 'I want you to be more than a Brigham.' Which is crazy; being a Brigham is good enough for anyone."

More than a Brigham . . . Dennis's father had told him to think big; he had told him to have dreams, but he had never shown him how to make them become real.

Tory's mother had given her a dream—to be Miss America. Tory now thought that it was one of the silliest dreams a human being could possibly have, and she resented, even hated, her mother for it.

But, Tory thought grudgingly, to give Marjorie Davidson her due, in the process of trying to be Miss America, during the practicing, the planning, and all that hard, hard work, at least she had taught her daughter how to achieve things.

DENNIS LEFT THE BAR SOON. Tory wasn't sure why he had come. Was it an act of defiance—showing Joe that he could still take over the playground? Or was it an attempt at self-punishment—needing to come to the one place where Joe was winning the King of the

Hill game? She didn't know, and she was sure Dennis didn't either. Those questions were the kind of intro-spection that residents of the coast, all so interested in themselves, indulged in endlessly, but that the people around here would think a waste of time.

A few minutes later, Joe and Davy came in. Tory pointed out the guy in the green parka to Joe. He went over to him and held out his hand. Tory went back to work.

A couple of hours later, after the afterwork crowd had left and just as the evening crowd was starting to come in, Tory noticed that Joe and the stranger were still there. Joe usually sat back from a table, with one arm hooked over the chair back, but tonight he was leaning forward, his elbows on the table. He was lis-tening intently, occasionally speaking. Tory won-dered what they were talking about.

A little before closing, the stranger put his parka back on. Joe stood up with him, walking over to the door to see him out, shaking his hand . . . almost as if this were his office. When he turned back toward the room, Tory smiled at him, inviting him over. "You must be starving," she said. "You've been here since before six."

Joe blinked. Obviously he hadn't thought about eating. "Why don't you serve food in here?"

"Too lazy." Tory handed him a bag of beer nuts. "Dinner's on the house."

As he started to tear the bag open, she asked, "What was that all about?"

He started to speak, then stopped.

"If you can't trust your bartender," she said, "who can you trust?"

So Joe told her. The green parka was a logger in Tramlet, the town Sweatshirt and Saturday Night had come from. He had a complicated story. His wife's sister—or something—worked in the bus station, which was where people picked up the Hertz cars, and she had seen some papers for long-term rentals for a bunch of guys from Industrial Policy Associates. "And you know what that means."

Tory apologized. "I'm sorry, but I don't. I've never heard of them."

They were union busters, he told her. Management would hire them to come in, then they'd force a strike and go to work on the rank and file, nurturing their complaints against the union, chipping away at morale until they had disheartened enough workers that someone would start a decertification petition, trying to force an election that would decertify—kick out—the union at that plant.

Decertification fights could be ugly, Joe said. They were worse than struggles with management because they were civil wars. One half of the union was pitted against the other, and he knew of towns where the social life had been poisoned for a couple of years after a decertification bout. Church suppers, bowling leagues, standing poker games, disintegrated as people took sides. It was an ugly, ugly business.

"Why did this man come to you?" Tory asked. "Is this going to happen in Sullivan City?"

Joe shook his head. "If IPA succeeds in Tramlet, the company might be tempted. But I know our management; they'll wait and see."

"So why did he come here?" Tory repeated.

"I think their local is a little like ours was five or six years ago, kind of sluggish and routine...it might even be worse."

If that local hadn't been good enough for Sweatshirt and Saturday Night, Tory couldn't imagine it being good enough for anyone.

Joe continued. "This guy tonight wanted to be sure that somebody told the International that they're going to need help, but he didn't really want to get involved." Suddenly Joe became just a little sheepish. "And I guess he'd heard about me..." Joe trailed off.

That you were the man who could handle it.

"So what are you going to do?"

"Tell Portland."

"Is that it?" she heard herself ask.

"Sure. What else would I do?"

"I wouldn't know what you could do, but it sure seems to me that you're a fool if you pass this one up."

Joe tilted his head. "What are you talking about?" he asked quietly.

Tory studied him. He really didn't know. She had once read that the difference between social classes in America was in planning. Rich people, the upper class, planned for three generations; poor people planned for Saturday night.

The people of Sullivan City weren't poor; they were working class. They planned for more than Saturday night; they planned their annual hunting trip. But they never planned their whole lives; they never planned careers—which was one reason that they didn't have them.

"Joe—" and suddenly here she was, telling him about herself again "—when I was three, my mother decided that I was going to be Miss America."

"Three?" He frowned. "That seems awfully young."

"Yes and no. One of Vanessa Williams's problems was that she didn't start thinking about it until a year before. Otherwise she wouldn't have posed for those pictures."

Joe looked confused. Clearly he didn't see what a dethroned Miss America's nude photos had to do with him.

"What do you want to be doing in five years?"

He drew back, frowning. "I haven't thought about it."

"No, surely a part of you has. Wouldn't you like to be doing more with the union, working on the staff of the International, something like that?"

He glanced away, a dull brick flush coloring his face, telling Tory the truth of her words. But his dreams embarrassed him; he thought them unrealistic, ridiculous. "Those are just fantasies," he said at last. "Everybody has fantasies."

"Of course, but if you choose carefully and work hard, fantasies can be ambitions."

He started to speak, but she wouldn't let him. "Now tell me the truth. When that guy was talking, didn't a little part of you wish that this was happening in Sullivan City, not Tramlet, so that you could be involved?"

She expected him to deny it. His whole background had told him that such a wish was hideously selfish. To

wish this fate on his own town just so he could have a
chance to prove himself... Well, yes, it might be selfish; Tory also thought it was very, very natural.

And Joe Brigham was unflinchingly honest. Reluctantly he nodded his head. Yes, he had thought it. He
was ashamed of it, but he had thought it.

"Then use this as an opportunity," she urged. "I
don't know what you can do, but surely you must. Get
involved up there. What harm will you be doing?
You'll be helping that local. So what if you're helping
yourself too. So what if your motives are a little im-
pure? Everyone's always are."

"I guess I could tell Portland that I'm willing to
help."

"No, don't even bother to volunteer. Don't give
anyone a chance to say no. Just act like it's a foregone
conclusion that you'll be doing whatever. And then go
and do it."

He didn't look convinced, but Nancy was at the
cocktail station with the last-call drink order. Tory
knew that she had to go. She lingered for a minute
longer, surprised at how much this mattered to her.
"Will you think about it?"

"Of course."

As she went through the routine of closing the bar.
Tory wondered if Joe would take her advice. She
didn't know. His background was so different from
hers—since she was three, she was told that she must
out-shine, out-sparkle all the other little girls—that she
couldn't gauge how difficult it would be for him to
step forward. He had done so at the robbery, but she
wasn't sure he would do it now.

"OH, JOE, I'm so sorry."

It was the next afternoon, and Joe had pulled up in front of the Oak Street rambler, expecting the blue-parkaed cannonball to come ripping out of the house. Instead Marianne opened the door and stepped outside, crossing her arms against the cold. Joe quickly got out of the Cherokee, and before he was up the sidewalk, she began to apologize.

"The dentist called just a few hours ago and asked if he could see Max this afternoon instead of tomorrow. I tried to call you at the union hall, but the line was busy—"

He had been on the phone to Portland.

She continued explaining, apologizing until Joe interrupted her. "It's okay, really it is."

And it was. If he had had to drive five hours to see his son for an afternoon, that would be one thing, but this was clearly another. So Max had to go to the dentist this afternoon; it was no big deal. Joe was only sorry that Marianne was so upset...and sorry that she didn't feel she had the right to tell the dentist or any other professional that she would not rearrange her schedule for his convenience.

At least she wasn't lying awake worrying about Christmas anymore.

"But do come in and see him," she was saying. "We don't have to leave for another twenty minutes."

Joe had not been inside the house since the night he had asked about the running shoes. He had felt much too uncomfortable to do anything more than pick up Max and then walk him back up to the door. But Joe knew that things had to get back to normal. They had to forget about what had happened—or at least pretend to forget. Joe knew that Dennis would never forget about the money, and that he and Marianne would never forget about what didn't happen on the sofa that night.

So forgetting hard, Joe came in and signed on as a carpenter's helper in a massive construction project Max and his Legos had going.

When it was almost time to leave, Marianne started apologizing again. "No, it's really okay," he tried to tell her. "I've got some other things I could do."

Joe walked Marianne and Max to the Capri and then got into the Cherokee, putting the key in the ignition, slowly turning it, wondering what he should do, if he should use this unexpected time to run up to Tramlet.

When he'd called Portland, Joe had done none of the things Tory had suggested. If anyone had asked for his advice, he would have given it. If anyone had asked for his help, he would have done nearly anything. But the International had listened very carefully to what he had to say, thanked him for calling, and said that they would get a field rep over to Tramlet by the beginning of next week.

But Joe wasn't sure that made sense. If a field rep suddenly appeared, everyone would know that something was up. Rumors would surge through the mill, and the members would get excited, suddenly deciding they either hated the union or loved it. There would be no way to assess how they really felt, no way to tell if the local really was doing what it should be.

But Joe knew that if he went, it would be different. He had relatives up there; it wouldn't be too odd if he dropped in on them to chat about their local. He could learn a lot more than an International staffer ever would.

What do you want to be doing in five years?

Tory had asked a lot of hard questions last night. He wished he could have talked to Marianne about them. No, that was crazy. Marianne would never understand. Her notion of a good job was one that was steady and not too dangerous, something that paid you decently and didn't leave you so wrung out at the end of the day you couldn't put one foot ahead of the next.

This job did leave him tired. There was so much to learn—about accounting, law, negotiating techniques—and some of the problems were tough ones whose solutions wouldn't make anyone happy.

But Joe loved it. It took—what did they call it?—problem-solving skills. He had them—at least that's what someone in Portland had said. He had probably gotten them from his father, who was the head sawyer on the green chain. Bob Brigham was the one who decided where each log should be cut. It was a responsible position; his mistakes were expensive. In the old days when the mills were small, the owner was always the sawyer. Other people didn't like that pressure, couldn't endure the unflinching concentration, but as Joe's father had once said, "Every log is different."

Joe had taken office in September and since then, every day had been different, with a different schedule, different problems. And, although he would never, not ever, admit it to anyone, he liked having power—the power to change things, the power to make a difference. With power you didn't spend the rest of your life feeling like a little kid watching your kite flutter in the tree branches, unable to get it back yourself, having to wait for someone else to do it for you.

Joe drummed his fingers against the steering wheel. What did he want to be doing in five years? He wasn't sure, but he certainly knew what he didn't want. He put the Cherokee in gear, but instead of driving up the street as he would if he were going back to the union hall, he made a U-turn, and headed north up to Tramlet.

JOE GOT THERE at quitting time. It didn't take long to find the right bar, and he stayed there until closing. Then he and a third cousin, Don Marsh, went back to Don's house and sat around the kitchen table, talking in low voices almost until dawn. Don was the only one he told about what was about to happen.

The Tramlet local was not a very strong one. All the members of their executive board were in their late fifties or even early sixties. The younger people rarely went to meetings. The women in particular felt like the union was a "boys' club," uninterested in their concerns. No one's grievances were pursued actively—

unless the grievance had been filed by a friend of one of the officers.

It was a tired, ineffective local, and Joe could see why the members might be dissatisfied. But the contract they were working under was the same as the one negotiated by the International with the Big Seven lumber companies. It was not a contract they ought to be taking for granted . . . and they were.

Joe had never known Don Marsh very well—they were only third cousins—but he liked what he saw in him now and decided to take a chance. When Don was walking him out to the Cherokee, Joe asked, "How much do you care about what other people think of you?"

"No more than most," Don answered, which, Joe realized, would have been exactly what he would have said himself.

"Then would you lie low for a while on this? Not say anything or commit yourself one way or another until you hear from me?"

"Sure."

Joe went back to Sullivan City and called Portland as soon as the International office opened. He told them what he'd found in Tramlet, and this time he made some suggestions, in particular that his cousin should pretend to go along with the union busters. "That way we can get decent information about what they're up to."

The hope was, of course, that Industrial Policy Associates would break some law and the union could get the National Labor Relations Board to serve a cease and desist order on them.

"So if you could get together all the details of the law," Joe continued, "I'll go over them with Don."

"And he'll report back to you?" the staffer asked.

Joe took a breath. "I think that will work the best."

JOE WAS NOT SURE how interested the International staff was in the Tramlet local—in some other unions, there was a tendency to let weak locals sink—but the staff was certainly interested in catching union-busting consultants breaking the law so a packet of materials was sent out to Joe on the afternoon plane. He picked it up at the little airport which Sullivan City shared with two other towns.

The union's attorney had warned Joe that some of the things they were sending would be heavy going, and they were right. The stuff was awful, full of long strings of words he didn't always know. At first Joe had to stop at the end of every paragraph and write down what he thought it had said and then read it again to be sure it said that. The pages in his paperback dictionary started to fall out. But he was determined that no one would ever get away with using big words and long sentences as a weapon against him, and after a while, it got easier.

He worked through the night again, finally going home sometime Saturday, pulling off his shoes and shirt, sleeping until it was dark.

He woke up after eight, hungry, but as usual, there wasn't much in the house. It was Saturday night; McDonald's and the Pizza Hut would be mobbed with teenagers. So he went to the diner, hoping that Lisa would be there—he felt like talking to someone. But she wasn't, so he ate quickly and then found himself on Fifteenth Street, heading out of town.

Tory's parking lot was full; there were even a couple of cars parked on the grass. Joe pulled up behind one of them. He had never seen the place so busy.

Inside, all the tables were full and all the seats at the bar were taken. Lots of people were standing. Both Tory and Rich's father were behind the bar, and Nancy was flushed, moving quickly among the tables. It was a different crowd than the one Joe was used to, there were more older men—his father's friends rather than his—and there were more women, some of the wives who didn't have kids yet, a couple of divorced women who worked.

Joe went around to the end of the bar, waiting, talking casually to some of the others. In a minute Tory came over.

He ordered a beer. "You've got a full house."

"It's Saturday. You've never been here on a Saturday night before."

"I haven't?"

She shook her head, handing him the beer. "Things quiet down later...stick around if you can." And then she was off.

He knew who most of the people in the bar were, even if they weren't people he'd ever been friends with. He talked about cars, sports, hunting, a little local union business...but all he could think about was Tramlet. He wished Davy were here so he could tell him all about it.

No, that was as crazy as trying to talk to Marianne. Davy wouldn't be interested in another local's problems.

Joe went over to the dart board to watch Mr. Halsey and Mr. Traker—that's how he thought of them since he had grown up with their boys. Then he felt a touch on his arm. "Joe? You're Joe, aren't you? Frank's brother?"

It was Cindy Swenson—no, she was Cindy Beebe now. She'd been in Frank's class. Joe said hello to her. "But what are you doing here? I thought you guys had gone south."

A number of people had left town during the layoffs a few years ago. Tommy Beebe had been one of them.

"Well, we did," she admitted, "but I'm back."

"Just you?"

"I've got the kids of course, but me and Tommy... well, we split up."

"I'm sorry to hear that."

"I guess I should be saying the same thing to you. I made a bit of a fool of myself when I ran into Marianne the other day."

Joe grimaced. "Yeah, she's married to my cousin now."

"That's a real surprise, not what you'd expect from the Brighams. Is her little boy yours or his?"

"Mine."

"He seems like a nice kid. Does she let you see him?"

"Nearly every day."

"That's nice."

She looked sad. Tommy Beebe must have said he was never coming back to Oregon, kids or no.

Gradually people started to leave. Joe found a place at the bar, and soon Tory came up.

"So what have you been up to?" she asked.

It was hard not to compare other women to her. Hard and not fair to them. "Oh, the usual." For a second, he thought she looked disappointed, but he couldn't really tell.

"What do you think of our Saturday nights?" she asked.

"Do you always know who comes in when?"

"More or less. And you usually come in here to work. Friday, Saturday nights, you're here for yourself."

Well, now that he thought about it, he guessed that that was true.

When he didn't say anything, she went on. "Who were you talking to? I don't think I've seen her in here before."

"You wouldn't have; she just got back in town." Joe sketched what he had learned about Cindy Beebe.

"She's divorced?"

He nodded.

"You going to start something in that direction?"

His surprise must have shown on his face because Tory smiled. "If I had to bet," she said, "I'd say it never crossed your mind."

He felt like he should apologize. "I don't know. I guess I'm going to be pretty busy the next couple weeks."

"Oh?"

And Joe heard himself saying that he had been up in Tramlet and then he went on and on, telling her about Don and all the laws he had been reading and—

Embarrassed, he broke off. "This must be boring."

"Are you kidding? I just listened to four fish stories."

Fish stories!

Well, he guessed there was a parallel. Ten years ago he was proud when he caught a big fish or shot a good goose. Of course, he didn't talk about it as much as the other guys did, but it made him feel good about himself, as if he had accomplished something.

It seemed odd now.

JOE SPENT MUCH of the next week working on Tramlet. He finished reading all the laws and regulations and went over them with Don. He met with the union officers there, told them what was about to happen and impressed on them how serious the situation was. He started talking to other locals in the area, suggesting that they appoint committees to organize support rallys so that when the hostilities began, the Tramlet local would know that the other locals were with them.

He loved it.

And a couple of times a week, he was back at the bar, telling Tory all about it. Sure, people still came there to talk to him, but he never left until he had talked to her. And no matter how crowded the bar was, she always seemed to have time to listen to him.

He supposed it was crazy, this need to tell her. But a man got used to telling things to a woman. If he were still married, he would be telling Marianne . . . Except if he were still married to Marianne, he wouldn't be doing any of it.

"You sure do seem to be having a good time," Tory said when he had finished one night.

"Yeah," he admitted. "I like this sort of thing."

Until this week, he thought his job as business agent was as good as a job could get—at least as good as any job he would ever have. But this—trying to avert a major crisis—was better, and there were people who did this for a living. In the job he had now, his responsibilities were to be sure that the local ran smoothly and that the company stuck to the terms of the contract negotiated with the Big Seven companies, and that was great for now, it really was—he still had tons to learn—but someday...

What would it be like to be one of the team who actually negotiated that Big Seven contract?

Joe had long resented how American culture had taught him to want. There were so many things pictured in ads, displayed in store windows: stereo TVs, personality dolls, electronic board games, inboard-outboard motors, personalized bowling balls, graphite baitcasting rods. You were taught to want it all.

But now he knew that along with the wanting came the other half of the American character—the energy, the drive, the persistence, the ambition. Yes, Americans knew how to want, but they also knew how to get.

Join a logging crew again? No way.

I don't know... coming from a large family, I've always wanted to do something that no one else has done.

Eighteen-year-old Lisa, everyone's baby sister, answered an inane beauty-pageant question with more insight than Joe had ever had into himself. But he felt the same as she did. He, too, wanted to distinguish himself from the crowd. There was more to all this than just being a Brigham.

Now that he thought about it, there were signs that this desire had been there for a while. Max's name, for instance. Tory had noticed it; it was an unusual name. Brigham children weren't named Max. They were Bill or Dave or Mike. And from the minute she had known she was pregnant, Marianne had said if the baby was a boy, she wanted to name him Joseph.

Just what the world needs, Joe had said then, another Joe Brigham. He had wanted something different, a more unusual name. Marianne had been reading a book called *Rebecca*. The hero's name was Maximilian. Joe had liked that.

And now when anyone in the family said "Max," a person knew who they were talking about. None of this "Bob's second boy" for Max. You didn't have to say "Joe and Marianne's Max," or "Dennis and Marianne's Max." Max was just Max; he was himself. That's what Joe had wanted for him.

No, that's what Joe had *thought* he wanted for his son. In truth, that was what he wanted for himself.

He had never been on a plane until the union had flown him to Portland. He had never been outside Oregon until he was twenty-eight and went to a regional convention in San Francisco. But now he knew that there were places to go, people to meet, decisions to be made, power to be earned.

So what if he was getting off to a late start? He would just have to move that much faster. Being like Frank and Dennis...that was the last thing he wanted now. Bob's second boy was going to soar alone.

ONE MORNING in late December, Joe stopped by Tory's to pick up some papers someone left there for him the night before. The bar wasn't open yet, but Joe knew Keith would be there cleaning and would let him in.

There proved to be no need for Keith. In the parking lot, the young driver of a florist truck was inching away from Tory. She was holding a red poinsettia, clearly trying to get the driver to take it from her. Joe got out of his car listening.

"Now, look," she was saying, not so much angry as amused, "the card says, 'Merry Christmas, from Tory.' I am Tory. I wouldn't send this to myself."

"But I don't read the cards." The kid was unhappy. "I just deliver them to the address." He pointed. "And that's your address."

"I'm not saying it's your mistake," Tory replied patiently. "Just that it is a mistake. That's the billing address. The plant was supposed to go to South Carolina. If you'll take it back, I'll call the shop and straighten everything out."

"But you already signed for it."

"Then can't I unsign for it?"

"Unsign?" Now he was genuinely bewildered. "I don't know what that is."

"Oh, never mind," Tory sighed. "I'll keep it."

The driver looked relieved and opened the door of his truck. "Have a nice day, ma'am."

"I'm sure I will," Tory answered. Then she looked over at Joe. "I just sent myself a poinsettia."

He held open the door to the bar. "It's a nice one."

"It was supposed to go to South Carolina."

"Then why did you sign for it?"

"Because I didn't know it was from me. It could have been from one of my suppliers. They're sending me all sorts of crazy stuff.'' She set the poinsettia on the bar, turning the foil-covered pot so the blossoms faced the room. ''There. You can die from nicotine poisoning,'' she told it. ''See if I care.''

''What are your suppliers giving you?''

''Food, mostly.''

''Whatever for?''

''Christmas gifts. A little commercial goodwill, one businessman to another, that sort of thing.''

Christmas . . . oh, of course. Joe hadn't been giving much thought to Christmas.

''I wish they would stop,'' Tory went on. ''Or at least stop sending food. They must think I'm raising twelve children. The nuts and the popcorn I can put out on the bar, but I haven't a clue as to what I'm going to do with the cheese and the fruit and the jams.''

''You really don't have any use for them?'' Joe knew people who were raising, if not twelve children, at least more than they could buy cheese, fruit, and jam for. ''The union puts together food baskets for Christmas, and we're always happy to have donations.''

''What a good idea! I should have thought to ask you in the first place. You always know what to do. Now aren't you here to pick up some papers?'' Tory went around the bar to get them.

Joe took them from her. ''Who's in South Carolina?''

''My mother. That poinsettia was supposed to be my big Christmas present to her.''

''What's wrong with that?'' Joe thought it sounded nice.

"What are you giving to your mother?"

Joe grimaced. "A new vacuum cleaner. We all chip in together, but it's what she wants."

"And she'll like it and she'll use it and she won't get ten of them. My mother will probably get at least that many poinsettias; a vacuum cleaner would be much more personal."

JOE DIDN'T CARE what Tory said. The next day he went to the florist and arranged to send his mother a poinsettia.

"Oh, Joe, you should have seen her," his little sister Lisa reported when he stopped by the diner that night. "She almost cried. I've never seen her cry. How did you know how much she's always wanted one? Even Dad said he had no idea that she liked them so much."

"I didn't," he admitted. "But I heard Tory Duncan say that that's what she was sending her mother, and I thought it sounded nice."

"Miss Duncan?" Lisa was suddenly interested. "She's really beautiful, isn't she?"

"Yes."

"Marianne said she was in the Miss America Pageant."

Joe nodded.

"Then she must have won her state pageant."

"I suppose so. I don't know much about it."

Lisa wanted to know what state Tory was from, if the pageant had been real scary, if her interview had been hard, if she had used her scholarship money to go to college.

"She did go to college." Joe had to admit ignorance on nearly everything else. "But I don't know about any scholarship money."

Lisa explained. The Miss America pageants, both state and national, weren't really beauty contests, she said seriously, they gave out scholarship awards. "It's the biggest scholarship program in the world—they told us that at the Miss Sullivan City Pageant. I won a few hundred dollars, but the people who do well in their state pageants and then in Atlantic City get really big ones."

"Well, Tory did well; she came in third."

"Third?" Lisa was awestruck. "You don't mean that, do you? There's someone in Sullivan City who was third in the Miss America Pageant?"

"Hard to believe, isn't it?"

Lisa didn't say anything for a moment, and then, "Cheryl says that you aren't going out with her."

Joe set his coffee cup down. "I beg your pardon?"

"Cheryl says that you aren't going out with her."

"And just when did Cheryl say this?"

"The morning after the Miss Sullivan City Pageant."

"Were other people saying I was?"

"No, I don't think so. We were all sitting around the kitchen talking about the pageant, and she just said it out of the blue."

Joe could imagine it. That's the sort of thing Cheryl would do. "Well, she's right. I drove Tory to the pageant because her car was acting up. I'm a customer in her bar, that's all."

Of course, he wasn't "going out" with her. That was silly. Sure he saw her a lot, and he did like talking to her, but she had been to college, she had been on TV, she had been married to some hot-shot executive type. Of course he wasn't going out with her.

But still, he thought, very much the younger brother again, where did Cheryl get off being so goddamn sure about it?

JOE MADE ARRANGEMENTS to pick up Tory's Christmas basket contributions Saturday morning. He had some other things to get on that side of town, probably more than would fit in the Cherokee, so his father was coming along, bringing the Buick.

His mother waved him inside, wanting him to come admire her poinsettia. Frank was sitting in the kitchen drinking a cup of coffee. "I thought I'd come along," he said.

"That's good of you," Joe said politely.

Frank finished his coffee, and standing up, held out his hand. Joe looked at it blankly, not understanding.

Frank snapped his fingers. "Keys, Joe, keys."

Oh. Frank was going to drive the Cherokee. Joe handed over the keys.

Joe rode with his father in the Buick. He wasn't about to be driven in what, at least on paper, was his own car.

"It's nice of her to donate things," his father said as they drove out to the bar. "I didn't know we could count on her like that."

Some businessmen were helpful, some weren't. "I suspect she's very generous," Joe answered. "People don't ask her much. Maybe it's because her place is outside the city limits."

"Or maybe it's because she's so good-looking."

A good point. "That's no reason to discriminate against her, especially when we want her to do us favors."

Tory was waiting for them, having come downstairs at the sound of the cars. She greeted Joe's father politely, calling him "Mr. Brigham," and shot Joe a teasing, questioning look when Frank got out of the Cherokee. He shrugged. Either this was the sort of thing you understood or you didn't. "You didn't have to come down," he said to her. "Keith could have shown us where it all is."

"I don't mind."

Joe didn't either. It was always nice to see her...and especially nice to see her in the daylight. She was so incredibly good-looking. He had gotten used to it in the bar, but out here in the bright light...

Frank stepped forward, throwing a shadow across her face. He thanked her, telling her how generous this was of her, acting like it was all his responsibility somehow. It was nothing, Tory kept answering. She had gotten the food free. Joe interrupted. "Is the stuff in the storeroom?"

Tory nodded, and Joe led his father inside and through the bar. Frank and Tory followed.

As Tory had said, there was much more than one person could ever use. There were several pyramids of oranges, apples, and grapes; some wooden trays of dried apricots, peaches, and pears; two or three wicker baskets crammed with artificial green grass and wedges of packaged cheese; and several ribbon-swathed boxes, each having three or four jars of jams, jellies, or honey—things that would add a little sparkle to the breakfast cereal and canned soup of the usual union food basket.

Tory helped carry the things out to the cars, and of course, Frank always managed to walk with her. They were chatting merrily. Joe quickened his step to listen.

"...and it was unbelievably cold..." Frank was saying.

He was telling the deer story. Joe shook his head. But then what else was Frank going to talk about? The Bible? No, meet an attractive woman and Frank would tell the deer story.

Four years ago, Frank had shot a record deer. There was no question about that. But it had been four years ago, and he was still telling the story. Hadn't he done anything since? And what made him think Tory would be interested?

Well, everything, Joe had to admit. She was nodding as Frank spoke, asking questions as if she thought it were something important.

Fortunately the loading didn't take long. "My wife will want to know if you want the trays and the baskets back," Joe's father said to Tory as he picked up the last fruit basket. Frank had already gone out.

"No," she answered. "Good heavens no. Throw them out."

"I don't imagine we'll do that." He started toward the door. "Check to be sure that we got everything, Joe."

Joe glanced over the shelf. "Do these go?" He picked up a small, brown-wrapped box and a thick, padded mailer.

"Oh, no," Tory stepped forward, taking them. "These are my personal gifts. This is from Mother—" she waved the box "—and this is from my ex," she said, indicating the mailer.

"Your ex-husband sends you a Christmas present?" It had never occurred to him to give anything to Marianne.

"Apparently," she answered, her voice a little tight. Then she changed the subject. "Your father doesn't talk any more than you do."

"No...Frank talks enough for the rest of us."

Tory raised her eyebrows. "I didn't know you Brighams said things like that about each other."

No, no, they didn't. What was the matter with him? What was he doing criticizing Frank to an outsider? Joe shifted uneasily. He knew what was the matter. He was jealous. He hadn't liked Frank walking with Tory, talking with Tory.

For God's sake, she was a bartender. That was her job, she had to talk to every bore who has enough change in his pocket for a beer. What was he trying to be anyway, the teacher's pet?

He knew the answer to that one too: Yes. He spoke quickly. "We really do appreciate your giving—"

She interrupted. "Do you have room for those?" She pointed to a stack of boxes.

"Sure. What's in them?"

"Exactly what it says. Coke."

Each box was a case of liter Coke bottles. There was no way Tory had gotten those free.

"Not exactly nutritious," Tory said, almost as if she were apologizing, "but it was all I could get on such short notice."

She had only had two days. "The kids will love you for it."

"Not as much as the town dentist."

"Don't be silly." And suddenly he wanted to be serious. "This was really nice of you." He wished he could touch her or something, show her that he really meant it, but of course he couldn't. "We didn't expect it."

"Nor did I," she said instantly. "Who would have thought that someday I would actually do something to help other people?"

Six

THE FOOD BASKETS had been packed and distributed; the union busters had gone back to California for the holidays, and as much as he would have preferred not to, Joe Brigham was now left without much to think about but his own life.

The thoughts were not pleasant. No matter how good he felt about himself, no matter how exciting his work was, nothing could stop one thing from hurting: Christmas is no fun for a man who doesn't live with his child.

It would, he could tell, be a happy Christmas for the people living in the little rambler whose mortgage had once been in his name. Marianne and Dennis wanted the same things—stability, security, comfort, peace—and together they were finding them. Joe didn't value those things as much as he once had, not at the price you seemed to have to pay.

Except maybe on Christmas. At Christmas, any price, any self-sacrifice, would seem worth it to be living in your own home with your own family.

He was certainly going to see Max during the holiday. On Christmas Eve, Joe had taken him over to Mom and Dad's for supper and had given him a Legoland Space Supply Station with a crew of helmeted space men. On Christmas Day, Dennis and

Marianne would bring him over to Grandma's for dinner. But between supper on Christmas Eve and dinner on Christmas Day, Max went back to Oak Street.

When Joe dropped Max off Christmas Eve, Max insisted that Joe come inside. He wanted to show Joe his stocking. Joe saw the stocking. Max said that Santa didn't need a chimney to come down. Joe confirmed that Santa could indeed use doors if he had to. Max said that Uncle Dennis had promised to leave the front door unlocked. Joe said that that was swell of Uncle Dennis. Max asked if Joe could tell which presents under the tree were for Max. Joe said that maybe Max should show him. Max did.

Max asked if they could play with the new Legos some more, but Mommy said no. It was bedtime. So Joe said good-night and told Max he'd see him tomorrow.

But by the time Joe would see him at Gran's the next day, Christmas would be over for Max.

Was this what being a father meant? Silently Joe drove the Cherokee home through the empty streets. It had started to snow, but not a nice, dry Christmas card sort of snow. Wet, fat snowflakes hit the windshield, the front walk was covered with a thick, muddy slush. Max wouldn't be able to wear the running shoes Joe knew were waiting for him under the tree. It was a lousy snow for Christmas.

At home, in the little boxy house he rented, Joe flipped on the TV, watched an hour of Jimmy Stewart in *It's a Wonderful Life*. They always reran that on Christmas Eve. Joe had watched the whole thing last year.

He wondered if Tory had it on in the bar. Or even if the bar were open. He didn't know what she had planned to do about holiday hours. It was a shame for anyone to have to work on Christmas, but there were people, the ones without families, who might like it if Tory decided to stay open. It was such a good bar, a warm, comfortable place. And it had Tory.

Joe went over to the window, peering through the glass at the thermometer. The temperature was dropping. The slush was probably freezing; there wouldn't be enough traffic on the streets to keep them clear, not on Christmas Eve. It was crazy to go out in weather like this.

No, it wasn't. He had a Cherokee Jeep, didn't he? Weather like this was the point of a car like that. That's why Frank had bought it.

SHE WAS DOWN to three customers, all sitting at one table. There had never been more than a handful this evening, and Tory had known beforehand exactly who her Christmas Eve customers would be. They were all watching *It's a Wonderful Life*. It made her think of Joe. In the movie, Jimmy Stewart wanted to get on a train and leave the small town he had grown up in. He wanted to travel, to build things. But he never made it out. Instead, he stayed home, married, had a family—all the things Joe had been raised to do, all the things he wasn't doing now. Tory wondered if Joe were watching too. No, he was probably at some family gathering.

When the movie was over, one of the guys at the table called to her. "Any time you want to close, Tory, just let us know."

"No rush," she said. She didn't have anywhere to go either.

Maybe she shouldn't have given Nancy a check for Christmas. Checks were fine for Keith and Rich's father, but her first impulse had been to get Nancy a sweater and a blouse. Nancy wore black and navy when she should be wearing greens, browns, and rusts. Tory had actually been in the store with her hand on a sweater when she'd stopped. The perfectly chosen gift that implied a criticism or a rebuke had been her mother's speciality, and Tory was determined not to do that. So she had come home and written Nancy a check too.

But it would have been nice to have had at least one gift to wrap. Tory had not bought a single sheet of Christmas paper this year. She had seen some beautiful papers—rich, muted colors with small designs. If she had bought a present for Nancy, she would have gotten that burgundy paper, the one with little silvery-grey rocking horses and teddy bears... but she hadn't bought a present for Nancy.

You aren't feeling sorry for yourself over wrapping paper, are you?

Yes, yes, she was. It was certainly possible to like your life 364 days a year, and then come Christmas, begin to wonder about it. But what could she do? Nobody came into a bar to hear a bartender's problems, did they?

Nancy would have liked the rocking horses and teddy bears; she adored children and children's things. For Keith, Tory might have gotten a blue paper— bright, but not very Christmasy. He would have liked that. Rich's father would have wanted a traditional paper, red and green with holly or Santa Clauses. And for Joe, a hunter green—

For *Joe*? What was she thinking of? He was a customer.

THERE WERE ONLY TWO OTHER CARS in Tory's lot. Joe had never seen it so empty. Inside, he stamped his feet in the vestibule, knocking the slush off, and then opened the inner door. Tory was behind the bar with her perfect welcoming smile. When she recognized him, her expression went wry, her smile not quite so even, not quite so perfect. And Joe couldn't help feeling very welcome indeed.

He took off his peacoat, shaking some of the snow off the wool. He hung it on one of the hooks, nodded to the three men at the table, and came over to the bar.

"What a nice sweater," Tory said as he crossed the room.

"Thanks." It was new, a crewneck pullover; he had never had one like it. Working out in the woods, you wanted wool shirts you could unbutton or sweatshirts you could unzip. "I just got it tonight. It's from my little sister; she drew my name."

"Is that how you all do it? Draw names so you don't have to buy for everyone?"

He nodded. "I was glad Lisa got me." When he'd opened the sweater, Frank had made a crack about "Joe College." Lisa had blushed, but Frank's jeer hadn't changed the way Joe felt. He liked the sweater. And who knows what Frank would have gotten him if Frank and Karen had drawn Joe's name? Probably something that Frank wanted a lot and that Joe didn't want at all.

"She has good eye for color," Tory was saying. "It's exactly the right shade of blue for you. Navy would have been too harsh. But come here, stick out your arms."

Obediently Joe extended his hands across the bar. Tory flipped up the cuffs of the sweater, settling them neatly, and with a light tug, pulled on the cuffs of his shirt so they showed below the sweater. She had never done anything like that before.

"There," she said when she was finished. "Now you look perfect."

Joe slowly lowered his arms. He couldn't help noticing: Tory did have pretty hands.

The other three customers got up to leave. Tory went down to the cash register, took their money, and wished them a Merry Christmas. Then she returned to where he was sitting. They were alone.

"So your family opens presents on Christmas Eve?"

"We do now. That way Cheryl and Frank and Jim can go over to their in-laws in the morning."

"Did you have dinner? What did you have to eat?"

Joe looked at her, finding it hard to believe that she was interested in this, but she seemed to be. "Ham. Gran will serve turkey tomorrow afternoon."

"Was your son there?"

"Of course." Joe didn't want to talk about that. "But what about yourself? Are you going to see any family over the holidays?"

She shook her head. "Mother's in South Carolina."

"Is that where the rest of your people are?"

"There aren't any more. I'm an only child, and my father died when I was small."

"I'm sorry to hear that."

"I was a baby; I don't remember him at all."

Was that supposed to mean that his dying didn't matter? "What about grandparents, aunts and uncles? Are they nearby? Will your mother go visit them?" People's mothers shouldn't be alone on Christmas . . . nor, for that matter, should their fathers.

Tory shrugged. "I never knew anyone except my mother."

He must have looked surprised for she went on. "All families aren't like yours, Joe."

How alone she was. "Have you opened your presents yet?" He remembered the two packages that had been in the storeroom last Saturday. "Or are you saving them for tomorrow?"

"More like January. Maybe February."

And then it occurred to him that when she did finally open her presents, she would be alone. Joe hadn't liked Frank jeering about "Joe College," and he hadn't liked having to take Max back to Oak Street afterward, but there had been a lot else to the family evening—the kids ripping open their presents, Mom moving her poinsettia from the dining table to the living room when they had finished eating, everyone admiring everyone else's gifts.

"Do you want to open your presents now?" he heard himself say. "I can supply the oh's and ah's."

She paused. "They're upstairs."

"Oh. Okay." That seemed to be the end of that. He looked down the bar. "My mother's poinsettia is doing better than yours."

"Everybody's poinsettia is doing better than mine . . . at least everybody who doesn't let people use them as ashtrays."

Tory's plant had been used that way. She hadn't seemed to care; otherwise people wouldn't have done it. It was nice talking to her like this, Joe thought, without all the usual noise, the usual interruptions. She wasn't having to make change, fill Nancy's orders, greet newcomers. It was nice to be the only person here.

The only person here. He was making her stay open. He stood up quickly, apologizing. "I didn't mean to keep you from closing. I'm sorry, I didn't think."

"You don't have to go."

"It's after eleven; you aren't going to get anyone else tonight, not on Christmas Eve."

"Joe, really, you don't have to go."

But he did. She shouldn't have to run up her utility bill for him. "It's good of you to be open at all. I think Robertson closed early."

"He has a family . . . Listen, Joe, is your offer to oh and ah over my presents still good?"

"Sure."

"Then give me a minute to close up and we'll go upstairs."

Go upstairs? Joe wasn't sure what to say. And when Joe wasn't sure what to say, he said nothing at all.

Tory was already flipping switches, disconnecting nozzles. "What can I do to help?" he asked.

She had him count the money and enter the total on a neatly kept cash sheet. It didn't take long, and in a few minutes, they were outside in the snow and she was unlocking the door to her apartment.

Upstairs she took his coat, and as she was hanging it up, Joe stepped past the little foyer wall and looked around with interest. The last time he had been up here someone had been pointing a gun at her, and he hadn't paid attention to much else.

The main room of her apartment was large, one continuous sweep of space soaring up through open beams to the sharply peaked roof. The floors and walls were pine, her upholstered pieces were pale. There were a few splotches of color: a scarlet and black wool throw draped over one arm of the couch, a pile of pillows in soft wool plaids. There was no television... and no Christmas tree.

It looked like a good place to live, comfortable but without a lot of fuss and clutter.

Tory crossed the room and knelt in front of the stone fireplace, turning a little handle, scratching a match to ignite the gas jets that shot blue flames up into the logs that were lying across the grate.

On the mantle above the fireplace was the one sign of Christmas, a green candle in a slender brass candlestick. Around the base of the candlestick was a perfectly tied red bow.

"Now what can I offer you to drink?" she asked. "I don't think I have anything alcoholic up here—I wasn't thinking, I should have brought something from the bar—but I think I have some coffee somewhere."

"Thanks, no. I'm fine."

"Do you mind if I make myself some tea?"

Of course he didn't.

Her kitchen was separated from the living room only by a counter. As she filled the copper tea kettle, its burnished curve reflected her blond hair. Joe watched her from the other side of the counter. It was a little like being down in the bar.

Except it wasn't. Downstairs, everything was clear; everyone had his own little niche. She was the bartender; they were the customers. It was safe downstairs. That's why they were all so comfortable.

"You don't have a TV?" he asked, just for something to say.

"It's in the bedroom. I don't like a television set in the living room."

"Then you're the only person in this town who feels that way."

"Actually, it's Japanese, so I have to hide it." She carried a tray into the living room, putting it on the low table which stood in front of the fireplace between the two small sofas. "Would you like some of this?"

There were two mugs on the tray. He sat down and took one from her. The tea was pale, straw-colored . . . and awful. "What is this?"

She was smiling. "It's herbal tea. I try not to drink caffeine. You don't have to finish it."

He didn't intend to. "Now where are these presents?"

She got them off a small side table and came back over to the fireplace. This time she sat next to him.

"Which one shall I open first?" she asked.

"We usually save the best for last."

"Does that mean the worst first?"

"I suppose."

"Then we start with Mother's." She picked up the smaller of the two packages. "This will be something very tasteful that I have absolutely no use for."

She started to ease the string over the corner of the package. Joe reached in his pocket, pulled out his knife, handed it to her. She slit through the packing tape. She took the brown paper off the box, smoothed it out, and then neatly folded it back up. The package was wrapped in gold paper. Once again, she slit the tape, smoothed out the paper, folded it up.

She was procrastinating. It wasn't that she hadn't wanted to open this gift alone, Joe realized; it was that she didn't want to open it at all.

She opened the white box, lifted a layer of tissue paper. "Oh, Mother..."

Joe looked in the box. It held a piece of china or something like that, pale blue with a raised white design, a little dish with a post in the center. He had no idea what it was.

"Wasn't I right?" she asked. "Tasteful, but useless."

"I can't say," Joe answered. "I don't know what it is."

"It's a ring holder, a Wedgwood ring holder," she explained. "When you take your rings off at night, you put them on this."

"Okay...do you take your rings off at night?" Marianne hadn't.

She held up her hands. "I don't wear rings...I can't. Not in the bar. My hands are in and out of water and detergent all the time, and I put on handcream about ten times a day. I wouldn't do that even to a diamond...shows you what my mother knows about running a bar." Tory set the delicate piece down on her rough-hewn pine table. It looked entirely out of place.

Joe wished there was something he could say, but there wasn't. Her mother's gift was all wrong.

The other package was the padded mailer. Tory pulled the tab and a strip ripped down the side of it, sprinkling little flecks of grey packing material across the coffee table. She reached inside and pulled out some kind of book, a large book, the spine was green with gold trim. Suddenly she stopped, laying the half-opened package down.

"What's the matter?" he asked.

"It's not a Christmas present...just something I left behind in Atlanta."

"You know what it is?"

"Oh, yes." She leaned forward, shoving it forward. "Look at it."

Puzzled, Joe reached out and took the book out of the mailer. It was a photograph album. He opened the cover. "Oh, are these your beauty contest pictures?"

"Scholarship pageant, Joe...scholarship pageant."

He was looking at an eight by ten glossy of Tory. She was wearing a white chiffon gown with a beaded bodice. She had on long white gloves and a lot of eyeliner. Her blond hair was teased and brushed back and up, held off her face by a rhinestone tiara, then descending to her shoulders in tiers of carefully constructed curls. She had a sash, declaring her "Miss South Carolina."

"It's pretty," he said. "I like you better now, but it's still pretty."

"I like me better now too."

Joe turned the page. The next picture was similar. She was in a different white evening gown, one with chiffon sleeves, and she again had on her crown and Miss South Carolina sash. Her hair was—

Her hair. Joe turned to the first picture and then flipped back to the second. "I don't get it. Your hair's darker in this one."

"What does it look like? I dyed it."

"You dyed your hair? I didn't know you dye your hair."

"I don't, but I did. This—" she flipped a finger through her light hair "—is my real color, like in the first picture. I really am blond, but I dyed it brown for the national pageant."

"You dyed it brown? Nobody dyes their hair *brown*."

"Miss America contestants do. Blond hair doesn't show up well in bright lights; it looks gray and faded. And the image of the wholesome All-American girl isn't a blonde. So my state pageant committee told Mother to have me dye my hair, and I did."

"That seems strange."

"Well, it gets stranger. The girl who won that year was a blonde, and she won as a blonde. Her state committee told her to dye her hair and she refused, had a fight with them about it. She wouldn't do it and she won anyway. I did it and lost."

"Did you mind much?"

"At the time."

It was hard to imagine Tory—independent, decisive Tory—letting people talk her into dyeing her hair. "Do you feel like you would have won if you hadn't dyed your hair?"

She shrugged. "It's a lot more complicated than hair color. To win that thing, you have to believe that you are going to win, that you deserve to win. I mean, at my state pageant, when they called the first runner up's name, when I knew I was Miss South Carolina, I wasn't even surprised. I was glad, but I had known all along that I was going to win. But somewhere between the state pageant and Atlantic City, I lost the confidence. The other girl, the one who won, the one who didn't dye her hair, she believed she could win whatever color her hair was, that she was that good. I didn't believe in myself like that."

This clearly wasn't something she wanted to remember. "Why did your ex-husband send these pictures to you?" It seemed cruel.

"I don't know. I suppose he means well, he's just too big of a jerk to know better. When I moved here, he sent me all my clothes. He really may think I want this stuff."

"How could he think that?"

"Don't blame him. How's he to know how much I've changed? It's not like I've made any effort to keep him up-to-date."

She made it sound like it was her fault, not his. "Is that how you feel about your mother too?" he asked.

She looked over at him. "Does your mother understand you?"

"My mother? Of course."

"Really?"

Joe hesitated. "Well, they weren't happy when I got divorced. They thought I should have quit the union work like Marianne asked."

"And now? What about all the work you're doing now?"

"We don't talk about it."

"That should tell you something. I bet none of your family understands you anymore."

She was probably right. "You make it sound like we're both so alone."

"I think we both are."

He shifted uneasily. "You aren't supposed to say things like that on Christmas."

"I don't like to pretend anymore . . . at least not to myself."

She had a point there. "You know," he said slowly, "that's the thing about you; a person doesn't have to pretend around you. He can be honest."

Which was pretty amazing when you considered what she looked like.

She was smiling. "Is that why you made such a face over my tea?"

"Among other things." Joe ran his hand along the arm of the sofa, then stopped, pulling his hand away, flexing his fingers.

Tory noticed. "What is it?"

"My calluses." He opened his hands and rubbed his fingers across his palms. "I'm losing them now that I'm working a desk job, and things feel different. It surprises me sometimes, that's all."

Tory was looking at his hands. "But you're getting a replacement." She took his right hand and ran her thumb along the side of his middle finger. "You're getting a callus there now, from holding a pen."

Joe didn't answer. A log in the fireplace sputtered and fell, dropping little chunks of orange-red glow onto the gray ashes beneath the grate. The glass fire doors were trimmed in brass that reflected, in its narrow lines and bands, a man and a woman.

Tory was wearing a white sweater with a lacy open weave. Under it she wore an orchid-colored turtleneck. Her head was tilted, her hair fell away from her shoulder. Her earring was a pearl, and in her throat, her pulse throbbed. Her hand was still holding his.

How easy it would be to tighten his hand, to pull her to him ... Joe broke free and stood up. "I'd better be going."

Tory looked up at him. Her eyes were green, a brighter green than he'd ever known eyes could be. He had thought that before.

"I'd better be going." He had already said that.

"You don't have anywhere you need to be, do you?"

"No."

"I thought we were being honest."

"About tea, maybe."

She was standing now. "Playing it safe, Joe?"

Yes, yes, he was. But what for? To go back on a logging crew? If he wanted to play it safe, he should have stayed downstairs. He put his hands on her shoulders. Her white sweater was soft. "I think about you. All the guys do."

"I know, but the difference is that I think only about you."

TORY WAS LOVELY, slender and strong. Joe could feel how lithe, how limber she was. She moved effortlessly, gracefully.

And at first most of the movements were hers. She seemed intent only on pleasing him, allowing him a passivity that was new to him. For a time he gave into it, but only for a time. There was a momentary contest of wills which he won because he had every intention of doing so, and as he felt her fingers lace through his hair, he knew that all was quite better than she had expected it to be.

Then just before they fell asleep, Joe learned something else about Tory Duncan. Hair color hadn't been the only problem. Her emerald eyes were a fake. She wore tinted contacts. Her own eyes were a soft and pretty hazel.

IT WAS SNOWING AGAIN, a lighter, dryer snow than last night's slush; Tory could see it through the skylight over her bed. The flakes brushed across the convex bubble, piling up around the sealed rim. She lay in bed, staring up at the little white drift bordering the circle of grey sky.

Well, so much for thinking of herself as his patroness, his aunt, his coach: they were lovers now.

He was asleep, lying on his back, one arm crooked behind his head. In the dim light, his hair looked almost brown. In the sunshine it would glint golden.

Maybe this could work. Maybe there was a way to handle it. If they kept their relationship apart, private, if he could run his local and she her business, leaving this for after hours, then it wouldn't take over the way marriage did; it wouldn't be something that would change you into something you weren't. They could just go on being themselves.

This fine notion lasted exactly as long as it took Joe to shower, dress, eat half a piece of the seven-grain substance that Tory called bread, and drink one third of a cup of the coffee she had hunted down in a corner of a cupboard.

He set his cup down. "Would you like to come to my grandmother's this afternoon?"

Tory looked at him suspiciously. "Your grandmother's?"

"It is Christmas. She has Christmas dinner at her place."

"That sounds—"

She stopped. *That sounds lovely,* she had been about to say, when in truth she thought it sounded awful.

Here Joe Brigham had done nothing more than shower, dress, eat half a slice of toast, drink a third of a cup of coffee, and already she was pretending, talking like a beauty queen again. She could imagine what would happen if she went to Grandma's. She would turn herself into Miss South Carolina again, pleasant, charming, interested in everyone. They would all like her, and she would hate herself.

"Do all the Brighams get together?" She was stalling.

"Oh, no. There's us and my aunt and my uncle."

"What's that, about six, eight people?"

"Eight?" Joe was shaking his head. "Not quite."

It turned out what Joe meant by "us" was not she and he, but she, he, his mom, his dad, his four siblings, their three spouses and assorted children. A similar entourage would be coming with his uncle, and a much smaller one from his aunt that included her

son, Dennis Colt, and his stepson, Max Brigham. Tory
had been in beauty pageants with smaller audiences
than that.

There was too much at stake here to do anything
except say no. She wasn't going to sugar-coat it, she
wasn't even going to hide behind the honest excuse of
having to open the bar. "No, Joe, I'm not going. This
isn't going to work if you start expecting me to take
potato salad to Brigham family picnics."

"Oh, you wouldn't have to bring anything."

"You know what I mean."

"Yes," he said slowly. "I guess you wouldn't fit
in."

No, she would fit in, she would make herself—and
that was the problem.

JOE'S MOTHER took his plate from him.

He thanked her. "I was trying to avoid going in
there." He glanced at the kitchen, which was full of
women, of sound. Sheets of aluminum foil ripped out
of long boxes were molded around casseroles, plat-
ters. Glasses clinked into soapy water were swirled dry
by terry-cloth towels. *Shall we save this?...Wasn't
there a lid for that?...Is this one Cheryl's or Marianne's?...There was so much...I hate to throw...Did
the kids eat any of the squash?* The usual noisy conclusion of a family holiday.

And only a few hours ago Joe had been sitting with
Tory in her quiet home with its sweep of pine and open
rafters.

"You look tired."

Joe looked down at his mother. "I'm okay, Mom.
Really I am."

"I don't know." She was shaking her head. "Your dad and I . . . we've been wondering if maybe you're working too hard."

"I don't think that's it."

"All this driving back and forth to Tramlet—it's good of you to help out, but surely there's someone else who can do it. There's no reason for you to run yourself ragged."

"I still have time for Max."

"But Dad says you didn't go hunting once this fall."

No, he hadn't, and earlier this afternoon when the other men had been talking about a new gun his uncle got for Christmas, Joe hadn't listened. It hadn't seemed interesting.

Eight-cylinder engines, electric drills, table saws, great big toys that made people feel powerful, people who didn't really have any power.

He kissed his mother and went down to the basement rec room. The second TV was on, tuned into one of the football games; most of the men were down there and some of the boys. Max was standing next to Dennis. Dennis was leaning forward, one arm around Max, the other pointing at the TV screen. He was explaining an official's call.

All the chairs were taken; Joe sat down on the steps and tried to concentrate on the game.

He really wished Tory hadn't said it last night, hadn't asked him if his family understood him anymore.

The basement door opened, and someone came down the stairs. Joe craned his head backward. It was Lisa.

"Hi," he said.

"Can I sit here?" she asked softly. She had been brought up not to interrupt football games.

"Of course." He moved over to give her room on the step.

She sat down. "You have your sweater on." She sounded pleased.

Joe looked down. He had folded back the cuffs just as Tory had done. "I probably won't take it off till spring. I hope you draw my name every year." And then, just because he wanted so much to mention her name to someone, he went on. "I stopped by Tory Duncan's bar last night, and she liked it a lot too."

"She did?" Lisa flushed. "Did you . . . did you tell her I picked it out?"

"Sure." Joe frowned, trying to remember exactly what Tory had said. "She said that this was the right shade of blue, that navy would have been too harsh, whatever that means. She said you must have a good eye for color."

"She said that about me?"

Joe nodded.

Lisa leaned more closely toward him. "Do you know that the newspaper called the other day and asked if I would give away an award?"

"An award?" Joe sat up. "Tell me about it. Is this part of being Miss Sullivan City?"

She nodded. "It's at a dinner for Paperboy of the Year or something like that, and they're even going to pay me—not much, of course. Actually, I'm going to lose money since I was supposed to work that night and I would make more at the diner, but I'm still going to do it."

"Of course, you should. It won't hurt you to take a night off."

Joe had never thought about it before, but Lisa was at the diner a lot. She did well there; she was so pretty and so friendly with the people she knew and so sweetly shy with those she didn't know that everybody tipped her as much as they could. Joe wondered why she worked so hard. Why should she need money? He didn't think she had a lot of clothes or a big record collection, but he had to admit he didn't know a lot about her life. It was hard to think of her as having her own life, but of course she did.

"How many hours a week do you work?" he asked.

"Mom and Dad say too many."

"Are they right?"

She didn't answer. "They say the same thing about you, that you work too hard."

"I expect everyone thinks that." Everyone except Tory.

"Exactly what are you doing up there? I don't really understand."

Joe was surprised. No one in his family had ever asked him exactly what he was doing in Tramlet. "Helping out" had always been enough of an answer. But Lisa seemed interested, so he explained it to her, telling her about the committees being set up, the rallies being planned, the money being raised, and without mentioning his cousin Don's name, he told her how they were trying to catch the union busters breaking the law.

Her eyes were wide. "Are you really doing all that?"

He nodded.

"It's hard to believe...but Marianne said there wasn't anyone who could do as good a job as you."

Marianne said that? "Well," he admitted, "sometimes a person from the outside can do more than someone on the inside."

"It must be neat, feeling like you are exactly the right person for something, and that you aren't just the most convenient available body. That must be really great to feel that way."

"It is," Joe answered slowly. "It really is."

They sat quietly for a while, half listening to the game. Then Lisa spoke again. "When you were my age, did Cheryl boss you around?"

"She still does," he pointed out. "Do you find it hard to take?"

"Only sometimes, and I guess I shouldn't complain."

"Well, it will—"

He stopped. *It will be over soon enough,* he had intended to say. But why would it? Yes, Lisa would graduate from high school this year, but why would that stop Cheryl from telling her what to do? She would probably live at home and work at the diner until she got married.

Live at home and work at the diner until she got married. Somehow that sounded a little sad.

The basement door opened again. "Is this a road block?"

The voice was Jim's—sunny, uncomplicated Jim, the one who had always been great with cars. Joe and Lisa each leaned to the side so Jim could hop over them. He strolled through the rec room, stopping next to Frank's chair. "Hey, I was sitting there."

"You aren't now," Frank answered.

Jim laughed, untroubled, and sat down on the floor and pulled one of the kids over to him.

"You know," Lisa said after a minute, "Jim has always worked long hours, and nobody complains about that."

She was right. Jim worked a ten-hour day at the garage, and then at home in the evenings he would work on the family cars. The family had never told Jim he worked too hard. After all, he was Jim; he had always been that way. He loved what he was doing, and he was so good at it.

Goddamn it, I'm good at what I do too.

_____ *Seven* _____

IT WAS TURNING into a mean January; there wasn't a speck of snow between Christmas and Superbowl week. Day after day, the sky was slate grey, and a sharp, drying wind sliced across the forest, stinging through the men's stocking caps and thermal underwear. Tory's regulars flexed their fingers as they pulled off their choppers' mitts, then fumbled through their pockets for Chapstick. It was a hard time with the Christmas bills coming in, the furnaces and the cars acting up.

Last January Tory had worked hard to be cheerful for them, warm and welcoming. This year she didn't have to try—she felt cheerful, she felt warm and welcoming.

Joe had come back Christmas night, coming in for exactly the same reason he had been coming to the bar for the last month. He had wanted to talk to her. Sex hadn't changed that.

She had been going to close early, and she had asked him if he could wait. He had come upstairs with her, had told her about his family holiday, and of course, had stayed.

After that, things seemed settled between them, at least for the time being. They did not see each other every day. Joe was busy; Tory stayed open late. But she took Mondays off, so as soon as he dropped off his son, he would come to her. She would make dinner, forcing him to share her low-sodium, low-cholesterol, high-fiber menus. But she did pollute her refrigerator with sausage and eggs, sweet rolls and bacon, so that in the morning he could have what he was used to.

If someone had asked her flat-out "Are you going to bed with Joe Brigham?" she would have answered honestly; she had done enough lying in her day. But no one asked, and she was glad.

It was, she told herself, more for Joe's sake than her own. Keeping things quiet would cut down on the explaining he would have to do when everything was over. "Yes, Mother, she's very pretty and keeps her house clean, and I'm sure that she's a good cook, but she's already blown one marriage and she hates her mother and probably has unresolved Oedipal complexes about her unknown father. She used to plan parties and was totally pathological about her appearance, and once upon a time, she could twirl two flaming batons in pinwheel pitches without setting her hair on fire. I just don't think there's a lot of future in the relationship."

THE SUPERBOWL was a disappointment. There were two East Coast teams playing, and no one at Tory's really cared who won. Last year's game had been great; a team was playing that people wanted to root for, and that brought a significance, a meaning, to the week. All things seemed to matter more that week because of the game. Tory now understood why sports were so important. Just as her regulars had no power, their lives did not have much drama or intensity either.

A pennant race, a good set of play-offs, made a difference.

Nonetheless her turn-out for the game was pretty good, and people probably drank more than they would have had they been intent on the game.

Joe hadn't come. She knew he wouldn't; he was watching the game with his brothers, but he'd said he would try to stop by later. As she was washing glasses after the game, she kept glancing at the door, hoping that each new arrival would be him. The bar was nearly empty, and when the door opened it was, to Tory's surprise, not Joe but his sister Lisa. She didn't come in, just stood there holding the door open, looking in.

"Is it okay if I come in?" she asked timidly.

"Of course, although I can't serve you."

"Oh, no." Lisa looked horrified at the thought. "I don't want to drink. I . . . I, uh—"

Clearly the girl wanted to talk to her. Rich's father was still on his shift, so Tory came out from behind the bar. She went to a table in the far corner and watched Lisa cross the room to join her. The girl needed to work on her walk.

Now, glide . . . look up and out . . . chins level please . . . relax those shoulders, girls, tuck those derrières in, and glide . . . glide. . . .

Tory shook herself. She was thinking like her mother.

"I saw your picture in the paper last week," Tory said as Lisa sat down. "It was a nice shot." Lisa had been pictured handing the "Newscarrier of the Year" award to some little paperboy. She had looked very good—or rather, very good for someone who did not know the first thing about making up for black-and-white stills.

Lisa thanked her, but didn't seem able to say anything else. Tory wondered how she had survived her pageant interview.

"Is there something I can do for you?"

Lisa flushed, but spoke bravely. "Do you know Erica Hicks?"

"Is she one of T.K.'s girls?" T.K. Hicks was the local contractor. He had done well for himself.

Lisa nodded. "She was home from college at Christmas—she's at the university in Eugene. I think she's majoring in drama or something like that. She says it's great."

There was envy in Lisa's voice. Tory sat up, suddenly interested.

"Anyway," Lisa went on, "Erica came down to the diner to see me and congratulate me on winning the pageant, which was really nice of her because of course she must have wanted Alison—her younger sister—to win."

Tory remembered that the first runner-up had been one of T.K.'s daughters.

Lisa continued. Apparently, Erica had won the Miss Sullivan City Pageant two years before, and the real reason that she had come to the diner hadn't been to congratulate Lisa, but to warn her, to tell her what the state pageant was like.

"She said it was awful, that she wasn't prepared at all, and she felt like she shouldn't have been there. And if she felt that way, what about me? I felt like that just during the local."

Tory knew. Oh, God, how she knew. That was one of the first things that happened in pageant rehearsals; long before the judges came near them, the girls sorted themselves out into winners and losers. From that moment on, the losers, feeling like they deserved to lose, never had a chance. Tory had always been one of the winners; she had known all the tricks to make another girl feel like a loser.

And Lisa Brigham was going to have every single one of them played on her.

"I know I can't win; I see that now. It was silly to even think about the sch—"

Lisa broke off, but Tory could fill in the blank: scholarship money. Of course. Lisa Brigham wanted to go to college, and she was going to need scholarships.

"Anyway," Lisa said quickly, "I may not win, but I don't want to make a fool of myself, and when I was telling Marianne—she used to be married to one of my brothers—"

"I know who she is."

"Well, she said that you almost won the Miss America Pageant."

"I did not almost win it; I wasn't close."

"And so I was wondering if maybe you could give me a few pointers so I wouldn't make a fool of myself."

Tory froze. "I beg your pardon?"

"It wouldn't have to take long, and I—"

She couldn't have heard right. "You want me to be your trainer? Me?"

"Trainer?" Lisa was bewildered.

"Yes, trainer. It's like race horses and boxers. Beauty contestants have trainers. Most girls go and live with theirs, and their parents pay them."

"Oh." Lisa paused. "I can't pay you actual money, but I'm a good waitress, I could come work for you until we're even."

"You're too young to work in a bar."

"Then I could clean after hours."

"I already have someone to clean, and he's on parole. He needs the job."

Tory was not going to do this. No way. She would never, not ever, have another thing to do with a beauty pageant as long as she lived. She had sat through one last competition, that had been her test. She had survived it so now she was through. Over, done, finished, dust to dust, ashes to ashes, clods dropping on the coffin, never again. She'd fire up one of her batons and torch herself before she'd do it.

And she meant it. "Now, Lisa—"

A shadow fell across the table. It was Joe, surprised to see his sister in the bar.

"Beat it," Tory said immediately. "We're having a conversation."

"No, no," Lisa protested. "You can stay. I don't mind if you hear this."

He sat down, but, true to form, said nothing.

"Lisa wants me to be her trainer," Tory said flatly.

"Trainer?" he asked.

She didn't answer, forcing Lisa to explain.

She wasn't going to do this. Going to Christmas dinner with three hundred Brighams was nothing compared to this. This was wrong, wicked. She would never take part in it. That was final.

"I didn't know that people got paid money for this," Lisa finished.

"Look, Lisa," Joe said, "Tory probably needs some time to think about this. Why don't you run along? She'll get back to you."

What was this "think about it"? Tory already knew. She wasn't going to have any part of this. She certainly didn't need time to figure that one out, and the sooner these two understood it the better. "Now, see here, I don't—"

"She'll get back to you," Joe interrupted firmly.

"I'd really appreciate it," Lisa managed. "I really would."

The minute they were alone, Tory turned to Joe. "I'm not going to do it."

"I gathered that."

"I mean, why should I?"

"Why don't you want to?"

Oh, Joe, you don't know what this does to people. Look at me, you don't want her to have to go through what I did. "I suppose you think I ought to do it because she's your sister."

"You said it."

"What difference does it make who she is?" Tory stood up. "I'm not going to do it, and that's final."

Joe blinked.

"Tell Nancy if you want another beer. I can't spend so much time with just one customer."

JOE WAITED UNTIL after closing time before going back. The bar was dark, but the lights in Tory's apartment were on. Joe parked the Cherokee next to the MGB. He went up the stairs and rapped on the door.

"Who is it?"

Who else visited her at this hour? "Joe."

He heard the rattle of the chain and then the door opened. She was wearing what looked to him like a floor-length sweatshirt. It was white cotton fleece with red ribbing at the neck and cuffs.

"May I come in?" he asked.

She stepped back. "I didn't expect you."

"You should have."

"After what I said?" She tucked her hands in the kangaroo pocket of her robe and looked at him directly. "I didn't mean it. You aren't just another customer. You know you aren't."

"I know, but it's still nice to hear you say so."

"I don't know why I said it; I'm really sorry."

She was clearly unhappy with herself. "When he was four, Max would sometimes get these terrible temper tantrums. His face would get all red, and he'd stamp his foot and shout that he was going to call you a 'dummy.' It was the worst word he could think of."

"I can think of lots worse words than 'dummy.'"

"Max can too now."

"Maybe if I'd had temper tantrums when I was four, I wouldn't have to have them now."

"All four-year-olds have temper tantrums."

"Not me, it would have mussed my makeup."

Joe stepped back, startled. "Mussed your makeup? At four? What are you talking about?"

"Oh, come on, Joe, I told you this."

"Not about wearing makeup at four."

"You remember, I said that Mother first started talking about the Miss America Pageant when I was three."

"Well, yes, but..."

She looked at him, her contacts caught the light, making her eyes seem brilliant. "Did you just think it was just idle 'what do you want to be when you grow up' talk?"

He nodded. What else could it have been?

"It wasn't just talk, Joe. We started right away. Your sister is off to a bit of a late start. I was out there competing before I could walk."

"You were actually entered in competitions before high school?"

She stared at him. "Before high school? Oh, God, yes. Joe, I thought you understood this."

"Apparently not."

And so, with her fists clenched inside the pocket of her robe, Tory told him what it had been like, all those years of twirling competitions and beauty pageants.

Her mother had taken her to her first "Beautiful Baby" competition when Tory was not even a year old. She had won, and her mother, barely twenty, was thrilled. They went to another competition and then another, and soon it was all that they did. Tory remembered the long drives, the canned meals heated over a hotplate in a cheap motel room, while from the curtain rod hung lacy little dresses stiff over layers of petticoats. Her mother would wind Tory's hair in curlers each night; she would put eyeshadow and lipstick on her little girl each day. Tory learned how to be careful so that she wouldn't chip her nail polish.

When she was Max's age, Tory was practicing her walk, her smile, standing still while her mother fit her for clothes. Then they looked for a talent. She had every sort of lesson while her mother searched for something Tory would be good at. She could catch a ball before any of the other children, but sports did nothing for a girl. She liked listening to music, but she couldn't sing. She could do all the things in Miss Amanda's ballet class, but Miss Amanda said she was "too athletic." Finally it was Mrs. Cato, the baton twirling instructor, who said what Tory's mother wanted to hear: "She's the best I've seen."

So the other lessons stopped, and Tory twirled her baton for two hours each morning and an hour at night, working as hard as she could because she knew Mother would have liked it better if she could have sung or danced.

She was entered in every "Little Miss" contest there was; she twirled in every local parade. If Joe had finished looking through her photo album, he would have seen not just Miss South Carolina, but the Little Dixie Darling, Miss Southern 500, the Pretty Peach Princess, Miss Teen AmVet, the winner of the Rule County Baton Twirling competition, children's division, junior division, and then senior division. There had been one competition after another, and one room at home had shelves and shelves of rayon sashes and chrome and plastic trophies.

Tory worked hard and adolescence brought endless fine-tuning from her mother, her twirling teacher, her charm school instructor, and then her pageant coach. Her accent was broken apart and then slowly pieced back together, so it was slightly Southern, but not too

Southern. "At least," she now said to Joe, "this was in the days before contestants had plastic surgery like they do now or who knows what I would have ended up looking like."

She was taught to be nice and friendly, open and vibrant. She could chat with anyone; she could seem interested in anyone, and she learned to smile—oh, God, did she learn to smile.

"'Be yourself, and don't forget to smile,' that's what they always told us, 'be yourself and don't forget to smile.' Nobody ever seemed to think that those two commands contradicted each other, but for me, they always did. How can you be yourself when you are trying to remember to smile?"

Be yourself, they said, and then made her dye her hair, change the color of her eyes. She knew what they were really saying—don't be yourself. Don't let them know what you are like. If the judges know what you are really like, if they know what you really think, feel, and believe, they won't vote for you. You must lie all the way through your interview. If you tell the truth, if you are yourself, you won't win.

So the dark side, the unacceptable side, the side that had opinions on things, that had tasted liquor, that wondered about sex, the side that was jealous, tense, competitive, the side that was all the things that beauty queens aren't supposed to be, started to feel more urgent, more real than anything else simply because it always had to be denied.

Yet through her marriage, Tory had continued to be the beauty queen, trying to be perfect when she was miserably conscious that she was not, accepting, even encouraging, Ned's criticisms because they felt more true than other people's admiration.

"You can't blame him for what was wrong with me," she said to Joe now. "If I hadn't wanted to be punished, if I hadn't felt like I deserved it, I wouldn't have married someone like him."

"You changed completely; that doesn't sound like you at all."

"Yes, but it was hard, hard work. And I just can't jeopardize who I am now. I like myself when I'm in the bar... and I don't know that I have ever liked myself before... at least not in the last decade. And it all started with the beauty pageants. They did such a number on me; I can't be a part of it, don't you see that? I can't do that to another girl."

Joe had almost forgotten Lisa's request. "Would you at least explain this to her? Would you tell her why you can't help her?"

Tory shook her head. "It won't mean anything to her. She wants it too much."

Joe did not believe that. He could guess why Tory had wanted to win all those pageants, why she had worked so hard to become this person that she now hated. She wanted to be loved. *Mommy loves you when you are a good little girl, Mommy loves you when you win.*

But it was different for Lisa. She was loved, and she had to know it. Yes, Mom and Dad had punished all five of them and sometimes rewarded them too, but never with love. Love wasn't a punishment or a reward. It was just there. Brighams loved their kids, whatever they were. This was, in part, why the kids always turned out as they did, good and decent people who achieved only one thing in life, raising another set of good and decent people. Brighams didn't win Nobel prizes; on the other hand, they didn't go to Washington and shoot the president.

"Are you sure?" Joe now said to Tory. "I wouldn't have thought Lisa wanted to be a beauty queen so much."

"Oh, no. It's not being a beauty queen. Actually that's pretty boring—you open shopping malls, sit at head tables, give stupid little talks. No, Lisa's probably got the sense to realize that this is her ticket out. She's eighteen—until now, she's had nothing to look forward to except a life like your sister's or your mother's, not in this town. It's not for Lisa; she's like you, Joe, she wants something different."

Live at home and work at the diner until she gets married… Yes, Joe could understand why Lisa would want more. "I'm not sure I see what the Miss Oregon Pageant has to do with this."

"Don't you see? This is her chance to gain some poise, to learn how to meet new people. I would be willing to bet that the women in your family are nervous about meeting new people, about walking into a room where they don't know anyone."

She was right. He had never thought about it, and he wasn't sure about Mother and Cheryl, but God knows it was true of Marianne. She was so easily intimidated by strangers.

"So Lisa wants this for poise and confidence?"

"And the scholarship money, no doubt. If she places in the state pageant, she'll at least get some of the runner-up money."

"Scholarship money? What does she want scholarship money for?"

"For college, Joe. Didn't you know? Your baby sister wants to go to college."

Lisa? College? Lisa wanted to go to college? "She told you that?"

"She didn't have to. I saw her face when she was talking about this other girl who was home from school."

College? "I had no idea..." So that was why Lisa had been working such long hours; she wanted the money for college. No Brigham had ever gone to college, but Lisa wanted to go.

For years, she had been the baby sister, and now she was Aunt Lisa, the world's best babysitter. When Mom had too many tomatoes last summer, Lisa had picked them and taken them around to Cheryl and Karen and Barbie. When Cheryl had thought Joe needed curtains, she sent Lisa over to hem and hang them. When Joe had bought his Christmas presents, he had asked Lisa to wrap them. Dad had given her the old Mustang and Jim had kept it running with the understanding that Lisa would run errands for everyone. She was convenient, useful, reliable.

She was also a young woman with a dream...and Joe thought it the best dream a young woman could have.

At least Dennis had had a chance. Yes, his dream had collapsed, his business had failed, he would never be his own boss. At least he had had a chance.

Shouldn't Lisa have a chance too?

Joe could help her with some things. The last few years had taught him how to organize and arrange, had given him the confidence to try to make things happen. He could help Lisa figure out the college applications; he could help her find a place to live, maybe even help her with the tuition.

But this was going to take more than money. There wasn't a college in Sullivan City. Lisa was going to have to leave home. Joe thought about how he and Marianne had been at eighteen. They had been wild to get married, but neither one of them would have had the nerve to leave town . . . and Marianne still didn't. Somewhere Lisa was going to have to find the courage to do that, to try something new. On that, Joe couldn't help her. But Tory could.

"Tory, will you help my sister?"

She drew back at the fervor of his tone, but she was still shaking her head. "Joe, no. You don't understand. Yes, you get poise and a certain kind of confidence. You can speak to large crowds; you can travel and go to new places; you can be on television without thinking twice. But real confidence about knowing who you are and liking yourself—I mean, look at me, you don't want her going through everything that I did."

"But, Tory, it's different. You started doing all this when you were a baby, but Lisa's nearly grown. She already knows who she is. She's a Brigham. That gives a person something—I don't know, a sense of responsibility, something to believe in, things like that. You aren't going to take those away from her by telling her about eyeshadow."

"Well, that's true," Tory agreed slowly. "I guess starting so late would make a difference. A big difference."

"Then you'll do it?"

"I will not show her how to make the other girls feel bad. That's a part of it, you know—psyching out the competition."

"It wouldn't matter if you showed her. She wouldn't do it." He paused and spoke again. "Tory, this is not going to hurt her."

"Well, even if it doesn't hurt her, I'm not sure that I can face all that, thinking about it all again."

"You went to her pageant that night."

"And I didn't stand up and start screaming, did I?"

"Not that I noticed...and I was watching you pretty carefully."

"No, you weren't," she said instantly. "You were watching your ex-wife."

How long ago that seemed. "You're changing the subject. Will you do it?"

She sighed. "Oh, Lord, I suppose so. But you have to come and keep me from turning into my mother."

JOE PICKED LISA UP after school the next afternoon.

Lisa seemed happy, excited. "It's so nice of Miss Duncan to help me. I can't believe she's going to do it."

"She knows how much it means to you."

"I just don't want to make a fool of myself," she answered. "You can understand that, can't you?"

Why didn't she say why she wanted the money? Did she think that no one would take her seriously? "Tory says you want the scholarship money for college."

Lisa gasped. "How...how did she know that?"

"She picks up on those things."

"You think I'm crazy, don't you?" She sounded defensive. "I know I'm just a mill kid, but—"

Joe interrupted. "Lisa, I have never been as proud to be a member of this family as I was when Tory told me this."

"Oh, Joe..." Lisa stared at him, her hand over her mouth. "You don't mean that."

"I really do—now don't cry, I want to hear about it. When did you start thinking about college?"

Lisa sniffed and tried to speak clearly. "I don't know, I guess a couple years ago. I really like school and I do okay—"

"You have a B average?"

"I've only had two B's since freshman year. The rest have been A's."

"Is that right?" He had no idea she was doing so well; it wasn't the sort of thing that the family would talk about.

When he was in high school, he had gotten B's. That's what Mom and Dad expected. They frowned at C's. A D and you were in trouble. B's were just right. The fact that Cheryl and Joe—especially Joe—didn't have to work as hard for their B's as Frank and Jim wasn't the sort of thing anyone paid attention to.

"What are your best subjects?" he asked his sister now. "What do you think you would want to major in?"

Lisa flushed again. "Well...I know girls aren't supposed to be any good at it, but I really like math."

Math. One year the math teacher had suggested that Joe sign up for algebra-trig instead of plain math. "You may be better at this than any of us know," he'd said.

But algebra-trig met during early period, and Joe, like his brothers, had a part-time job. He pumped gas from six to eight four mornings a week. That seemed more important than algebra-trig. It hadn't even been a hard decision.

What a waste. Now he could tell he had a head for numbers. He made sense of them faster than other people, but he was having to learn it all on his own. That was harder.

"I like numbers too," he told Lisa. "If I had ever done more school, that's what I would have studied—maybe accounting, something like that."

"Really? You would have?"

"We—you and I—may have a lot more in common than we ever realized."

Now why that would make anyone look like she was about to cry again, Joe did not know. He was grateful they had reached Tory's, and Lisa had to compose herself.

"I'm glad you're coming with me," she said as they got out of the Cherokee. "I think I'm a little afraid of her."

"There's no reason to be scared of Tory," said Joe, shoving aside the thought that he had been probably been a little afraid of Tory once. But she would make Lisa comfortable soon enough...as long as she didn't show Lisa her closets. Lisa would probably never recover from that.

The wall between Tory's bedroom and bathroom was entirely closets. One of them was banked with floor-to-ceiling white wire baskets that slid in and out like drawers. In the baskets were her turtlenecks and sweaters, arranged by color.

It was a little like looking at the racks of thread in a fabric store; Joe felt that same dizzying fascination with the array of colors, with their subtle gradations of shades. Tory's blue sweaters alone filled five baskets, the colors ranging from navy to a blue so pale it was almost white. There were grey-blues, purplish blues, turquoises, and aquas.

"Do you wear all these clothes?" he had had to ask.

"Not really...I mean, no, not at all. I thought I told you. Ned sent them. I only unpacked the casual ones, and even so I don't wear all of them. Do you realize I have nine swimming suits with matching high heels? Can you imagine a grown woman needing nine swimming suits with matching high heels?"

But as soon as they were inside, it was apparent that Lisa was not going to have to look inside Tory's closets. The former Little Dixie Darling had already spread their contents across her apartment. A rack of plastic swathed suits had been wheeled out next to the oak table. Evening gowns lay piled on the couch in a froth of white and pastel chiffon. The counter separating the kitchen was covered with scarves and hats and other things Joe didn't recognize. The oak table looked like a chemistry lab with little bottles and pots of strange brews; the mirror with its lighted stand suggested that these chemicals might be makeup, but Joe could never have sworn to it.

"What's all this?" he asked.

"Clothes," Tory said unnecessarily. "We must wear about the same size, and there's no reason for her to buy a whole new wardrobe of things she'll never wear again when I have clothes running out of my ears."

"But can't I just wear what I wore to the local pageant?" Lisa asked, still in a bit of a daze.

"No, you can't. Your evening gown looked like you had worn it to the junior prom, and you also need rehearsal clothes and sitting-around-scaring-the-other-contestants clothes. I showed up in Atlantic City with eleven suitcases and twenty-three pairs of shoes."

"Eleven suitcases?" Even the blue sweaters hadn't prepared Joe for that.

"And I still lost. But you're lucky. I was doing all this back in the days when everyone was wearing micro-mini skirts, and pageant rules said our skirts had to be two inches above the knee. Nobody manufactured clothes like that then. You couldn't even let hems out enough. So we had to have everything custom made. Fortunately Mother and I could sew, but for some of the other girls, it was unbelievably expensive, and then you never wore any of it again."

"That doesn't make sense," Lisa said.

Tory smiled, not her perfect TV-ad smile, but the wry, mocking one that Joe preferred. "Lisa, my dear, if any of this ever makes the least bit of sense to you—even for the briefest second—you are to tell your brother instantly and let him take you out in the woods and shoot you. That's a far better fate…which brings me to the first point—" Tory waved at them to sit down "—you don't want to win this thing."

"She doesn't?"

"I don't?"

"No. If you win, you go to Atlantic City, and you don't have a prayer at Atlantic City. You're too young; you're too green. You'd be cannon fodder. You need a couple of state pageants under your belt before you have any chance at winning the national—"

"Me? Win the Miss America Pageant?" Lisa was stunned. "Me?"

"Why not?" Tory said calmly. "You're tall enough. The plan for state should be for you to make five—"

"Make five?" Joe asked.

"Finals, making the finals. Making five means being a finalist. Making ten, the semis, isn't good enough; you don't get scholarship money until you make five. So that should be your goal. But you don't want to win. That ruins everything because you can only go to Atlantic City once."

Lisa looked dumbfounded, and Joe sympathized with her.

"It's nothing to worry about," Tory said in what she probably imagined was a reassuring tone. "You won't win. The judges would never send somebody who's as young as you to Atlantic City; they'll pick someone they think can win. So just go to state, don't be spooked by the obvious winners because you don't want to win. Your goal is get some money and decide if you like doing this enough to try for Miss America."

Besides pulling out all her clothes and makeup, Tory had been on the phone. "Margaret Sumner is your chaperone for the state pageant. She'll go to Seaside with you. Do you know her?"

Lisa shook her head.

"Her husband is the senior vice-president of the company," Joe explained.

Lisa looked a little sick.

"Anyway," Tory went on, "she's never really done anything to help the girls prepare, but she says she's certainly willing to if we just tell her what. So she's setting up a bunch of practice interviews. Her friends will act like judges, asking you questions."

Tory started listing names, and Lisa shook her head. "I can't talk to those people."

Joe could see her point. Until a very few years ago, he couldn't have talked to those people.

"Maybe you can't now," Tory agreed, "but two months from now, you'll know how to take control of the interview so they can't help but ask you the questions you want them to ask. The year she won, Phyllis George spent her whole interview talking about her pet crab. The judges were so overwhelmed they had to vote for her."

Joe was beginning to think that maybe he should enroll in the Tory Duncan School of Charm, Poise, and Borrowed Clothes.

"Now, Lisa, down to work. The city girls will kill you on makeup if you don't start learning about it so—"

"Can I leave?" Joe pleaded. And when neither female seemed to hear him, he did.

THE NEXT WEEK, Joe got a call from the vice-president
of labor relations at the company, a man Joe reluctantly admired. Brian Ross had to make and explain
some tough, unpopular decisions, particularly during
the lay-offs a couple of years back, and he had done
so with grit and grace.

But at the moment, Ross was miserable. He had
been an interrogator on one of Lisa's practice interviews, operating under instructions from Tory that
made him feel like the sort of person who tied tin cans
to puppies' tails. "We folded the rug under so that she
tripped when she came in the room, and I was supposed to call her by the wrong name just to rattle her."

Joe admitted he would have a lot of trouble doing
that to an eighteen-year-old girl.

"Then I had to ask her questions about abortion
and Indochina, while somebody else was asking her all
these mindless questions about why was it good to help
other people."

"How did she do?"

"Better on my questions than on the mush...
although I did throw her one fat pitch, Joe."

"Oh?"

"My last question was about gyppos."

Joe laughed. Gyppos were crews of non-union loggers that some companies hired for contract work. The union did not, to put it mildly, approve. "What did she say?"

"She spouted some nonsense about safety."

"Good for her."

Sunday night Joe teased Tory about her tactics. "What if she had broken her leg on that rug? Weren't you worried about the vengeance of the Brighams?"

"She wasn't going to break her leg."

Tory's voice was tight. Joe waited a moment. "What's wrong? Are you having second thoughts about doing this?"

"Second? Are you kidding? I've run out of fingers and toes; I'm having to use eyelash hairs to keep track of my 'second' thoughts."

"What's the problem?"

"Have you talked to her recently? She sounds so phony, so pleased-to-meet-you smiley all the time. To hear her talk, all she cares about anymore is clothes and makeup. She's obsessed with stocking colors; last month she was perfectly happy to wear nude-colored pantyhose from the Safeway and now we're into blueberry ice and fussing about the difference between vanilla and cream. Your mother must be so sick of hearing about it that she's probably ready to strangle her... or me."

Joe shook his head. "Stuff like that doesn't get to Mom. She's glad that Lisa is having such a good time."

"See if she still feels that way when her baby turns into a party consultant."

"I don't think we need to worry about that."

"Well, sure. You don't have to worry about it, because you know perfectly well I'm doing enough worrying for the both of us...and not just for you and me, but for your entire family—all fifty-seven thousand of them. They're so fortunate to have Tory Duncan sitting out here doing their worrying for them; they have no idea how lucky they are."

"They probably don't," Joe admitted. "Look, even if all Lisa cares about right now is having legs the color of food, she'll remember soon enough why she's doing this. Anybody who tells Brian Ross off about gyppos can't have gone all bad."

"I suppose."

Tory didn't sound convinced. "What else is bothering you?"

She sighed. "Oh, I guess it's that I care so much, that I so want her to do well. I feel like I would do anything to be sure she gets that scholarship money."

"What's wrong with that?"

"Do you realize I got angry the other day? I mean, I never get angry. Last year, the beer people completely screwed up, and I spent a whole Sunday without any domestic beer, without a thing on tap. And it wasn't just any Sunday, but a *play-off* Sunday. I had to sell the bottle imports at a terrible loss, but I didn't get angry then. But last week I got angry."

"Who did you get mad at?"

"The high school music director. I went to ask him if he would help Lisa with her song, because that's where I'm weak, and he said he couldn't. That what with funding cuts, he had the orchestra, the band, and the chorus, and he couldn't take the time to help a student who had never enrolled in any of them."

"I think he has a point."

"I know that," Tory said impatiently. "That's why I'm so mad at myself—for getting angry over it."

"What's wrong with getting angry once in a while?"

"Don't you think it a little odd that after going for years and years without getting mad at anyone except myself, the minute I get into the pageant business again, I start hooting like a crazed rooster? It's happening, I know it's happening—I'm turning into my mother."

Joe knew now this was one of her worst fears. "Maybe you finally care enough about somebody to get angry."

"About somebody winning a beauty pageant?"

"About somebody going to college. Now tell me the truth, what if Keith's parole board decided to revoke his parole because he worked here, wouldn't you be angry then?"

"They promised they wouldn't do that."

"But if they did, wouldn't you be angry?"

"I'd kill them."

"My point exactly."

She didn't say anything. Then after a minute she stood up. "It's a good thing, Joe Brigham," she remarked calmly, "that I know you are an ignorant logger; otherwise I might listen to what you have to say."

He smiled at her. "Now are we done talking about the color of Lisa's legs?"

"I suppose . . . if you can think of something more important."

"Max."

"Max?" Tory always seemed interested in Max. "What about him? What's he up to?"

"His usual lunatic self. But he and I are going sledding tomorrow afternoon. Do you want to come?"

Tory sat down again. "Sledding?" she said carefully. "I've never been sledding."

"What do you mean, you've never been sledding? What kind of person has never been sledding?"

"Persons who grow up in South Carolina, that's who. No snow, no hills—it sort of cuts down on the opportunities."

"You've got a point there."

"And even if I'd grown up in Denver, I probably wouldn't have gone sledding. Baton twirling isn't much of a talent, but sledding has got to be worse. Can you imagine trying to put on a sledding demonstration in Atlantic City in September?"

"Well, we don't have to go sledding." Actually Joe thought Tory would enjoy it a lot. "There are plenty of things we can do."

"Oh, no, I'd hate to have you change your plans on my account."

"The plan was for you to meet Max. It doesn't much matter what we do."

Tory was sitting at one end of her living room sofa. She turned away from him and examined the potted plant on the end table next to her. She fingered one of the green leaves, then pulled it off, spread it along the arm of the sofa and started to pierce a little design in the glossy surface with her fingernail. It wasn't like her to fidget.

"I'd like you to meet my son, Tory."

She crumpled the leaf. "Oh, Joe, don't ask. Please don't ask me to do that."

"Why not?"

"I just don't think it would work out, that's all."

That was hardly an answer, but Joe was a patient man, he could wait. He found Tory's background incomprehensible; he couldn't imagine growing up without any relatives except a domineering mother, but he supposed it would have to give you some strange ideas about family life. He wanted her to meet Max, but he was willing to wait.

The surprising thing was that Tory kept bringing the matter up.

A week or so later they were sitting in her living room again. "You know," she said suddenly, "this business about my not wanting to meet your son...I hope you don't take it personally."

"No," he answered, not quite lying. "Of course not."

"It's just that I don't know anything about children. I've never been around them. I mean, I don't know what I would have in common with him."

In common with him? Since when did a person need to have anything in common with a six-year-old? Who would want to? "Okay."

"It's not that I have anything against him," she went on. "I just don't see how if we got together that he would have a very good time."

Max had a good time putting money in a vending machine. "Okay."

"If it were important, of course I would meet him, but it sounds like we would all be in for a lot of unnecessary awkwardness."

It also sounded like she knew perfectly well that it was important. "Okay."

"Are you just going to sit there and say 'okay'?"

"Yes."

LIFE CONTINUED. More snow fell. Joe's brothers and uncles went ice-fishing. His youngest cousin was having a good season on the high school basketball team. Jim's wife was pregnant again. Lisa read *Time* every week and watched the evening news every night to prepare for her interview. Tory was using the word "derrière" in normal conversation. A puller on the green chain broke a couple of fingers, but he was going to be all right. A gyppo logger across the mountains had a bad accident, he wasn't going to be all right, and he didn't have any health insurance. Don Marsh continued to report from Tramlet. Max started moaning for a dog. Marianne and Dennis told him he could have one as soon as school was out.

Joe wasn't seeing much of his old friends, and he almost felt guilty one Sunday afternoon in March when he ran into Davy in Tory's parking lot.

"Long time no see," Davy called out.

"If you hadn't skipped the monthly meeting last week, you would have seen me there."

"Well, if you hadn't—"

Davy stopped, and Joe realized he had been about to say something about Tory. No one had said one word to him about her, although people certainly must know. In this town you kept track of a person by where his car was parked, and the Cherokee had done a lot of time in the bar's parking lot when the bar wasn't open.

Joe knew that if he were dating any other woman in town, he would have come in for his share of ribbing and teasing. But because he and Tory didn't "date," because they didn't go out in public or do things with other people, no one knew what to say. This wasn't a courtship; it was an affair, clandestine and therefore flagrantly sexual. To talk about it was to talk about sex, and people didn't do that.

So now he and Davy talked about their cars.

The minute they were in the bar, Davy stopped so suddenly that Joe nearly bumped into him. "Will you look at that?"

"At what?" Tory looked spectacular, but that was no reason for Davy to comment on that. Tory always looked spectacular.

"At Nancy, you idiot. Doesn't she look different?"

Joe looked across the room at her. Yes, there was something different about her, but he had no idea what it was. Maybe it was her hair, but looking at her now, he couldn't remember how she had worn her hair before.

Davy stopped her. "You look very pretty today, Nancy."

She flushed, but she didn't turn away. "T-t-t-t-tory helped me with m-m-m-makeup."

Apparently Nancy had heard about Lisa's lessons, and she had finally asked Tory if she could watch. Tory spent a couple of hours with her, and then they had gone shopping together. "T-t-tory says I shouldn't wear n-n-n-navy blue."

Nancy's sweater was a soft rust color, which looked nice with her brown hair and eyes. Joe was surprised that color and makeup could make such a difference. He had always thought that a woman was pretty or she was not. Showed you what he knew.

Nancy was still standing with them.

"H-how's Max", she asked.

Joe was impressed. Nancy had been answering people regularly for a couple of months now, but he had never before heard her try to make small talk. "He's great. As crazy as ever. The latest thing is that he's decided he'll die if he doesn't get a dog."

"Who wants a dog?"

It was Tory. She had come over, wanting to know what they were talking about. Joe had to put his hands in his pockets to keep from touching her.

"Max does."

She smiled politely and moved away.

Joe didn't have a chance to talk to her alone that afternoon, but as usual he came over on Monday evening. "Nancy looked great yesterday," he said. "It was nice of you to help her out."

She shrugged. "I probably should have done it a year ago."

"Why didn't you?"

"I don't know, I just didn't."

But Joe knew. A year ago, she didn't believe she could help someone pick out a new sweater without turning into the stage-mother monster her own mother had been. These sessions Tory was having with Lisa might well be helping Tory even more than they were helping Lisa.

"Tory, I think it's time for you to meet my son."

She sat down. "Oh, Joe..."

"You know that you should."

She didn't deny that. "But what if he doesn't like me?"

"He's going to like you."

"You don't have any way of knowing that."

"Why are you so worried about it?"

"I'm not worried."

That was a lie. She was worried about it. Why? Surely she didn't think whether or not Max liked her would change the way Joe felt about her. Or did she? Was that what was bothering her?

Before he could say anything, her phone rang. She apologized and went to pick it up. She answered, and then suddenly her expression froze. "Oh, Mother, hello."

Joe sat up, listening. Tory's mother.

"Fine, how are you...that's nice...very well, thank you . . . yes, business is good—"

This was hardly a heart-to-heart conversation.

Tory was examining her manicure. "Are you really? Portland?"

Then she listened for a long time, her face as blank as the mannequin in the window of J.C. Penney's. She looked like that only when she was upset.

"No, that wouldn't work out," she said at last. "I just don't think it would, maybe some other time... yes, Mother...yes, of course...goodbye." Tory hung up and looked down at her nails again. "I don't think I like this color. Do you?" She held out a hand.

Joe ignored it. "You didn't say much."

"To her? What's to say?"

"What was that about Portland?"

"Nothing."

Joe didn't believe her, but he didn't say anything. He just looked at her.

"Oh, all right." She sounded exasperated. "She's got to be in Portland pretty soon. She wanted to come visit."

"Here? When?"

"It doesn't matter. She's not coming."

"Is that what you were talking about when you said 'it wouldn't work out'?"

Tory nodded.

Was that the only reason she had given: "It wouldn't work out"? What kind of thing was that to say to your mother? Even if your mother were like Tory's.

Joe decided to let the subject drop. "When the phone rang, we were talking about you meeting Max," he said.

"We were?"

Joe knew that she hadn't forgotten. "Yes."

Suddenly she stood up, impatient. "For God's sake, Joe, why do you bother? I mean, what's the point?"

"The point of what?"

"The point of it all. This business with you and Max...he's in another family now. Can't you accept that?"

"Are you asking me why I bother with my son?"

"Yes. Don't you know what's going to happen? He's not going to turn out like you want him to. Nobody's kids ever do." She sounded glib, flippant. "But especially him, living with Dennis and Marianne like he does. He'll grow up to be like Dennis or Frank, and you'll be disappointed. So in ten or fifteen years, you'll find some substitute, some other kid who lives up to your expectations. Cut loose now and save yourselves both a lot of grief.''

Joe was not going to listen to this. He simply wasn't. He didn't care why she was saying it, what problems she had; he wasn't going to listen. Without saying a word, he stood up and left.

JOE ALWAYS STOPPED at the 7-Eleven for coffee on his way to work. The rest of Monday evening had been long, and the night even longer, so on Tuesday morning he bought a larger cup than usual, balancing the paper cup on his leg, prying the lid half off, sipping as he drove to the union hall.

He had been angry with Tory, angry with her for the way she treated her mother, angry with her for the way she had spoken about his son. He had spent the drive back into town indulging his anger, wallowing in it.

But when he got home, he forced himself to calm down. He knew why he was angry. Tory got angry when she cared; he got angry when he felt powerless. At Christmas, he had come to understand how people around here were basically powerless, how their cars and snowmobiles were substitutes for power. And that's why so many of them got angry easily, because they didn't have any control over what was happening to them. During the lay-offs, everyone had been very short-tempered. The whole town had felt frightened, powerless; there had been nothing to do to get the company to stop laying people off.

That was why he was angry now, why he had been angry about the child support last December. He had been powerless then, he couldn't force Marianne and Dennis to spend Max's money on Max. And now he was powerless again. Here he was in his job, learning how to change things, learning how to make things happen, but there was nothing he could do about Tory. He didn't know how to change her. Whenever she felt uneasy or threatened, she grew glib and mocking. She had done it before, she would do it again. He had always forgiven her, as he had again this time, but he didn't know how long he could go on.

He turned down Jefferson, the side street the union hall was on, and glanced up the block to the Exxon station to see if there was much of a line at the pumps. There were a couple of cars; he would get gas later. He started to swing into his usual parking spot.

In front of the union hall was a little green MGB. There was only one of those in town.

Joe parked, turned off the engine, set the brake, took a breath and got out of the Cherokee and came around the M.G., watching Tory get out.

"You're out early," he said.

"I couldn't sleep." She was looking around, almost as if she were nervous. Joe took the lid off his coffee cup and offered it to her even though she almost never drank anything with caffeine. She shook her head. It was cold for this time of year, and the steam from the cup formed a soft, wispy cloud.

"Me neither," he answered.

"I never should have said those things about Max."

The foam cup was warm. Joe set it down on the hood of Tory's car. It took him a moment to balance it there. "You don't have to apologize." That sounded stiff, cold. "Yes, I was mad at you," he admitted, "but that doesn't change the fact that I love you."

At last he was telling her he loved her, and where were they? Outside the union hall, across the street from the Daylight DoNuts and the Exxon Station. Tory's face was expressionless, that perfect television oval, her eyes, the brilliant green contact lenses, were polite and waiting. She was miserable.

"You know that I love you."

"I know that you *think* you do," she admitted.

"But that if I knew the real you, I wouldn't?"

She didn't answer. She didn't have to. Of course, that was what she thought. She probably didn't think anyone had ever loved the real her, only the dressed-up, curled, smiling, one-piece bathing suit with matching high-heels her.

Joe started to put his arm around her and then noticed that Daylight DoNuts had just released a few people, most of whom were named Brigham, and at least one of whom was also named Joe. He didn't know what he was doing, but he knew he didn't need his family for audience.

"Come on," he touched her arm. "Let's go in."

He led her down the hall that ran alongside the big meeting room to his office.

"What about some tea?" he offered, not knowing what else to say. "It wouldn't take too long."

She shook her head again and Joe helped her with her coat. She sat on one of the chairs in front of his desk, and he leaned against the desk, looking down at her. She sat like a beauty queen, legs to the side, crossed at the ankle, but when she spoke, she was herself again, forthright, direct.

"I wasn't talking about you and Max, Joe. I really wasn't. I don't know what came over me... No, I know. All that business with substitutes—that wasn't you and Max, that was Mother and me."

Tory's mother: who had put rouge on a three-year-old. Who had entered her child into the Little Miss AppleMaid Apple Juice contest. Who had driven her to the hairdresser to have her hair dyed brown.

Joe Brigham was afraid of very few things, but if Max grew up to hate him, if Max did not want to see him, if Max felt betrayed, inadequate...if Max felt all the things that Tory did, Joe did not know how he could live with himself.

"I don't know why she wants to see me," Tory was saying. "She doesn't have time for anyone who isn't perfect. All she would do is come and disapprove. And you— Good Lord, Joe, she's going to hate you."

Joe didn't care. "Tell me, has she really found a substitute for you?"

"Oh, God, yes...haven't I told you what she does for a living?"

"I didn't even know that she worked."

"She's one of Miss America's traveling chaperones."

Joe blinked. "I beg your pardon?"

"She travels with Miss America, making sure that no one spills a drink on her or kisses her. Mother watches out for the luggage, gets them places on time, all that."

Joe supposed he should have known that there would be someone like that, but your own mother...

"She and another lady alternate months," Tory continued. "So now she's got the perfect daughter...every year she gets a new one."

"What's so wrong with you? Just that you were second runner-up?"

Tory shook her head. "No, I was never quite right. It wasn't easy turning me into a beauty queen. I couldn't sing, and the sponsors like it when a queen can sing. We had to work so hard, and finally the summer before Atlantic City when we were doing nothing but getting ready for the pageant, I started thinking if I really were good enough, then this shouldn't be so hard, we shouldn't have so much to do."

"Why didn't you quit?"

"It was our whole life. We didn't have anything else, just the pageants."

"Why was she like that? Your mother, I mean."

Tory didn't answer.

"You can see how something like that might start," Joe went on. "Lots of women whose husbands die young do strange things for a while." Rich Miller's wife had had troubles for a couple of years after he had been killed in Vietnam, but she was okay now.

"I'm not so sure my father died."

Joe drew back, amazed. "What do you mean? Do you think your folks were divorced?"

"No... I'm not sure they were married. I think I'm illegitimate."

"Ille— Tory, what are you talking about?"

"Well, I don't know for sure, but—"

"What do you mean you don't know? How can you not know?"

"Easy. If your mother tells you your father died when you were a baby, it's a while before you think to ask for the death certificate and the marriage license.''

''Be serious.''

''I am. It's why I didn't win.''

Joe was having trouble keeping up with her. ''Win what?'' But then he knew. The Miss America Pageant. ''Did the judges find out?''

''No, but I found out.''

It had happened at her last practice interview. She had been waiting outside the door, and the people inside were laughing about the questions they were going to ask her, and then one said, ''I know, let's ask her if her mother is really *Mrs.* Davidson.''

It had taken Tory a minute to understand what he meant.

She did beautifully in the interview, but that night she lay awake. ''It all added up. We never had any family—none. I told you that. No cousins, aunts, grandparents. It was just the two of us, like we had been shipped in from Mars.''

And so during those hot August days, while she was shopping, practicing, getting her hair dyed, Tory grew to feel like a fraud, and she just wasn't able to provide that last bit of sparkle needed to win. '' 'Be yourself!' How was I supposed to be myself? I didn't even know what my last name was. Mother probably picked it out of a hat ... along with my eye color and my hair color.''

''Why didn't she put you up for adoption? That's what people did thirty years ago.''

''I don't know. I can't exactly ask her. I guess it's because she's proud. She was probably determined to show everyone—even if no one was watching—that she could raise a perfect child. I had to be perfect. I ruined her life.''

No, Joe thought, Tory's mother had ruined her own life . . . and Tory's too. "I can see why you don't want to see her.''

"I certainly don't . . . Nonetheless, I called her and told her she could come here.''

"You did? Why?''

"I just did, and I'm willing to meet your son this afternoon if that's what you want.''

Joe drew back. He didn't like this, this sudden change, these efforts to do exactly what she thought he wanted her to do, to be exactly what she thought he wanted her to be.

I love you. Don't you understand what that means?
No, she didn't.

"Shall we do it this afternoon?'' she was asking.

"I usually pick Max up about three.''

"Fine.'' Tory picked up her purse, getting ready to leave. "I'll see if Rich's father can come in early.''

"If he can't, don't worry about it. Max will be happy enough looking around the bar.''

Joe walked her out to her car. It was quarter to eight. There were still cars at the gas station, people in the doughnut shop. He opened her door for her, waited as she started her car, pulled away.

What could you do about a person who didn't know anything about love? She probably needed to start over, but she was almost thirty; no person could ever love an adult with the unquestioning, overwhelming devotion that babies get. No person . . .

But a dog loved you. That was the thing about dogs. You could snap at them in the morning, step on their tails, shove them off the couch, but in the afternoon they were wriggling, squirming, delighted to see you. That's what Tory needed, a dog—a dog who would never judge her, never criticize her, never expect her to be something she was not.

But Tory with a dog? Immaculate, fastidious Tory housebreaking a puppy?

Well, why not? If she couldn't cope with human love, maybe they should all slide down a notch or two.

Joe reached for the phone.

Nine

JOE PICKED UP MAX at the usual time and issued a very stern lecture. Max was getting his dog when school was out in June. And there was nothing he could say or do that would get him the dog one minute before. Nothing. Did Max understand that?

Max did.

Now Daddy wanted to take Max on a very special trip in which something very nice was going to happen to someone else, but if Max complained or whined or felt sorry for himself, he would have to go home instantly because that would show Daddy that Max wasn't old enough for special trips. Did Max understand that?

Max did.

TORY WAS IN THE STOREROOM, counting gin bottles. She finished counting the bottles and carefully entered the figure on her inventory sheet. And then glanced back at the shelf. There was no way on earth there were 347 bottles up there. What had gotten into her? She couldn't even count bottles anymore.

She gave up and went out front. Nancy was just coming on duty. She was wearing a new sweater; it was olive green and looked good on her.

"That's a great sweater," Tory said as soon as she had thanked her for coming in early. "The color is perfect for you. Did you buy it by yourself?"

Nancy nodded. "S-s-s-someone will p-p-probably spill a drink on me."

"Isn't that the truth?" Tory was impressed. Nancy almost never offered little pleasantries like that one. She was really trying to change; maybe it would soon be time to bring up the speech therapist. "But don't worry about it. Every time someone spills a drink on a waitress's new sweater, God drops everything and makes another bottle of Woolite."

Nancy laughed and went off to get her apron and tray.

Tory had stopped at the library on the way home from the union hall. It wasn't open, so she went around the corner to the drug store and looked at nail polish and over-the-counter medicines for an hour. Then it took her a long time to find the sort of book she wanted—she certainly wasn't going to ask for help; in fact, she didn't even check the book out. She just stood in the dusty stacks, flipping between the index and the text, reading the parts that explained how an almost thirty-year-old, divorced ex-baton twirler was supposed to treat her Gentleman Caller's children.

Don't buy them presents. Okay, she could do that. *Don't criticize them to their parent.* She would never dream of it. *Don't expect them to like you immediately.* Tory could acquit herself there; she didn't expect Max would ever like her. *Remember that children are natural, so just be yourself.*

What terrific advice.

Now, as she was waiting to put this advice into action, Tory stood behind the bar, watching the Budweiser clock for an hour. Shortly after three, the door opened. She looked up. It was Joe.

Oh, gee. He wasn't perfect, Tory knew that. There were many things wrong with him, starting with the fact that he didn't always hang up his towel after he showered. But still . . .

Something catapulted into the bar. Tory had a blurred impression of light hair, blue jeans, and astonishing velocity. Joe caught it, stopping it. "Tory, this is Max."

Yes, this was Max. It had to be. The boy had Joe's face, Joe's eyes, Joe's hair. And for a moment, Tory felt a stir. Joe had a son, a child, someone who was a part of him.

But she quickly corrected herself. That the boy looked like Joe was nothing to get sentimental about. The least unique thing about Joe was his appearance. This boy might look like Joe, but he also looked like his stepfather Dennis, his uncle Frank, his uncle Jim, etc., etc.

"Hello, Max," she said politely. "How are you?"

Max was much too absorbed in looking around the bar to answer. He tugged on Joe's sleeve. "Look at all those bottles. Have you ever seen so many bottles?"

"Say hello to Miss Duncan," Joe replied.

Max regarded her with interest. "Are those bottles yours?"

"Ah . . . yes, I suppose they are."

"What do you do when you're done with them?"

"My janitor takes them to a recycling center." Tory never expected that she would have to defend her ecological habits to a six-year-old.

"What does he do with them there?"

Haltingly, Tory tried to explain recycling, which was not a process she particularly understood. Finally Joe interrupted. "I think Max wants to know if all the bottles have to go there."

"Why, no, I don't—" And then Tory finally grasped the point of this conversation. "Would you like some bottles?"

"Oh, yes."

So much for not giving presents. She had known her Gentleman Caller's son for four minutes, and she was already promising him empty liquor bottles.

"But Max understands," Joe was saying, "that you have to take the labels off the bottles first."

"I do?" Then Tory realized that Marianne might not want Max starting a collection of bottles with liquor labels. "Yes, I do have to take the labels off."

"Why?" Max asked.

Tory was stumped. She had thought she could answer any question put to her, but not this one. Why did she have to take the labels off her empty liquor bottles? No one had ever asked her that in a pageant interview, "Because I just do," she finally said.

Surprisingly, Max accepted that, probably because his attention had switched to the padded bar stools. Joe noticed and reached out a hand to help him, but Max pushed him away. "I can do it myself," he announced and launching himself off from the foot rail, clambered up on the stool. "Hey, Dad, look at this. It spins around." Max gave himself a push.

Joe sidestepped quickly and avoided being thwacked by two electric blue running shoes.

Only six minutes and Tory was exhausted. But she remembered her manners and lifted up the power nozzle which dispensed the soda and soft drinks and looked at Joe inquiringly. She knew you were supposed to spell out words like *cookies*, *sex* and *joint custody* in front of children, but she imagined that every kindergartner in the United States knew exactly what "C-O-K-E" spelled. Tory hoped Joe understood her gesture because she doubted her ability to spell her way through "carbonated non-alcoholic beverage." That's why she could never have kids; she couldn't spell well enough.

Joe signaled that Max could have a little one. Tory took out a whiskey sour glass, thinking that Max might have never used a stemmed glass before, and, because she was such a thoroughly swell human being, she put two cherries, an orange slice and a swizzle stick in the Coke.

Max could hardly believe it. "This is a *great* special trip, Dad."

"It hasn't even started," Joe said mysteriously. Then he asked Tory, "Is Rich's father here?"

"Not yet." She glanced at the Budweiser clock. "He couldn't make it. But I did ask Nancy to come in early."

Nancy had drifted over to the bar and was listening to Max; Tory knew she liked children a lot. Joe turned to her now. "Nancy, do you think you could manage the bar alone for an hour or two?"

Tory straightened. What was he saying? Leave Nancy here to manage alone? Was he crazy? Tory began to speak, but with a quick gesture, Joe cut her off.

"Can you handle things?" he asked Nancy again. "Max and I need Tory for a while."

Well, they may need her, but they weren't going to get her. She wasn't leaving Nancy here by herself.

Nancy seemed to agree. "B-b-b-b-b-but I n-never have. I don't know how to m-m-m-m-mix drinks."

"You can draw beer and mix Seven-and-Sevens and bourbon and gingers."

Nancy nodded. She could.

"And if anyone wants anything else," he continued, "either tell them that they can't have it or that they have to mix it themselves."

What a great way to run a bar. Then Tory noticed Nancy looking at her, her eyes asking.

Oh, Lord, what could she say? She didn't have a choice. "Of course, you can manage; I won't be gone long, and you'll do fine. I trust you completely."

Nancy flushed and looked pleased. Terrified, but pleased.

Tory got her jacket and as soon as they were outside, started to protest. "That was a horrible position you put me in, Joe Brigham."

"You'll survive."

"And I don't know why I promised I wouldn't be gone long; I don't even know where I'm going."

Joe didn't answer, but instead called out to Max, who was already halfway across the parking lot, "Get in the back. Let Miss Duncan have the front."

Tory winced. "Ah...could we cut out this 'Miss Duncan' business, Joe?"

"Why? It's your name, isn't it?"

"No. 'Duncan' is my married name."

He apologized. "I keep forgetting that."

"Well, don't remember by starting to call me Mrs. Duncan. I'll have a ton of explaining to do. Can't he call me Tory?"

Joe shook his head. "Marianne doesn't think he should call adults outside the family by their first names." He grinned. "What about Aunt Tory?"

"Just try," she dared.

"You're from the South. We could call you Miss Tory."

"We could," she replied calmly. "We could also chop our tongues out and then we wouldn't have to call anyone anything."

They were at the car, and, laughing, Joe opened the back door for Max, the front door for Tory, then slid into the driver's seat.

"Might I know where we are going?" she asked.

"Is your seatbelt on?" Joe answered.

"No."

"You *have* to put your seatbelt on," Max announced from the back seat. "Dad won't start the car until everybody's got their seatbelt on." He appealed to Joe. "She has to put her seatbelt on, doesn't she, Dad?"

Tory wondered what Dad would do if she refused. She probably didn't want to know. She put her seatbelt on. "At the risk of being a bore, could I again ask where we are going?"

He didn't look at her. "We are going to buy you a dog."

"We're *what*? A dog? Me?" Had he lost his mind? "Oh, no, we're not."

He said nothing.

"Joe!"

He continued driving, flashing his brights and tapping the horn as he pulled out to pass another car.

"Have you run mad?" Tory glanced over her shoulder at Max, then lowered her voice. "I don't want a dog. What on earth would I do with a dog?"

"Take care of it."

"I don't know how."

"You can read. We'll buy you a book."

"I'll show you how," Max piped up. "I know."

That had to be a lie, but Tory turned and thanked him anyway. Then she glared at his father again. "This is just—"

Max interrupted. "Dad, can I tell you a secret?"

"Not while the car is moving, and don't interrupt," he told him and then spoke to Tory again. "Nancy Smith has more guts than you do. Right now she's doing something she's never done before, that she isn't sure she can do, but she's willing to give it a try."

He certainly fought dirty. "It's hardly the same."

"No, but it's similar. She's never been in charge of anything, and you've never taken care of anything."

"What are you talking about? I take care of tons of things." Like her hair, her cuticles, her skin, to say nothing of her clothes. She took great care of her clothes; her dry cleaning bill was—

"That's not what I mean," Joe said.

No, she supposed not. He meant good, old-fashioned, womanly nurturing, and Tory had to admit that that wasn't exactly her strong suit—although she had just put two cherries, an orange slice, and a swizzle stick in a Coke for this man's son. If that wasn't nurturing, she didn't know what was.

Which was probably Joe's point; she didn't know.

"How about a fish?" she proposed. Surely she could spell well enough to have a fish. "Or a turtle, something like that? I think I could manage a turtle."

He pretended not to hear. "I was thinking about a golden."

"A golden what?" A golden bracelet would be nice, or a pair of earrings.

"A golden retriever," he said.

That meant nothing to Tory. "Are they big?"

"Sort of. But you don't want a small dog."

That was certainly true. Tory didn't want a dog at all. If she had a dog, having a wet floor because Joe didn't hang up his towel would seem like the good old days. "What if I make a complete and total hash of it?"

"If it's really not working out after a couple of months, I'll take the dog or Jim will. Debbie—his wife—is crazy about dogs. But you'll do a good job."

Tory thought Joe was the crazy one. "At least I'll be good at throwing sticks," she sighed.

They had driven all the way through town and now were a mile or so north of Sullivan City on the road to Tramlet. They turned off the road up a long driveway. Max seemed to recognize the place and launched into a complicated saga about what happened when one of Aunt Debbie's dogs had had her babies. Tory tried hard, but she was entirely unable to see his point. As soon as they parked in front of the aluminum-sided rambler, Max abandoned his narrative and went ripping off around the garage.

A man came out of the garage. Joe shook his hand, then turned to introduce her. "Tory, this is Sonny Snow."

Wonder of wonders. Sonny *Snow*. This wasn't a Brigham.

Joe continued. "He's my brother's wife's uncle."

A virtual stranger. Tory put out her hand and smiled nicely.

"Joe here said that you wanted a female," Sonny told her, "so I washed up a couple of pet-quality ones."

Tory was suspicious. "What do you mean 'pet quality'? What's that?"

Sonny explained the difference between pet dogs, show dogs and field dogs. At least he probably thought he was explaining the difference. All Tory got out of his account was that pet-quality dogs were somehow second—maybe third—rate.

"And I should tell you," he continued, "that the mother is Daisy; lots of people don't want her pups."

"Oh, that is a shame." Tory turned to leave.

Joe grabbed her arm. "You've never heard of Daisy."

That was true. "Of course, I have," she said anyway. "It's a drink, you make it with grenadine and lime juice; unless you're using brandy and rum, then you use curacao."

Apparently, Daisy was the town joke. She was, by all accounts, a sweet-tempered dog who was a disaster on the hunting field. She chased a few butterflies and then fell asleep.

''We didn't mean to breed her,'' Sonny said, ''but these things happen.''

Tory supposed they did. But she liked the idea of a mother who chased butterflies and then fell asleep. She wished her own would have done more of that . . . just admitted she had a pet-quality daughter and stopped trying to turn her into a show dog.

''So,'' Sonny continued, ''I can't promise that the pups will know what to do if you take them out with a gun.''

''That's okay.'' The last time Tory had been taken out with a gun, she hadn't known what to do either, and she had a feeling that that episode had landed her where she was right now, with Joe Brigham rummaging around her psyche, hunting for nurturing instincts.

Ah, here we go, I found it, at last, Tory, here are your nurturing instincts. . . No, Joe, that's an old paint rag . . .

The pups were in the garage. Tory followed the men inside, and before her eyes were accustomed to the dark, Sonny had reached into a wire cage and pulled out a very tiny animal. He was holding it out to her, expecting her to take it.

''What if I drop it?''

Joe was trying not to laugh. ''You aren't going to drop it, Tory.''

Well, he had a point. That was one thing about being a baton twirler; you didn't drop things. So she held out her hands and received the puppy. It was little and warm, with brown eyes and a soft, short coat the color of butter. Before Tory had a chance to ask it why it wanted to help other people, Max barreled in and squealed at the sight of the puppy.

"Be careful," she said automatically. And then looked around, expecting Bert Parks to pop out of one of the cages, singing, all ready to crown her the Nurture Queen.

Max was careful, gently stroking the puppy's little spine as Tory held it. "This is *exactly* what my puppy is going to be like," he told her. "Only *mine* is going to be bigger."

"Would you like to look at the others?" Sonny asked.

"No," Joe answered for her, "They'll all look alike to her."

Sonny started to tell Joe that he was just trying to recover his costs because of the puppy's pathetic ancestry, and Joe was pulling out his wallet. Tory could not get to her purse since she was holding her little fragment from the Wild Kingdom. Then suddenly Sonny was telling her all sorts of frightening things about feeding and housebreaking.

Max wanted to carry the puppy out to the car, which was just fine with Tory. Joe said he had to be careful so they walked down the drive very slowly.

"Now, Max," Joe said when they got to the car. "She's Tory's dog, so Tory gets to hold her on the way home."

"Oh, no," she said instantly. "I don't—"

"Max is a big boy," Max's father said. "He knows how to share."

Tory doubted every word of that sentence, except possibly "boy," but Max handed the dog over to Joe obediently.

Tory got in the car, averted another crisis by fastening her seatbelt, and sat very still while Joe set the little animal in her lap.

"What if she pees on me?"

"You'll get wet."

Max bobbed up from the back seat. "What are you going to name her?"

Tory hadn't given it a bit of thought. Most of the dogs in her hometown had been named Rebel, but that did seem like a boy dog's name. "What would you name her?"

Max thought. "Wags."

"Wags?" This was exactly the tone in which her mother had once said, "Loggers?"

"Sure, because of the way she wags her tail."

"Now, Max," Joe put in, "Tory may want to think about it for a while. There are already a lot of dogs named 'Wags.' "

There were? That surprised Tory; why would anyone name anything "Wags"? It was a horrible name. And Joe was trying to catch her eye, signaling to her that she did not have to name her dog "Wags."

Who was he to complain about common names? If she was going to let him bully her into having a dog, then the least she could do was let his son bully her into giving it a terrible name. "Who cares if other dogs are named 'Wags'?" she said with determined good cheer. "If you like it, Max, then it's good enough for me."

It was an eventful trip home. Wags got carsick, but had, in Tory's opinion, the good grace to whimper beforehand. Joe promptly stopped the car and they piled out and gathered around the side of the road to watch the puppy throw up.

"I'm glad we had time to stop," Tory remarked.

"Oh, I expected that this might happen," Joe said calmly.

"You what?" Had he knowingly handed her this volcano? Max had offered to hold Wags, and while Tory had only known Max for an hour or so, she felt reasonably certain that he would not mind it in the least if a dog threw up on him. For her part, she would mind.

Back in the car, Wags nestled comfortably in her lap, and, exhausted by these traumas, was within moments falling asleep. And Tory had this really horrible feeling that she was falling in love.

Finally Joe pulled up to the curb in front of a small yellow rambler. "I always go up to the door with Max," he said softly. "Do you want to wait here or come in?"

Since going inside undoubtedly would mean a pleasant chat with Marianne, Tory thought she would pass. "Oh, we don't want to wake up the dog," she said airily and moved her purse, hoping to hide the fact that the animal was already awake.

But Max had inherited more than his looks from his father. He wasn't easy to fool. He had already unfastened his seatbelt and was leaning over her shoulder. "No, look, Wags is awake. She really is. So you can come in, and you've *got* to come in. Mom will want to meet Wags, I just *know* she will."

Tory could hardly say no to that so she relinquished Wags to Max. As she got out of the car, she saw Marianne open the front door and step outside.

"Look, Mom," Max shouted. "This is Wags. Her name is Wags. I got to name her."

Marianne straightened. "Joe!" She sounded shocked, angry. "How could you?"

Obviously she thought that the dog was Max's, that Joe had bought the dog for him even though she and Dennis had told him he had to wait.

Joe didn't answer until they were up on the concrete slab that served as a front porch. "It's Tory's," he said quietly. And then he looked at his ex-wife. "I would never get him something until you say he can have it . . . and you know it."

She colored. "I know that; I'm sorry," she apologized. She touched his arm, and he covered her hand.

Tory wasn't exactly crazy about this little scene.

Joe stepped back and gestured to Tory. "You remember Tory, don't you?"

Marianne flushed. "Yes, of course. Won't you come in?"

Joe held open the door, and Tory followed Max in. She looked around. The living room was very much what she would have expected. She smiled at Marianne. "What a comfortable room."

"Why, thank you." Marianne sounded a little breathless, but pleased.

Actually Tory had chosen the word 'comfortable' out of desperation; she couldn't bring herself to call the room attractive. But clearly she had used the right word. Marianne wanted her home to be comfortable...and it probably was. Tory and her mother had wanted the Atlanta house to look perfect. They had never cared whether or not it was comfortable.

Max put Wags down on the floor. The puppy scampered around while Max provided a noisy play-by-play commentary on her movements. Tory started to worry, dreading that Wags might disgrace herself on Marianne's carpets.

Was this what nurturing involved? Worrying about your nurturees going tinkle on other people's rugs? If so, she'd done well to avoid it all this time.

"Why did you decide to get a dog?" Marianne asked.

For the second time that day, Tory was hard-pressed for an answer. *Your ex-husband bullied me into it* seemed inappropriate. "I've never had a dog before," she said, stalling for time.

Marianne nodded as if Tory had said something reasonable, which Tory herself did not think she had. "I know. If I lived outside of town, I'd want a dog too."

Tory had never thought of that and looked down at Wags, wondering how much protection this four-pound animal could provide. "Well...I was robbed once."

Wags was sitting upright, her front paws resting on Max's wrist. He was scratching her little chest. She seemed to like it. She liked it so much, in fact, that she forgot what little she knew about muscle control and rolled over backward. Tory thought about her two robbers, Sweatshirt and Saturday Night. Wags would have fit right in.

Joe said it was time to go, and Max groaned. A look from his mother silenced him, and he asked if he could carry Wags out to the car.

"Can you do what?" Marianne asked.

"Could I please, *please*, carry her to the car?" he amended.

This was fine with everyone, and Max, who apparently was one to press his advantage, turned to Tory and pleaded, "And can I come see her tomorrow? *Please*?"

Tory blinked. "Well, sure...I mean, it's fine with me," she added quickly. "But you'd better ask your mother or your father if they have other plans."

She felt like a model citizen; the library book would have approved.

"Oh, Mom, can I? Please can I?"

"We'll see," Marianne answered. "You don't want to be a bother to Miss Duncan."

Max carried Wags out to the car. When she was safely stowed on Tory's lap, he gave Joe a hug and dashed back into the house. Joe stood on the walk, watching him until he was inside the house. When Joe got into the car, he looked a little tired.

"You don't like this part, do you?" she asked. "Leaving him off like this."

"I'm luckier than most divorced fathers. I get to see him as much as I want."

He was trying hard not to feel sorry for himself. Tory reached across the car and touched his arm. He covered her hand with his, squeezing it warmly. And then when he let go to start the car, Tory realized that that gesture was exactly the same as one he and Marianne had shared.

Well, for heaven's sake, she wasn't getting jealous, was she?

Embarrassed, Tory looked out the window. All the houses on the block were ramblers, not much different from each other, each with their little concrete slab, their little front walk. It reminded Tory of some parts of the forest, the parts that had been clear cut twenty years ago.

When an area is clear cut, everything is removed. The sagging, half-dead trees and the tiny pale green sprigs are bulldozed so that the healthy ones can be logged easily. And all the underbrush, the ferns, the holly, the dense twists of wildflowers and brush, are stripped away, leaving the land bare and ugly.

Then the company plants new trees, row after row of perfectly spaced pine trees, all the same height, all just the right distance apart. The new forest would have neatness without beauty, order without variety... just exactly like this neighborhood.

"You lived here once, didn't you?" she asked Joe. It was hard to imagine.

"Yes."

"Does it seem like a long time ago?"

"Some days." And then he put the car in reverse and changed the subject. "I think we better get back and see how Nancy's doing."

"Oh, my God, yes!" Tory had completely forgotten. She had been so agitated by Joe Brigham's efforts to thrust an animal into her life that she had not only survived meeting his son, but she had forgotten about her business. She would have to watch herself; she could hardly neglect her source of livelihood. She was a woman of responsibilities now. She had a family to feed.

There were quite a few cars outside the bar, and the place was still standing, so Nancy must have done something right.

And indeed, she had managed just fine. Some strangers had ordered Manhattans and white wine spritzers, which weren't drinks often served in logger bars, but Nancy had asked Davy to make them.

"I c-c-could have looked them up," she said, "b-b-but I was too busy."

"Well, you did great," Tory said. "I knew you would; I wasn't one bit worried."

Everyone was crowding around Wags, admiring her. Tory was, she was ashamed to admit, pleased to pieces.

Junior Rogers was shaking his head. "We've got a golden; it's hard to remember when he was that little."

"How big is he now?" Tory asked.

"Oh, about seventy pounds, I think."

"Seventy pounds!" Tory stared at him. Seventy? "You're joking!"

He shook his head.

"Wags is going to weigh seventy pounds?" What was she going to do? Seventy pounds, that was huge.

"Oh, females weigh less, she'll probably be about fifty-five or sixty."

That wasn't much better.

Wait a minute. She had asked Joe, and he'd said that goldens were "sort of" big. Since when was sixty pounds only "sort of" big?

Davy was laughing. "Did Joe forget to take you around back where Sonny keeps the adult dogs?"

"Yes, I guess Joe 'forgot' to do that." Tory glared at him. He smiled back.

"Well, if you got her from Sonny," Ed said, "he'll take her back."

Take her back? Take her back? "You might as well rip my heart out," Tory announced, hoping that someone would believe she was exaggerating.

TORY WOULD HAVE BEEN boiled in oil—or at least started using cheap mascara—before she would have admitted it to Joe, but she adored Wags. Her little chin was so soft, and she looked so cute when she was waking up, yawning and blinking, and she snuggled up to Tory so cozily. When Joe wasn't there, she slept on the bed, her little body firmly wedged against Tory's.

She "helped" Tory do her exercises every morning, barking at her heels when Tory was running in place, crawling all over her while she was doing sit-ups, catching the strap to the leg weights in her teeth and refusing to let go so that Tory could not do leg lefts without hauling Wags up too.

Tory took her down to the bar every afternoon. She had a little basket behind the bar where she slept, and when she woke up and started to cry, Tory would pass her over to one of the regulars who would take her out.

Wags made getting to know Max surprisingly painless. He would play with Wags, so absorbed in the dog that Tory and Joe were only expected to "watch this" every so often.

Of course, life with an animal was not always easy. Wags couldn't make it through the night without creeping over to Tory and whimpering that she had to use the ladies' room. So Tory would have to get out of bed, take her outside and down the stairs, and stand there in the middle of a chilly spring night, waiting for Wags to attend to herself. And Wags was afraid of the vacuum cleaner. Every time Tory wanted to clean her apartment she had to take Wags downstairs and ask Keith to babysit.

When Tory did have to leave her by herself, Wags got lonely and consoled herself by chewing Tory's things. She chewed up one sandal, two left running shoes, a week's worth of cash register tapes, one box of Kleenex, three unpaid bills, and half of a potted plant. Why this made her feel better Tory did not know.

"You need to start disciplining her," Joe said at last.

"But, Joe," Tory protested, "she's only a baby."

Finally she caught Wags starting to take a bite out of an electrical cord, and she knew it was time for some discipline. Miserably she tapped the puppy's rump and told her that she was a bad girl, a very bad girl indeed.

"She forgave you, didn't she?" Joe said when Tory confided her woes to him.

"She forgot all about it."

"Tory, she loves you, and she won't stop just because you show her what she should and shouldn't do."

"You think I'm turning into a real marshmallow, don't you?"

"No, I just think you don't see any middle ground between letting a dog do anything and forcing a little girl to twirl a baton for three hours a day. You can teach Wags how to obey without teaching her a lot of useless tricks.''

This had to be the most that Joe had ever said in his entire life, and Tory looked at him suspiciously. ''That's not why you thought I should have a pet-quality dog, is it? So that I wouldn't start taking her to beauty pageants?''

''Why, no,'' he said innocently. ''It never crossed my mind.''

Tory couldn't decide whether or not to believe him. But she didn't care if Wags's head was too small or if she wouldn't know what to do with a gun. Tory wouldn't have traded her for all the world.

_____ *Ten* _____

ON THE LAST MONDAY IN APRIL, Tory turned thirty.
It didn't bother her, not in the least. She was pleased
with her life, happy with the bar, with her dog, and
with Joe. If she were in Atlanta, still married to Ned,
turning thirty probably would have depressed her, but
then if she were in Atlanta, still married to Ned,
getting up in the morning probably would have depressed her.

An early morning delivery brought a flower arrangement. It was lovely, a splash of spring flowers—
irises, daffodils and tulips. Tory fumbled with the
little envelope, wondering if they were from Joe. But
how could they be? Joe didn't know today was her
birthday. The flowers were from Ned, but they were
still lovely.

The U.P.S. man came an hour later with a small
package from her mother. Tory opened it quickly. The
box held a pair of earrings, which she had to admit
were tasteful and stylish. She put them on. They
looked great; her mother was rarely wrong about
things like that.

But ten minutes later the phone rang, and when
Tory picked up the receiver, she immediately realized
that the earrings were about as useless as the Wedgwood ring holder. The prongs were too long, and she

couldn't answer the phone wearing them. One thing about having your own business was that you wasted a lot of time on the phone.

The call was from Joe, reminding her that he was bringing Max over in the afternoon. "We'll be here," she said.

Joe and Max came over almost every Monday afternoon, supposedly to help train Wags, and Tory looked forward to their visit. She liked Max in part because she could see so much of Joe in him. Of course, Max was much louder than Joe had probably ever been, and he talked more, but he had his father's unrelenting independence and determination. Joe fought to hide those qualities, Max wore them on his grubby little sleeve. Countless times Tory had seen his small body stiffen and his face go red as he tried to reach something too high or carry something too heavy; he would not ask for help. And he had to know everything—he was unendingly curious, asking questions until some exhausted adult would say "Just because, that's why." If he became tired or confused, he would brag, claiming that he already knew *that*, everyone else was just *stupid*.

Tory, who had absolutely no other data on the subject, thought him everything that a little boy ought to be, and he seemed to like her in return…although not nearly as much as he liked her dog.

So when she heard their knock on this Monday afternoon, she moved to the door quickly.

"Happy Birthday," Max shrieked. "Happy Birthday." Tory felt something being thrust at her. "Here. This is for you. We made it for you. You're going to *love* it."

Shocked, Tory looked down at it. Max was poking her in the stomach with an oblong package, wrapped in yellow paper that had Happy Birthday written all over it in orange letters. It was a birthday present. Joe and Max had brought her a birthday present. She looked over the boy at Joe. "How did you know?"

"I saw you filling out some form," he said calmly, putting out his foot so that Wags wouldn't get out. "Can we come in?"

"Of course." And then she noticed that he was carrying what looked for all the world like a plate covered with aluminum foil. "What is that?"

"What do you think?" he replied.

Wags certainly had an opinion on the subject. She was dancing around Joe with the sort of glee she felt only in the presence of food. Whatever was on that plate, she wanted.

"It's your cake," Max told Tory. "Your birthday cake. It's only cupcakes, because Mommy said you might not want a whole cake, but she said cupcakes were just as good and we brought candles and everything. You don't mind cupcakes, do you? They're okay, aren't they?"

"Oh, no...I mean, yes," Tory answered faintly. This wasn't just a present, it was a party. Joe and Max were throwing her a surprise birthday party. "Cupcakes are just as good...but your mother, did she make these?"

"She did *not*. I did." Max didn't want there to be any mistake about that. "I made them. She was just there, though I guess she did stir some, but only a little bit. Dad said we would buy a cake at the grocery store, but when I told Mom and Uncle Dennis about it, they said the grocery store cakes weren't any good and we could make one for you.''

Tory could hardly believe it. She supposed that her ex-husband was dating, and that was fine with her, but she could not imagine any circumstance under which she would offer to bake a birthday cake for one of his girlfriends. These Brighams...

Joe and Max deposited their burdens on her round oak table. Max took the aluminum foil off the plate and began to solemnly lick off the chocolate frosting that had stuck to the foil. Joe took some candles out of his pocket, and when Max was finished with the foil, he stuck one in each of the twelve cupcakes. Then Joe went over to the fireplace and got some matches.

Twelve cupcakes—what on earth would she do with twelve cupcakes? She almost never ate sweets.

"Can I light them, Dad?" Max asked.

"If you're careful."

Max was so careful that the first one had almost burned down by the time he finished the twelve. Tory went over and stood in front of them and obediently took a breath.

"Don't forget to make a wish," Max whispered loudly.

Tory exhaled without disturbing the candles. A wish. What should she wish for? What didn't she have? She had the bar, Wags, and a man and a boy to give her a birthday party. She could only wish to hold on to it all.

But as she leaned over to blow out the candles of the first birthday cake she'd had in more than twenty years, as she thought about all that was right with her life, she remembered, just for a moment, her mother's face.

Max started to sing, his young voice high and thin, and Joe joined in a quiet baritone. Tory listened to the familiar words, staring at the twelve chocolate cupcakes and the yellow package with the orange letters, and she realized she was blinking, that she was about to cry.

Tory Duncan . . . crying?

Yes. When they finished singing, she had to clear her throat before she could speak. "Thank you. Thank you very much. This means a lot to me." It did. She had never expected anything like this. If they had asked first, she would have said she didn't want it, but . . .

Joe reached over and covered her hand with his. "Happy Birthday, Tory."

And he sounded like he meant it, like he truly wanted her birthday to be a happy one.

Max started chattering. Tory was glad of the distraction. "Hey, Dad, can I tell Tory about when Granny turned a hundred?"

Joe straightened. "Of course," he answered, "But she was only eighty."

"No, she was a *hun*dred." He turned to Tory. "We had this big party and Grandma and Aunt Cheryl put a hundred candles on this *huge* cake, but they didn't think that Granny could blow them out so they had me and Mike and Billy stand around the cake and we were supposed to blow exactly when she did so that no one would know we were helping. We did a great job, didn't we, Dad?"

"Yes, you did," Joe agreed.

"That's a good story," Tory told Max although she was a little confused. "What's the difference between Granny and Grandma?" she asked Joe.

"Granny is my grandmother, his great-grandmother. He has three great-grandparents—Marianne's mother's mother is still alive."

Tory couldn't imagine having that much family. "Can he keep them straight?"

"He doesn't need to."

Max wasn't interested in this conversation. He shoved Tory's present over at her. "Open this now. You're really going to like it."

She was glad he was so sure. She seemed to have a history of not liking the presents people gave her. Gingerly she slit through the tape and unfolded the paper. Her present was flat and white. She had absolutely no idea what it was.

"It's a tray," Joe said quickly.

So it was. The tray was a piece of plywood, edged with ogee molding and painted white. She looked at it a moment and then realized what was going on. "Did you make this, Max?"

He looked very proud. "Well... Dad had to help. He cut the big board, but I sawed the edge pieces. I mean, he held them in the—what was it, Dad?"

"The mitre box."

"That's right. He held them in the mitre box, but I did the real sawing, and then we glued the little pieces on. I did that myself, didn't I, Dad?"

"Yes, you did."

"And then we painted it."

"It's beautiful," Tory said. "It really is."

"But you haven't turned it over yet," Max said. "You have to turn it over. That's the best part."

Tory turned it over. Written across the back with a felt tip pen in such staggering capital letters that it took her a minute to read them was "To Tory and Wags, Love, Max."

Except for his own name, Max could not read or write yet, but he could print the alphabet. Joe must have spelled out the words, waiting patiently as Max formed each letter. It would have taken them a very long time.

"Don't you like the commas?" Max pointed to one of them. "I've never made commas before. Dad told me about them. They mean you are supposed to stop and take a breath." Max repeated the tray's legend, stopping for huge gulps of air at each comma. "Aren't they great?"

"They're beautiful." And they were. The whole tray was wonderful, the nicest present Tory had ever received, and suddenly she felt her eyes burn again and she had to lean over and pick up Wags, something that was getting harder every day. "Look, Wags, see what we got."

Wags sniffed the tray for half a second and then tried to wriggle out of Tory's arms so that she could crawl across the table to the cupcakes.

Max laughed. "Wags wants a cupcake. I know she does. Can she? Can we give her one?"

"Oh, why not?" Let everyone celebrate. Tory picked up a cupcake and started to peel the paper cup off it. That was what was wrong with the parties she had planned in Atlanta; people didn't get cupcakes for the dog.

TORY USED MAX'S TRAY every single day, and she wrote him to tell him so. Of course, she had to write the note twice because the first time she had automatically written it in cursive. She had the envelope sealed and stamped when she remembered—all on her own, the library book had mentioned nothing about this— that Max's grasp of the regular alphabet was shaky enough, the cursive alphabet was entirely beyond him. If she printed her note, he would at least be able to pick out the letters.

Joe said that Max had been thrilled. He had never gotten a letter before.

Tory looked at the letter she had just received from her mother. "Well, he can have some of mine."

"YOU'RE QUIET THIS MORNING," Joe said. It was a Monday morning, several weeks later.

"No, I'm not," Tory responded.

. "Is there something the matter with Wags?"

"No—not unless you count aggravated hysteria."

"Then what is it?"

Last fall this had been her role, prodding him to tell her what was troubling him. Some days she wasn't sure that the change was any improvement. "My mother gets in today."

"Tory!" Joe almost dropped his cup. "Today? Why didn't you tell me?"

"It's too awful to even think about."

"Is she staying long?"

"Only two nights, but still . . . I don't know, everything's been going so well, and I know something's going to happen if she comes. I just know it."

"What could possibly happen? She's not going to burn down the bar, is she?"

"No, but she won't approve of it. Or you. Joe, she'll hate you."

"I don't care about that. And you shouldn't either. You can't rebel against your mother and then be miserable because she doesn't approve of what you're doing."

"You want to bet?"

He smiled. "Do you want me to drive to the airport with you?"

"I thought the field rep was coming into town."

"I can shake loose for a couple of hours."

Tory shook her head glumly. "No, I think I'll be better off facing this alone."

Joe stood up. "Well, call me if you need me."

"I'm more likely to need the rescue squad."

"Then have them call me."

He kissed her goodbye, then, as she always did on the first Monday of the month, she sat down at her desk to go over last month's books. She uncapped her pen, opened her ledger, took out her receipts. Then capped the pen, closed the ledger, put away the receipts, and started to clean. She vacuumed under every piece of furniture, she inched her bookcases away from the wall so she could dust their backs, she straightened the fringe on her carpet, she used rubbing alcohol on the chrome in the bathroom and kitchen, she hid Joe's toothbrush and razor. And then she got to the airport forty-five minutes early.

Oh, Lord, here she was, thirty, and still trying to get her mother to like her.

THE ESTRANGEMENT from her mother had come about gradually, starting, Tory supposed, the summer before the pageant, when she had first wondered if her mother had lied to her. With that came an uncertainty, a questioning, that she tried hard to stifle over the next few years. She was the busiest Miss South Carolina ever, and her mother traveled with her to almost every appearance. When Tory married and got the house, her mother helped her, as interested in the furniture catalogues and rug samples as Tory was. But during all that, there were times when Tory would lie awake at night wondering if she weren't just her mother's Barbie doll, all grown up now, living with Ken in Barbie's Dream House.

They had last seen each other two years ago. Tory had left Ned and taken a furnished apartment on a week-by-week rental. Ned called her mother, and Marjorie came, shocked at the news. She was horrified at the stained carpeting, the nylon upholstery, and she wanted to know what had happened, what had gone wrong with Barbie and Ken, how this could be better than the Dream House.

Tory had no way of telling her. Beauty queens never learn how to talk about the unpleasant, the ugly. And even if Tory was able to explain, how could her mother understand? Tory left Ned because she couldn't stand the part she was playing, the part she began learning at age three from a script her mother handed her.

Her mother's whole life had been a masquerade, Tory kept thinking during that awful weekend. Both of them were nothing. Neither of them had natural personalities, spontaneous emotions, or genuine reactions. They just had wonderful clothes and spectacular manicures. They were both Barbie dolls, and Tory blamed her mother for that.

Right after that visit Tory had gone out to the West Coast with only her leotard, two pairs of jeans and three sweaters. She hadn't seen her mother since then; she didn't want anything to do with her, but Marjorie got her address from Ned and she kept up, calling and sending Tory notes and gifts. The notes were about the places she had been to, the people she had met. The gifts were tasteful and useless. Tory wondered why her mother bothered.

TORY CHECKED THE BOARD behind the ticket agent's shoulder. The afternoon flight was indeed expected on time. She went over to the line of molded plastic chairs and sat down on a turquoise one. She sat upright, her legs crossed at the ankles, her hands folded in her lap... Just like a beauty queen.

She got up quickly. There was no gift shop, no newsstand. She looked at the vending machines. Coffee, Coffee Light, Coffee Light with Sugar, Mr. Goodbars, Snickers Bars, Reese's Peanut Butter Cups. How could people eat such things?

Someone said the plane was coming. She went over to the plate glass windows to watch. It was a twin-engine Beechcraft, able to carry about twenty passengers. The steps came folding down out of the fuselage. A groundsman, clad in overalls, waited at the bottom. The passengers began to come out, holding the stair railing, looking at their feet as they climbed down. Marjorie Davidson was the fifth or sixth. She had on a pale green spring coat—not a trench coat like everyone else wore in the spring, but a fabric coat that wasn't doing double duty as a rain coat. Tory watched as the pale coat and beige heels crossed the tarmac. Her mother's blond hair stirred lightly in the wind that was rumpling everyone else's.

She was smaller than Tory, really only an inch or so shorter, but she was slighter, with a lighter, more delicate build. Tory was stronger, more limber, more athletic.

The passengers were coming into the terminal and soon Tory's mother came through the door.

"Tory!"

"Hello, Mother."

They didn't touch or embrace.

"Did you check your luggage?" Tory asked, although obviously she had. She wasn't carrying any.

"Yes," her mother said pleasantly. She always said everything pleasantly. "I hope you don't mind the wait. I thought that in a small airport it wouldn't be so bad. You certainly have to wait a long time in the bigger ones."

This was exactly the sort of thing her mother would have said to a complete stranger, to the head of the Rotary hospitality committee who had been delegated to pick Miss America up at the airport. Tory didn't say anything.

In a moment her mother spoke again. "We had an interesting flight. It was cloudy in Portland, but cleared up just as soon as we crossed the mountains."

"It usually works that way."

The groundsman came through the door, carrying some luggage. Marjorie shook her head; it wasn't hers.

And then again it was she who spoke. "Is there a lot of logging around here? I thought it looked that way from the air."

"It's our major industry."

More luggage, again not Marjorie's.

"I like your hair. Is it easy to take care of?"

Tory answered reluctantly. "I have to blow it dry."

"Is that all? How nice."

"Actually it takes longer than I'd hoped it would."

"Perhaps with a light permanent and a very good cut, you could let it air-dry."

And where in Sullivan City was she going to get a very good cut? "Perhaps."

Mother, I've changed. I'm totally different. My values are different, my habits are different, my friends are different, everything is different. Why are we talking about my hair?

They claimed Marjorie's luggage. Tory offered to carry it, but her mother had a little collapsible cart for it. She set her suitcase on the rack, fastened it with shock cords, and followed Tory to the car.

"I made you a reservation at the motel," Tory said. "I live over the bar, and I didn't think you'd like that."

"I'm sure whatever arrangements you've made will be fine."

Tory waited for her to ask about the bar. She didn't. Not a word. Tory put her hands in the pocket of her jacket. Nothing mattered to her as much as her bar. She had started her own business and made a success of it . . . and her mother didn't even ask how it was doing.

They came to the car. Tory opened the trunk, put the luggage in. "The door's not locked," she told her mother.

"Isn't it nice how safe small towns are?" her mother responded.

It had nothing to do with that. "Anyone who wants in an M.G. can unsnap the roof."

Tory felt sick. How was she going to endure this? Through dinner this evening, then all day tomorrow, breakfast, lunch and dinner as well as the hours in between, and then breakfast again on Wednesday.

She wanted to sit here, silent, numb. Let her mother talk, let the bright, empty words swell and crash against her own sullen silence. Maybe she could say nothing, maybe she could just let it happen without being a part of it, without letting it swamp, overwhelm, poison her, maybe...

But Tory knew it was not going to happen that way. She would talk to her mother. She would talk about her hair, her nail polish, her clothes, about Elizabeth Arden's newest lip product, Vidal Sassoon's latest hair treatment. She would ask her mother about this year's Miss America, she would ask about her pale green coat—maybe it was some miracle fabric that would stand up to rain. She would talk this way this evening, all of tomorrow, and then again on Wednesday morning.

The last two years might as well have not happened. She was right back where she'd started.

JOE KEPT QUIET during the meeting. He usually did. He sat up at the front table with the executive board, gave his usual Financial Secretary's report, then lis-

tened. The various committees reported—the grievance committee, the safety committee, the publicity
committee. The president encouraged people to volunteer to work on the committees. Reports came in
from the softball team and the bowling team that the
local sponsored. The field rep, Gil Jenkins, gave his
talk, reminding everyone they were brothers and sisters to the Tramlet local. The usual people had their
usual reactions. Joe knew that some of them weren't
saying much, but once a month these people had a
place where they felt like someone was listening to
them. That had to be worth something.

After the president adjourned the meeting, Joe saw
Davy and Ed waiting by the door. Davy caught his eye,
clearly asking whether or not Joe wanted to go to
Tory's with them. Joe shook his head. He needed to
talk to Gil Jenkins.

He and Jenkins were meeting Joe's cousin, Don
Marsh, at the Sullivan Inn, the town's only decent
motel. Don was pretty excited because he'd found out
that the California consultants had broken the law a
couple of times in the last week, but to Joe, the inci-
dents sounded more like missteps than any persistent
pattern of flagrant illegality. He argued for waiting
until their case was stronger before going to the
National Labor Relations Board. "We don't want
them thinking we're just being nuisances."

Don was a little disappointed, but Gil Jenkins
agreed with Joe.

The motel's bar closed at midnight, but the night
manager was married to a sister of one of the other Joe
Brighams. He plugged in a coffee pot and told them
to stay as long as they wanted. Don left around two,

and then Joe was pretty blunt with Gil Jenkins about how the International had to take some of the blame for the Tramlet situation. The smaller locals were feeling ignored and were beginning to resent the dues that went to Portland. "They aren't sure what they're getting for the money."

"You know that four times a year the locals get copies of our audit," Jenkins answered.

"Yes, but nobody in Tramlet understands them. They just stuff them in a file. I'm sure the executive boards of the bigger locals can cope with them, but even here nobody could make heads or tails of them until last year."

"Last year being when you started looking at them."

That was true. "Yes, but you guys helped me a lot." In fact, Joe had been impressed with how willing the staff accountant had been to answer what had to be the most basic questions. The International was great at answering whatever questions were asked; its staff wasn't as good at answering the questions people were too embarrassed to ask. Joe thought they needed to be, and he said so now.

"I'll pass this along," Jenkins said. "And they'll listen to you. I can't tell you how many times a day I hear the name 'Joe Brigham.'"

"There are three of us in town. So a person's bound to hear the name three times as much."

Jenkins didn't bother to smile. "What's your family situation, Joe? You're divorced, aren't you?"

"Yes."

"What about your ex-wife? Is she pretty dependent on you?"

"She's remarried . . . why do you ask?"

"No reason." Gil Jenkins stood up. "It's late . . . no, it's early. A few more nights like this and you'll learn to keep a razor and a clean shirt in your office."

"I already do."

Joe walked out to the lobby with him. Guests were already arriving for breakfast. Joe and the field rep shook hands, said goodbye. Then Jenkins turned back with one more thing to say.

"Oh, by the way—" his voice was casual "—you know Chuck Bigelow, don't you? Of the R and E staff?"

Joe nodded. He had a fair amount of contact with the Department of Research, Education and Collective Bargaining Coordination. They did a good job. Increasingly he could see a few things they could do better, but, for the most part, he had a lot of respect for their staff.

"Well," the rep continued, "he's fixing to retire before the start of hunting season."

Joe didn't say anything for a moment. "He is?"

"He doesn't look seventy, does he? We'll probably move Wesley Clark up to his job, but I guess we need to think about finding someone to replace Wes."

"Must be a nuisance," Joe said, "having to hire people."

"It can take a lot of time . . . Well, goodnight."

"Goodnight." They shook hands. Gil went through the back door on the way to his room. Joe left by the front.

Retire . . . replace . . . Joe knew what that conversation had been about. He had known right away. Gil

Jenkins was asking, "Should we think about replacing him with you?"

Oh, yes. Oh, God, yes. The R & E staff—did he want *that*? How could he not want it?

Joe had been aiming for Jenkins's job. He knew that Gil was getting a little tired of the traveling and probably wouldn't stay on for more than two or three years. Or if that didn't work out, Joe was hoping for something with the Regional Council. But this was the International staff...the R & E department... Portland. And this fall, not in two or three years, but *this* fall...

To be living in a city, getting to know people he hadn't grown up with, people who were interested in something besides cars and sports, people like Tory.

Joe longed to tell her. He glanced at his watch. It was almost six-thirty. She wouldn't be up yet, but she wouldn't mind if he woke her, not for something like this. She was going to be thrilled for him. This was so exactly right for him...and maybe for them.

Portland...he was going to Portland.

He started toward his car. It was a cool morning. The motel was on the outskirts of town, just where the drooping black power lines and grey cement met up with the pine forest.

Portland...

He walked along the edge of the parking lot toward his car, automatically looking through the plate glass windows of the coffee shop, checking to see who was there. Mostly businessmen and one family. Three people from the company's financial staff having a breakfast meeting with someone Joe didn't recognize—he would know who it was before the day was out.

Portland...

The waitress, Mary Hammond, had just finished pouring coffee for a lady. Joe didn't know the lady either, she was older, blond, very well dressed—

Good God, he had completely forgotten. That was Tory's mother. It had to be.

Joe was not afraid of confrontations. He didn't thrive on them as some men did—he thought lots of confrontations could be avoided if people just started working earlier and stayed calmer longer—but he was not afraid of them. And if Tory's mother already hated him, he had nothing to lose.

He turned around and went back inside the coffee shop. He nodded at Mary and went straight up to Tory's mother. "Mrs. Duncan?"

She looked up, her expression very polite. "My daughter is Mrs. Duncan. I'm Marjorie Davidson."

Joe winced. He kept forgetting that Duncan was Tory's married name. "My name's Brigham, Joe Brigham. I'm a friend of Tory's."

"Are you?" she said pleasantly. "How nice."

His name meant nothing to her. Tory had not mentioned him.

Mrs. Davidson gestured to the chair across from her. "Won't you sit down? I'm expecting Tory any moment."

"Thank you." He sat down and signaled to Mary to bring him some coffee. There wasn't any doubt where Tory got her looks. Her mother was beautiful. She was wearing a white linen suit with a pale pink blouse. The notches on the blouse collar lined up perfectly with the notches on the suit collar, and her nail polish was the same color as her blouse.

Joe thought about his own mother, whom he loved and respected. She wore flowered overblouses and polyester knit slacks with elasticized waistbands. But her children would never have put her up in a motel.

"I hope you had a good flight yesterday," he said.

"Yes, thank you. It was very smooth."

Tory was thirty so her mother had to be somewhere around fifty. She didn't look it, not even close. "It was a clear day," he said.

"Yes," she agreed, "it was very pretty. Is this weather typical for this time of year?"

Joe could not recall when he had been in a more boring conversation. "We have better weather on this side of the mountains. Over in the west, it rains much more."

"Then your vegetation must be different."

"Yes, the Douglas fir doesn't grow here, we're mostly pine and . . ." Joe realized he was in the hands of a master; Marjorie Davidson could probably keep this conversation going for a couple of weeks if she had to. He was willing to bet that this was one lady who would never forget to smile. And he was also willing to bet that this was exactly the sort of non-conversation she and Tory had had over dinner last night.

If Tory had talked at all, that is.

Well, Joe was not here to talk about the weather. "Did Tory take you to her bar last night?"

"No, she says that she doesn't work on Mondays."

Right, and they barricade the door so she can't go in.

"You should try to stop by," he said instead. "It's a nice place."

"I am sure that it is."

Joe decided he was very close to not liking this woman; she was so careful, precise and proper. "Tory gets a good crowd . . . most of us are loggers."

"Yes, she told me that some time ago. Are you a logger?"

He shook his head. "I was on one of the crews for a while, but mostly I worked down at the mill." He couldn't imagine that she was interested in his progress up from carrier driver, and he certainly wasn't going to try to impress her by saying what he did now.

She must have misunderstood his tone because she spoke quickly. "That's nothing to be ashamed of."

"I'm not."

"It really isn't. It's an honest way to make a living."

Why was she making such a big deal out of this? He wasn't in the least bit ashamed of the years he had spent in the company yard. And if he ever had to go back, he would be disappointed, but not ashamed. He changed the subject. "Tory tells me that you are one of Miss America's chaperones."

"Another woman and I alternate months. I enjoy it a great deal; we see many different places and meet many interesting people."

That one was really wrenched from the heart: *We see many different places and meet many interesting people.* It sounded like a sixth-grade essay; did she talk like that all the time?

Well, maybe she'd been going to different places and meeting interesting people her whole life and so she didn't have the sense to value it, but Joe had just started in the last three years and he cared too much about those opportunities to chit-chat about them with this woman.

But you didn't have to approve of people to talk to them. "My sister is going to the Miss Oregon pageant next month."

"She is?" Mrs. Davidson looked surprised. "She's a contestant?"

"Yes, apparently she really is eager to go different places and meet interesting people."

Mrs. Davidson was quick. She caught the quiet criticism in his voice, and for a second or two, she looked directly at him, and Joe felt as if she were silently apologizing for her glibness.

But in a moment, the smile returned. "Beauty pageants are certainly one way to do that."

Then he heard Tory's voice, more drawling, more Southern than usual. "Well, Joe, I didn't expect to see you here."

He stood up, and as he was pulling out her chair, she said softly, "Giving up shaving, are we?"

He ran his hand over his chin; he had forgotten, but he hadn't been home in almost twenty-four hours. "I was in the motel bar all night."

"How nice."

Tory was speaking slowly with a slightly bitter edge to her voice. She was nervous.

"Good morning, Tory," said her mother.

"Good morning. I see that you met Joe."

"Yes, he was kind enough to introduce himself. We've been having quite a pleasant conversation."

"I can imagine."

That was sarcasm, but Joe could understand. Her mother was very hard to take.

"I hope you slept well," her mother said to her.

"I slept fine," Tory answered.

Joe didn't believe her.

Mrs. Davidson tried again. "That's an attractive polish color."

"Thanks." Tory opened her menu. "I wonder if they have cottage cheese or plain yogurt."

"It isn't the color you were wearing last night, is it?"

Tory shook her head without looking up from the menu. "No. I redid it when I decided to wear this shirt."

That wasn't like her, changing her nail polish so it would match a particular shirt. The Tory Joe knew would have put on a different shirt. That was less trouble.

She was looking at her hand now. "The color's not quite right, but I suppose it will do."

"I think there's a Charles of the Ritz shade that would be a better match," her mother said.

"We can't get that brand here." Tory flipped over the menu as if she expected to find cottage cheese or yogurt listed among the desserts. "I told you that last night." She was sitting in the sun. Even in the bright light, her complexion was nearly perfect, her skin smooth, finely grained.

"I was offering to send it to you."

Tory didn't seem to hear. "They must have cottage cheese. I'll ask the waitress." She turned, looking around the room, as if getting cottage cheese were the only thing that mattered.

Joe looked at Marjorie Davidson. She seemed perfectly composed, her face beautiful, expressionless, just like Tory's was sometimes. She lifted her coffee cup, took a tiny swallow, set the cup down, and carefully patted her lips with her napkin. It was exactly the sort of thing Tory did when she was upset.

And Joe realized that Marjorie Davidson was upset too. She knew how badly this meeting was going, and she was just as tense and sick about it as Tory was.

She had been trying. She had been trying to talk to Tory. She had been going about it all wrong with this talking about clothes and makeup. Maybe that's what Tory had been interested in once, but it was the worst way to reach her now. Like the Wedgwood ring holder . . . Marjorie Davidson knew nothing about her daughter.

But Joe was a parent too. He understood why she was here. He prayed that he and his son would never end up like this, two strangers trying to make conversation. But if they did, he knew he would be doing just what Mrs. Davidson was doing—trying, even if it seemed pointless, even if he knew he was going about it all wrong, he would go on trying. They could be standing at the edge of the world, and he would still try to get Max to talk to him.

As Tory asked Mary about the cottage cheese, Mrs. Davidson spoke to him. "Tell me about your sister."

Joe was better at this question than he'd been when Tory had first asked it in December. "Her talent is singing, and she's got nice legs and a very good back."

"What about her clothes and makeup?"

"Tory is helping her—"

Coffee flooded across the table. Tory was on her feet, untangling the strap of her purse from the back of her chair. "If the two of you are going to talk about beauty pageants, I'm leaving."

"Tory...baby..."

Her mother's voice was pleading, but Tory ignored it. She swung her purse over her shoulder and was gone.

The people at the next table had gotten their breakfast. Forks clinked against china, and napkins rustled. Through the window, Joe could see Tory, fumbling with the door to her car. She started the car and backed out without looking. Another car slammed its brakes; the tires squealed, but there was no collision. Tory shot out of sight.

Joe knew what had happened. Tory was alert, she had sensed the sudden sympathy he felt for her mother. Then he had started talking about beauty pageants. He, her lover, her friend, had gone over to the enemy camp. She felt betrayed.

Reluctantly he looked at Tory's mother. She was staring out the window although the M.G. was long gone.

"She hates me," Mrs. Davidson said flatly.

Joe shook his head. "I think she hates herself."

"I'd rather that she hated me."

"I can understand that."

She shot him a quick questioning glance, and Joe explained, "I have a son." And yes, he would rather that Max hate him than hate himself.

Joe wasn't sure if he should say anything. He wasn't one for interfering in other people's business, but this was so important. "You know," he said slowly, "Tory's changed. A lot."

"What do you mean?"

"She can't stand it when people think of her as a beauty queen."

"I wasn't doing that."

Joe didn't say anything.

She grew still. It took her a moment to speak. "All that talk about polish color...it must sound like I only care about her appearance."

"Yes."

"But it's not true. Yes, the way she looked used to matter a lot, but not now."

"Then why talk about it?"

She smiled faintly. "Do you want the truth?"

Oh, yes, he did.

"It's because I don't know what else to say to her. I am never uncomfortable with anyone, but I am awkward and miserable with my daughter. That's why I asked you to sit down, I dreaded being alone with her."

How sad it was.

Mrs. Davidson spoke again. "I take it you aren't just one of her customers."

Joe shook his head. "No, I'm not." *I love her. She doesn't believe it, but I do.*

"Tell me about her. What's her life like?"

"She's happy here. I mean, she doesn't exactly have what we think of as a normal life with friends and family, but she cares about a lot of people, and she's very proud of her business, that she's made such a success of it."

"What's her bar like?"

"Why don't you ask her yourself?"

"She doesn't want me to. I used to ask her. Every time I spoke to her, I would ask her how it was, but she just said 'fine' and changed the subject. So I don't ask anymore."

And Tory probably now resented her for not asking. "Did she tell you about Wags?"

"Wags? I don't believe so. Who's Wags?"

"It's her dog, and she's—"

"Her dog? Tory has a *dog*?"

Joe didn't imagine that Marjorie Davidson interrupted people very often. "Well, no. Wags is a dog, but Tory has a baby."

"Tory mothers her dog?" Mrs. Davidson clearly couldn't believe it.

"It's quite a sight. Ask her about Wags. That's one thing she will always talk about."

"I will...but what an odd name."

"My son named her," Joe apologized.

Mary came over to clear the table, and Joe glanced guiltily at his watch. He had to get moving. "What are your plans for the rest of the day?"

"I hardly know now. Originally Tory and I were going to spend the morning together and then I was going to go shopping while she had to work."

Shopping? In Sullivan City? That was an idea conceived in desperation. "Let me take you to the bar then. About five-thirty, when the after-work crowd is there."

"I'd like that."

"I can't make it any earlier because that's when I see my son and—" Joe broke off. "What are you doing around three?"

"Meeting your son, I hope."

Eleven

AS SOON AS HE GOT to the union hall, Joe called Tory. Her line was busy. Five minutes later he got through.

"Since when did you start pulling out of a parking place without looking?" he asked as a greeting.

"That's none of your business. But tell me, what did you think of her?"

Tory was, Joe thought, capable of being very direct.

"She certainly made a rather plastic first impression." He was capable of being very indirect. The union had encouraged that.

"Why did you tell her about Wags?" Tory asked.

That must have been her mother on the phone, calling to chat about the dog. "Well, I had to talk to her about something . . . I couldn't charge out like you did."

She made a very un-Miss America noise. "Not very good form, was it?"

Joe was not going to criticize her. "No, but understandable."

"I'm seeing her later this morning. We're going to take Wags for a walk. I'll try to be less of a maniac."

It was clear that Tory felt bad about the way she'd behaved. "What are you going to do when Wags eats one of her shoes?"

"Gloat . . . but, listen, I'm expecting the beer truck any second. Was there something else?"

Joe was tempted to say there wasn't. He would have liked to share his news at a less complicated moment, when she wasn't upset, when he was with her, but he couldn't stand the thought of walking around all day with him knowing and her not. "I do have some news. It seems like the International staff is looking at me for a job in Portland."

The line was silent for a moment. "Will you say that again?"

"Somebody on the R and E staff is retiring and there will be a vacancy in the fall. I got the impression they're considering me."

"Are you kidding? Oh, Joe, that's *great*. I don't believe it. Is it in Portland? That's just perfect for you. When would it start? What would you be doing? Tell me *everything*."

Joe wished they were together. She would come to him, laughing, sparkling, her hands sliding up his arms to his shoulders . . . "Well, there's really nothing to tell. So far only one person has mentioned that someone is retiring . . . but he said it right after asking me if I was tied to Sullivan City for the rest of my life."

"So a million things could go wrong," she said, realistic as always. "But at least you know they've noticed you. That's the first step...now tell me about it, at least until the beer truck comes. Did you know this this morning? Why didn't you tell me?"

"At breakfast?"

She laughed, seeing his point. "Okay, maybe that wasn't the best time. Now what did you say it was— the R and D staff?"

"No, R and D is what corporations have," he told her. "This is R and E—education." As he explained the R & E Department, he could picture her listening. She was probably standing by the window, waiting for her delivery, the receiver tucked under her ear, the phone itself dangling from one hand.

She was thrilled for him. She truly was. And Joe hoped she'd be thrilled for herself too... because he was going to ask her to come with him.

THAT AFTERNOON Joe picked Max up first. Max loved going to new places, and Joe didn't think he had been in the Sullivan Inn before.

Next year, son, I'll be showing you Portland.

Inside the Inn, Joe called up Mrs. Davidson's room while Max explored the intricacies of the lobby's Mediterranean furniture. He examined the legs of a side chair. "Did somebody do this with a knife, Dad?"

"I don't think so. They used a machine and packed wood particles into a mold that would make it look like carving."

"Why?"

"Because it's cheaper that way."

"Why?"

"Because it would take someone a long time to do that with a knife, and if you paid him a decent wage for his time, the chair would end up costing more than anyone could afford."

"Why?"

Joe took a breath. Max had started asking "why" at three. Marianne had said that it was a stage and that he would outgrow it. So far he hadn't.

Before they could get much further in this discussion of the economies of mass production, Mrs. Davidson came into the lobby. Joe took Max by the shoulder, pulling him away from the chair. It was probably made in Japan, anyway. "Mrs. Davidson, this—"

"Please," she interrupted, "call me Marjorie."

Joe wasn't sure he could. "Okay...Marjorie...this is my son, Max. Max, this is Mrs. Davidson."

"Who are you?" Max asked with his usual charm and tact.

"I'm Tory's mother," she answered. "Do you know Tory?"

"Sure, I know Tory. We gave her a party, and she wrote me a letter."

"Well, I'm her mother."

Max looked suspicious. He had not, despite his frequent claim to know everyone and everything, gotten hold of the fact that grown-ups have parents too.

"You know," Joe explained, "like Grandma Lou is Mommy's mother, and Grandma June is my mother, Mrs. Davidson is Tory's mother."

Max understood grandmothers . . . and approved of them. "Whose grandmother are you?"

"No one's," Marjorie confessed. "My daughter doesn't have any children."

"Why not?"

"She just doesn't," Joe said. "Now do you want to stay here for a while or go to the house?"

He had been speaking to Marjorie, but, of course, Max answered. "Oh, let's stay here. This place is *great*."

"Okay, we'll go into the coffee shop and get a Coke since you didn't have one yesterday, but you'll have to keep your voice down."

They got a table, and Mary brought tea for Marjorie, coffee for Joe, and a Coke for Max.

The Coke was a major disappointment. "Look, Dad," Max complained. "There's no stuff in it. Tory always puts stuff in Cokes."

"What sort of stuff?" Marjorie asked, interested.

"Cherries and oranges and lemons and those green things...limes...cherries and oranges and lemons and limes. And ice. Lots of ice. And a stirrer stick...what are the stirrer sticks called, Dad?"

"Swizzle sticks."

"That's right...swizzle sticks."

"That must be a very nice Coke," Marjorie said.

"It's *great*." Then Max sobered. "But Mom says I can only have one on Mondays. If we see Wags and Tory on another day too, then I can't have one. But it's okay because Tory has juice-in-a-box."

"Juice-in-a-box?" Marjorie was puzzled.

"It's just like regular juice," Max explained seriously, proud to be the source of information. "It can be apple or grape or orange or anything, but it comes in a little box and you get to stick a straw in the box. It's super, but Mom never gets it because she says it costs too much that way."

The rest of the tea party was devoted to Max's chatter. It was not until they were in the car that Joe was able to ask Marjorie about her visit with Tory and Wags.

It had been better than breakfast. They had only talked about Wags. "But I like dogs; I grew up around them," Marjorie said.

"So you didn't mind it when she ran your stockings?"

"Not in the least."

When she said that, she sounded exactly like Tory.

"Did you see her place?" he asked. "It's nice, isn't it?"

"I didn't see it. She came into town, and we went to a park."

At Joe's house, the three of them played a rousing game of Candyland. Max was competitive and, at one point, told Marjorie that she was a "stinky ape," which didn't seem to bother Marjorie any more than it would have bothered Tory. Then they put some paint on the birdhouses that Max was now making for his grandparents. Marjorie swathed her white suit in one of Joe's old shirts, which turned out to be an unnecessary precaution. She did not get a drop of paint on herself. Joe knew only one other person who could have managed that.

She came with him to take Max home, even coming up to the door. Marianne, although clearly intimidated, invited them in, and Marjorie immediately started asking her about the crocheted afghan that was folded over the arm of the couch. Had Marianne done it herself? It was lovely. Had it taken long? etc., etc. It was the sort of conversation that would have driven Tory mad, would have made her feel like a patronizing hypocrite, but Marianne liked such talk, and soon she was relaxing, enjoying meeting Marjorie.

"Well, are you ready to hit the bar?" he said when they were back in the car.

She sighed. "I suppose...but why couldn't she have opened a nice clothing shop?"

Joe could imagine what sort of shop Marjorie had in mind. "Because she'd have gone broke in six months...at least in this town she would have."

The parking lot was about three-quarters full, and Joe knew that the bar would be crowded with people coming straight out of the woods, dressed in green twill work pants, stained, even torn. There would be men in hob-nailed caulk boots, in zippered sweatshirts, worn flannel shirts, work shirts with the sleeves ripped off. That's why people came here; you could be comfortable at Tory's.

Joe pulled open the door and let Marjorie go in first. The place grew suddenly quiet, and he imagined everyone was staring, but he was only interested in watching Tory. As soon as she had seen her mother, her face had gone blank. It was as if she were waiting for the TV cameras to start rolling before she came to life.

But when they sat down at a table, Tory went down to the end of the bar, ducked under the hatch, and came over.

"Hello, Tory," her mother said.

"Hello, Mother, Joe. I didn't expect to see you here."

He didn't hear any sarcasm in her voice. "We felt like getting drunk," he volunteered.

Tory almost smiled. "I'm sure."

Marjorie ordered white wine, and Joe a beer. Tory went back to the bar and sent the drinks over with

Nancy. The waitress put down the drinks without saying anything. Joe thanked her, she smiled, turned away, then turned back. She took a breath, and obviously determined to say something, she haltingly asked Marjorie if she were Tory's mother.

"Yes, yes, I am."

"P-p-p-pleased to meet you."

"And I couldn't be happier to meet you," Marjorie replied immediately.

Nancy seemed pleased with herself. Marjorie leaned toward Joe, the sleeve of her white suit almost touching his arm, and spoke softly. "She works here?"

Joe nodded. "She's Tory's only waitress."

"And she stutters?"

"Yes, and the other bartender is hard of hearing, and the janitor is out on parole."

Marjorie raised her eyebrows without saying anything, and then she turned to watch Tory.

Tory was doing the usual, mixing drinks, drawing beer, making change, chatting with the guys at the bar, telling them about her car, making them laugh, smiling in return. Joe sensed a certain self-consciousness about her, a slight exaggeration to her gestures as if she knew she were being observed, but it was so slight he doubted that anyone else would notice. Basically she seemed to be trying to make the best of things . . . and naturally she was doing a good job.

They didn't stay long. Marjorie and her pink silk blouse were a little too much like having the teacher watching at recess. People were much quieter than normal and started to leave before they usually did.

Marjorie guessed it. "I think we should go before Tory loses any more money." She asked to be directed to the ladies' room, and Joe went up to the bar to pay the check.

Tory shook her head. "It's on the house." Then she glanced around and, leaning forward, spoke softly. "I'm sorry I had to hang up this morning. Can you come back after closing and tell me more about this job?"

"Do you know when I slept last?"

"Ditch your date," she suggested, "and go home and take a nap."

Just then her mother returned. "You certainly have a nice ladies' room, Tory."

Tory shrugged. "Thanks, but I can't take much credit for it. Keith cleans it and Nancy checks it every hour."

"Well, it's very nice."

No one said anything for a moment. Then Tory spoke. "You have the early plane, don't you? I'll be by about six."

"That would be fine," Marjorie answered. Then they all said goodnight and left.

On their way back into town, Marjorie spoke. "How long have those people worked for Tory?"

"Since she opened up...why?"

Marjorie paused. "I don't know if she ever told you, but when she was younger, Tory was in a lot of beauty pageants, and—"

"She told me about them."

"Did she tell you about the interview part of a beauty pageant? About what you always say?"

"That's where you say you want to help other people even if the question is about some civil war somewhere."

Marjorie didn't laugh. "Yes, and those were just words to Tory. 'Helping other people'—she had no idea what that meant. How could she when I didn't know? But look at her now. She really is helping people, and not just her employees. Everyone who comes in that door probably feels better when he leaves. That's more than most beauty queens ever do."

Joe could not believe it. Here she was telling him the sort of thing Tory had probably spent her whole life wanting to hear, dying to hear, and what had she told Tory? That she had a nice ladies' room.

He didn't say anything.

"What's wrong?" she asked.

He shrugged. "I don't know . . . just that maybe it makes more sense to say these things to her, not to me."

"Oh." And then about a mile later, she spoke again. "I am an ambitious, competitive woman."

Joe didn't see that there was any answer to that.

"But," she continued, "I no longer compete with my daughter. But if I still did, Joe Brigham, I'd start with you."

Joe laughed, pleased. "She said you would hate me."

"Then she insults us both."

JOE SUGGESTED they eat at the diner. "It's no worse than the motel food, and my sister Lisa might be working."

"Then, by all means, let's go there."

Lisa was thrilled to meet Tory's mother and was almost speechless when she learned what Marjorie did for a living—Tory had never told her. But, Joe noticed, Lisa recovered quickly. She talked to Marjorie with a poise that surprised him. All that tripping over rugs had done some good. She was neither shy, as she used to be around strangers, nor gushy, as she tended to be with the family sometimes. She sat down with them at her break, and the conversation rapidly became too technical for Joe.

"Pink?" Marjorie asked. "I would have thought mauve would work better on you, but I'm sure Tory knows best."

"Oh, no, you're right," Lisa exclaimed. "That's what the label says, mauve. I just forget and call it pink."

Joe didn't listen until Marjorie began asking Lisa about her college plans. Lisa grew a little hesitant. She had been accepted by the University of Oregon, even though she had applied late, but she hadn't told them whether or not she was coming. She hadn't talked about it to her parents too much since she wanted to wait and see what happened at the pageant.

"Have you looked into other scholarships?" Marjorie asked.

"Yes, but I didn't start until Tory suggested it, and by then, it was too late for most of them. You had to apply in the fall, and I missed the boat because I didn't really understand that other people would give you money to go to school. I mean, I had heard about it, but it never occurred to me that it would apply to me."

Joe frowned. He hated to hear her say that, hated the fact that his sister might miss the chance to go to college because she hadn't known how to go about it right, because she hadn't believed that it was possible.

But it was possible. You could get beyond what you were raised to be. Lisa was going to college, and he was going to Portland.

IT WASN'T LATE when Joe turned into the parking lot of the Sullivan Inn. He pulled into a space and turned off the car, starting to get out to walk Marjorie in.

But before he had his door open, she stopped him. "I wanted to thank you for taking me to the bar tonight. It told me a lot about Tory."

Joe had hoped that that would happen. At least there wouldn't be any more of those blue things—what were they called?—Wedgwood ring holders.

"And meeting Lisa," she continued. "I had no idea that Tory was helping her so much."

"Don't forget Max," Joe put in. "He loved meeting you. For the next three days, he'll be telling everybody how you didn't know what juice-in-a-box was."

She smiled. "No, I won't forget Max . . . In fact, he reminds me of myself."

"Max?" Joe was startled. "Max? He reminds you of yourself?"

She laughed lightly. "When I was a girl, yes. Oh, I was quieter...and cleaner, but one thing was the same. I always wanted everything of mine to be the biggest, the fastest and the best. I had to know everything."

Joe nodded. Max was like that.

"And I lived in a town like this one," she continued. "Actually it was much worse. Lisa may be eager to get out, but I was desperate."

Oh. So she was a small-town girl. She certainly didn't seem like one now. But maybe that was the point. "Were you from working people?"

"My father drove a forklift in a furniture factory."

And now she looked like she was married to a neurosurgeon. "So you used Tory's beauty pageants as a way out?"

"It was the only way I knew. There are many, many ways to make something of yourself, and if I had known what I know now, I wouldn't have used pageants. But no one had shown me any of the other ways, and the very tragic part is that when I was eighteen, when I was one of the mill girls, I didn't even know about pageants. I thought my only chance was to run away with a boy."

Joe didn't say anything.

"Have I shocked you?" she asked.

"No, I was thinking about my son, hoping he will know how to get out."

"Oh, but he has you to show him."

JOE WENT INTO THE LOBBY with Marjorie, saying good-night, even kissing her cheek. Then he walked back out to the Cherokee slowly, his hands in his pockets. He drove home, not tired anymore, and for a long time sat at the curb in the cooling Jeep, his arms folded across the steering wheel.

First he thought about his father. His dad didn't love his job. He didn't mind it, and as long as he had to work in the mill, he was glad he was the sawyer, but he didn't love it. But Bob Brigham had never felt restless or frustrated because he knew exactly why he was working. He worked so that his children could have a better life than he did. That's why men—and women—worked around here, so that their kids could have better lives than they did.

But that was no longer the reason why Joe was working. He was working for himself.

Then he thought about Max, remembering one family gathering perhaps two years ago when Max and one of Jim's girls had been playing with blocks. Janie had been building long straight roads, putting one block end to end with another. Max had been building towers, daring himself to add one more block until the towers fell down. He was unhappy, frustrated and Marianne told him not to build them so high, then they wouldn't always fall down.

But that wasn't what Joe wanted Max to grow up hearing. He wanted him to go on building towers just as high as he could, because one day one of them wouldn't fall down.

Tory had said it. *There's not a chance he'll turn out like you want him to... especially living with Dennis and Marianne.*

THE NEXT MORNING Tory was outside, halfway to her car, when she stopped, went back upstairs, unlocked her apartment, told Wags not to get so excited because this was only temporary, went into the bedroom, and changed her earrings, putting on the pair her mother had given her for her birthday. She guessed that this was what Joe would want her to do.

He hadn't come after closing last night. She tried not to mind. He had probably taken her mother back to the Inn and then gone home and fallen asleep. He said he'd been up all night Monday with the field rep. He must have been tired.

He was going to love living in a city. Tory's regulars were all afraid of change, of the unfamiliar, but not Joe. The new was a challenge to him. Like introducing himself to her mother—who else would have done that? A new city, a new job...it was perfect for him.

And godawful for her.

During her first year in Sullivan City, she hadn't minded not having anyone to talk to. Being busy and productive had felt so good that she didn't mind not having anyone to share it with. But now everything was different. She had gotten used to Joe, and oh, how she was going to miss him.

HER MOTHER WAS READY, waiting in the lobby of the Inn. They exchanged greetings, went out to the car, and, as Tory was opening the trunk, she heard her mother say, "Oh, you have your earrings on! Do you like them?"

"Yes, I—"

Tory stopped. She had been about to lie, to say that she loved them, to gush that they were just the prettiest things, that she had never, in all her living days, seen anything so pretty. But what would that get her? More earrings like this every birthday, every Christmas.

She didn't want to hurt her mother's feelings; she didn't want to attack her, but she did want to tell the truth. "I think they're lovely." That was true. "But I can't talk on the phone in them so I can't wear them as much as I'd like to."

Her mother winced. "Oh. I hadn't thought about that. I suppose with a business you must spend a lot of time on the phone."

"Sometimes I feel like my ear will drop off."

When they were outside town, her mother spoke again. "Joe Brigham is certainly an exceptional young man."

Tory ran a hand across the top of the steering wheel uneasily. This was too fast for her. She was just managing to talk to her mother about her earrings; she wasn't ready to talk about Joe.

Marjorie went on. "He took me to meet his son."

"You met Max?" This was okay; she could talk about Max. "What did you think? Isn't he great?" Then it occurred to her that Max might not be to her mother's taste. "I guess he is a little loud sometimes."

"He's very loud, but he seems to be a wonderful child."

"You liked him?"

"A great deal. It's not often anyone calls me 'a stinky ape.'"

"He called you that? What did you do to deserve it?"

"I landed on green and got to pass over the Rainbow Trail and miss the Pepperstick Forest and Gumdrop Mountain. We were playing Candyland."

"He's not the world's greatest loser, is he?"

"Give him time. He'll learn a lot from his father...and maybe from you."

"From me? What could he learn from me?" How to twirl a baton?

"I don't know specifically. But he seems very attached to you. He told me all about the wonderful Cokes you concoct and how you buy very expensive juice."

"That's not why I buy it." Tory was instantly defensive. "It only makes sense since I don't drink processed juice and the boxes are one serving and they keep—"

"Tory, I wasn't criticizing you."

Tory shut up. No, her mother hadn't been criticizing her.

"Is something bothering you?" Her mother's voice was gentle.

Tory wanted to lie. But what would be the point? Anyone who had twitching fits over juice-in-a-box was clearly not intact. "Oh, Mother, I don't know..." This was something she hadn't even talked to Joe about. "Max's stepfather's business failed last fall so things are still really tight for them, and there are so many things that Max doesn't have. He doesn't have a soccer ball, his baseball bat is one they sawed down. He'll talk about television characters or sports stars, but he doesn't have any of the products—the lunch boxes or the action figures. I mean, I know kids don't need Trailblazers T-shirts, but still..."

"You'd like to buy them for him."

"But I don't think it's good to have him thinking of me as a fairy godmother. He's demanding enough already. On one hand, I can't imagine that it would hurt if I bought him one T-shirt, but I have no idea where to draw the line."

"You should talk to his mother. Let her decide what's appropriate."

"Talk to his mother?" Tory had not seen or spoken to Marianne since the day they bought Wags.

"Yes, I met her. I found her very pleasant, very easy to talk to."

Tory grimaced.

Her mother smiled. "Of course, your situation isn't the same. It's bound to be a little awkward. But if Max is important to you, you should at least be on speaking terms with his mother. I'm sorry I didn't know this. The three of us could have had coffee together yesterday."

Coffee with her mother and Marianne? What an extraordinary notion. "I don't drink coffee," was all Tory could manage to say.

TORY DROVE HOME SLOWLY, thinking about what her mother had said. She was probably right. Tory should talk to Marianne about Max, find out what presents she could give him, find out if she were unknowingly doing something that Marianne didn't like. That way they could—

What on earth was she thinking about? It was all irrelevant. Joe was going to Portland.

She turned into her parking lot. Joe's car was there; he was leaning against it. He straightened as she pulled up, then came over, opening her door for her. He looked tired, and she reached up and brushed his hair off his forehead. He pulled her to him, holding her tight. She rubbed her cheek against his chest.

How she was going to miss him.

She stepped back. "You look like you could use some coffee."

"Yes."

They went upstairs and did their best to cope with Wags's delight at seeing them. Tory went into the kitchen—her incredibly clean kitchen that she had never invited her mother to see—and started coffee for him and herbal tea for herself. As she was waiting for the water to drip through the grounds, she looked across the counter at Joe. He was down on one knee, scratching Wags. Wags was in ecstasy, but Joe didn't look like he was paying attention. He said exactly one word since she had driven up. Even for Joe, that was quiet.

Tory carried the mugs into the living room. Joe stood up, taking his from her.

"Tell me more about Portland," she said.

Joe paused. "Let's sit down."

"Why? What's wrong?"

"Let's sit down," he repeated.

They sat opposite each other. Joe tasted his coffee. Tory waited. He would talk when he was ready.

"I don't think there's going to be anything in Portland, at least not yet."

"Oh, Joe..." Tory ached for him. "What happened? Did you hear something else? Aren't they interested in you anymore?"

"No, this is my decision. If they offer me the job, I won't take it."

Tory had been about to take a sip of tea. She held the cup against her lip for a moment and then set it down with a sharp little thud. "Won't take it? What are you talking about?"

"I'm going to tell Gil Jenkins that I can't leave Sullivan City. At least not yet."

"What do you mean you can't leave Sullivan City? How can you not leave?"

"Easy. I just don't go."

His voice was flat. What had come over him? "Why are you talking like this? This has got to be exactly right for you."

"Oh, it's right for me."

"Who else is involved but you? Who else matters?"

"My son."

Oh. Yes. Max did change things, but still... "I know you'll miss him. Of course you will. Change is hard, it always is, but—"

He interrupted. "That's not it. This has nothing to do with whether or not I'll miss him."

Tory had no idea what he was talking about. "Then you'll have to explain it to me."

"You don't understand?"

"No, not in the least." Tory could hear herself; she was starting to sound crisp.

Joe stood up. He went over to the fireplace and ran a hand across the mantel. The firebox was clean. Tory had swept out the ashes, mopped the dust. They hadn't had a fire in weeks.

He didn't turn when he spoke. "The last couple of years—ever since the divorce—I've never felt that Max needed me. Dennis was doing everything I would have done. Max isn't going to grow up careless around tools or guns or cars. Dennis does things right and he will make sure Max learns right, just the same as I would have. I see Max so much because I want to, because I need to, not because I thought he needed me. But then I met you."

"Me? What do I have to do with this?"

Joe was facing her now. "Everything. Tory, I've learned so much from you, and I want Max to grow up knowing the things I'm having to learn now. I want him to know how to plan, how to take risks. You know what he's going to hear from Dennis. Play it safe, don't stick your neck out . . . that's what he's going to hear. You were the one who said it—growing up in that house he will turn out just like Dennis and Frank.''

Tory was stunned. ''I didn't say that. When did I say that?'' Then she remembered, it had been after her mother called, wanting to visit. ''Joe, I was mad at my mother. I'll say anything when I'm mad at my mother.''

''Perhaps, but that doesn't mean you weren't right.''

''You can't listen to me.'' Tory was frantic. ''Not on something like this. How can you listen to me? What do I know about families?''

''You were the one who said how sad it was that Dennis's father told him to be more than a Brigham, but never showed him how to do it. I need to be here to show Max how.''

''But, Joe, children learn by example. Dennis didn't learn how to plan, how to take risks, because his father never planned or took chances. He just stayed in the same old job. And what about me? Why do you think I didn't know how to be anything but a beauty queen? You met my mother. That's all she knows how to be. So what's Max going to learn from you if you rot away the rest of your life in Sullivan City—if he doesn't see you taking chances?''

''It won't be the rest of my life. As soon as he's old enough to travel on his own—''

"He's six. Six-year-olds travel on planes by themselves. I've seen them."

"Marianne would never let him...and I wouldn't either. Once he's nine or ten, then I'll go. I need more time with him. If I go now, I'll be like Rich."

"Rich? You mean, Pete Miller's son?" Tory stared at him. "But he's *dead*, Joe. He's been dead for fifteen years."

"And he's this vague ideal to his kids, something the boys are supposed to be like, except, of course, neither of them have any idea how to be a military hero. That's why they get in trouble. I want to be Max's father, not a cross between the Superbowl quarterback and Santa Claus. In another couple of years, I'll be willing to trust things to weekends and summer vacations, but not just yet."

Tory could hardly believe she was hearing this, that he was saying this. Everything he had worked toward this year, all his plans, his dreams, his ambitions, he was turning away from. "Joe, don't you see?" She was urgent, intense. "You're making my mother's mistake all over again. You're sacrificing everything for your child; you'll be living entirely through him. It will be the ruin of both of you."

"I'm not sacrificing everything for him. I'm just putting a few things on hold for a while, that's all. I know that in the last year I've changed, and my job—"

"It's not a job; it's a career."

"All right." He acknowledged her point. "Maybe I do have a career now, maybe I am working more for satisfaction than for anything else, but even so I'm still working class enough that my own satisfaction doesn't matter as much to me as my son's."

"Do we need to make this into a class struggle?"

"Class is a part of it. It's how I grew up."

"And now it's what's trapping you."

TORY COULD NOT SLEEP that night and could remember almost nothing of the day that followed. She must have opened up, she must have tended the bar, talked to customers, made change, but all she could remember was thinking how Joe was making her mother's mistake.

He didn't come to the bar that evening, nor did he come in Thursday. He came Friday, but before he had crossed the room, two people stopped him, drawing him to a table, and later he left with them. So he and Tory didn't speak until he came in when she was opening on Sunday. The bar was empty; he must have known it would be.

"Hi," she said. He looked tired.

"Hello."

"Would you like some coffee? It's fresh." *Is this all you have to say to him?*

"That would be nice."

Tory went over to the coffee-maker and slid the glass pot out. She had thought that the water had finished dripping, but as she poured Joe's coffee, a few more drops fell through, landing on the hot burner. They sizzled, then burnt dry, leaving a bitter smell and little brown rings on the burner.

As she put the pot back, she heard him speak. "I was going to ask you to come to Portland with me."

Tory set his coffee down in front of him, black, the way he took it. "That's hardly relevant now."

"I guess not."

For the first time since she'd known him, Tory wished someone would interrupt them. She looked down, away from Joe. On the ledge below the bar was a dish of cut limes, covered with plastic wrap. There was a little wrinkle in the plastic. Tory picked up the bowl and lifted one corner of the wrap, pulling it tighter.

"Tory, I want us to get married."

The bowl clattered, limes spilled across the ledge. "Married?" She stared at him. "Joe, what are you talking about?"

"I've been thinking about what I want and then about how much of that I can have."

There were lime wedges everywhere—on the ledge, on the floor. "I never wanted to get married again."

"I'm asking you to change your mind."

Tory started to pick up the limes, then stopped. "Could we talk about this tonight? Upstairs?"

"Why? There's no one here."

That was true, but she didn't want to talk about marriage down here. She probably didn't want to talk about it at all.

Marriage. She didn't want to be married again. Marriage changed you, turned you into something you were not. Joe was already trying to turn himself into something he wasn't anymore; now he wanted to add marriage to that. What did he have in mind? That they move into one of those little boxes down the street from his parents and go over for supper every Sunday night? So everyone would know exactly when they left for work, when they came home, how often they went to the grocery store, how many things they took out to be dry cleaned.

"Why can't we go on as we have been?" she asked.

"It's not enough, not anymore."

"What's not enough about it?"

"We never go out in public; we've never been to a movie or out to dinner."

"I work nights."

"That's not the reason. I love you, but we aren't a part of each other's lives. When I needed help picking out ties, I asked Lisa even though you would have been much better at it. When you needed to have that kitchen outlet fixed, you paid Keith to do it; it would have taken me ten minutes. You've never even seen where I live. Don't you think that's a little strange?"

"I've been to Marianne's."

"Once."

"I was going…" *to go again. I was going to talk to her about Max. Really I was.*

Tory stopped. Why was she being defensive? Joe wasn't attacking her. She took a breath, letting the air out slowly, steadily. It was—God help her—what she had done when a pageant wasn't going right.

And the trick still worked. "Maybe the texture of our relationship is a little unusual, but it's been right for us." She had loved it—the privacy of things, the separateness. "That's what counts, it being right for us."

"At first it was right," he admitted. "We were so different, our experiences, our backgrounds—"

"Will you stop talking about that?"

He ignored her. "We didn't know how to fit our relationship into our normal lives. But that was last winter, I'm ready for more now."

And more was marriage, a home, children. "As long as I have the bar, I'll always have this crazy schedule." She said that even though she knew that her schedule had almost nothing to do with it.

"I'm not asking you to give up the bar. I can deal with your hours so long as we're living together in our own home, planning a future together. Sleeping together half the night two or three times a week isn't enough anymore."

"Is this some kind of ultimatum, Joe?"

"No. It's a proposal. I love you and I want us to be married."

"I don't know what to say."

"It sounds like you do."

TORY WOULD HAVE GIVEN ANYTHING if she'd been able to do what she had done once before—show up at the union hall before seven on Monday morning, to apologize, to tell Joe she was sorry, wrong, that she was willing to do anything to make it all right again.

But how could she? She was sorry, very sorry, but she wasn't wrong. She couldn't get married. She just couldn't.

She thought of suggesting a compromise, a counteroffer. The union had taught him how to negotiate. She would suggest that they live together. Not get married, not plan a future, not be Brighams, just live together.

But she knew that was pointless and insulting. Joe hadn't been negotiating; he hadn't been playing a game. He had said that he loved her, that he wanted to marry her. He wouldn't settle for anything less. There was only one thing he wanted to hear if she were outside the union hall in the morning—that she was ready to be a member of a family—to be a wife, a daughter-in-law, a stepmother... a mother.

So Tory didn't go to the union hall.

IT WAS OVER. They tried for a little longer, but there wasn't much reason to. All they were doing was trying. Joe felt that he couldn't talk to her about his job anymore; she didn't think he should still be in it. They were uncomfortable talking about Max. And in bed, it was like Christmas Eve again with Tory putting on a performance, doing her best to please the judge, and Joe couldn't get her to change.

He supposed he understood why she didn't want to settle down to a more normal life. All she knew of the life he was talking about was a marriage to an insecure, competitive man and her mother's engulfing, driven love. She believed this half-secret affair was all she was capable of.

Finally they had to admit that it wasn't working anymore.

Joe quit going to the bar. He couldn't bear it, to see her, to listen to her. People would have to understand that if they wanted to talk to him, they must call him at the union hall. It took them a week or two, but they figured it out. The months he had spent coming to the bar had taught them that the union did want to hear from them.

And they knew why they had to call him, why he had quit coming to the bar. No one knew what to say, so for the most part, they said nothing, which was absolutely fine with Joe. When he took Max home one day, Marianne dropped her eyes, fiddled with the doorknob, and asked Joe if he was all right. He didn't pretend that he didn't know what she was talking about and said that he was okay. When Frank said, "Must have been something while it lasted, huh?" Joe did pretend that he didn't know what Frank was talking about.

Jim said that Tory had brought her car in—she was having problems with the electrical system and was considering selling it. "I don't know why she's put up with it for so long."

"Beats me," Joe answered.

Lisa reported that she and Tory had finished selecting the pageant wardrobe. "Wait until you see the dress I'm going to sing in. It's gorgeous—all sequins, raspberry sequins. I tried it on in January, but it didn't fit, it was too tight across the seat. But now it fits great, and I haven't really lost any weight. It must be all those exercises she's made me do."

"That's nice," Joe answered.

It was so different from the time after he had split up with Marianne. He had lost so much then—his home, his wife, his son. He had never tried to sort out how much he missed Marianne from how much he missed Max and the house. It had been all one blank, incomprehensible absence.

But this time it was just Tory. He didn't miss her cooking, she had never done his laundry, his grocery shopping, his errands. It was she herself he missed—her company, her companionship.

And her body. He hated to admit it, but he missed that. It had been difficult, after Marianne had asked him to leave, to get used to that part of not being married, and now he was having to get used to it all over again.

ONE MORNING in early June Joe was walking down Main Street on his way back to the union hall when he noticed Marianne's Capri parked in front of the drugstore. He went in.

She was alone at the prescription counter. He said her name.

She turned, surprised. "Why, Joe...hello."

It was the first warm day of the year, and she had on a sleeveless dress, yellow with little white flowers; it was pretty against her brown hair. "That's a nice dress. Is it new?"

She flushed. "Yes, yes, it is. Do you like it?" She smoothed the skirt with her hand. "I just got it, it was on sale after Memorial Day, but now, of course..."

She stopped. Was she regretting buying herself the dress? Joe hoped not. It was time she was getting new things for herself. He waited until the pharmacist gave her her change and moved away. "Is something wrong?" he asked.

"Oh, no, not at all... In fact, I was going to tell you when you came to get Max this afternoon...since we thought you should know before he did..."

"Know what?"

She glanced around. "Do you mind coming outside?"

Of course, he didn't. They didn't say anything until they were at the door of her car. Then she turned to him, seeming a little hesitant. He waited.

At last she spoke. "I'm...we're going to have a baby."

A baby.

The Capri was clean. The sun glittered across the hood, and the windshield reflected the power lines overhead. Dennis must have just washed it.

Marianne was pregnant.

She was laughing, smiling, blushing, looking happy...and so far away.

Joe tried hard. "That's really wonderful news. You must be beside yourself."

"Oh, we are. Dennis is just thrilled."

Joe supposed he was glad for Dennis. "What about Max? How did he take it?"

She winced. "As I said, we haven't told him yet. It's going to be a big adjustment for him."

That was for sure. Max was hardly perfect brother material. "It will probably be the best thing that's ever happened to him. Being a brother is hard," Joe said, thinking of his own brothers. "It's time he learned how."

"Still, he's lucky he has you," she replied, "that you like being with him so much. I think that will be important to him when the baby comes—to know he's still first with someone."

Yes. But if Joe had taken the Portland job, he would have been gone before the baby came. That would have made it doubly hard on Max. He looked down at Marianne. She was so happy. "I bet you want a little girl."

"We don't care," she lied, "as long as it's healthy."

Joe opened the car door for her and waited at the curb as she backed out. He began to walk back to his office. He was past the movie theater, almost at the grocery store when he noticed he hadn't turned down Jefferson, the side street the union hall was on. He turned around and started back.

He remembered when Marianne had found out she was pregnant with Max. He too had been beside himself. He must have been...what?...twenty-three. That seemed so young.

It was funny about Marianne—sweet, reliable Marianne. She hadn't changed. She had matured, gone from being a girl to a mother, without really changing, not the way he had, or the way Tory had.

There was nothing wrong with that. Change wasn't the be-all and end-all of everything, but two people who had both changed...well, you understood each other, and Joe knew no one who had changed as much as he had, no one except Tory...and her mother.

He turned down Jefferson, walking quietly, looking down the street. In front of the pumps at the Exxon station was a blue van. He thought it belonged to the Kossers, but he wasn't sure. In a minute the van pulled away. On the other side of the pump was a green M.G.

A boy—somebody from the high school voc-tech program, Joe guessed—was at the car window, waiting while the driver signed the charge slip. When the boy moved away, Joe saw the gleam of Tory's hair.

She started the car, but instead of leaving the lot, she pulled over to the air pump. She was untangling the hose when Joe got there.

"Here, let me do that for you."

She stepped back, slipping her hands in the back pockets of her jeans.

"What do they take?" he asked.

"Twenty-six."

"Front and back?"

"Yes."

Joe set the gauge on the air pump and knelt down at one of the front tires. "Jim says you're thinking of selling this."

"I was, but he's got it running so well that I'll keep it at least through the summer. He put in a whole new American electrical system."

He stood up, jerking on the hose, moving to the back tire. "Next thing you know, you'll be buying a whole new American car."

"Maybe."

That would be a change for her. The air shot into the tire with a sharp hiss. Too bad more couldn't change. "I just saw Marianne," he said.

"How is she?"

"Pregnant."

Joe stood up, flipping the hose over the top of the little car. It caught on the windshield. Tory reached over and freed it. "I imagine they're thrilled," she said.

"Yes, they are."

"How did Max take it?"

Joe appreciated her asking that. "They haven't told him yet."

"But she's told you?"

"Like it or not, I'm a part of that family, and I'm grateful that they know it." Joe stood up. He was finished with the tires. He started to coil up the hose. He didn't look at Tory.

"A little ambivalent about this baby, Joe?"

How did she know? "Well, yes. I mean, I wouldn't trade places with Dennis for the world, but . . ."

"But you like kids."

"Yes."

With everyone else, he was going to have to pretend, he was going to have to be pleased. And if Dennis tried to rub it in a little, Joe was going to have to bear that with good grace too. He could do it, there wouldn't be any problem, it was no big deal . . . but still it was nice that Tory was here, someone with whom he didn't have to pretend, someone to whom he could say, "I know I've got no right, but yes, I feel a little strange."

Tory was still standing by the pump, not making any move to get back into her car. He tried to think of something else to say. "I guess Lisa's off to Seaside next month."

Tory nodded. "She wanted me to go as her chaperone."

"Oh?"

"I would have, Joe, I really would have. But I own a bar. Pageants are so strict about liquor that it might have hurt her chances."

"Oh."

Neither of them said anything for a moment. Then Tory spoke. "I got her graduation announcement."

"Lisa's?" That was stupid, who else was graduating?

"I'm thinking about coming."

"She'd like that." And Joe almost offered to come get her, but stopped himself. Her car worked now. She could drive herself.

He wished he could think of something else to say. There was much he wanted to say—how hard being apart was, how much he missed her, how he wished that everything could be different—but what was the point?

She spoke. "I'd thought about going away for a week or so."

"Why didn't you? It might have done you good." As far as he knew, she hadn't taken a vacation since she'd opened the bar.

She shrugged. "I don't know. I guess I couldn't think of anywhere I wanted to go. And I wasn't sure what to do about the bar."

"Have you ever thought about hiring an assistant manager? It would give you more time for yourself."

"Have you been talking to my accountant? That's what he says."

"If you ever get serious about it, will you let me know?"

"Why? Do you have a fourth cousin who needs work?"

"He's a first cousin, and he doesn't need work. He's at the mill, but I think he would be good at it and would probably like it a lot better than the mill."

She smiled, her wry, crooked smile, the one Joe liked. "I should hope." And now there was a teasing light dancing behind her emerald contacts. "But listen, I don't want him if he's going to unionize my shop."

Now she was laughing and the sun was bright in her hair. This was how it had once been, so warm, so easy. Joe stepped forward, but before he could touch her, he heard someone call his name. He glanced across the street. It was Bud Plummer, the president of the Tramlet local. Joe smiled apologetically at Tory, she smiled in return, and he went back to work.

THE SITUATION in Tramlet was looking better by the day. The union busters continued to violate various regulations. They hadn't done anything wildly wrong; Don Marsh's list was all very nickel-and-dime sort of stuff, and there probably wasn't anything on it that would merit a cease-and-desist order. But it was a long list, and the International hinted about it to management, prompting the company to wonder if it weren't spending a great deal of money to get itself into a great deal of trouble.

Life went on. Joe started to look for another place to live—he couldn't stand that empty little box anymore—but he wasn't having any luck. Nothing seemed right. There was a piece of property for sale outside town, just beyond the bar. It would be nice to be living out of city limits, people wouldn't know quite so much of his business. But it seemed silly to build a place just for himself.

Tory did come to Lisa's graduation. She didn't sit with the family, but Joe and Jim went over and talked to her afterward, mostly about her car. She gave Lisa a hardback dictionary, which seemed like an odd present to Joe until Lisa whispered that the dictionary made her feel, for the first time, like someone who might go to college.

A week later, Joe went to Tramlet, to talk to some of the members who were working on various committees. One was a woman, divorced, three kids, no child support. She had a sad but sensible air that Joe found vaguely appealing. He asked her to dinner.

They had a nice time. She was happy someone wanted to take her to dinner, wanted to open car doors for her. They talked about their kids, and she was relieved that he didn't expect her to go to bed with him.

He asked her again, but the second evening wasn't the same. By then someone had told her about Tory—not about how warm and funny and generous Tory was, not about how forthright and realistic she was—no, this report had only been of Tory's beauty, and the other woman grew nervous. She couldn't imagine that a man who had known and loved a beautiful woman would want her. She was tense, defensive. Assuming that Joe would reject her, she pushed him away. It was sad, but Joe didn't know what he could do.

He was lonely. He would meet up with the guys who had been his friends since they were all boys—Davy, Ed, and the others—but he wouldn't have anything to say. They had nothing in common anymore. He would be with his family, and he would feel as he had at Christmas, the outsider sitting on the stairs.

But he went on in his usual quiet way, working hard, seeing Max as much as he could, helping Cheryl's husband reroof their house, letting Frank borrow the Cherokee. Everyone thought he was doing just fine.

What they didn't know was how often he had to remind himself to smile.

_____ *Thirteen* _____

ON THE LAST FRIDAY IN JUNE, when the union busters turned in their Hertz cars for the weekend, they
told the girl at the counter that they wouldn't be back
on Monday. By Saturday, the news was all over the
county.

"What does it mean?" Tory asked her regulars. She
knew a lot less about the situation in Tramlet than she
once had.

"Joe says that the company canned them," someone answered.

So he had done it. Joe had done it.

"Yeah," someone else was saying, "and Joe's not
one for talking crazy."

No, Joe wasn't one for talking crazy.

The voices went on. "I bet he did most of it. He's
really good at this sort of stuff."

"We're damned lucky to have him."

This had been going on ever since Joe had quit
coming to the bar, this praising him. At first Tory had
been puzzled; her regulars rarely praised one another.
Then she had understood. They knew something had
gone wrong, and they minded. She was touched; she
didn't realize they cared so much.

The baseball game that Saturday afternoon was a
good one, a pitching duel. People were clustered along
the bar, standing behind those who were sitting,

watching the TV. The bar itself was crowded with mugs, bottles. Tory could not see the door.

And when someone called out, "Get my man a beer here," she automatically slid a mug under the tap without knowing who it was for. Then looking over the tap handles, she saw him . . . Joe.

The mug seemed to take a long time to fill.

She took it over to him. "Hello, Joe."

He reached through the people seated on the stools. "Hello, Tory."

It was too crowded to say anything more. Tory went down to the other end of the bar. Two batters from the East Coast team drew walks, then there was a homer. Everyone grunted and booed. It wasn't such a good game anymore. A couple of customers left the bar, going to the tables. A stool opened up near the hatch. Joe came over and sat down.

Tommy Halsey got up right away, leaving the seat next to Joe empty. Ed Bauer, who had been next to Tommy, turned to ask Hank Kenny something.

They were giving Tory and Joe a chance to talk.

"I heard about the IPA people leaving Tramlet," she said. "That's great."

"It is good news," he said mildly.

It is good news. Six weeks ago he would have told her everything.

She spoke suddenly. "I hear you've been seeing someone."

He almost smiled. "How many people told you that?"

"Only three."

"Then you heard it once more than it happened."

He sounded like he always did, quiet and firm. She believed him.

"By the way," he continued, "there's something I need to tell you. That's why I came today."

"Oh?"

"Max got his dog today, and—"

"He did? That's great! Is he thrilled? What kind is it?"

"That," Joe said, "is not quite clear. But it's black, and he is thrilled to pieces."

"I can imagine," Tory laughed. She would have liked to have been there. "What did he name it? And what is it—a boy or a girl?"

"It's female."

Tory made a face at him. "Listen, buster, if I want to call my dog a little girl, I can call my dog a little girl . . . so what did Max name this female?"

"Tory."

"Yes?"

"No, that's her name. He named her 'Tory.'"

"You're kidding!" She could not believe it. "He named his dog after *me*?"

"That's right."

"And you let him?"

"I wasn't there, and I think Dennis and Marianne were too stunned to know what to do. Marianne finally said he would have to ask you. So I'm the advance party, sent to warn you."

"What do you want me to do? Do you want me to tell him that he can't?"

"It's entirely up to you. If you want to have a dog running around with your name, I don't see that it's anyone's business but yours and Max's."

Tory liked the idea that she and Max had some business that was just theirs. She liked Max, she missed seeing him. "Are we talking about a pet-quality dog here?"

"Just barely."

"It's not a poodle or anything like that?"

"She might have some poodle in her, but there's no telling. She's a mutt."

That sounded good to her, a mutt named Tory. Now Sullivan City would have two Torys of uncertain parentage.

Later on that evening, during the supper lull, Joe called and put Max on. The boy was subdued, obviously feeling a little shy about using the phone. His voice sounded light and very young. "Mom says I have to ask you if it's okay if I name Tory Tory."

Tory was glad this call had been preceded by an advance translation. "I'd be delighted."

"Mom said I had to ask."

"You can tell her that it's okay." Tory waited a moment, but Max said nothing. She could hear him breathe. "Is she a nice puppy?"

"She's *great*." He now sounded a little more like himself. "But Mom says I have to keep her in the kitchen and put newspapers down otherwise she'll pee on everything."

"I had to do that with Wags."

"Do you want to see her?"

"Well, yes." What else was she supposed to say? "Yes, of course."

"Can you come tomorrow?"

"Oh, Max, I don't know...." And suddenly, now that she was talking to Max, Tory thought about how much she liked him and how much she missed spending time with him. Did ex-girlfriends of non-custodial fathers ever get visitation rights? "Are you home? If you'll put your mother on, I'll ask her about it."

Max dropped the phone without saying anything, and in a moment Marianne was on the line. She had heard Max's invitation and said that of course, it would be all right if Tory stopped by and saw her namesake.

"I'd like to come by in the early afternoon." This was going to be awkward enough without running into Joe too. "What time does Max get out of school?"

Marianne paused. "It's summer. He's not in school."

Tory felt like an idiot.

ON MONDAY MORNING, Tory drove into town, feeling stranger by the instant. On the coast, when you told a man you didn't want to see him again, that's what happened. You didn't see him again. His friends didn't praise him to you; his son didn't name a dog after you; you didn't have to go visit his ex-wife. What a strange town this was.

No, it was the coast that was strange. Most of the country was probably like it was here. Maybe she should get used to it.

She parked in front of the little yellow rambler and was barely out of the car when the door opened and Max came charging out, shouting her name.

He looked wonderful, so solid, so deliciously little-boy. Tory wanted to hug him, to let him know how happy she was to see him, how much she cared about him, but Marianne had come outside, and Tory felt awkward.

As soon as they were in the house, Marianne suggested to Max that he take "Miss Duncan" and "the dog" out to the backyard.

"Oh, *Mom*," he groaned, "her name's Tory."

"I hope you don't mind that he calls you by your first name," Marianne apologized as they went through the newspaper-carpeted kitchen to the back door.

"Not at all . . . and anyway," she heard herself say, "it isn't *Miss* Duncan. Duncan is my ex-husband's name."

"Oh." Marianne sounded surprised. "I didn't know you'd been married."

"Most people don't. I got tired of explaining."

"Goodness, I never thought about that.... I mean, everyone in town knows what happened to us. I can't imagine if I had to *explain*—that would be awful."

"Are you coming?" Max shouted from the backyard.

Tory, the puppy, was a little black thing, compact and wriggling, with a band of yellow polyester lace hem tape around her neck. "That's so she can get used to a collar," Max said proudly.

They romped around the backyard for nearly twenty minutes, which was a long time for Max to do one thing. He issued all sorts of commands to the dog, telling her to sit, come, stay, shake hands, roll over, play dead. She couldn't do one of them, but she still seemed like a nice little girl.

Finally Marianne came to the back door and called them in. "I put coffee on," she said to Tory, "would you like some?"

"And we made cupcakes," Max said. "We got up extra early and did it this morning. I iced them all."

Caffeine, sugar... But Marianne had picked up most of the newspapers off the floor, and the table was set with cups and saucers, a sugar bowl, a jar of Cremora, the stainless steel electric percolator and a plate of messily frosted chocolate cupcakes. Everything was spotless.

Tory wished this weren't happening, she wished that Marianne hadn't gone to such trouble, getting up early to make cupcakes. "That sounds lovely," she said, and for the first time in years, she wished her mother were with her.

Max gulped down his milk, made very quick work of his cupcake, and acted stunned when he was told he couldn't have another. "Well, *God*, why not?"

"You know why not," Marianne said calmly, "and don't swear in this house."

"Then may I be excused...please?"

"Yes, but clear your plate and glass."

As soon as they were alone, Marianne apologized to Tory for Max's profanity. "I hope you don't think I wasn't severe enough with him, but Dennis and Joe both think we shouldn't react very strongly to it, that he's just saying those things to get a reaction from us."

Tory ran a bar. If people started to apologize for other people's profanity, they'd be in line all the way back to the men's room. "Has he said...ah, the F-word yet?"

Although Tory heard the "F-word" word several dozen times a day and had, on occasion, been known to use it herself, she had never before stooped to calling it the "F-word."

"Not yet," Marianne answered. "But the day he does is the day I wash his mouth out with soap."

Did people actually do that? "You would?"

"Oh, yes. I don't care what Dennis and Joe say. I'm doing it. My mother did it to my sisters and me the first time we talked back."

It certainly sounded like Max had a mouthful of bubbles in his future. "Do you think it will stop him?"

"It's the sort of thing you only want to go through once," Marianne answered. Then she sighed, looking more natural than Tory had ever seen her. "But with Max . . . who knows?"

Tory laughed and took a bite of her cupcake. "These are very good cupcakes," she said, not really lying. Like the ones at her birthday party, these weren't bad.

"Thank you," Marianne replied. "It's the new Duncan Hines. They are good, aren't they? So much moister than the old mix."

The new Duncan Hines? Tory didn't know what the old Duncan Hines tasted like. She had nothing to say, absolutely nothing. But there was frosting. She could ask Marianne how she made her frosting.

Tory couldn't care less about frosting.

So she wasn't going to ask about it. She wasn't going to be a beauty queen. She shifted uneasily, sipped her coffee, and then, to her relief, thought of something to say. "I heard that you've had some very exciting news—you're going to have a baby."

Marianne flushed. "Yes . . . we're very happy about it."

"How's Max taking it?" She and Marianne might not be soulmates, but they did have one thing in common—Max. He was someone they both cared about.

"Fine now, but all he's thinking about is Tor—his dog. I'm sure it's going to be a big adjustment for him."

"The timing on the dog worked out well then."

"It worked out well for him. Can you imagine having a puppy and a newborn in the same house . . . and in the winter, no less?"

Tory could not. "I'd leave town if I were you. Let the men deal with it, and come home in the spring when everyone's toilet trained."

It took Marianne a moment to understand that Tory was joking, but she managed. "I'm sure there will be days when I'll feel like it."

IT POURED ON THE FOURTH. Tory spoke to Lisa, who was leaving for the Miss Oregon Pageant the following Sunday, and Lisa said that the Brighams had had to cancel the annual clan gathering. "They'll probably have it next week," she added wistfully. "It will be the first one I've ever missed."

"You're going to have to get used to missing things," Tory said gently.

On Tuesday, July 5, Nancy began a second job. It was morning work, helping out in a rather informal day-care center that one of the local mothers ran in her home. The pay was terrible, but Tory knew Nancy was going to like the job a lot. On Wednesday, when they talked about how her first day had been, Tory mentioned the speech therapist down in Klamath Falls, saying she'd be glad to go along to the first consultation. Nancy didn't answer, but a couple of hours later she asked Tory for the address. Tory had her call. The therapist was just back from vacation and could see Nancy on Saturday morning.

"Y-y-you don't m-m-mind coming with me?" Nancy asked.

"Not a bit," Tory answered instantly. She could see that Nancy looked relieved.

Tory set aside Thursday morning to work up a day-by-day schedule of stocking colors, accessories, and hair styles for Lisa. On Saturday afternoon, Lisa was coming over while they packed the clothes. Tory wanted to be sure that everything was packed properly so that Lisa and Mrs. Sumner wouldn't have to do a lot of ironing in the motel room.

Tory had just finished listing what Lisa was to wear on the plane Sunday when the phone rang.

"Tory, this is Ned."

Ned? Tory dropped the pen. Her ex-husband? Why was he calling? "This is a surprise . . . how are you?"

"I'm fine, but I've got a message for your mother. Do you know where to reach her?"

"Mother? You have a message for Mother? Who's it from?"

"A Mrs. Lynette Morris."

"Never heard of her. How did you get it?"

"Mrs. Goodman—the lady from the Miss South Carolina Pageant. She said that this Mrs. Morris was looking for your mother, and all she knew about her was that you had been Miss South Carolina. So she called the pageant committee, and they called me—I guess you never told them that we were divorced."

Telling the Miss South Carolina state pageant committee that she had left her husband had never occurred to Tory. "No, I didn't. But what's the message? I'll track Mother down."

"Oh, Tory . . . why don't you just let me call her?"

Tory was instantly alert. This was Ned being nice. "Tell me."

"Well...apparently your mother's father died, and her mother wants her to know that the funeral is on Friday."

FOR YEARS Tory had had a number she could call if she needed to find her mother. She had never used it before. She called now. A secretary flipped through some itineraries and said that her mother was at a Holiday Inn in New Mexico with a noon flight to Arizona. They would be in Arizona for the weekend, then in the Seattle-Takoma area for the early part of the next week, and then in Oregon.

"Oregon?" Tory asked. "Where in Oregon?"

"Seaside, the state pageant there. We had a cancellation in Montana so we're sending her there."

That was interesting. Her mother would be at Lisa's pageant. She would be able to tell Tory how Lisa was doing.

Tory thanked the secretary and called New Mexico. Marjorie wasn't in her room; Tory left a message and went back to work on her list.

Twenty minutes later the phone rang again.

"Tory, what's wrong? What's happened? Are you all right?"

Marjorie sounded almost frightened. "Nothing's wrong," Tory assured her. "I'm fine, really I am."

"Is it Joe?...Max?"

"No, no, they're both fine."

"That's a relief. I nearly panicked when I saw your message. I was sure something was wrong."

Tory hated to admit it, but her mother's panic was justified. Tory wouldn't have called her unless something was wrong. "I do have some bad news," she said, wanting to give her the news slowly. "It's about your father."

"My father?" Marjorie didn't speak for a long moment. "Is he dead?"

How had she known? Had she guessed that this was the only way she would ever hear anything about him? "I'm afraid so," Tory said as gently as she could.

"How did you find out?"

"A Mrs. Morris called Lee Ann Goodman, and she called Ned, thinking to reach me. I guess I never told her—" Tory stopped, she was chattering. "Anyway, the message was that the funeral is on Friday."

"I suppose that's to be expected."

How cold she sounded. "Are you going?"

"No, of course not."

"But, Mother," Tory heard herself say, "don't you think you should?"

"I haven't been back in thirty years; why should I go now?"

Tory didn't know. She wasn't exactly experienced in advocating family solidarity.

Marjorie continued. "I'm working this month; I can't up and leave."

"Surely there are contingencies for family emergencies."

"Yes, but I've never used them."

Because we've never been what you could call a family. "Then start now."

"Tory, this is silly. There's no point in talking about this. I see no reason in the world why I should go."

Again Tory had no real answer, just a notion that this was the right thing to do, that this was part of what funerals were for. "Maybe your mother needs us."

A sharp breath came over the line. "Us?"

"I'd go with you."

That, too, wasn't something she had planned to say. "We've been to enough strange places together. Why not one more?"

There was a pause. "Tory dear... I can hardly believe you're offering to go, but there are... you see, there are things about this you don't know." Marjorie's voice was strained.

Tory had been trained to answer anything. Those practice interviews had given her pretty answers for every question. But not this. No one had ever taught her how to say this.

So she just said it. "If you're talking about me being illegitimate, I know."

The line was quiet. Tory wished they were together. She wished she could see her mother's face.

"You know?"

"I've known for a long time, and it's nothing that would keep me from going. As you said, it's been thirty years. Who's going to think about it now? And if they do, what do we care what they say about us?"

Her mother didn't speak for a while. "We may not get there in time."

"If we're late, we're late. That's better than not going at all. And we might make it; we've got twenty-four hours. How far is this place from an airport?" Tory realized she didn't even know what state they were going to.

"We'll have to fly to Charlotte and then rent a car. It's almost two hours from there. If you can hold on a minute, I've got a Pocket Flight Guide."

Tory waited as her mother, obviously experienced at these matters, worked out a route from Sullivan

City, Oregon, to Charlotte, North Carolina. "It's going to be awful, but it will work. If you take the evening flight out of Sullivan City, then you can get a red-eye from Portland to Atlanta. You'll have to stop in Salt Lake, but it's not a change—and then we can catch the same morning plane to Charlotte. Why don't I make the reservations? I'll call you if there's any problem."

"Fine, but shouldn't we tell someone we're coming?"

"I guess . . ."

"If you give me the number," Tory volunteered, "I'll call."

Her mother recited a number. "At least that's what it was thirty years ago."

A moment later Tory had hung up and was dialing the North Carolina number. Halfway through, she had to stop and call her mother back. She didn't know her grandmother's name.

"Kellogg, Frances Kellogg."

Tory dialed again. A woman's voice answered.

Tory didn't know what to call her. Grandmother? Grandma? Granny? "Mrs. Kellogg?"

"She's not here right now." The voice wasn't very warm. "Can I take a message?"

Tory took a breath. "My name is Victoria Davidson. I am Marjorie's daughter."

"Oh, my goodness . . . and here I thought you might be trying to sell something." The woman was now much friendlier. "People do that, you know, check the obituaries and then catch the family when they aren't thinking straight. Not that Herb's obituary is out yet since our paper is a weekly and all, but still people have a way of finding out."

Tory wasn't sure what to say. "I'm sure they do."

"Oh," the woman exclaimed. "I haven't introduced myself, now have I? I'm a neighbor, Lil Patterson. Fran's down at the funeral home, making sure
everything's set up for the viewing this evening. She
said that the minister's wife was trying to call you all.
I didn't know how she was going to, but you know
Lynette—no, I guess you don't—she's good at that
sort of thing."

What a talker this lady was. "We just got the message an hour ago, and we wanted to let someone know
we will both be in sometime tomorrow morning."

"Tomorrow? But you'll miss the viewing…oh, well,
I suppose that can't be helped, not if you only got the
message an hour ago. Are you coming into Charlotte? I can send Bud or Billy to pick you all up if you
want."

"Oh, no, thank you, but Mother said we would rent
a car. Could you tell me the name of a nearby motel?"

"A motel?" Lil Patterson sounded surprised.
"What do you all want with a motel? We don't have
a motel, not unless you count the Dixie Belle, which I
certainly do not. Fran expects you to stay here. Just
before she left, she said we better make up the sleep
sofa in case Marjorie comes."

Thirty years. Marjorie hadn't been home in thirty
years, and yet her mother was making up the sleep
sofa for her.

"Mrs. Patterson, the message I got was very brief.
It didn't say anything about…well, about what happened. Was it sudden?"

"You mean Herb? Oh, no, not at all. It was a
blessing, really, a blessing. He had a stroke three years

ago, and he's been bad off ever since. He had another one a couple of weeks ago, and Dr. Rider said right away that he wasn't ever going to come out of the coma. I thought we ought to call you all then, but Fran wanted to wait.''

Why? Why wait? Had Marjorie's quarrel been with her father, not her mother?

Tory exchanged a few more polite words with Mrs. Patterson—or rather Tory exchanged a few of her words for a great many of Mrs. Patterson's—then hung up. She wondered what this was going to be like. She sketched a rectangle around her grandmother's phone number. Awful, probably. She drew a circle around *ice* and then one around *blue*...

Ice blue stockings... This was Lisa's list, the list of the clothes she was to wear next week. And the ice blue stockings were for Monday afternoon; Tory had the rest of the week left to do—this list... and packing Lisa's clothes and her own... and Nancy's appointment with the speech therapist, Tory was supposed to go along... and Wags, she had to find somewhere for Wags to stay... the bar... all this and she was leaving on the evening plane.

How was she going to get it all done?

She was going to have to close the bar. There was no way around it. Neither Nancy nor Rich's father really knew how things ran. Nancy was bright enough to manage the daily things, but only if Tory explained first, and Tory didn't have time to explain. And Nancy had enough stress this week with the new job and the appointment in Klamath Falls. It was too bad. Tory would pay her employees anyway, and her regulars would understand, but still...it was a shame she didn't have an assistant manager.

But Wags... what was she going to do with Wags? Tory looked over to the sofa where Wags was sleeping. Wags opened one eye, saw that Tory had no food, and went back to sleep.

She could take her to the vet. They boarded dogs in those awful little cages. Wags hated the vet; in the waiting room, she whimpered and trembled. Tory didn't think she could stand to leave her there. Surely there was some nice place outside of town with nice people and special runs and things.

Who would know? Sonny Snow, the man she got him from, he would know...or Junior Rogers, he had a golden too, he might know.

But both Sonny and Junior would be at work. There was no way to reach them. The only people who would be home were women... and Tory didn't know very many women.

So she called the one she knew—Marianne Colt.

"I'm sorry to bother you," Tory said, "but I've been called out of town for... well, I don't know for how long, and—"

"I hope nothing is wrong." Marianne sounded concerned.

"My grandfather died."

"Oh, how awful. I'm so sorry."

"No...it was a blessing really," Tory repeated Mrs. Patterson's words without knowing whether or not they were true. "He had been sick for a long time."

"I understand... it was like that with my grandfather. What can I do?"

"Nothing really. I just need to know a good place to leave my dog. Do you know of any, besides the vet?"

"Oh, I don't, I'm sorry...but Debbie would know. That's Jim's wife. Can I call her? Then I'll call you right back."

Tory remembered Joe saying that this sister-in-law loved dogs. Sonny Snow was her uncle. "If you give me her number, I'll call her myself."

Marianne did. "And will you let me know if there's anything else I can do?"

Tory thanked her, hung up, and called Debbie Brigham. She was obviously surprised to hear from Tory, but she knew all about Wags.

"For heavens' sake," Debbie said when Tory explained what she needed, "you aren't going to pay to have someone take care of your dog."

"That's what people do, isn't it?"

"Not really, at least not around here. People take their dogs with them or leave them with family. So, why don't you bring her over here? Jim and I will be happy to keep her."

They would keep her? The thought had never occurred to Tory. "No, no. I can't let you do that. I don't mind paying to board her, I really don't."

"But there's only the vet."

And Wags hated the vet. Tory didn't like to take favors; asking the Brighams to take care of her dog would make her very uncomfortable, but leaving Wags at the vet would make both of them miserable. "If you're sure you don't mind..."

"Not at all. One more dog isn't going to make any difference around here."

"I hardly know what to say. This is so generous of you. When should I bring her by?"

Debbie thought. "I have some errands to do this morning...why don't I just come out and get her in about half an hour? You must have a million things to do without coming into town.''

Tory protested again, but she had to admit it would be a relief.

So that took care of Wags. Now about Nancy's appointment. Nancy was counting on her. She would worry so much less if someone else were in charge of finding the building, parking the car, knocking on the right door. Nancy still allowed all those little things to frighten her. Reluctantly Tory picked up the phone again, dialing a number she knew very well.

He answered.

''Joe, this is Tory.'' And then she went right into it, saying it bluntly, baldly. ''My grandfather died, and Mother and I are going to the funeral. It's tomorrow.''

He was quiet for a moment. ''Tell me what I can do.''

Tory appreciated that. He had to be surprised. He alone knew how extraordinary it was that she and her mother were going anywhere together, much less to her grandfather's funeral. But he hadn't said a word.

''Nancy's got her first appointment with a speech therapist on Saturday. Would you go to Klamath Falls with her?''

''What time? Where?''

It was a two-hour drive. They would have to leave at seven, wouldn't be back until noon at the earliest. It would ruin his Saturday, but he hadn't even bothered to say yes.

''Now what else?'' he said. ''Do you want me to come get Wags? Max and I will take care of her.''

"Oh, thank you...but—" and Tory was a little embarrassed to have to admit it "—your brother and sister-in-law are going to keep her."

"They are? Jim and Debbie?" His voice deepened. "I'm glad you asked them."

Tory wanted to explain that she hadn't really, that she had only called Debbie for information about kennels, but before she could say so, Joe continued. "What are you going to do about the bar? Can Nancy and Rich's father run it?"

"No. Nancy's working another job, and Pete doesn't have the stamina."

"And they would panic in an emergency."

Tory would not have admitted this to anyone else. "Yes."

"So what are you going to do?"

"Close. I don't know how long I'll be gone, but surely I'll be back in a few days, maybe even by Saturday, depending on how things go."

"I wouldn't count on being back by Saturday, not with the funeral on Friday," he said. "Do you want me to ask my cousin to come in nights?"

"Your cousin? What cousin? What are you talking about?"

"My cousin Doug. I told you about him when we were talking about an assistant manager for you. I'm sure he'd be willing to take on a second job for a week or so. I've seen you cash out any number of times, and he's plenty sharp. Between the two of us, we could figure things out. He probably doesn't know anything special about making drinks, but he's level-headed and won't fall apart if you are held up again."

It would have been perfect. That's all she needed, someone who didn't mind being in charge. "But, Joe, I can't turn my bar over to someone I've never met."

"Ah... well, I can't blame you for that."

Except that she could. If Joe thought this cousin was level-headed and sharp, then he was level-headed and sharp, that's all there was to it. This wasn't the sort of thing that Joe would ever be wrong about.

"Do you think he would do it?"

"I'm sure. I'll go out and catch him as soon as the mill closes. I'll explain the situation, and I'm sure he'll be happy to help."

"I hate to make you do all this."

"You know I don't mind."

Yes, she did know that.

"Tory?"

"Yes?"

"You will call, won't you? Let me know how things are?"

She nodded... even though he couldn't see her. "Yes, Joe. Yes, I will."

She had hardly gotten back to work on Lisa's list when she heard a knock. At the door was a vaguely familiar, rather pregnant strawberry blonde who must be Debbie Brigham. She was accompanied by Marianne Colt.

"Marianne," Tory said, hiding her surprise. "How nice to see you."

It turned out that when June Brigham—Joe's mother—had learned that Tory had to leave town, she urged Debbie to tell Tory that she should forget about Lisa's clothes.

"She said that Lisa could wear what she wore to the pageant in town," Marianne added. "But I know she's very excited about your clothes, she talks about them all the time. So Debbie and I thought perhaps we could pick them up now. Lisa's at work, or we would have brought her too.''

"But they aren't packed yet," Tory apologized.

"Oh, we'll help," Marianne volunteered. "That's why we both came."

"And we don't care how long it takes," Debbie added. "We left the kids with June. She'll give them lunch and, to be perfectly frank, there's nothing I would rather do today than be away from my children."

"Okay, let me make a phone call and then we can get to work."

Tory called Pete Miller's daughter-in-law and asked her to ask him to come in as early as he could. "My second bartender will be stopping by for the key so he can open up," she told Marianne and Debbie. "Shall we get started?" She picked up the list she had been working on and explained what it was. "Could one of you write things down as I tell you?"

"Marianne will," Debbie said quickly. "She has such pretty handwriting."

Tory knew that many of her regulars were self-conscious about their penmanship. They wrote so little that their letters were unformed, childlike. It seemed sad to Tory; handwriting was such an unimportant thing to be embarrassed about.

The three of them set to work. Marianne was the secretary: she wrote out the schedule as Tory dictated. Debbie was in charge of the tissue paper; she folded and crushed it into all the intricate shapes that Tory needed for padding sleeves and fattening creases.

It took them several hours. "What about your own things?" Marianne asked Tory when they had finished Lisa's packing. "Let us help you pack."

Tory felt as if it were too late to be quibbling about little favors. She opened her closet to find something appropriate for a funeral. Debbie started to fold more tissue paper.

"Don't do that for me," Tory said quickly. "I don't pack like that for myself. It takes up too much space. That's just for beauty queens."

It took only a few minutes to get Tory's suitcase packed. Then, as she explained Wag's foibles and habits to Debbie, Marianne watered plants, took the yogurt, cottage cheese and bean curd out of the refrigerator, checked the dishwasher for dirty dishes, and carried the kitchen trash out—things Tory wasn't sure she would have remembered to do herself.

This must be why people had sisters.

KEITH LET TORY OFF at the airport nearly forty-five minutes before the plane was due to take off. Thanks to Debbie and Marianne, she had managed to get everything done. She had even had time for a long phone conversation with Lisa, telling her that all her clothes were in order, assuring her that she was going to do fine. She had been able to sit down with Pete and Nancy and assure them that they too were going to do fine. They had both met Doug Brigham before, and even though they didn't know him well, they were happy he was going to help out. Tory wished she had had time to meet Doug, but she kept reminding herself that Joe's word ought to be enough.

She waited quietly, knowing she had done everything she could have before leaving. Now she could start thinking about what she had to face. There was a pile of tattered magazines on the chair next to hers. She picked up an issue of *Family Circle* that had an elaborate gingerbread house on the cover. She started reading an article on how to make her own Christmas ornaments: tiny lace wreaths, crocheted gingerbread men, knitted candy canes. The gingerbread men were actually rather cute. She thought about the gingerbread man who had been last year's Christmas ornament, Joe Brigham. Tory doubted that *Family Circle* would have anything to top that, at least not until she learned to knit or crochet.

"Tory?"

She looked up. In front of her was a man in his early twenties. No, it wasn't a man, it was a Brigham. She had no idea which one it was or even if she had ever seen it before.

"I'm Doug Brigham."

"Doug Brigham!" Tory stood up so quickly that the *Family Circle* slid to the floor. "How did you get here? I mean, how did you know?"

He laughed. "Joe kidnapped me as soon as I came out of the gate, and he said if we hurried, there was a chance of catching you. He's parking the car now."

"Did he tell you what's going on?" Of course he had. "Are you willing to help me out?"

"I think it will be a ball. I'm thrilled that you thought of me."

Doug had an easy, self-confident manner. He seemed livelier, more outgoing than Joe, and if first impressions counted for anything, Tory thought he would make a terrific bartender. He sat down and pulled out a list of questions that he and Joe had come up with in the car. Tory answered as quickly as she could. Joe came in as she was explaining what she did when she decided to stop serving someone. She was glad that Doug had thought to ask that.

She could have managed without the Brighams. Wags could have gone to the vet; Lisa could have packed the clothes; the bar could have closed. She would have managed...but it certainly was better this way.

When she had to leave, Joe picked up her suitcase and walked over to the door with her. Doug acted as if he were suddenly fascinated by the vending machines.

"He's terrific, Joe. I do appreciate your bringing him out here."

Joe shrugged. "I thought you might feel better if you met him."

"I do, I really do."

"That's good."

Neither of them said anything for a moment and then Joe asked, "You must be feeling a little strange about this trip."

"I haven't had a moment to think about it," she answered honestly.

"I'm a little surprised that your mother asked you to go with her. I'd have thought she was pretty self-reliant."

"She didn't ask. I volunteered."

Joe didn't say anything. Tory looked up at him. His lower lip had tightened, his eyes glowed. This was how he looked sometimes when he talked about something Max had done in school or when he talked about Lisa's college plans...when he was proud of someone.

He was proud of her. He thought she had done the right thing, and he was pleased, proud, impressed. He would never say it, but she knew.

He handed her the suitcase. ''Give your mother my best, will you?''

''I will.''

It was awkward. Was she just supposed to say goodbye and go through the door? That didn't seem right. She wanted to touch him, to hug him, to have his arms around her, to feel safe for a moment before she set out. But they wouldn't embrace, they weren't lovers anymore.

Joe had his hands in his pockets. She knew he was feeling the same way.

''You'll miss your plane if you don't hurry,'' he said at last.

''Well . . . goodbye, Joe.''

''Goodbye, Tory.''

And she went through the door, across the runway to the plane, without having touched him.

TORY WOULD NOT HAVE THOUGHT it possible, but it was. Three rows behind her, a baby screamed all the way from Portland, Oregon, to Atlanta, Georgia. She felt sorry for the baby; she felt even sorrier for herself.

The child took an intermission while the plane was on the ground at Salt Lake. "She has a bad ear infection," the stewardess confided to Tory. "They shouldn't have ever brought her on a plane."

When Tory walked back to the rest rooms, she took a look at these fellow passengers. The baby was asleep; screaming across three states had to be even more tiring than listening to screaming across three states. The thirtyish parents were—or rather had been—well-dressed, in expensive white shirts and khaki slacks. Tory imagined that stowed in the overhead compartment were navy blazers and a determination not to let a child interfere with their life-style. She felt angry with them. They weren't being fair to the baby; they weren't being fair to the other passengers.

But when Tory got off the plane in Atlanta, she saw two eager grandparents. Grandpa had a Polaroid, Grandma was standing on her toes, bending this way and that, trying to catch the first sight of the white shirts and khaki slacks and the lovely bundle they carried.

It must be hard sometimes to know what to do.

TORY'S MOTHER WAS WAITING at the gate assigned to their flight to Charlotte. She stood up as Tory approached. "It was very good of you to come on such short notice."

"I didn't mind. It wasn't a problem."

Tory winced. So far the first polite lie had been hers.

Marjorie shook her head. "I find that hard to believe."

Which was also polite, but at least it was true.

Marjorie had already gotten their seat assignments; Tory only had to show the agent her ticket to get a boarding pass. Then she sat down next to her mother.

"Now tell me," Marjorie said, "how did you manage to leave? What did you do with Wags? Did you have to put her in a kennel?"

Her mother remembered Wags's name. Tory was surprised and pleased. "No, Joe's brother and sister-in-law took her."

"Oh, how nice. What about the bar? Can Mr. Miller and Nancy run it themselves?"

Apparently she remembered a lot. "I don't think so," Tory answered. "Especially since Nancy has taken a second job. A cousin of Joe's is going to look after things for me."

"What a good thing that you have Joe."

But before Tory could tell her that she didn't "have" Joe anymore, Marjorie continued. "Did you say that Nancy has a second job? Tell me about it."

Tory explained about the day-care center and the speech therapist, thinking that as soon as she was finished with Nancy she would tell her mother about what had happened with Joe, but then the agent announced that the flight was ready for boarding, and they were gathering up their luggage, checking their tickets, and it just didn't seem like a very good time.

In the plane, Marjorie asked more questions about the people in Sullivan City. Tory reported on Marianne's pregnancy and Max's dog. They talked about how the new baby was going to affect Max, and Tory knew she should say that she wasn't a part of these people's lives anymore, but she couldn't seem to bring it up.

It wasn't a long flight. The airline served coffee, juice and nearly icy sweet rolls. A rental car was waiting at the Charlotte airport. Marjorie had reserved a Cutlass, roomy and comfortable, an utterly American car.

Tory volunteered to drive, and in a few minutes they were heading west on Interstate 77. "What's this town like?" Tory asked.

"Stuartsville? It's nothing much. A little furniture factory town. Furniture is an important industry in North Carolina because there's such good hardwood on the slopes of the Smokies and in the western Piedmont."

Furniture is an important industry in North Carolina . . . Her mother was sounding like a guidebook. She must be dreading this. Tory wished that there was something she could say. But how could she say that everything was going to be all right? She had no evidence for that at all.

They drove quietly. The countryside was covered with small farms—some cattle, but mostly apple orchards billowing up and over the gentle slopes of this rolling country. This was the Piedmont, the easy hills at the foot of the Blue Ridge.

After a while, Marjorie spoke. "You said you knew. How did you find out?"

"Knew?" Tory was puzzled. "Knew what?"

Her mother didn't answer.

But the silence said enough. It was what her mother had been thinking about while Tory had been thinking about Joe, while they had been talking about Sullivan City. Her mother had been thinking about what Tory had revealed on the phone—she wouldn't have thought of anything else.

"I never had a clue," Tory explained. "Not until a month or so before Atlantic City. While I was waiting for one of my practice interviews to start, I overheard someone say something and then it all fit together.

"I suppose I should have told you myself. Did it bother you very much?"

"Not being illegitimate. It seems irrelevant somehow. But it did bother me that we were pretending to be something that we weren't."

"We were doing that . . . did you say this happened about a month before, sometime in August?"

Tory nodded.

"That makes sense," her mother said. "I noticed something happening to you then. For the first time it seemed like you didn't believe that you were going to win. I didn't understand it."

Tory spoke quickly. "Oh, Mother, it wasn't just finding out. That was only the symbol for everything else we were pretending about—dyeing my hair, wearing tinted contacts, lying to the judges, having to work so hard. That's what made me feel like I didn't deserve it, not that I was illegitimate. I don't care about that. I don't feel like less of a person for it."

"I did."

That was understandable. "That's why you left Stuartsville?"

Marjorie nodded. "My father said he never wanted to see me again."

She had been eighteen. Her father worked in a furniture factory, her mother clerked in the grocery store, and Marjorie had wanted out desperately. "I'd read magazines and go to movies and it would seem like there were worlds and worlds of exciting things happening, but none of them were happening in North Carolina. When I graduated from high school, I got a job in a drugstore. I couldn't stand that, a lifetime of that, and so my mother suggested that I go to beauty college at nights. Then a boy from the next town asked me to go to Richmond with him . . . and I went."

"Was he athletic?"

Marjorie looked at her, surprised. "How did you know?"

"I have a lot of basic athletic ability. I don't use it much, but it's there. Where is he now? Do you know?"

"He is dead. That part is true. He died when you were around five—a car accident. He must have been drinking. He always drank too much. You didn't call a young person an alcoholic in those days, but I'm sure he was one."

"It sounds like we were better off without him."

"We probably were."

"Why didn't you give me up?"

"For a while I thought he would marry me, and then when it was clear that he wouldn't, I swore—" She stopped.

But Tory knew what she was going to say. "You swore that you would raise a perfect child."

"Yes."

Tory glanced over at her mother. It was hard to imagine this elegant blond woman in her lilac shirtwaist as a small-town unwed mother, but that's what she had been. How determined she must have been since then, how driven. "And you haven't seen your parents since?"

"My mother did write me once."

It had happened exactly as Marjorie had always imagined it. Her mother had been watching the Miss America Pageant, and she had seen Tory and she had known. "Apparently you look just like her younger sister. Of course, she didn't contact you because she assumed that you'd been adopted since 'Davidson' isn't their last name. I had made it up."

"Then how did she find you?"

"She came to one of your Miss South Carolina appearances later that year and saw me there. She didn't say anything to me, but she wrote to me in care of the pageant."

"Is that all? Didn't she try and see you...us?"

"My father wouldn't let her."

That seemed unforgivable to Tory.

In a few minutes, her mother directed her to an exit off the interstate. The Dixie Belle Motor Court was at the end of the ramp. Tory could see why Mrs. Patterson hadn't counted it as a place to stay. The management probably hadn't changed the sheets since Marjorie had left town.

Up the road was a dirt speedway, a half-mile track in the middle of an empty field. The grass around it was flattened and brown. Marjorie stared out the window at it. "We used to come here. Cars would pull up around the track and leave their headlights on."

"Would you sit on the hoods and drink beer?"

Marjorie shook her head. "No one could afford beer. They drank cherry bounce."

"Cherry bounce? What's that?"

"You put wild cherries in a gallon jar, pour sugarhead over it, and leave it for a week or so."

This was the first time Tory had heard mother reminisce. "Sugarhead?"

"White lightening, moonshine...people in the mountains still make their own liquor."

Tory wasn't fond of paying liquor tax, but she certainly preferred it to the alternative. "And you drank it?"

"I didn't, but everyone else did. In fact I hated coming here. It seemed so pointless...but there was nothing else to do."

Four or five miles farther off the interstate was the furniture factory, a one-story, corrugated tin building, which sprawled across several acres. As they approached town, they passed a couple of auto body shops, a Dairy Queen, and a gas station that advertised groceries. Tory slowed as they came to the downtown. There was a hardware store, a small grocery store, a lunch counter that also served as the bus station. Downtown was only two blocks long, and a third of the stores were vacant. They passed some frame houses, three churches, a couple of trailers, and then they were out in the country again.

"Is this right?" Tory asked.

Marjorie started. "My goodness, no. I forgot to tell you where to turn."

Tory pulled over on the shoulder of the road, waited for a semi to rumble past, then made a U-turn to go back into town. This time her mother told her to turn off Main Street onto a residential street.

The houses were all alike. They had only one story and were made of frame with cement steps leading up to front porches. On hot nights, people must sit out; there were rockers and straight-backed chairs on the porches. The houses were painted white or grey with green trim, but here and there was a pink door, a turquoise railing. The houses were set on cinder blocks, and few of them had any foundation planting, although several had gardenia and althea bushes on the lot lines. Some yards had little birdbaths in a ring of zinnias and marigolds; others had dirt and dandelions.

"Are these company houses?" Tory asked even though she was sure that they were.

Her mother didn't answer.

Sullivan City was much better than this, bigger, less squalid. In Stuartsville, the poor and working classes lived closer together, the line between them was more fragile than in Sullivan City. One house would have a neat fence, a pick-up or a van; the next would have a car rusting at the curb and an angry dog barking on the front stoop.

They went another block and then Marjorie pointed. "There it is." Tory pulled up to the curb. She turned off the engine and set the emergency brake even though the street was completely flat.

She looked at the house her mother had grown up in. "The yard is attractive," she said. It was. Masses of azalea bushes hid the cinder block foundation, and the flower borders were pretty, carefully weeded. The Kelloggs were clearly one of the "nicer" mill families.

The screen door opened and a woman stepped out onto the front porch. She was dressed in navy knit slacks and an overblouse of some synthetic print. She was Tory's grandmother.

She could have been Joe's.

"You made good time," she said as they came up the concrete walk.

"There wasn't much traffic," Marjorie answered.

You made good time...there wasn't much traffic... Thirty years and they didn't even say "hello."

Tory's grandmother squinted at her. "So you're Victoria."

"Yes, but people call me Tory."

"I thought you had brown hair."

Tory remembered that her grandmother had seen her in the Miss America Pageant. "This is my real color, but I was a brunette for a while."

"You look better this way."

Tory felt uncomfortable. She didn't want anyone weeping and embracing her, but she couldn't help thinking that there ought to be a little more than this.

Her grandmother stepped back to hold open the screen door. Tory followed her mother into the living room. In the center of one wall was a big color television, tuned to some morning talk show. Magazines, many magazines, were carefully stacked on the lower shelves of the coffee table and the end tables. The area rug was a variegated green shag.

"Would you like some iced tea?" Frances Kellogg asked. "Or there's some biscuit from breakfast."

"Iced tea would be lovely," Marjorie said. "But let me help."

Tory spoke quickly. "No, Mother, sit down. I'll help."

She followed her grandmother toward the kitchen. It was a shotgun house—a bullet fired through the front door would go out the back window. Tory saw the doors to what were probably two bedrooms and a bathroom.

In Tory's Atlanta house, the kitchen opened into a breakfast nook which in turn opened into a family room. Her grandmother's whole house would have easily fit inside just those rooms.

Her grandmother had already taken three tall iced tea glasses out of the cupboard and was running water over the ice cube tray. "The tea's in the icebox," she told Tory. "And the pink sugar is in that bowl."

"Pink sugar?"

Her grandmother took the lid off the sugar bowl. It was crammed with little blue packets of artificial sweetener. "The old stuff, saccharine I guess it was, was pink. But there's real sugar in that canister over there if that's what you want."

Tory drank tea unsweetened, and she imagined her mother did too. "This will be fine."

Her grandmother refilled the ice cube tray and walked around Tory to put it back into the freezer. Tory watched her.

Frances Kellogg didn't wear any makeup and her figure had grown a little thick, but her bone structure was exceptional, probably better than Tory's, and at seventy, or however old she was, her coloring was still delicate. Tory guessed she had been blond too, and now her hair was a softly greyed silver.

"What would you like me to call you?" Tory asked.

Her grandmother picked up the tray of glasses without looking at her. "I don't know... Fran, I guess. I suppose it's a little late for anything else."

Fran started out to the living room, and as she followed her, Tory decided that her grandmother was every bit as uncomfortable as she and her mother were.

Tory sat next to her mother on the sofa. Fran took the small club chair. The largest, most comfortable chair, a leather-grained vinyl lounger, remained empty. Tory imagined that it had been her grandfather's chair. A quiz show came on. A model in an evening dress swished about, showing off prizes. Marjorie seemed to be very interested in the quiz show—something Tory knew to be impossible. Fran picked up a magazine. It was going to be a very long day.

Of the three of them, Tory had to be the least uncomfortable, the one with the least at stake. If anyone was going to talk, it would have to be her. But she was determined that it would not be small talk. Impersonal, yes, but not small. She hadn't come all the way across the United States to talk about the weather. She thought for a moment. "Mother says that this is pretty much a company town."

Fran only nodded, but she did look up from the magazine.

"Do you have a strong union?"

Fran looked surprised, as if she didn't expect such a question from Miss South Carolina. "Don't have one at all. North Carolina's not much for unions. The textile people make a lot of noise about it—like that movie with the girl who used to be the Flying Nun—but not much ever happens."

"What about your owners?" That was one thing about Sullivan City. The McKechnees still lived there and still owned most of the company; that made a difference to a town. "Are they any good?"

"They're out-of-state," Fran said. "Lots of our money is, but enough about that. Tell me about you. Last I heard you were Miss South Carolina."

"I'm not anymore. I'm a bartender. I'm divorced, live in Oregon and have my own bar."

"Do you have any kids?"

"No."

"That's too bad. How old are you?"

"Thirty."

"You don't look it," Fran said flatly. "You don't either, Marjorie—look your age, I mean."

"Thank you," Marjorie said.

That was probably the third thing Marjorie had said since they had arrived. "What's the schedule for today?" Tory asked.

"The funeral's at two, but Lil Patterson's having us over to lunch first."

That sounded like an excellent idea. With Mrs. Patterson around, they would not have to worry about what to say to one another. "Then I think we'd better start getting ready," Tory said. "I'd like to take a shower if I could. We've been traveling all night."

They took their suitcases into what had undoubtedly once been Marjorie's bedroom. It was furnished as a den now, with a sofa, a sewing machine, a couple of TV trays with towering stacks of junk mail, and more magazines, piles and piles of magazines—*Road and Track*, *Ladies' Home Journal*, *Family Circle*, *Ideals*, *National Geographic*, *Reader's Digest*, *Southern Living*. "Herb didn't like to throw anything out," Fran explained.

Tory showered first and then did her makeup standing in front of the full-length mirror that was screwed into the closet door. When Marjorie returned from her shower, Tory turned the mirror over to her, leaving the closet door open so that she could unpack.

She was arranging her white slacks on a hanger when she noticed her mother watching her, mascara brush in hand. Tory could feel herself start to tense. "What is it?"

"Are you going to wear those while you are here?"

Don't tell me what to do . . . don't tell me what to wear . . . "Not to the funeral, but maybe sometime. Is there a problem with that?"

"Oh, Tory, I am sorry to criticize you."

Why not? You always have.

"I really am," Marjorie continued. "I love the way you dress now; it's such a casual and fresh look, but . . ."

Tory forced herself to relax. She had to be less defensive. Her mother was trying. She knew that Tory wasn't a Barbie doll anymore. She tried to speak pleasantly. "What is it? I'd like to know if I am doing something wrong."

"It's not exactly wrong, but it's not very tactful."

"Tactful? What's tactless about a pair of white slacks?"

"If you're about to meet a room full of women with weight problems, it isn't very tactful to show up dressed in a pair of snug white slacks."

Oh. Her mother was right; of course, she was. Tory hadn't thought.

Tory dressed for herself, kept fit for herself. During the year she'd spent on the coast, she had eaten junk food and wore the same shirt and jeans day after day. It had taught her that being overweight and ill-kempt made her feel even worse about herself. So now, although she dressed casually, she chose her clothes carefully and made sure she still looked good in snug white slacks. She did it for herself; she didn't need to impress pageant judges anymore... and she certainly didn't need to make other women feel bad.

"Am I supposed to pretend to have saddlebag thighs?" she asked lightly.

Marjorie went back to her mascara. "In a word... yes."

Tory laughed, and they chatted pleasantly while they finished dressing. Her mother could dress very quickly, and in a few minutes she was standing in front of the mirror again, checking her hem, settling her collar. Tory went and stood beside her, looking at the two of them.

"Don't we look the berries?" she said.

They did. Neither of them looked good in dark colors so they were both wearing slim-skirted suits in light but muted shades, Tory in a Williamsburg grey-blue, Marjorie in heather. Their silky blouses were white, their stockings lightly tinted, their shoes taupe. Marjorie had an antique gold stickpin in her lapel, and Tory wore her wedding pearls.

Tory thought of what it had been like when she was growing up, all those years until the last one, when they had gone to pageants together, driving all night, sharing a bed in a small motel room, eating in the room while Marjorie ironed Tory's ruffled dresses. They had been everything to each other, they had been a team.

"We'll show them, Mom," she said suddenly.

"We will," her mother answered. Then she turned to pick up her purse. "The sad part is I'm not sure I want to anymore."

THE FUNERAL WAS in the Baptist Church. It was a yellow brick building, probably built before the Depression. The style was, Tory guessed, a little Moorish, but even that made it sound better than it was. It had a big square bell tower with one great garish stained glass window. Spurting off to one side was a round polyp of a building, the Baptistry. Tory pointed to it, asking her mother, "Were you baptized there?"

Marjorie nodded. "I was eleven. We wore white gowns, and the minister held your nose while he pushed you all the way under."

It was a long funeral, the longest Tory had ever attended, lasting an hour and a half, with lots of prayers and several eulogies, one by someone from the factory, another by the local politician, who was some sort of County Commissioner. At least the casket was closed; Tory was glad of that. There were two flower arrangements from the factory, one a cross, the other a wreath. The rest of the floral tributes were garden flowers that people had picked and brought to the church—zinnias, marigolds, gardenias, even a few roses.

Bud and Billy Patterson—the husband and teenage son of Fran's neighbor, Lil—were among the pallbearers. Lil's conversation at lunch had suggested that the other pallbearers were more Bud's friends than Herb Kellogg's. It sounded like Herb had not had too many friends.

When she'd been living in Atlanta, Tory had gone to the funeral of Ned's boss's mother. The pallbearers had been the grandsons and the granddaughters' husbands. There had been more young men than coffin handles so a few of them had just walked behind the casket respectfully. Funerals in Joe's family must be like that.

At least this minister had known her grandfather. Tory imagined that in an increasing number of American funerals, the minister had to say, "Although I didn't know..." If she died tomorrow, that's what hers would have to say.

After a brief service in the graveyard, everyone went back to the church basement where congealed salads and cakes were lined up on tables covered with white vinyl cloths. People wanted to speak to Tory and Marjorie, but no one really knew what to say. Tory couldn't decide if she would rather be here in this basement, smiling an appropriately funeral smile, agreeing that the sermon, turn-out, food and weather had been lovely, just lovely, or if she would rather be back in that little magazine-encircled living room, listening to the TV, trying to think of something to say to her mother and her grandmother.

Actually she knew she would probably be happiest in the parking lot. A good number of the men kept slipping out the church's back door to "get a breath of fresh air." It didn't take long for her to figure out that the "fresh air" probably came in a bottle and was concealed in a brown paper bag.

After the funeral, there was nothing to do but go home, change clothes and eat again. The food had all been brought in by neighbors: ham, fried chicken, deviled eggs. Tory ate half a cup of very mayonnaisey macaroni salad without realizing it. She didn't know what they would have done without the television. Listen to each other chew, no doubt.

"I haven't had any exercise today," she said as soon as they had finished the dishes. "Is it safe to go for a walk?" It was eight o'clock and getting dark.

"What could happen to you here?" Fran answered. "Some high school boys might try to pick you up, but I suppose you could handle that."

Tory thought that she could.

"Would you like me to come with you?" Marjorie asked.

"If you want, I'd love to have you, but I'll be fine alone."

Marjorie admitted she was weary. "I think I'll sit and read for a while."

Tory turned back to Fran. "Do you need anything while I'm out?"

"There's bacon and eggs for breakfast."

"Would you mind if I got some cottage cheese or yogurt?"

"The grocery store's closed," Fran answered, "but there's a dairy case at the gas station. They might have some, but be sure and check the pull date. They sometimes keep things forever at that place. If you need some money, my purse is over there."

Tory said it was okay, she could manage.

It was a warm July night, with a light wind that stirred through her hair and pressed her shirt against her shoulders. A block ahead, white neon spilled out of a cinder block Laundromat, falling on the beer cans and candy wrappers that littered the little parking lot. Three adolescent boys were leaning against a Chevy with a crumpled fender; two more were sitting on the curb. They grew silent as Tory approached, watching her as she passed.

Her mother must have walked this street. She would have dressed carefully, dipping her comb in water as she pulled her hair back into a ponytail. Her skirt would have been a dark circle over layers of white petticoats, and her bobby socks would have been folded so that each sock was exactly like the other. Every scuff would have been polished off the white of her saddle shoes.

The boys in the parking lot would have had hair slicked back in ducktails, T-shirt sleeves rolled over a pack of cigarettes. They wouldn't have been silent as Marjorie passed. They would have known her, been half-afraid of her, thinking she was proud, stuck-up, full of herself.

And she would have been; she must have hated this town, the Laundromat, the dirt speedway, the beer cans, the candy wrappers.

The little store at the filling station would not have been part of Marjorie's walk. It was newer than that. It stocked mostly snack food: barbecued potato chips, nacho cheese taco chips, pillow-shaped bags standing upright in wire racks. The meal-time food was canned or packaged: chili, macaroni and cheese. On the back wall was a bakery rack well-filled for the weekend trade. Tory supposed that by Sunday night, there would only be two or three boxes of doughnuts and a stray package of hot dog buns left. She moved on to the dairy case, glancing past the milk, the onion dip, the American cheese slices. Yes, they had cottage cheese. She picked up a carton. The pull date was for Monday.

Hopefully by Monday, she would be gone.

She paid for the cottage cheese and went back outside. Neon lamps arched over the gas pumps, dropping slabs of light across the oil-spotted pavement. She passed the rack of motor oil, the Coke machine, to what she now realized she had come for—the phone.

She closed the glass door and set her cottage cheese down on the grey ledge next to the phone. She looked at her watch. It would be five-thirty in Oregon. She gave the operator her credit card number and the number of the union hall. Joe might have already gotten back from seeing Max.

He answered.

"Hi, it's me."

"Tory." His voice was quiet, deep…and very much his.

She wasn't sure what to say. She looked out through the glass wall of the phone booth. "How are things at the bar?"

"I'm sure they're fine. Doug should be getting there right about now."

Doug hadn't even started. She had only been gone for twenty-four hours. Why was she calling? "Did Lisa get the clothes all right?"

"Mom says so."

"And you won't forget about Nancy's appointment?"

He didn't answer. Of course he wasn't going to forget; she knew that.

Then he spoke. "Has it been hard?"

"Oh, Joe…" She sank down on the booth's little corner seat. "Mother and Fran, they hardly speak. They don't even look at one another."

"Fran is your grandmother?"

Tory nodded. "Yes, she is…although you wouldn't know it."

"What did you expect?"

"I don't know... At least that they'd be glad to see each other."

"Were you glad to see your mother in April?"

No, she hadn't been. "What are you saying, Joe?"

"I'm not criticizing you."

But he was pointing out something, and he didn't have to say anything more. For the last two years, she had tried to shut Marjorie out of her life just as Marjorie had, with much more success, shut out Fran. And if she continued, she and her mother would end up like this, seeing each other only at funerals.

HER MOTHER WAS SITTING on the front porch, reading a magazine underneath the yellow bug light. "Did you have a nice walk?"

"It wasn't bad. I called Joe."

"Did you?"

Marjorie sounded pleased. Tory sat down on the other chair. "Mother, we split up."

The magazine dropped. "Oh, Tory, no. I'm so sorry. It didn't happen tonight, did it?"

Tory shook her head. "No, it was last spring, late in the spring."

"Baby, what happened?"

"I don't know... it's hard to explain."

"Could you try? I would really like to know."

Tory forced herself, telling her mother about the job in Portland, about how perfect it was for Joe, how he wasn't going to take it, how he was going to stay home with Max.

"And you can't support him in that decision?"

Her question made Tory feel bad. Joe needed her support. "If we could keep things as they were, it would be fine, but he's decided he wants a home again, he wants to be married, have a family, kids, the whole works.''

"And you don't?''

"It's not so much a question of not wanting it, as of . . . well, I haven't exactly had a lot of experience at it.''

"Is that a reason not to try?''

Tory didn't answer. She couldn't.

It was a moment before her mother spoke again. "I don't think you're right, Tory, about not having much experience with families, at least not anymore.''

Tory wasn't sure what she meant. "If you're talking about the Brighams, I really haven't had much to do with them . . . except yesterday when I was getting ready to go. They came through then.''

Her mother was shaking her head. "I wasn't talking about them or even about you and me, but about your own family, the family you've created for yourself.''

Tory stiffened. The family she had created for herself? "I have absolutely no idea what you're talking about.''

"Your grandfather wasn't buried today,'' Marjorie answered. "He's out there in Oregon with a hearing problem. And you've got a brother who's conquered a drug problem and is trying to straighten his life out, and a little sister who's got her first speech therapy appointment tomorrow. You've created a family for yourself. You've even got a baby.''

"A baby?''

"Your dog. Wags, she's your baby. You treat her like a baby.''

"I don't." Just because Marjorie had gone out and gotten herself an annual substitute daughter didn't mean that the whole world did things like that.

"I'm not saying that it's wrong or bad." Marjorie was leaning forward in her chair. "It's actually quite a positive thing. Being a part of a family is important to you, and you are very good at it."

"Or perhaps all these substitutes are the best I can do." It really did seem pathetic, that she had to go out and hire a bunch of people to pretend to be her family.

"Maybe they were a year ago," her mother admitted. "But you aren't giving yourself enough credit .. Oh, Tory, I was so proud of you when I saw you in your bar; it was so successful and you were making people happy and—"

"It's just a bar, Mother. I'm not exactly Albert Schweitzer."

"But maybe Sullivan City doesn't need Albert Schweitzer; it needs you."

Tory shook her head. "You actually believe yourself."

"Yes, I do, and someday I hope you will too." Marjorie stood up. "It's been a long day. Let's go to bed.

Inside the house Fran was watching television.

"Do you want to use the bathroom first?" Marjorie asked.

"No, you go on. I'll sit with Fran for a while." Tory was determined to have some kind of conversation with her grandmother...if only to show her mother she could talk to someone who wasn't on her payroll

Tory sat down on the sofa. Fran's program was one of the prime-time soaps about unhappy rich people

Tory wasn't sure which one it was, she always got them confused. She watched a few scenes, looking at the clothes. When the commercial came on, she spoke.

"Is this a dry county?" she asked, thinking of the "fresh air" and the fact that she didn't recall seeing any bars.

"There's a package store over in the county seat," Fran answered, "but that's it. We're all good Baptists."

"And good Baptists don't drink?"

"Not officially. Don't you know why Southerners drink so much iced tea?"

"I haven't a clue."

"Because it's the same color as bourbon. It makes things very convenient."

Tory laughed.

"Didn't you hear," Fran went on, "people this afternoon saying that you ran a bakery?"

"That I *what*?" Tory sat up, amazed. "A bakery? Where did that come from?"

"Not from me. It sounds like Lil Patterson. She tends to clean things up a bit. I've always been one for putting it like it is, but I figure you've got to let everyone do it their own way."

Putting it like it is... let everyone do it their own way... Tory had been struggling to learn that for two years now. Fran made it sound so simple.

They watched the rest of the program together, this time exchanging comments. It was a rerun so Fran didn't mind talking through it. Tory could guess what the clothes cost, which pleased Fran no end, even though she clearly thought all the characters were unbearably silly and deserved every inch of misfortune that befell them. "I mean," she said after explaining a plot twist to Tory, "would you ever do anything like that?"

Even Tory could profess innocence on that score. "If they're all so crazy, why watch it?"

"Because I'm even sillier than any of them. Now hush up, there's a big love scene up next."

Fifteen

TORY WASN'T SURE what the three of them were going to do with themselves on Saturday. But then she discovered one advantage of having a grandmother. Your grandmother told your mother what to do; your mother told you what to do, and then you didn't have to worry in the least about spare time.

"Let's get these dishes done," Fran said the instant Tory had taken the last spoonful of her breakfast cottage cheese. "I figured that with you all here, it would be a good time to clear out some of Herb's things."

Tory swallowed hastily. "We'd be glad to help."

She thought that they would be folding sport shirts, throwing out unmatched socks, looking through the pockets of a suit or two, and then taking a neat parcel to the Salvation Army. She was wrong.

Her grandmother sent her off to the grocery store for boxes. She had intended to get four or five, but when she identified herself to the owner of the store, he immediately started wedging one box inside another. Soon the trunk of the Cutlass was a brown jigsaw puzzle of carefully arranged boxes.

"That's all I have," the owner said at last, "but I'd guess Dick Fraser down at the drugstore has been saving boxes for Fran all week, the same as I have."

So Tory went to the drugstore...and left with boxes on the back seat, boxes on the floor, boxes on the passenger seat stacked so high that they threatened to topple over on her while she drove home. "We can't possibly need all these," she had protested.

Mr. Fraser had smiled and signaled to his clerk to bring out more boxes. "You didn't know Herb, did you?"

She learned fast. In the backyard was an aluminum-sided, prefab tool shed. It was very neat and very full. In two hours, they threw out seven broken toasters, two broken waffle irons, three electric clocks, five transistor radios, three picture frames with cracked glass, six boxes of folded-up brown paper grocery bags, seven or eight carefully coiled, dangerously frayed extension cords, three shower curtains, a collection of expired North Carolina license plates dating back to the early forties, three spare tires from cars that had been sold years before, five pairs of rusted pruning shears. Herb Kellogg didn't like to throw anything out. Tory now understood the piles and piles of magazines in the house.

Fran and Marjorie packed the boxes. Tory carried the full boxes through the yard, loaded them into the Cutlass and then, on her return trip, brought back more empty boxes. When the Cutlass was full, she started on her grandmother's Buick. Early into the second hour, she thought her arms were going to fall off.

Now why would Herb have saved these? her grandmother would ask. *What did he think he was going to do with a pair of woman's arms?*

Don't ask, her mother would reply as she packed them into a box.

Marjorie and Fran began the day's work as silently as ever. They were both methodical and organized, not moving from a spot until the task there was completed. Tory had always known she had learned to be systematic from her mother; she had never wondered where her mother had learned to be systematic. Now she knew.

The silence between Marjorie and Fran could not last. They had to talk about the packing, who would do what. Marjorie had to ask Fran about something, should she keep it? Then Fran asked Marjorie about her job, and Marjorie asked Fran about some of the people in town. They found it easier to chat when their hands were busy. Eventually they relaxed enough that Tory heard her elegant mother called "Marjie."

At noon, Tory and Fran drove the cars out to the dump while "Marjie" assembled lunch out of the donated food. A group of three teenage boys were hanging around the dump so desperate for something to do that they helped unload the car. Tory wondered if they could adopt one of them. She was sure whatever trouble an adolescent male could cause, however many smelly socks, speeding tickets, wrecked cars, pregnant girls he might generate, it would be worth not having to carry all those magazines out to the car herself.

But they didn't get to the magazines. When they finished the tool shed, they started on the neighbor's tool shed where Herb had also stored stuff. The two cars each made three trips to the dump. Tory had thought she was in good shape, but when she woke up Sunday morning, she felt a great sympathy with the physically disabled. Never in her life had she been so pleased that the Lord had rested on the seventh day. Sitting in church—sitting anywhere—sounded wonderful. She wasn't sure she would even be able to lift the collection plate.

But when church was over, they went right back to work.

The more tired they got, the more natural they became, and the constraint eased with each hour, especially between Tory and Fran. Tory found that she liked her grandmother a great deal. She could understand why Fran and Marjorie had not gotten along when Marjorie was young. Fran was forthright, practical to her soul, not the least sentimental or imaginative, and to a young Marjorie, desperate with dreams, Fran must have seemed hostile and unsympathetic.

But Tory enjoyed Fran's dry wit, her candor, her shrewd insight. In fact, these were the qualities she had been struggling to develop in herself.

In the time since her marriage, Tory had never had a map, she had never known what sort of person she had wanted to be, she had only known that she wanted to be different from what she was. She had changed, but it had been hard; it would have been much easier if she had had a role model, someone from whom she could have taken lessons.

And the irony was that there could have been someone, this grandmother back in North Carolina whom she had never met.

BY MIDAFTERNOON, they had finished with the tool sheds and were ready for the inside of the house. This was a little more difficult as Fran—rather reluctantly, Tory thought—did have to acknowledge that perhaps two percent of what Herb had saved had been worth saving.

When she was taking a break from hauling magazines, Tory idly flipped through one of the "save"
boxes. She picked up an old black-and-white photograph of a family lined up in front of a small, neat
farmhouse. "What's this?" she asked.

"Herb's family," Fran answered. "There he is, and
that's his mother, his father and his two sisters, Edna
and Florence."

"Where are they? Is that their house?"

Fran nodded. "They had a farm northeast of here."

Marjorie looked up. "I didn't know that."

"No, Herb never said much about it. It near killed
him when they lost it."

Tory continued looking at the picture. These were
her relatives, her grandfather, her great-aunts, her
great-grandparents. "When did they lose the place?"

"During the Depression, like everyone else."

Tory was interested, and she kept asking questions
until Fran told her the story.

Both Fran and Herb had grown up on small farms.
Farming was all they knew; it was the life they wanted.
But when Fran was expecting Marjorie, Herb's parents lost their place, and there was no room for them
with Fran's family. They moved here, and Herb found
work in the factory.

"We were lucky to have work at all, no question
about that, but things were never the same. We were
farm folks, and we were raised strict, to be good,
honest people. A lot of folks around here are down
from the mountains, and some of them are right
shiftless, not thinking about tomorrow or planning for
what's to come, not taking care of their places. I don't
know, I could accept it, but Herb, well, he never
could."

"Never?" Tory asked. "You mean all this time he always hated living here?"

Fran nodded. "That's why we only had Marjie. Herb always said he didn't want to have young ones to grow up in a place like this. He didn't want them turning out like the kids from the hills."

Marjorie was listening. Apparently this was a story she had never heard. Now her back was turned again and she was packing another box, but her hands, normally so quick and decisive, were moving slowly, hesitantly.

Then she spoke. "When I got . . . I mean, just before I left, that's what he said to me, that I had turned out like a slutty girl from the hills. He said he never wanted to see me again."

Fran went back to work too. "But you chose to believe him, Marjie. He didn't mean it, but it was what you wanted to hear. Sure there were some rough spots between—"

"Rough spots?" Marjorie whirled, facing her mother. "Rough spots? He *hated* me. I wanted out of here, and he hated me for it. I would read a movie magazine, and he would tell me I was getting uppity. I would buy a lipstick, and he would keep asking me what I hoped to gain from it."

"And you've never forgiven him?"

"No, never." Marjorie slapped together the flaps of her box, picked it up, and then was gone.

The late afternoon light slanted through the window. Their packing had stirred the dust and the air was grainy. Fran was still working. Tory was not. She sat down on the arm of the sofa. "If Herb hated this town so much, why wasn't he more sympathetic to her wanting to leave?"

"He had given up." Fran stopped packing and looked over at Tory. "It's a sad thing when a man gives up at twenty-two, but when we came here, he did. He quit trying to be anything else. And here was Marjorie, hating it all so much. She didn't mean to, but she reminded him of what a failure he was. He resented her for it. She was willing to do anything to get out, and all those years he had done nothing. He couldn't stand being reminded that he had quit, and Marjorie, she didn't quit."

No, Marjorie didn't quit. That's the one thing she had taught Tory, perhaps the strongest lesson that had emerged from all those years of competition, was that you never, not ever, quit. *Don't forget to smile*—yes, it was a message of hypocrisy and pretense, but it also said, "Don't quit."

That was part of what had kept Tory in her marriage—the belief that she shouldn't quit. And she hadn't bought the bar and made plans to leave the coast until she had realized that leaving Ned had not been quitting, but this year of lethargy and purposelessness—*that* had been quitting.

And leaving Joe . . . had that been quitting too?

Tory picked up a box and went outside to find her mother. Marjorie was bent over the trunk of the Cutlass.

She looked up as Tory approached. "Don't you think if we turned all these boxes lengthwise, we could get a few more in?"

Tory started to consider it, then stopped. Who cared how many boxes they could get in? "Mother, are you all right?"

Marjorie glanced away. "Did I make a scene in there?"

"Not by normal standards, but it was a little surprising coming from you. But that's okay; this can't be easy on you."

"I blame him for so much."

"You'd be happier if you could forgive him."

"I wouldn't even know where to start."

Tory looked off to the west. Over the roofs of the little houses she could see the peaks of the Blue Ridge. The sun would soon start to set behind them. "Sometimes it helps me if I try and understand why people have done what they've done. Did you meet Keith, my janitor?"

Marjorie shook her head. "But Joe told me about him."

"Well, he went to Vietnam and it would be a nice, pretty story if he had come back a hero, but he didn't. He picked up a heroin habit. But he came from a miserable home with abusive parents, and then at eighteen he went to this war he didn't understand. Who are we to judge what he did there?"

"It's much easier to forgive someone who hasn't hurt you."

"That's true." *But, Mother, I'm learning to forgive you.*

AFTER SUPPER THAT NIGHT, Tory went back to the gas station and called Joe. Fran's phone was right in the living room.

Everything was fine at home, he reported. Nancy had survived her appointment, and nothing undue had happened at the bar Saturday night. Joe and Max had stopped by Jim's and could attest that Wags was well.

How nice he was. "Is she really? She's not homesick?"

"A little. She seemed awfully glad to see Max, and Debbie says that she's permanently attached to a pair of socks that I guess are yours."

Tory melted. She did miss her own little puppy. "She hasn't forgotten me?"

"Not a chance."

"And what about Lisa? She left this afternoon, didn't she? How did she seem?"

"Fine. She tried on that red dress for us all last night—the one she's going to sing in."

"It's not red, Joe. Do you know what I look like in red? It's raspberry. How did she look?"

"Pretty grown-up."

The dress was sequinned with a slit nearly to mid-thigh. "That's the point. You're supposed to look twenty-eight; even the twelve-year-olds are supposed to look twenty-eight. But seriously, what did you think?"

"I'm her brother and I'm not going to answer that."

Tory laughed. It was good to talk to him. "Then it sounds as if she looked exactly like she's supposed to."

Joe groaned and changed the subject. "How are things out there? What have you been up to?"

"Packing boxes." Tory told him about Herb's accumulated junk. "But it's been interesting. I'm starting to understand my mother better."

"You are?" He sounded pleased.

"This has been hard on her. I'm surprised she was willing to come."

"She probably went because you said you would."

Tory had a feeling that he was right.

"But what about your grandmother?" he continued. "How's she doing?"

"It's hard to tell, but I think she's okay. She had a long time to get ready for him dying, and I think getting rid of all this stuff is sort of cathartic."

"How's she fixed for money?"

Tory stopped. "You know, I don't know."

"Maybe you'd better find out. There could be a lot of medical bills left, and if she's living in a company house, she may have to leave."

"My God, you're right. I'm so glad you thought about that." Tory might not have much experience with families, but she did know you weren't supposed to leave your grandmother on the street.

As soon as she got home, she pulled Marjorie back into their bedroom.

Marjorie had already thought about it. "I know we need to find out. I'd want to help her if she doesn't have enough."

"So would I," Tory agreed. "So would I."

"So you will ask her?" Marjorie suggested smoothly.

"Me?" Tory sat up. "Why me? Why don't you do it?"

"She'll take it better from you."

"Forget it. I only met her three days ago. I can't ask her how much money she has."

"Of course you can."

"Maybe I can, but I won't. She's your mother, not mine. When you get old and grey, I'll have to ask you, and I'm not doing it but once."

"Then we'll ask her together."

"That's not fair," Tory complained, "because I'm going to have to ask you all by myself."

"That's your own fault," Marjorie pointed out. "You could have had a daughter."

THE NEXT MORNING they asked her together. Fortunately Fran took their questions in good part. If she hadn't, she wouldn't have told them a thing.

She proved to be adequately fixed. Herb had been in the hospital throughout his coma so the insurance and Medicare were taking care of the bills. The company was letting her keep the house, her car was paid for, she got Social Security, Herb had had life insurance, and before she retired from the grocery store, she had always saved most of her own paycheck.

"Why haven't you spent some of this?" Marjorie asked, looking up from the passbook.

"What would we have spent it on? We already subscribed to every magazine that was willing to come to North Carolina."

"You could have traveled," Marjorie suggested.

"Herb didn't want to travel."

"You could start now," Tory suggested. Fran had read all the Time-Life books on the regions of the United States, and the only magazine she was asking them to save was the *National Geographic*. That had to mean something.

"Where would I go?" Fran asked. "You aren't going to catch me on one of those buses full of yammering old widows."

"You could," Tory heard herself say, "come back to Oregon with me. I'll put you to work in the bakery."

WHICH WAS HOW Tory found herself in the Charlotte airport on Wednesday morning handing the ticket agent three tickets instead of two.

Fran had never been on a plane before. In fact, Tory and Marjorie had finally gotten her to agree to come to Oregon by accusing her of being scared to fly, a notion she found so insulting that she had to go if only to prove them wrong. They let her have the window seat, and it was soon altogether clear that she was enjoying it much more than she would ever admit.

The three were flying as far as Portland together. From there, Marjorie would go to Seattle, pick up Miss America, and bring her down to the Miss Oregon Pageant at the end of the week.

"You'll let me know how Lisa's doing?" Tory asked her mother while they were en route. Fran had gotten up to go to the rest room simply because, Tory was sure, she wanted to see an airplane rest room.

Marjorie looked up from her magazine. "Of course I will. How do you think she'll do?"

Tory sighed. She wasn't sure. "She hasn't had much performing experience."

"That's important. You really want her to do well, don't you?"

"I don't want her to win. I don't want her to be a beauty queen, but I want her to get a scholarship. That's the only reason she's entered, for the money."

Tory knew that she sounded a little hostile, but her mother answered smoothly. "There's nothing wrong with that. Actually it's better that way. I can see it in the queens. The girls who are using the pageant as a stepping stone to something, those who have some sort of goal—whether it's a singing career or more schooling—have a good year and adjust well afterward. But the girls for whom being Miss America is all they ever dreamed of, they have some trouble the year after their reign. Winning took so much energy and discipline and drive and then suddenly they don't know what to do."

"Mother..."

Marjorie turned a page of the magazine. "If you're asking me if I know which sort you would have been, the answer's yes, I know."

"Mother..."

"And I also now know that all the little-girl pageants don't help. I think there's only been one Miss America who entered many of them, and she didn't start as early as you did. I don't think any nationally successful models or singers entered any of them either. You need performing experience, but that's not the way to get it. Now where's your grandmother? She's been gone a long time."

Tory glanced to the rear of the airplane. Fran was standing in an empty row of the smoking section, intently watching the stewardesses work in the galley.

Fran could take care of herself. Tory was not going to let her mother stop talking about this. "Tell me, how did we get started?"

Marjorie stared at the tray table locked into the seat in front of her. "I was so young when you were born, and I was alone. You were an easy baby, you slept well and didn't fuss, so it was as if you were a doll. I was working in the fabric store and they let me use the sewing machines. I would dress you, and everyone always said that you were the prettiest baby they had ever seen. A customer told me about a contest, and it sounded like fun, going to a different town, meeting new people, and she said she would drive. That's how it got started, it was as simple as that. If she hadn't been willing to drive, I probably wouldn't have gone. But you won, and it was so exciting I kept going to others, and then the contests became the reason to get out of bed in the morning.''

"And you never wondered if it was a good thing to be doing?''

"No, never. I didn't really understand that you were something separate from me, that your needs might be different from mine. I was enjoying it, I liked it, that's all I could see. But—" Marjorie began to sound like she was defending herself "— I never said you were my sister. You said you hated how we were pretending about everything, but I never pretended about that.''

"About what?" Tory wasn't sure what her mother was talking about.

"Other mothers did, you know. When the girls got to be ten or so, they would say that their daughters were their little sisters so people wouldn't think that they had girls that age. No one believed them, but they said it anyway.''

"I did," Tory admitted. "I believed them." In fact, she had always been a little envious of those girls, thinking that she would have liked to have a big sister. But it must have been awful for them to hear their mothers deny them. "And you never yelled at me when I lost.''

"No, I didn't. I knew it would destroy your confidence.''

"Mother, why are you in this job?''

Marjorie paused. "I don't know. At first, I wanted to travel, but now I guess I want the girls to have some perspective on what it means to be Miss America, how it is a wonderful and exciting year, but not necessarily the best year of their lives. I've learned so much I didn't know when you were growing up, things I want to share.''

"It sounds to me like you're punishing yourself," Tory said bluntly. "Staying involved in the pageants, you just keep reminding yourself of . . . well, of all the mistakes you made with me."

Marjorie's eyes met hers, then dropped. This was a new idea. "I did make a lot of mistakes with you."

"Maybe you did, but who wouldn't in your shoes? It seems to me that you should forgive yourself and go on with things."

"What do you mean?"

"Quit this job. Do something that is more than just atonement, do something that will really make you feel good about yourself."

"I don't know what else I would do. This is what I know."

Tory couldn't believe that. "That's not true. You have other skills. You're the most organized, efficient person I know. Don't you remember that one pageant—I don't remember which one it was—but we got there and found that nothing was ready?"

Rehearsals hadn't been organized, the judges had no instructions, there was no one to work the lights, the M.C. had been drinking. Marjorie had pulled Tory out of the pageant and the two of them had organized it. In less than a day and a half, they had made arrangements that should have taken a month. And, Tory thought now, it was probably her favorite of all the pageants.

Her mother was shaking her head. "I don't think my taking out a franchise to stage Little Miss pageants is the best course."

"No, of course not. I meant that you're organized, you can run things. Open a business."

"A business?"

"Why not? I did. You can do it, you know you can."

"I never thought about having my own business."

"Well, think about it."

"I might," her mother answered slowly. "I just might."

TORY HAD CALLED KEITH from Portland and asked him if he could meet the evening plane. He was waiting for them in Sullivan City's little airport. What she didn't expect was that he would bring a friend.

Tory had just spotted him when he jerked and nearly stumbled. Between his legs appeared a soft golden head, a pair of brown eyes and a pink tongue.

"Wags!"

Forgetting baggage, purse and grandmother, Tory dropped to her knees and Wags came rushing toward her, wriggling and squeaking. Tory hugged her, scratched her head, her tummy and her fuzzy little chin, telling her that yes, she was glad to see her, she missed her so much. Had Wags been a good girl? Had she had fun? Wasn't she glad to be going back to her own little puppy home?

"Marjie said you had a dog."

Tory looked up. Her grandmother and Keith were both standing over her. A little embarrassed, Tory stood up and introduced them. Then she turned to Keith. "This is great. I can't believe it. On the plane I was thinking that I might not be able to get her until tomorrow. What ever made you think of it?"

"It didn't take much to figure out you'd want to see her," he pointed out.

On the way into town, Fran sat in the front seat, and
Tory climbed in back with her half-grown animal.
Wags leaned against her and after a while, curled up
on the seat with her head in Tory's lap and let out a
nice, doggy sigh. Tory felt very loved.

"Did anything exciting happen while I was gone?"
she asked Keith.

"The sink behind the bar backed up."

"That's exciting?" Fran asked. "Did I fly all the
way across the country to visit somewhere where a
clogged drain is exciting? I could have stayed home for
that."

"You're supposed to be admiring the scenery,"
Tory told her. "What happened?" she asked Keith.

"Carey Bonner had a snake in his car so he and
Doug got it running in a minute or two. We really need
to get ourselves a good snake; I hadn't thought about
it before."

"Fine. We've been lucky with the plumbing, haven't
we?"

Keith nodded, and Tory started to scratch Wags's
head, thinking fondly of her plumbing...and her
regulars. What if she had been running a fern bar in a
city somewhere? Her clients would be better dressed,
they would have more money, they would have talked
about more interesting things, but would any of them
have carried a plumbing snake in his car?

The parking lot wasn't too full when they turned in;
it was near the end of the suppertime lull. Fran looked
around interestedly, not saying anything, which Tory
now knew meant that she approved. Keith helped
carry the luggage upstairs, but then he left quickly.
The parole board didn't want him around when the
bar was open.

"This is a nice place," Fran said after looking around. "Where do I sleep?"

"The sofa in the office makes out into a bed." A bed that had never been used because in the entire time she had been in Sullivan City, Tory had never had an overnight guest, except Joe. "We'll have to put some sheets on it. I didn't know you were coming."

"You didn't know I existed," Fran pointed out. "But why don't we make up some iced tea first?"

So like good Southerners, they brewed up a pitcher of iced tea. Or rather Fran brewed while Tory apologized for not having pink sugar and for having only herbal teas. "We'll go to the grocery store first thing tomorrow morning," she promised.

"We certainly will." Fran had already examined one or two of the strange packages Tory had sent in from a health food store in Portland and dismissed them with a crisp "You call these food?"

As soon as they had Fran settled, Tory said that she should run down to the bar for a few minutes. "Just to see how everything is. Would you like to come or will you be all right here? I won't be gone long."

"I'll be fine. I'm going to sit down, have a glass of iced tea, and look at pictures of you."

Tory had been getting the tea out of the refrigerator. She stopped. "Pictures of me?"

"What's so funny about that? I am your grandmother. That's what grandmothers do, isn't it?"

"I don't really know."

"Well, I do. I've looked at enough pictures of other people's granddaughters. I figure it's my turn."

Tory put some white sugar in a bowl, set it, a glass and the pitcher on Max's tray, and carried them all into the living room. "I really don't have any...

Mother has all the baby pictures and such, even my wedding album, I think. All I have is one book of pageant glossies, but they're pretty silly.''

"Haul them out. I'm not fussy."

Tory had stowed the album on the upper shelf of a closet. When she returned to the living room with it, Fran was examining Max's tray.

"A little boy I know made that," Tory explained.

"He did a nice job. Who is he?"

Tory decided to ignore the second half of that remark. "I think his father helped him a lot." She handed Fran the book. "Here's my life . . . both as a blonde and as a brunette."

TORY'S ABSENCE HAD NOT AFFECTED the size of the Wednesday evening crowd at all. There were plenty of customers, and everyone was delighted to see her. Pete Miller waved; Doug Brigham came out front and shook hands with her. He certainly did look like Joe.

"I heard you were coming back tonight," he said. "I wasn't sure if you wanted me to come in."

"No, I'm glad you did; I just popped in for a second . . . but how did you hear I was coming back?"

"My cousin Jim's wife said that Keith picked up your dog this afternoon."

"Oh, of course." Every Brigham on earth would know that she was back. "How did things go? Did you have a good time?"

"I had a terrific time. In fact," he confessed, "I'm a little sorry that you're back."

"Actually my grandmother came with me, and it would be nice if I had some extra time for the next week or so. Is your wife about to shoot you for never being home?"

He shook his head. "I'm not the only person in town working two jobs, and Katie's a good sport. She knows I'm having fun. Except I can't be here Sunday afternoon. My family's having its annual picnic, and I need to put in an appearance."

"I thought you all were doing that last weekend."

"I did too," Doug admitted. "But, believe me, the men do not make these decisions."

Tory laughed and let him go back to work. As she waited for Nancy to have a free moment, she watched him. Everyone liked him. He was cheerful, relaxed, easy-going. He wasn't as fast as she and Pete Miller were, but he was faster than she had been after one week of tending bar... and she had been to bartending school. Tory wondered if he would quit the mill and come work for her full-time.

Finally Nancy came over. She was fine. The day-care job was wonderful. Yes, Joe had driven her to Klamath Falls last Saturday. She was going by herself this week. No, she hadn't minded it. The therapist was a nice lady. She had been, Nancy added shyly, very impressed at the kind of jobs Nancy had.

They didn't talk very long; Nancy still believed that the sun wouldn't rise tomorrow if a customer at Tory's had to wait to be served. Tory went around to the tables, chatted briefly with some people, and then left. Outside she automatically glanced around the parking lot even though she already knew who was here.

Except there was one surprise, one dark green Cherokee Jeep. Tory looked up at her apartment suspiciously. She went up the stairs and eased the door open.

Her grandmother was speaking. "—always wondered if things would have been different if we'd had a union."

Tory heard a little thud and the jingle of Wags's tags. "Oh," she heard Fran say, "Tory must be back."

Wags came trotting around the corner, her tail wagging happily. Tory patted her for a second and then went into the main room.

Joe stood up. He was wearing a sport coat over his jeans; he must have been to a meeting. "Hello, Tory."

"Hello, Joe."

It felt odd—just as it had at the airport last week—to see him without touching him, to say hello without running her hand up his back, without having him crook his arm around her neck and kiss her hair.

"I heard you were coming back this evening," he said.

"Because Keith picked up Wags?" she asked.

"Of course."

There was a second iced tea glass on the coffee table. Someone had taken the sugar bowl off the tray, and the tray was sitting at the edge of the table. Apparently it had been emptied, picked up, and discussed. Tory glanced over at her grandmother. Fran was sitting back, watching them with a bland expression that Tory did not trust for one instant. She knew that as soon as Joe left, the questions would start.

"I take it you met my grandmother," she said to Joe.

"Yes," he said. "We've been having a nice talk."

That was exactly what Tory was afraid of. Oh, well, what could she do? "What do we hear from Lisa?" she asked. "I tried to call you Tuesday, but I couldn't seem to track you down."

"She says she's fine."

"Is that all? Just that she's fine?"

"No, there's more…wait a second, I took notes for you." He reached into his breast pocket and pulled out a small spiral notebook. As he flipped through it, looking for the right page, Tory started to tell Fran who Lisa was, but Fran already knew. Tory wondered what else she had learned.

Joe found his notes. "Miss Gold Beach is very pretty so is Miss Medford. Miss Corvallis isn't. Miss Portland has terrific clothes, but no better than Lisa's. A whole bunch are already in college, but not Miss… Do you need to hear all this?"

Tory would have liked to. "No. How did rehearsals go?" Rehearsals had been Monday, Tuesday and today. The first round of actual competition would be on Thursday, the second on Friday and the finals were scheduled for Saturday night.

"Fine, I guess. Lisa says that she was feeling like she was the only person who hadn't had, quote, a thousand years of ballet lessons, but then when she saw some of the other girls try the dance steps, she decided either they were lying or the lessons hadn't taken real well."

Tory laughed. "I'm glad it didn't rattle her too much, and the dances won't be hard. They never are."

"Maybe for *you* they weren't."

All in all, it sounded like Lisa was having an absolutely wonderful time, meeting everyone, walking up and down the beach. She was really glad, Joe reported her as saying, that she wasn't supposed to win because there were girls who wanted to win, and they were tense and nervous and not having a good time at all. "She says that she's sorry they're competing with each other; she wishes they were all just getting together to have fun."

What a good way to feel. "Mother's going to be there. She says she'll call and let us know how Lisa's doing."

"That's nice of her." Joe stood up. "Now I've got to be going. Gil Jenkins, our field rep, is in town tonight."

The field rep...the one who had offered him the Portland job. Tory got up too. "I'll call you as soon as I hear from Mother."

"Okay." Joe turned to Fran. "Good night, Mrs. Kellogg. It was nice to meet you."

Fran smiled blandly. "Why don't you walk him down to his car, Tory?"

Walk him down to his car? Was Fran worried that he couldn't manage the steps alone? Tory glanced over at him. He was trying not to smile...and, she would like to point out, not trying hard enough. "Come along, child," she said. "We can't have you taking a tumble."

She didn't say anything once they were outside. Being silent was usually his trick, but she was going to get there first this time.

"Your grandmother was looking at your pictures," he finally said.

"She claimed that that's what grandmothers do."

"Yes, but those?" Clearly he was remembering how much the pictures had upset her at Christmas.

Christmas was a long time ago. "They were all I had... I bet you were a little surprised when she answered the door."

They were at the Cherokee now. "It wasn't exactly what I'd expected," he admitted. "But she seems great."

"She is."

"So you're glad you went?"

"I'm very glad I went."

"Then I'm glad too...even though—" He stopped.

"Even though what?"

"I don't know...I guess it just seemed like you were gone for more than a week."

THE NEXT MORNING Tory and Fran went into town. "You have a fabric store," Fran noticed. "That's nice. I wish we had one."

"Do you want to go in?"

"Do they have yarn?"

"I don't know. We don't have a knitting shop so they probably do."

"Good. I haven't knit a thing since Herb's first stroke." And before Tory knew what was happening, she was in the store with her arms stretched out, being measured for a sweater.

Two years ago, she would have strangled anyone who had done this—pulled her into a shop and told her to hold out her arms. It was like being a life-sized Barbie doll again. But that was two years ago; now she thought it was funny.

As soon as they got home, Tory called Joe. "Have you heard anything more from Lisa?"

"Not yet. Why don't I have her call you directly?"

"Would you?"

So early Friday morning Lisa called. "I hope you don't mind," she said right away, "my calling collect, that is. But Joe said I should call you and that you wouldn't mind, but that he would pay you back if you did."

"It's fine. I'm delighted you called. How is everything?"

"Oh, wonderful, just wonderful. And thank you for the flowers. They were really beautiful—I mean, *roses*—they're so expensive, you shouldn't have. But let me tell you about the best thing that just happened, the very best thing . . . you aren't going to believe this, and it didn't just happen once, but twice. Two times. Isn't that incredible?"

"I'm sure it is," Tory said politely.

"Oh, what a nitwit." Lisa laughed at herself. "I haven't even told you what it is, have I? This morning, one of the other high-school girls—it was Miss Medford—asked me where I was going to college, and of course I said that I didn't know yet. Then she said that if I decided to come to Eugene—like I would *decide* not to if there was the least chance that I could— anyway, she asked me if I wanted to be her roommate . . . her *roommate*. Isn't that wonderful?"

"Yes. Yes, it is." Nothing would make Lisa's adjustment to college easier than knowing that someone wanted to room with her.

"And then just an hour later, Miss Willamette Valley asked me the same thing, but she's going to Lewis and Clark, and of course, I didn't even apply there because it's so expensive, and I told her that flat out. I'm not pretending to be rich . . . even though lots of people think I am because of your clothes, but I tell them they aren't mine."

As a pet-quality human being, Tory approved of Lisa admitting that the clothes weren't hers; as a beauty pageant trainer, she thought it was a terrible idea. But still she was delighted that Lisa seemed so happy.

"Was that Joe's sister?" Fran asked when Tory hung up.

"Yes. What would you like to do today?"

"He certainly seems like a very nice young man."

They had been through this. "He is, but he's not *my* very nice young man."

"Did I say that he was?" Fran asked innocently.

Tory made a face at her.

Tory went back to work that afternoon. People were happy to see her, and it was good to be back. Doug Brigham came in just as the evening crowd was arriving so she took an hour off to have supper upstairs with Fran. She usually ate standing up in the storeroom, hurriedly swallowing some yogurt and a few unsalted nuts. Taking a regular dinner break probably made sense.

"Are you sure you don't want to come downstairs?" she asked when they were finished.

Fran sniffed. "No. I'm not one of these old people who can't tell when they aren't wanted."

"Mother came."

"She did?"

"Yes, Joe brought her."

"Joe?" Fran began to pick up her knitting. Apparently anything Joe Brigham suggested was to be acted upon unquestioningly.

Tory installed Fran at a corner table and, although it was too dark for her to knit, she had a splendid time, watching and listening. Tory's regulars had all found Marjorie intimidating, but Fran looked exactly like a grandmother was supposed to look. Pleased that Tory had an approachable relative, some of them went over and spoke to her. Because it was Friday, there were more women in the bar; a few of them even sat down and talked to Fran for a while.

At nine the people going to the late movie started to leave. Tory was making change for them when Doug called her to the phone. She had to turn away from the room and put her hand over her other ear to hear.

The call was, as she had hoped, from her mother. "Are you and Mother getting along?" Marjorie asked.

"We're fine. She's knitting me a sweater. But tell me," Tory asked quickly. "How's Lisa doing?"

"She's very pleased. I just listened to her sing, and one of the organizers told me that she looked very good in the swimsuit yesterday. She herself said that her interview went very well. She will make ten without any problem at all."

Ten wasn't good enough. The money started at five. "She's not going to be one of the runners-up?"

Her mother paused. "Oh, Tory... her inexperience showed in the song. She was too conscious of being judged."

Tory bit her lip. She had worried about that; Lisa just didn't have the experience. Other girls would have been in piano and ballet recitals since age five. "So it's going to keep her out of the money?"

"I'm afraid it will." Marjorie's voice was gentle. "She'll do great next year, she really will have an excellent chance then."

"But she needs that scholarship now."

"I'd talk to her about the song if I thought it would help, but I imagine it would only make her that much more self-conscious when she does it again tomorrow night."

"Yes, I guess it would."

Tory thanked her mother and hung up. She turned back to the bar and tried to get to work.

She remembered what it was like. She remembered when her name had been called for second runner-up, that awful moment when she had known she had lost, that awful, numb moment when all she could think about was that she had to keep smiling.

This would happen to Lisa tomorrow night. One minute she would still have a chance, she would still be thinking about college, about going to Eugene and rooming with Miss Medford, and the next minute she would be left standing in the line with the four other girls who hadn't even made runner-up. It would be—

"I'm going to get another keg."

Tory looked up. It was Doug. "Fine."

He looked at her closely. "Are you all right?" He sounded concerned.

"Oh, yes. I'm fine." She tried to smile. "Maybe I'm a little tired. I guess I'm still on East Coast time."

She watched Doug hoist the empty keg to his shoulder. He grinned at something someone said, the quick expression making the standard Brigham face seem entirely his own. Doug was good at this. It was exactly right for him. He could make people laugh, he could make them feel welcome.

But he had not sought this job, he had not come to Tory, asking her if he could try it. Doug Brigham would have worked out his thirty years at the mill, without ever considering anything else, without knowing how to consider anything else. He had been programmed for a particular niche and would have stayed there if Joe hadn't handed him a way out.

Was this going to happen to Lisa? Would she come home from the pageant, feeling like a failure? Would she get a job at the K mart, then get married, and in a few years be washing her kids' mouth out with soap? That couldn't happen. Tory wouldn't let it. She simply wouldn't. She reached for the phone.

It was too noisy in here. She would go upstairs. She looked around for Doug; he was still back in the storeroom. She went over to Pete. "Can you and Doug manage alone for a while?"

"What's that?"

She said it again, louder.

"Sure. Take your time."

On her way out, she stopped by her grandmother's table. "Mother just called. Joe's sister isn't doing as well as we had hoped. I'm going to run upstairs and call him. I'll be right back."

"Why don't you go see him?"

"See who? Joe?"

"You shouldn't trust important things to the phone."

"Oh, Fran..." Now was not the time for matchmaking. "I'm going to call."

But as soon as she was outside, she realized that Fran was right. It would be better to see Joe. Did she have her keys? Yes. Did she know where he lived? No. How could she not know where he lived? What kind of relationship had they had that she didn't know where he lived? What had been wrong with her?

There was a pay phone in the entryway. She jerked open the phone book. God, but there were a ton of Brighams. *Frank, Henry, Hugh, Jr., Hugh, Sr., James, John, Jr., Mrs. John, Sr. Here we go: Joseph.*

Well, curse the man. There were three Joseph Brighams. Why couldn't he have his own name?

The door to the bar opened. Carey Bonner and John Steckler came out. They were surprised to see her. She didn't care what they thought. "Listen, guys, do you know where Joe lives?"

"Sure," John answered. "He's renting one of Dr. Hobart's places. It's on Hoover, between Fifth and Sixth."

"Do you know the number?"

"No, but it's grey, I think...or white. But it's the one right next to the schoolyard. You'll recognize his car."

Yes, she would.

JOE'S HOUSE was little, even smaller than the one Dennis and Marianne lived in. It did indeed border on the playground of an elementary school. It must be awfully noisy, but Tory didn't suppose Joe was there enough to mind.

She walked up to the door slowly, hoping that she wasn't making a mistake by coming here without calling. But she had been home for two days. She would have heard if Joe's life now included a woman who spent Friday evenings at his house.

She knocked. The door had a little window at eye level, and as the door knob turned, she looked through it, expecting to see Joe. She didn't, which was odd.

The door opened. "Tory!"

She looked down. Joe did have a Friday night date—Max. He had opened the door and was already turning away from her, shouting over his shoulder excitedly, "It's Tory, Dad. Look, it's Tory."

"Ask her in."

The house had no foyer and Tory could see Joe standing up from the sofa to greet her. Max's puppy had been sleeping on his foot. She rolled over, blinking and confused.

A board game was spread out on the coffee table. They must have been playing it when she knocked. "That's Monopoly, isn't it?" Tory asked. She couldn't think of anything else to say.

"Yeah, and it's *stupid*," Max announced. "Really stupid. Stupid Monopoly. Stupidopoly. That's what I'm going to call it. Stupidopoly." Max started stamping around the room, chanting "Stupidopoly, Stupidopoly." The puppy scooted over and started barking at his heels. She still had a high-pitched, little puppy yip.

How could you talk to a man when his son was stamping around the room, chanting "Stupidopoly"?

"That's enough, Max."

"But, Dad…" Max sank down to the floor, his face red. "It's a stupid game."

"Maybe it is. We don't have to play it anymore. Anyway, it's bedtime."

"Oh, Dad…Tory just got here."

"You can talk to her some other time."

"But I want to talk to her now. We never go see her anymore."

"Max." Joe's voice was low, but Tory felt sure if he ever spoke to her like that, she would do exactly as she was told.

"Do you need to take him home?" she asked. "I can come back."

"No, Max gets to spend the night here tonight. And," Joe added pointedly, "he promised Mommy he would go to bed without a fuss."

Max didn't say anything, he looked fierce and determined, but he started to stalk out of the room.

"Max," Joe reminded him. "You need to see if Tory has to go outside."

"Outside? Why would I—" Tory stopped. Joe had been talking about the dog.

Max frowned and shifted course, moving into the kitchen. "Come on, Tory." The puppy scampered after him.

The human Tory heard the back door open. "What's wrong with Monopoly?" she asked Joe softly.

"It's my fault. The game's too hard for him. You know Max, he's never going to admit that, so the game's stupid."

In a minute Max and the dog were back inside.

"How did she do?" Joe asked.

"Just number one," Max reported.

"That's fine. Did you put newspapers down in your room?"

Max nodded and Joe pointed toward the little hall that probably led to the bedrooms. Max moaned, picked up his dog, and marched off.

Tory looked at Joe, wondering how to start.

"I'm taking my shirt off," Max shouted from the other end of the house.

"Good for you," Joe called back. "I think," he told Tory, "we're about to get a play-by-play of Max getting ready for bed."

And they did. Every few seconds, Max shouted that he was doing something else, taking off his shoes, his socks, his jeans, putting on his pajamas, brushing his teeth. These activities were accompanied by generous sound effects. Other conversation was impossible.

"This is going to bed without a fuss?" Tory asked.

"For Max it is."

At last Max announced that he was in bed. Joe stood up. "I'll go say good-night to him. It will just take a minute."

"Don't rush."

Tory sat down and waited, listening to the low murmur of Joe's voice and the diminishing decibles of Max's. She looked around the living room. It was barren, nearly ugly. Joe didn't belong here.

But he knew that. He didn't belong, but he was staying.

"Tory?"

She looked up. Joe was standing just inside the hall, speaking softly. "Would you mind coming in to say good-night to Max? He asked if you would."

She stood up. "I'd be glad to."

Max's room was nearly dark, but there was light coming in from the hall, and plugged into the outlet closest to his cot was a small night light.

How odd, that Max, with all his bravado and daring, should be afraid of the dark. But that was all right, he was still a little boy. Tory looked down at him. He was lying on his side in a sleeping bag; his six-year-old body didn't do much more than put a big wrinkle in it. The other Tory was curled up like a kitten, asleep on his discarded shirt.

She knelt down next to the cot. "Good night, Max," she said softly.

"Good night, Tory." His voice was light, a child's voice. He nestled into his pillow. "That's funny, both your names being Tory."

"I like it," she answered.

"How's Wags?"

"She's fine. You and Tory will have to come see her."

"When can we come?"

"Soon," she promised. "Next week."

"Do you mean that? You aren't just saying it?"

"No, I mean it." And as she looked at him, at his light blue Brigham eyes, eyes that were asking for assurance, Tory finally realized why Max had named his dog after her.

She heard Joe come stand behind her. "Max," he said, "it's time for you to go to sleep now."

"Will you leave the door open?"

"A crack."

As they walked back down the narrow hall, Tory was very aware of Joe, the way the cuff of his dark T-shirt fit across his biceps, the way his hair fell down his forehead. In a moment, he would push it back. He always did.

"Can I get you something to drink?" he asked when they were in the living room.

"No, I'm fine."

They both sat down. Joe leaned back, his arms hooked over the back of the sofa, his legs crossed, waiting patiently, silently, for her to say why she had come.

"Max minds that we split up, doesn't he?"

"Yes."

How like him, to answer so simply, so honestly. "I never thought about that happening."

"I imagine that the divorce affected him more than we knew. He may worry about losing people, about his life becoming fragmented."

"I wish it hadn't happened like this," she said.

Joe shrugged. "It was you who thought meeting him wasn't such a good idea. I was the one pushing for it. I don't know... I guess I was like a kid; I never thought about us splitting up."

His tone was quiet, even, and he had tilted his head back, looking up at the ceiling as if he didn't find any of this interesting or important, but Tory knew better. He felt it very deeply. She didn't know what to say—there wasn't anything to say.

Then she remembered why she had come. "I talked to my mother this evening. Lisa's going to lose."

Joe turned his head, looking at her. "Lose?"

"Well, not *lose* lose. She'll make ten, but not five."

"People around here won't call that losing."

"But she will and she won't be getting any money."

Joe didn't say anything for a moment. "Is your mother sure? How does she know?"

"She just does." Tory had complete confidence in her mother's judgment on this. "She says that Lisa's having trouble with her song. She's thinking about the judges as authority figures, not people to be wooed, enticed. That takes experience, and I knew she didn't have that kind. Anyway the point is that she's going to come back here thinking like she's failed. She won't have the money to go to college, she won't have the confidence that comes from doing well."

"Lisa may think she's done well; I think she has. This is her first time away from home alone; she hasn't been homesick or scared. I think she's doing terrific."

"Yes, but, Joe, you don't know what it's like to lose a beauty pageant ... And what about the scholarship money? She wants to go to college."

Joe started to pick up the Monopoly game, scooping up the little silver-colored roadster and terrier that had been their pieces. "And she still can."

"But how? She's not going to get this scholarship."

"She has lots of other options." Joe was sorting the pastel-colored money. "There are community colleges, work-study programs, all sorts of things we didn't know about before. Next year won't be easy, but I'll chip in something and I'd bet that Jim and Mom and Dad, and maybe even Frank, would too. And after that, the union has a couple of really good scholarships. If Lisa applies for one next year, she's bound to get one—I looked up the winners this year, she's got a much better record than they did."

This was the Joe that Tory knew ... the Joe she had loved. Joe with his manner so calm, so offhand, his method so determined, so enterprising. He was going to make sure that Lisa got to college.

And she knew that she had been afraid he wouldn't be like this. That was why she had come tonight. She had been afraid that he had started to persuade himself that Sullivan City wasn't so bad, that he would say that if it were good enough for him, it was good enough for Lisa, that he was starting to sink back into the bog of Brigham conformity.

But she had been wrong. He wasn't her grandfather; he wasn't going to quit as Herb Kellogg had. Lisa might be the first Brigham to get out of Sullivan City, but Joe was going to be the second ... and Max the third.

Joe was picking up the property cards. Mediterranean with its royal purple band was on top—Mediterranean, the cheapest property on the board. Tory watched as he straightened the cards with a quick tap, snapped a rubber band around them, and placed them in their little compartment.

She must have touched him—she didn't know—but when he sat back, one arm closed around her, and she leaned against him. His other hand touched her face. He was kissing her. And however the kiss may have started, it soon grew slow and dizzying just as kisses always did when Joe—

He stopped, lifting his head, taking his arm away. He cleared his throat and then spoke. "I'm sorry."

It was a moment before Tory could speak. "Don't be."

"Max is here," he explained. "Marianne would shoot me if he went home with tales of how you spent the night."

What unending compromises he had to make. Each day must be full of such moments, when he set aside his own wishes to do what would fit in. Tory wondered how he could stand it, but she knew that he could, that he would go on standing it for another three or four years until that little boy sleeping in the next room needed him less.

And he shouldn't have to do it alone.

"Maybe Marianne would think he was talking about his dog," Tory said.

He smiled. "She'd ask if I put newspapers down . . . and anyway, what would your grandmother say if you stayed out all night?"

Tory had a feeling that she would be thrilled.

Joe walked her out to her car. The neighborhood was quiet, and the low mass of the school building was a dark shape in the warm July night. As she started the car, she looked at Joe. Over his head, through the power lines, she could see the stars.

_____ *Seventeen* _____

SATURDAY MORNING Tory went down to the bar to talk to Keith about Doug Brigham. Keith was not around during operating hours, but he cleaned up the next morning, and that told him a lot. "There's your good-time clutter," he would say, "and then there's your rowdy clutter." Some people read tea leaves; Keith read clutter.

The clutter-meter reported only good things about Doug, and Tory went back upstairs, knowing that this little substitute family of hers was about to get a new uncle. That was good; being a single parent had been tiring.

"You got a call," Fran said as soon as she was inside. "It was Mrs. Brigham."

That was hardly enough. "Which Mrs. Brigham?"

"Joe's mother."

Tory had met June Brigham at the Miss Sullivan City Pageant and since January had spoken to her on the phone when calling Lisa. "I wonder what she wanted."

"To invite us to a picnic tomorrow. A Fourth of July picnic. I guess they have one every year and they got rained out this time."

It sounded like this phone call had gone on for a lot longer than it should have. "I know that, but why is she inviting us?"

"Because it's now a 'Welcome Home' thing for Lisa... I said we'd go."

"Fran! You did what? But I have to work!"

"Now, Tory," Fran said with what she probably hoped was a pathetic air. "Don't you want me to meet some other senior citizens? Don't you want me to have some friends to talk about dentures with?"

There was a wolf hiding somewhere inside this grandmother. "I do not."

Fran gave up on the pathos. "Well, it's too late now," she said briskly, "so get your purse. We need to run into town. I said we'd bring potato salad."

Tory supposed that anyone who had once worn sequins on her rear end had no right to complain about being forced to do strange things, but Sunday morning felt bizarre indeed. She started off by apologizing for not belonging to a church and then spent the rest of the morning peeling and slicing potatoes for a nice bowl of potato salad.

Her mother had indeed been right about the pageant. Joe called Tory at the bar after midnight on Saturday to report that Lisa had phoned home. She had indeed been in the top ten, but not the top five.

"But my family's thrilled," he added.

"I hope someone's prepared in case she's not."

"I suggested to Dad that maybe he and I should go to the airport to get her instead of leaving Margaret Sumner to bring her home, and your coming to this picnic will help a lot."

He had probably known that she was going to the picnic before she had known it herself.

Sunday afternoon was supposed to be clear and warm, the sort of day that was lovely for human beings, but not so good for bars—people were going to do their drinking in their backyards. Tory knew that Pete and Nancy could manage without her. So at one o'clock, she took off the white shorts she had been peeling potatoes in and, telling her thighs that they should pretend to have nice, dimply saddlebags, put on a sundress.

"That's a pretty dress," Fran said. "You don't wear many dresses, do you?"

"Not anymore." Tory suspected that she owned high heels and a handbag that had been dyed to match this dress, but that was a suspicion she didn't care to verify. "Are you ready?"

Fran said she was, and Tory picked up the aluminum-foil-covered bowl of potato salad. "What did you put in here?" she asked. "It weighs a ton."

"It's that blame bowl; that's what's making it heavy. You need some Tupperware."

The "blame" bowl was hand-thrown pottery with an intricate three-color glazing. Tory had paid a startling amount of money for it at a crafts fair out on the coast. It was beautiful, but she supposed that Fran was right. There are moments in life that call for Tupperware.

Tory was standing by the front door, waiting for Fran to come open it; the potato salad took both arms. "What are you looking for, Grandmother dear?"

"Wags's leash. Where did we put it?"

"You weren't planning on taking her, were you?"

"Of course. Everybody takes dogs to these things."

Tory guessed that Fran knew more about "these things" than she did, and anyway, she was always happy to have an excuse to take Wags places. The problem, she discovered four minutes later, was that when she had bought her M.G., she had never antici-

pated that one day she would be hauling a dog, a bowl
of potato salad and a grandmother. There was barely
room. Fran held the potato salad, and Wags, who was
getting to be a big girl, had to sit in the little well behind the seats. Wags hated that and kept trying to
creep around the gear shift so she could sit in the potato salad. Fran swatted her, and chastened, Wags
more or less stayed where she belonged. She hunched
forward, resting her chin on Tory's shoulder, and
moaned all the way into town. It was not a particularly relaxing drive.

North Park was crowded and full of Brighams. A
team of them was spread across the softball diamond
with another team at bat; many of the players had
light brown hair. Some girls were playing hopscotch.
Other people were playing horseshoes and catch.
Three barbecue grills had been set up, and a man and
a boy were setting up a fourth. Some streamers with
brightly colored triangular flags, the kind used for
filling station openings, were strung up between the
trees. Between some other trees hung a banner—Welcome Home, Aunt Lisa—painted in green tempera
paint. The green changed hues several times, signaling the moments when the artists had had to mix new
paint.

A woman hurried over to the car to greet them. It
was June Brigham, Joe's mother. Tory introduced her
to Fran.

"Bob and Joe are picking Lisa up at the airport,"
June said. "They should be back any minute. So why
don't you take that bowl over to the tables and I'll introduce your grandmother around."

The picnic tables were already crowded with plastic
containers and foil-covered casseroles, and there was

a cluster of ice chests under one tree. "This is potato salad," Tory said to a woman who seemed to be as much in charge as anyone.

"Here, set it right here," said the woman, un- doubtedly either a Mrs. Brigham or a former Miss Brigham. "Oh, my, what a beautiful bowl. I do hope it doesn't get broken."

"It won't be the end of the world if it does," Tory answered. And it would serve her right for bringing it to a picnic.

Tory was surprised at how many people she recog- nized. There were a few people who came into the bar occasionally. They didn't look like Brighams; they must have married Brigham girls. The two men who had picked up extra money by painting the bar before she opened it were playing horseshoes. The teenage boy who loaded her groceries into the car was wres- tling a Frisbee away from her shampoo girl.

"Tory! Tory!"

It was Max. He broke away from a group of other children and came running over to her. His puppy was scampering behind him; the pair of them were tied to- gether with a cord that went from Max's belt to the puppy's neck. Tory wondered how many people they had tripped.

"Tory! Tory! This is *great*!" He stopped in front of her. "No one said you were coming. Look, Tory has a collar."

Tory looked down. Her namesake's end of the cord was attached to a bright blue collar that had a little bell on it.

"It's a cat collar," Max announced proudly. "We couldn't find a dog collar that was small enough. How come you didn't bring Wags? You should have. She would have had a *great* time."

"I did. My grandmother has her."

"Your grandmother? You have a grandmother?"

He couldn't have been as surprised about it as she had been. "Yes, she's over there." Tory pointed at her grandmother just in time to see Fran bend over and unfasten Wags's leash. Tory watched with a sick feeling, but Wags headed straight for a group of other dogs, not straight for the street as Tory had feared.

"Oh, good," Max exclaimed, "we'll go see her. Tory will like that. Come on, Tory, let's go see Wags."

Tory grabbed his shoulder, stopping him. "Is your mother here?"

"Sure, she's around here somewhere." And with that helpful remark, he raced off.

Tory looked around and soon spotted Marianne sitting on a lawn chair talking to a woman Tory didn't know. She started toward them, but was intercepted by Doug. He wanted her to meet his wife, Katie. She chatted with them for a while. Then Debbie joined them, once again thanking Tory for the steaks she had sent.

When she had been in North Carolina, Tory had wondered what she could do for Jim and Debbie to thank them for keeping Wags. She had mentioned it to her mother, and Marjorie had said she knew of a place in Nebraska that air-freighted wonderful steaks. Tory had called Nebraska, and Jim and Debbie were now the proud owners of twelve six-ounce filet mignons.

"Will you hush up?" Tory admonished Debbie now. "I was so happy you could take her."

"I heard that you brought your grandmother back with you. That was nice of you."

Tory glanced around the park, looking for Fran. She was standing at the food table with a few other women, one of whom was bent over the table, writing something. They were probably exchanging recipes.

Fran did not need any help. She fit in better than Tory did. So Tory did exactly what Tory wanted to do, which was to settle down with Debbie for a long chat about dogs.

They were good people, these Brighams—generous, conscientious, kind. Their dreams, their interests seemed paltry and materialistic to Tory; they talked about boats and cars, they wanted microwaves and dishwashers. There was no self-analysis, no introspection. They were uneasy with outsiders, uncomfortable with the different, unlikely to do more with their lives than their parents had done. Although she admired, even envied their family spirit, she did not want to be like them.

But then there wasn't much danger of that, was there?

Debbie and Tory were soon interrupted by a shout. Lisa was coming. Lisa was coming.

A Buick pulled into the empty space in front of the fire hydrant. The passenger door opened. Joe got out, opening the back door for Lisa. Tory stood on her toes, trying to see the girl's expression, but she was engulfed with people hugging and kissing her.

Then Debbie pointed. "Who is that?"

Tory looked. And stared. "Good God, it's my mother."

Mother? What was she doing here?

Marjorie was coming around the back of the car, chatting pleasantly with Joe's father. Tory hurried over. "Mother!" She still didn't believe it. "What—I didn't expect you."

"No, and I wasn't planning on coming, but my month was up—you know we always switch around the fifteenth—and I couldn't help thinking that it was silly for me to go back to South Carolina when you and your grandmother were here. I just decided for sure this morning, and so—"

Marjorie did not sound like herself. Tory interrupted. "I'm glad you came. I wish I had thought of it myself." Suddenly she stepped forward. If she could hug her dog, she could hug her mother. "It really is good to see you."

And it was.

"Now tell me about Lisa. How is she?" Tory looked over at the girl. She was still surrounded.

"I can't really tell. She's been quiet, but she may be tired. You'll have to talk to her later. Now where's your grandmother? Is she all right?"

That was a little like asking if Mt. Rushmore were all right. "She's fine. She's over there." Tory pointed over to the tables. Fran was now shooing some children away from the desserts. "But let me speak to Joe first."

"Of course." Marjorie moved off quickly, not about to interfere with such a moment.

Tory turned toward Joe, but his father was handing him the car keys, obviously asking him to park the car.

Oh, great. Here you get all steamed up to say something nice to a man, to tell him that his family isn't so bad after all, that being at a picnic with them

*is really almost pleasant, that you don't know how you
can live without him, and he is off parking his father's Buick.*

"Dad, Dad . . . wait."

Max was charging toward the car, his puppy trying
hard to keep up with him. Joe had been about to get
in, but he stopped, straightened, and looked across the
car roof at his son.

"Tory and I want to come too. Can we, Dad? Can
we, *please*?"

Tory couldn't hear Joe's answer, but he gestured at
the passenger door as if to say it was open. Max tugged
the door open and hurled himself in. Joe's father
moved quickly to save poor little Tory from being
strangled. He handed Max the dog and tucked the
cord inside the door before closing it.

Tory watched them drive off together. Max was
right. Tory did want to go with Joe.

She felt a nudge at her leg. It was Wags. Tory knelt
down, scratching her puppy's head, burrowing her
fingers in behind Wags's ears. "Are you tired, sweet-
heart? Did all those other doggies wear you out?"
Wags closed her eyes and sagged against Tory.

Yes, Wags was her baby, and she had loved having
a baby.

The two of them went over to the tables where Fran
and Marjorie were talking to some other women. At
their approach, Marjorie stepped aside.

"Fran's having a good time, isn't she?" Tory said
softly.

"Yes, she is. I can't quite believe it. In fact . . ."

Marjorie stopped, but Tory knew exactly what she
was thinking. *Yes, it's hard to start seeing your mother
as she is, hard to push aside all the resentment and*

anger that you may feel and see her as another woman. Hard, but worth every bit of the effort.

Wags was clamoring for Marjorie's attention. Marjorie bent down, patting her. "When I stop traveling, I think I would like to have a dog."

Tory looked at her own pet fondly. "Yes, dogs are great."

Marjorie didn't look up. "I'm going to tell them in Atlantic City this year."

Tory was puzzled. "Tell them what?"

"That I'm leaving the pageant organization. As soon as they can find someone good to replace me, I'm going to quit."

"Mother!" Tory was shocked. Yes, they had talked about it on the plane, but that was only five days ago. "Mother, are you sure? How can you decide so fast?"

"It was easy. Once I started thinking about it, it seemed so clear. I've enjoyed this job a lot, but now I'm ready to do something more than support and organize someone else."

"What are you going to do?"

"You always did what I told you to, now I'm going to do what you tell me. I'm going to open a business—a clothing shop."

"You'd be good at it."

"It's not the kind of shop you're thinking of. It would be a half-size shop, for full-figured women. The manufacturers are finally starting to make nice clothes for them, but many of them have such poor self-images that they always wear navy and have never developed any notion of accessorizing or putting together a whole look—the right jewelry, stockings, all that. That's where I could help."

"You certainly could." Marjorie could make any-one look, if not great, at least a whole lot better. "Are you thinking of an upscale place or one for women with less money? You probably shouldn't try to do both at once."

"I haven't decided yet. I first need to decide where to locate and then do some basic market research."

Tory did not have to worry about her mother blundering into a business blindly. "You aren't going back to South Carolina?"

"Not necessarily. I could, but I don't feel tied there. I think I might like to move. I'll certainly look into Houston, Atlanta, places like that."

"If you pick Atlanta, we can force Ned to do a lot of free P.R. work for you, but Mother, why don't you think about Portland?"

"Portland?"

Tory suddenly felt uneasy, not quite sure of what she was saying. "Well, Joe will probably be moving there in a couple of years. And who knows? He might be married to someone with a terrible weight problem."

"Tory." Her mother's voice was gentle, firm. "Don't joke about that."

She couldn't help it. "On the other hand, he might be married to someone who could help manage her mother's growing chain of stores."

"Tory!" Marjorie turned to face Tory directly. She took her by the shoulders. "Baby, what are you saying? Are you and Joe going to get married?"

"Oh, Mother... I don't know, I guess so. All my reasons for saying no keep disappearing. I can't even remember what they are."

Marjorie hugged her. "Oh, honey, I'm so happy for you. Now where is he? Let me go hug him too."

"Ah, Mother... Do you think you could wait? I haven't told him yet."

Marjorie stepped back. "May I ask why not?"

"Well, what do you expect? I've only known for about nine seconds myself. I haven't had time."

"Maybe you'd better go find him."

"How can I? They all look alike here. I'll find someone I think is him, and it'll turn out to be his fifth cousin Oscar, and I won't find out about it until a year after the wedding."

"Tory." Her mother's voice had a "be serious" tone.

"Okay, okay, I'm going."

SHE FOUND JOE playing horseshoes. He had just finished a turn. "How are you doing?" she asked.

"How do you think?" he grumbled. "Frank's killing me. He always does."

"Does it still bother you that your brother beats you at games?"

"Yes." Frank ringed one, and Joe grimaced. "I'm not going to watch anymore." He turned away from the game, looking down at her. "That's a pretty dress. It's nice to see you in a dress now and again."

"My mother's been ordering me around again."

Joe looked concerned. "She has? What does she want you to do?"

"She says I should stop telling people that we're going to get married until I've told you."

He went pale. "Tory—"

"I love you, Joe."

And just then Max rushed over and started tugging at Joe's arm. "Come on, Dad, it's your turn. You can't miss your turn. Come on."

Joe allowed himself to be pulled away, but he looked over his shoulder. "You have great timing, sister."

Tory moved forward to watch him throw. He was intent, concentrating, swinging his arm back, letting the horseshoe fly. Jim, standing halfway to the stake, had to jump out of the way. And that was his best throw.

When he was done, he came back to her side. "That was your fault."

"I'm sorry."

"Oh, well, Max needs to learn that when it comes to games, Uncle Dennis is a better bet than me. Now about—"

Someone interrupted. "Excuse me, but could I talk to you guys for a minute?"

It was Lisa. Joe dropped his hand from Tory's arm. "Sure. Do you want to talk now?"

"Please."

So Joe called to Jim asking him if he would finish out the game, and over the sound of good-natured catcalls about quitters and losers, the three of them went over to one of the far picnic tables.

Lisa sat down between Joe and Tory. "I know that everyone here thinks I did great at the pageant," she said, "but you both know that I went to win money and I didn't."

Tory tried to reassure her. "Beauty pageants aren't that important. Even if you don't do well in them—"

Lisa interrupted. "But, Tory, I did do well. I didn't think so last night, then I felt really awful, but on the way home today, I was thinking. Some of those girls have been doing this sort of thing their whole life, and me, I don't even sing in the school choir. For someone who doesn't like to sing and who was wearing borrowed clothes, I think I did okay, more than okay, I did great.''

Joe put his arm around her. "I knew you would feel that way," he said quietly.

"And I still want to go to college…now more than ever. I figure I can do one of two things. I can work for a year and save all my money and apply for all those scholarships I didn't know about and go to the university in Eugene next year. I know that everyone will think once I start working, I'll forget all about going, but I won't, I know I won't."

"I believe you," Joe said. And Tory did too.

"Or," Lisa went on, "I could go to one of the community colleges. Their tuition is so much less, I couldn't believe it. With all I've been saving and my Miss Sullivan City money, I've got enough for almost all the first year."

"What would you do about room and board?" Tory asked.

"I don't know, but I was thinking…I'm really good at home, at around-the-house sort of things, so I thought maybe if there was some family with nice little kids, maybe I could live with them and cook and clean and babysit like I do for everyone here… I don't know how I would find a nice family though."

"We could contact the local in whatever town you'd be in," Joe said. "They'd find a good family."

"Oh, I never thought of the union," Lisa exclaimed. "They'd help me, wouldn't they?"

"Of course, but I wouldn't give up on the university so fast," he advised. "You should talk to Mom and Dad first. Now that you're so sure of what you want to do, maybe you should tell them, see if they can help."

"But they didn't help any of the rest of you like that."

"None of us wanted that. And now that we're all out of the house, they've got more money."

Lisa stood up, and Tory couldn't help contrasting her with some of the adolescents she had encountered in Atlanta, kids who thought that their parents owed them the world.

As soon as they were alone again, Tory turned to Joe and spoke flatly. "If she goes to the university, she's going to be in the dorm her first year." The Brighams wouldn't know this. "It's one thing at a community college, but at a four-year school, half of going to college is living in the dorm."

"Tory, forget Lisa. Things will work out for her."

Yes, they would.

Joe put his arm along the back of the picnic table. "Now what were you saying—"

"Dad! Dad! Could you hold Tory?" This time it was Max, running up to them, his puppy scurrying valiantly behind him.

"Yes, Max, I'll be glad to hold Tory." Joe held out his hand for the cord that Max was untying from himself.

"No, no, let me tie her to you. I don't want her to get loose. Mommy says if I let her loose, she would run out in the street and *die*. That's why Uncle Dennis tied her to me."

"Okay, I'll tie her."

"No, no, I can do it. Uncle Dennis is teaching me how."

Obediently Joe stood up and held out his arms while Max threaded Tory's cord through one of his belt loops. Tory herself was sniffing at Joe's shoe, her little bell tingling.

"Okay," Max said, as he did something with the cord. "This is the tree, and there's this hole underneath it. The rabbit comes up out of the hole like this. And then he goes around the tree like this, and then he—" Max stopped, frowning. "What does he do now, Dad? Go up out of the hole or down in?"

Joe peered down at the knot-in-progress. "Down in. How can he come out of the hole? He just went around the tree."

This was one of the strangest conversations Tory had ever heard, but it seemed to be making sense to the two of them. The knot was soon finished; Max gave the cord a good tug, and then ran off.

Joe looked down at the puppy for a moment and then sat down. He put his arm along the edge of the picnic table. "I think you were saying something about—"

"Oh, Dad." Max was back. "I almost forgot. Grandma says she wants you to come cook the hamburgers."

"I'll be there in a minute."

"No, she wants you right *now*."

"Tell her I'll be there in a minute," Joe said firmly.

"And Tory's supposed to come eat."

"She'll be there in a minute."

"Okay... but you better hurry or the food will be all gone."

Tory rather doubted it. But Max looked like that was a risk he wasn't willing to take, and he ran off. Tory leaned back against Joe's arm, looking up at him, laughing.

"It's always going to be like this," he said, "these interruptions…at least for as long as we're here. I may not fit in very well anymore, but they're still my family."

"I know that."

"And I'm not interested in what we had before. I want a lot more."

"I know that too. I'd even be willing to throw out some of my clothes so that you can have some closet space."

"Thanks, but I'm not sure that I want us living over the bar. I'd like a little more privacy so the whole world won't know every time I work late."

"But it will be worse if we live in town."

Then he told her about a lot not even a mile beyond the bar. "I suppose everyone will think we're crazy to build when we're only going to be here for a few more years, but I think we'll be happier if we do."

It would be nice to have more space. If she and Joe did manage to produce a puppy-substitute, nothing would keep Marjorie and Fran away. "You have worked this all out, haven't you?"

"Once someone told me something about fantasies and ambitions—"

"*Dad!* Grandma says you are to come now."

Max was standing with his hands on his hips, looking impatient and important. Joe sighed. "There are probably forty men here who get called 'Dad' by someone. Why is my son always the one you hear?"

"Because he's loud," Tory answered. *And because many, many people will probably hear from him someday.* "You had better go grill your hamburgers. Do you want me to take Tory?"

"Would you?"

Joe untied himself from the dog and knotted her cord in a loose loop around Tory's wrist.

"Sometime you're going to have to tell me what made you change your mind," he said as they walked toward the crowd.

"Someday maybe I will."

Joe went over to a grill and took his father's place. Tory saw Fran getting in the food line and went up to join her, trying not to let the other Tory get too tangled up in her cord. Marjorie got in line a few minutes later. Tory waved at her.

"Who's this?" Fran asked, looking down at the puppy.

"Wags's stepsister. She's Max's dog."

They picked up paper plates. Tory scrutinized the crowded table looking for something to eat. She got a chicken leg, some green salad, and, hoping there weren't forty tons of sugar in the dressing, some bean salad. Suddenly her grandmother scooped something onto her plate. It was a molded salad with nuts on top, layers of purple alternating with layers of white. The purple had canned peaches in it, the white canned pineapple.

"Fran, I don't eat Jell-O."

"Today you do. Joe's grandmother made it."

"Did you spend the last two hours finding out who made what?"

"Yes."

They reached the end of the line of tables, and under her grandmother's gaze, Tory picked up a brownie and a lemon square. "Are you happy now?"

"Max helped make the peanut butter cookies," Fran answered.

"You might have told me that before I got the lemon square." Tory took a peanut butter cookie. At this rate, there wouldn't be any pretending about the saddlebag thighs. She would end up not as her mother's assistant manager, but as her customer.

Joe's father had seen them going through the line and was waiting to escort them to a blanket. He got a lawn chair for Fran and tied Max's puppy to a tree so they could eat.

Tory picked up her drumstick and eyed it carefully. Maybe if she took off the skin . . . She glanced up and saw Fran looking at her with surprising seriousness. "What is it?" she asked.

"I guess I was thinking I would have liked to see you grow up."

Tory smiled. She would have liked that too.

"You're interesting," Fran went on. "Most pretty people aren't. They're boring."

"I was probably a boring child," Tory answered. "But you might have a second chance."

Fran scooped up a spoonful of Joe's grandmother's salad. "What do you mean?"

"I'm going to marry Joe."

"You're *what*?" Fran dropped her spoon. Little gobs of purple Jell-O and white Kool-Whip splattered across her green slacks. "Now look what you made me do." She put down her plate and started blotting at the spill with her napkin. "Have you ever tried to get stains out of polyester?"

"Not recently," Tory admitted. "I'm sorry."

Fran glared at her. "You don't look it. You look tickled pink."

"I am. And are you just going to complain about the stain or are you going to say that you're happy?"

"I've only known you for a week," Fran answered. "What's it to me what you do? You should be worrying about whether your mother likes him, but," she added, contradicting everything she had just said, "I wouldn't let it bother you if she doesn't."

"She likes him even better than I like him. But here she is now; you can ask her yourself."

"Ask me what?" Marjorie handed Tory her plate, which was not, Tory noted, nearly as filled as her own, and gracefully arranged herself on the blanket, no mean trick for someone in a straight skirt.

"Did you hear that this girl is getting married?" Fran asked.

"I heard that she was about to propose to someone; I hadn't heard that he accepted."

Fran frowned at Tory. "You proposed to him? What did he say?"

"Not much. We kept getting interrupted, but he didn't run screaming into the bushes."

"Well, that's something. Are you going to invite me to the wedding?"

Tory blinked. She had given absolutely no thought to a wedding. "Sure. You can even give me away if you want."

"Me? Give you away? We'd look like a pair of fools."

"No, we wouldn't, but I don't imagine anybody's going to be giving anybody away. If Joe comes equipped with nine hundred thousand relatives, the least he can do is swallow the two of you.''

Marjorie reached over and patted Tory on the leg. ''It's nice to hear you say that, baby. Now, have you thought about the reception? Even if you don't want to have the official one there, you might have a party or an open house at the bar.''

The official reception? An open house at the bar? Her plans weren't exactly that far along.

''Mother—'' she acted shocked ''—it isn't a bar. I don't run a bar. It's a bakery.''

''If that's a bakery,'' Fran declared, ''I'm not eating any of the wedding cake.''

They were all laughing when a shadow fell across the blanket. ''What's so funny?''

Tory looked up at Joe. ''Wedding cake. We're fighting about who's going to make it.''

''Not you, I hope. Wedding cakes are supposed to have white flour and sugar. You'd probably put zucchini in it.''

Tory would have made a face at him, but she noticed he had someone else with him. She smiled politely.

Joe introduced them. ''I want you to meet my cousin Joe.''

So this was another of the three Joe Brighams. Tory handed her plate to her grandmother—let her eat the Jell-O—and stood up. ''Hello, Joe,'' she said. ''It's nice to meet you.''

''I hope you still think that in a minute,'' Joe Brigham said. ''My little girl heard from Lisa that you used to be a baton twirler, and she's been about to die ever since. She's brought her baton and she would love it if you would come watch her.''

Tory looked at Bob's second boy, the one whom she guessed she was now supposed to call "her Joe." He was trying not to laugh. "Why, sure," she said. "I'd be glad to." And she went off, across the green park crowded with horseshoes, baseball gloves, Tupperware and aluminum foil, filled with grandparents sitting in nylon-webbed lawn chairs and small children toddling around with sagging diapers, to watch Joe Brigham's daughter twirl a baton.

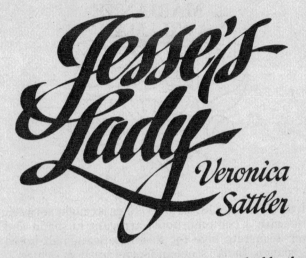